A SEASON AT THE CLIFF HOUSE

ALSO BY BROOKE L. DAVIS

Adventures of an Urban Homesteader
Without You, I Would Be Nothing

A
SEASON
AT THE
CLIFF
HOUSE

a novel

BROOKE L. DAVIS

GALLATIN RIVER PRESS

Published by Gallatin River Press, Highlands Ranch, CO

Book cover and interior layout by Roseanna White
Cover images: The Cliff House – Library of Congress; Border and all other decoration - iStock.

Library of Congress Control Number: 2023922339
Publisher's Cataloging-in-Publication data

Names: Davis, Brooke L., author.
Title: A season at the cliff house / Brooke L. Davis.
Description: Highlands Ranch, CO: Gallatin River Press, 2024.
Identifiers: LCCN: 2023922339 | ISBN: 978-1-7366758-3-0 (paperback) | 978-1-7366758-2-3 (ebook)
Subjects: LCSH San Francisco Bay Area (Calif.)--History--20th century--Fiction. | Women--Fiction. | Cliff House (San Francisco, Calif.)--Fiction. | Historical fiction. | BISAC FICTION / Historical / 20th Century / General | FICTION / Women | FICTION / Family Life / General
Classification: LCC PS3604.A85 .S43 2024 | DDC 813.6--dc23

A SEASON AT THE CLIFF HOUSE

ONE

I sabelle Hamilton stared out at the Pacific from the Cliff House balcony and hoped her cousin Grace wouldn't be yet another conventional and unimaginative young woman.

In the distance, gulls floated overhead on a cool breeze, and the sun sparkled on the water. Behind her, the Cliff House, a gleaming white, palatial Victorian structure with "gingerbread" trim and four floors lined with endless windows, rose like a beacon toward the clouds from its perch atop a rocky outcropping. Isabelle laid a relaxed palm on the thick concrete balcony parapet. The Cliff House was where she dared to dream; it stood as a reminder that not all had been destroyed on that dreadful day a little over a year ago.

Grace Hamilton and her aunt Cora were to arrive the next afternoon after a two-day train trip from Denver. While Cora would return home the following week, Grace would be with the family for "an extended stay after a difficult situation with a suitor." Isabelle had frowned in concerned curiosity when her father, James, had announced the reason for Grace's visit. When pressed, he had waved a hand and dropped the subject, unwilling to provide more details. Despite his dismissal, Isabelle was most excited not only to have a visitor but also to have one so close in age. She had recently turned twenty-one; Grace was twenty.

Footsteps sounded behind Isabelle, and Josephine, her older sister, joined her.

"We're about to go into the women's parlor." Josephine tapped an impatient forefinger on the parapet, a devious gleam in her eye. "I wonder what delicious tidbits Harriet will have to share with us today."

Isabelle sighed. Josephine, along with their mother, Margaret, enjoyed the gossip that was spread as liberally as jam on toast in the women's parlor. Isabelle found it exhausting and silently prayed that Grace would too.

"Really, Isa, why can't you at least pretend to care about what's going on in society?" Josephine teased her sister.

Isabelle scoffed in protest. "It's not that I don't care. It's that I care about different things. *Important* things."

Josephine tsked and cast a sidelong glance at Isabelle. "Still thinking about our guest and more than a little excited to have someone other than Mother and me to talk to?"

Isabelle chuckled. "Yes."

"Well"—Josephine arched her brows—"don't scare her away with all your chatter about the Red Cross and saving the world. I'm sure she'll have interesting stories to share about living in Denver. And since she's coming because, well, you know . . ."

Isabelle tilted her head. Her father had shared the reason for Grace's visit, but doubts still niggled at Isabelle. What *had* happened with Grace's suitor?

"What I'm trying to say is," Josephine continued, her face the picture of cautious optimism, "we need to make sure she has a pleasant time."

Isabelle recognized Josephine's expression; it had flickered across the faces of both sisters during the rare bright moments of the previous year.

"We will," Isabelle assured Josephine, who turned and walked away.

Isabelle inhaled the salt air and focused her attention on Seal Rocks, a lump of boulders sprouting up from the ocean in the distance. She had learned long ago she could never hope to be Josephine. With innate elegance and an ease with social graces, Josephine was what every parent wanted as a daughter. When Josephine walked into a room, those within noticed. Isabelle simply arrived without fanfare. Josephine's smoldering beauty also didn't help; her dark hair and eyes and her consistent choice of rich, jewel-toned dresses did nothing to downplay her looks. The reflection that usually stared back at Isabelle in the mirror was that of a bright and passably attractive young woman with piercing green eyes and a pert upturned nose. Isabelle, however, struggled to keep her dresses unwrinkled, her long honey-blond hair presentable, and her eagerness in check. She often felt like the more awkward of the two.

Isabelle gripped the edge of the parapet and closed her eyes. She grimaced, envisioning the roaring stretch of flames that had licked the clouds on the morning of the tragedy.

At least Josephine was alive.

One of the largest earthquakes on record had destroyed nearly 80 percent of San Francisco thirteen months prior. Houses had collapsed, water lines had burst, thousands had wandered wounded and bloodied in the streets, and the city had burned for three days. Isabelle scrubbed her arms, a shiver worming its way up her spine. Through sheer luck and overindulging during Isabelle and Josephine's parents' anniversary party, Josephine and her husband, Henry, had stayed at Isabelle and Josephine's parents' home the night before the terrible temblor.

The terrific shaking had awoken them the following morning. As the blazing inferno had filled the sky with enormous black plumes of smoke, Isabelle had tried to comfort her terrified, wailing sister. Henry and Josephine's home on Nob Hill, their staff, and their beloved King Charles spaniel, Muffin, had perished.

In the months that followed, Isabelle found her calling. Though the Hamiltons' home had been damaged, it remained standing, alongside a handful of other Victorians on the west side of Van

Ness Avenue. Still, Isabelle's entire family had lived in a tent across the street from their home in Lafayette Park, alongside many other displaced residents, until their house had been deemed safe for them to return. During that time, Isabelle had helped neighborhood women distribute food and supplies. She had watched carefully and finally assisted the nurses who treated those suffering from smoke inhalation, lacerations, and burns. Her desire to help others and a chance encounter with a short notice in one of her father's recently discarded *San Francisco Call* newspapers had determined her fate; she would become a nurse.

Unfortunately, her mother vehemently disapproved. Women belonged at home, doting on husbands and nurturing children. Financially supporting charitable causes was one thing, but outside of being pressed into duty due to a disaster, voluntarily working on the front lines was out of the question. Isabelle, however, thrilled at the idea of being in the thick of the action instead of relegated to the sidelines, where she was forced to mingle with other social-climbing women who cared more about being seen than about making a difference.

Isabelle stole a glance over her shoulder; she would not be Josephine. She had no interest in idle gossip, had no idea if she wanted a husband, and couldn't imagine anything more tedious than having her time dictated by a prescribed schedule of domestic and societal duties.

Instead, unbeknownst to her family, she had set a plan in motion.

With any luck, this would be the last summer she would spend in San Francisco, maybe for a very long time.

TWO

Grace Hamilton clutched her *Ladies' Home Journal* and relaxed against her padded bench seat aboard the Overland Limited train bound for San Francisco. She would rather have been reading the copy of Arthur Conan Doyle's *The Hound of the Baskervilles* that she had snatched from her younger brother, Jacob. Unfortunately, Aunt Cora would have disapproved, and Grace had left the book in Denver. Grace smiled as the train trundled on, and the faint smell of leather and cigarette smoke wafted forward from the back of the car. She hadn't remembered how much the pine-swathed foothills and rolling expanses of green in Northern California resembled Colorado. She absentmindedly checked the pins in her upswept pale blond hair; nary a strand was out of place. The sapphire hat that matched her dress sat intact at the proper angle on her head, much as it had for the duration of her trip. To her right, Aunt Cora, a plump, nervous woman with a penchant for eating too much bread and potatoes, sat, engrossed in her Bible.

Grace had met Isabelle and Josephine briefly several years ago. They all had practically been children then, but vague memories of both cousins bubbled in Grace's mind. Josephine had been elegant and poised, almost beyond her years. She was a gracious natural beauty with an innate confidence Grace had envied. Josephine had undoubtedly married well and seamlessly blended into upper-class society. Isabelle had contrasted with her sister, given her bubbly and gregarious personality. Much to Aunt Margaret's consternation,

Isabelle shared her progressive opinions and often quoted lines from the latest book she was reading. A straightforward young woman seemingly eager to make friends, Isabelle had tried, and somewhat succeeded, in putting Grace at ease. Grace sighed silently. She wanted her trip to San Francisco to be an adventure. She didn't want to think about how miserable she would be biding her time in a strange house if Isabelle turned out to be a bore.

Grace tried but failed to enjoy the beautiful scenery that slipped by outside the window. Images of the near miss on that fateful night with her former beau flashed through her mind, and she squeezed her eyes shut. She attempted to calm her nerves by reminding herself that that was all behind her now. Grace laid a palm on the window and allowed the warmth from the glass to seep into her body. She wouldn't miss cold Colorado: the bone-chilling snowy winters, her stern and distant father, her silent, wilting mother. Grace gripped her magazine with steely resolve. She would not stay in Denver, marry a man her father approved of, and give up her dream of becoming a kindergarten teacher.

Instead, unbeknownst to her family, she had set a plan in motion.

When the train slowed, Grace snuck a glance over her shoulder. Her heart pattered, and she bit her lip. *He* was still there, engrossed in his newspaper. *He* was still there, dapper in his chocolate-brown suit, just as he had been when he had boarded the train in Cheyenne and tipped his hat to her and Aunt Cora.

A bespectacled conductor strolled up the aisle. "We're coming into the station now."

Grace startled and stared out the window across the aisle. Buildings rose like jagged teeth beyond the sparkling harbor. A pleasant tingling sensation spread throughout her body. She smoothed her hair and stuffed her magazine into her bag. Today was the first day of the rest of her life, and she couldn't wait to be reunited with her cousins and begin her new journey.

THREE

Henry Rothwell stood before the armoire mirror in his wife's childhood bedroom and adjusted his ruby-colored necktie. The room retained much of Josephine's elegant charm: the lavender ruffled spread atop the sturdy four-poster bed, the dainty footstool with its needlepoint rose top that Josephine had completed as a child, and a small aged-bronze foal sculpture that she still adored. Across the street, afternoon sun bathed Lafayette Park, a crisp breeze rustling through the sparse maples and blue gums that dotted the rolling, grassy open space in Pacific Heights. Henry smoothed his thick, clean-cut dark hair with both palms and walked to one of the large windows. Despite the new buildings that had sprouted up down the hill, he shuddered.

It had been, to put it mildly, a rough year.

Fire had consumed his home and killed his staff and dog. Henry swallowed hard and tried to push aside the memories of life immediately after the quake: the constant low din of too many people forced to live in tents alongside one another, the racking coughs of those who had inhaled too much smoke, the interminably long food lines, and the grubby hands that passed tattered newspapers amongst their neighbors.

To make matters worse, James had also barely escaped being implicated in one of the most notorious scandals of the modern era. The corruption trials that would eventually send the mayor of San Francisco and Abe Ruef—the corrupt political boss convicted of controlling local politics through bribery—to jail had caused a nationwide sensation. Henry had been sickened by it all. As the bookkeeper for his father-in-law's real estate holdings company, Henry couldn't pretend he didn't know more than he should have about the inner workings of James's sometimes questionable land deals. Mercifully, James kept what he could from Henry to prevent him from being implicated should trouble arise. But inevitably, Henry found himself privy to far more unsavory details than he would have liked.

One challenge businessmen in San Francisco now faced was that the inferno had swallowed city hall and all of its records. Birth certificates, real estate deeds, and titles had been incinerated, while police records had escaped unscathed. One's criminal record remained, but best of luck trying to prove age, identity, or property ownership.

Two robins hopped along the iron fence that skirted the narrow front yard, and Henry smiled. He and Josephine were fortunate. Thanks to James's connections and generosity, Henry and Josephine hadn't needed to worry about unscrupulous land sharks contesting ownership of their property.

The bedroom door opened, and Josephine swept into the room. Henry's heart swelled at the sight of his wife. She had always been the most beautiful woman he had ever known. Today, her lilac dress molded to her curves, the shade of cotton nearly matching the ruffled spread that lay atop the bed opposite the armoire.

"Father and George have gone to the train station to get them." Josephine pressed a kiss onto Henry's cheek and seated herself at her dressing table, which sat between the two windows that afforded a view of the park.

Henry sat down on the edge of the bed, the end of his mouth quirked up. Of all the men in San Francisco—and there were plenty of eligible bachelors of class, to be sure—Josephine had chosen him. She had made him the happiest man alive by becoming his wife, and Henry had every intention of giving her the life she deserved. He admired her as brushed on a pale shade of pink lipstick. The color reminded him of another woman, a fortune teller who had once frightened him as a child. His mother had gone for a reading and on the way out the door, the fortune teller had clutched his hand. He had tried to pull away, but the woman had held him fast and proclaimed that he would one day save someone whom he loved and it would bring him a life of luck. Henry instinctively laid a palm over his heart; he had been unable to save his mother. Instead, he had saved Josephine, and she had brought him his good fortune.

Josephine turned in her chair and faced him, her brown eyes sparkling.

"What kind of difficult situation do you think Grace could've gotten herself into with a suitor?" she asked, her voice pitched low, her tone conspiratorial.

Henry raised his eyebrows. The unspoken answer was that Grace had found herself in a family way but he strongly doubted it. Women in that condition were still spirited away to spend extended summer vacations with sympathetic relatives, but Henry sensed something else had happened.

"I'm not sure, but it must've been something big for her parents to send her here for the entire summer."

Josephine shook her head. "I've tried to wheedle it out of Father, but every time I ask, he waves his hands and sputters. I'm not sure if he knows what happened, or if he's only repeating what Uncle told him."

Henry bit the inside of his lip to keep from chuckling; he understood why James had shared nothing more than scant details about the reason for Grace's visit. Playing host to his niece was one thing; knowing the sordid details of her love life was another.

Josephine returned her attention to the mirror and patted her lips with a forefinger. "It's too bad for Grace. It can be so hard to find someone good and kind to love."

Josephine winked at Henry in the mirror, and he blushed at her compliment.

"Well, whatever it was, I'm sure her time here will be a welcome fresh start." Josephine rose from her chair and walked to the door. "I'm going down to wait. Will you be along soon?"

Henry rose from the bed and nodded. He returned to the armoire, a wry smile forming on his lips. He recalled courting Josephine: the stilted conversations, the almost overwhelming desire to kiss her, the not knowing if he would measure up to an unspoken set of standards he imagined she had set for him. Henry stared hard at himself in the mirror, well aware of the pitfalls of being a suitor. A man did not simply show up and pretend to be charming, polite, and proper. A man had desires and feelings and ambitions, much as a woman did. Only a man was supposed to hide his feelings, control his desires, and ruthlessly pursue his ambitions, all unenviable and sometimes impossible tasks.

Henry grabbed his black suit coat from a hanger inside the armoire. He put the coat on and licked his lips, nagging thoughts lingering in his mind. Grace could have had any number of "difficult situations" with a suitor. The real mystery was, had her suitor also found himself in a difficult situation with her?

FOUR

race and her aunt Cora stepped onto the Oakland Station platform to the sounds of hissing steam and thumping luggage being pulled from the train cars by porters. Butterflies danced in Grace's stomach as other passengers hurried past her. She had finally arrived, in more ways than one, and couldn't help but smile. Uncle James, a portly man with a balding pate, the top of his head reflecting the sunlight much like his watch chain, strode toward her. A much older wiry gentleman dressed in a plain suit followed.

"Ladies, welcome. We're thrilled to have you with us," Uncle James said, beaming. He shook Aunt Cora's hand and enveloped Grace in such an unexpected bear hug she feared the side seams of her dress might burst.

George, the aging butler, retrieved the ladies' luggage and trundled along behind Grace and Aunt Cora as they followed Uncle James back to the car. With the luggage loaded, Uncle James helped Aunt Cora and Grace into the spacious backseat of the Winton Model K. Uncle James parked himself in the front seat and lit a cigar. As George drove the family through the maze of streets to the Hamiltons' home, Aunt Cora struck up a conversation with Uncle James. Grace struggled to keep her mouth from dropping open in wonderment.

San Francisco was *alive*.

The faint moans of foghorns drifted in from the bay. Dinging cable cars rolled by, hammering from construction sites rang out, and the nasal honk of automobile horns sounded as their engines strained up steep streets, all of them signs of the ongoing herculean effort to resurrect one of the West's largest cities. Once away from the major thoroughfare, the car climbed past entire blocks filled with the burned-out, broken skeletons of homes and charred piles of rubble. Grace swallowed hard, tears pricking her eyes. How horrible it must have been to lose one's home and to have one's life torn apart.

At the top of the hill, George finally pulled the Winton to a stop. He gathered their luggage while Uncle James helped Aunt Cora and Grace out of the car. Across the street, a lush park of rolling green grass dotted with trees spread out before her. Grace turned and gazed up at her aunt and uncle's elegant home.

The lavish lemon-chiffon three-story wood-framed Italianate Victorian welcomed her with its wide front steps, contrasting blue trim, ornate dentil molding, and black parapet. Low junipers and climbing rose canes framed the iron fence around the narrow front yard. Grace and Aunt Cora ascended the steps. Midway up, the front door swung open, and Aunt Margaret stood in the doorway, a broad smile on her face.

"It's so good to finally have you both here." Aunt Margaret, radiant in a petal-pink dress, welcomed Grace and Aunt Cora into an expansive marble-floored foyer. "I'm sure the trip was quite tiring."

Uncle James motioned for George to carry the luggage upstairs. Uncle James trailed behind Aunt Margaret, who ushered the ladies into the sitting room.

The rich mahogany-stained paneling and green color palette of the room soothed Grace. An emerald-colored settee sat beneath the picture window opposite an imposing fireplace with brass andirons. Two pastel floral upholstered armchairs flanked a low round table, and tall Tiffany lamps glowed in the far corners of the room. When Aunt Margaret hugged Grace, a sense of ease and relief washed over her. Aunt Margaret's soft, rose-scented eau de toilette reminded Grace of the color of her aunt's dress. Aunt Margaret's sturdy frame complemented her clearly well-fed husband's.

"Josephine and Henry are with us for the time being." Uncle James motioned to his eldest daughter and her husband. "And you remember Isabelle."

Grace painted on her best smile. Josephine was as elegant and beautiful as Grace had remembered. Henry, a tall man with a thick shock of black hair and twinkling eyes, was the picture of polite well-heeled kindness, his arm wrapped gently around his wife's waist. *He's devoted to her. That's the kind of man I'm going to marry.* Grace greeted them with warm yet proper handshakes. Isabelle's wide grin and contagious energy, evident in her jovial hello, hadn't changed since the cousins had last seen each other.

Aunt Cora shook hands with the trio, her eyes searching the room as if she had lost something. "The train ride was quite long, and the car was very warm. We've also had nothing to eat since lunchtime."

Aunt Cora plopped down onto the settee with an unladylike harrumph, and Grace's cheeks flushed. She quickly tried to wipe the appalled expression from her face. She and Aunt Cora had eaten fine meals en route, and it was only late afternoon; her aunt couldn't be that hungry. The woman had been parked on her backside for the better part of two days yet sounded as if she were an ox who had just pulled a wagon over the Sierras.

Aunt Margaret sat down next to Aunt Cora and patted her hand. "You rest now. Eleanor's making up some tea and goodies. We're going to take you to the beach for some air."

"The ocean, how exciting," Grace breathed, her eyes widening in anticipation.

Aunt Cora shot Grace a withering stare, and Grace averted her gaze to the floor. *If only she weren't here to ruin the fun.* Grace's parents had insisted that her mother's sister accompany Grace to

San Francisco because it was entirely unsafe for young ladies to travel alone by train. Though Aunt Cora would only be staying a week, Grace suspected that time would drag on for what would feel like an eternity.

Aunt Margaret clasped her hands together and rose. "Isabelle, can you get them settled? I need to check on what's taking Eleanor so long."

Isabelle motioned for Grace and Aunt Cora to follow her out of the sitting room. Once upstairs, Isabelle led the women down a hall adorned with rich burgundy wallpaper and brass wall sconces. Isabelle opened the third door on the right and ushered them inside. Grace nodded in approval at the thick navy velvet curtains and opulent mahogany four-poster bed covered in cornflower-blue damask. A washbasin and a dressing table with a bouquet of white rhododendrons sat between two large windows on the far side of the room. A wardrobe dominated the wall opposite the bed.

"This was Daniel's room." Isabelle's voice shook.

Grace stared out the window, wanting desperately to avoid Isabelle's sorrow; Isabelle and Josephine's younger brother had died several years ago of pneumonia.

"With Josephine and Henry with us, we don't have rooms for both of you, but hopefully this can do for the week," Isabelle continued.

"It'll suit us very well, thank you," Aunt Cora assured her.

Distracted by the beautiful flowers and fresh breeze wafting in through the open window, Grace wandered toward the dressing table. "Why are Josephine and Henry living here?"

Aunt Cora cleared her throat, and when Grace turned, she was met by her aunt's pursed lips.

Isabelle bowed her head and shifted her weight uneasily from one foot to another. "Their house was destroyed in the fires, but it's being rebuilt."

Shame suddenly tightened its grip on Grace, and she pressed

her hands together in front of her mouth, nearly unable to breathe. "I—I'm very sorry, Isabelle. I'd forgotten that Father had told us they'd lost . . . I hadn't realized it'd take so long to rebuild. I apologize. This room is lovely. It'll do fine for Aunt Cora and me."

Isabelle mustered a smile and motioned to their luggage, which George had placed next to the armoire. "Please join us again after you've settled in. The bathroom is down the hall on the left." Isabelle quietly excused herself and clicked the door closed behind her.

Grace sank onto the edge of the bed, her cheeks burning. The silence between her and Aunt Cora grew loud, but Grace sensed it wouldn't last long.

"You're a selfish girl, Grace. You always have been. You shouldn't have asked." Aunt Cora grabbed her small suitcase from beside the armoire and thumped it onto the bed behind Grace.

Grace gritted her teeth and rose. "I am *not* selfish."

Grace retrieved her suitcase and placed it on the bed, her defiant tone drawing another hard stare from Aunt Cora.

Though she hated the accusation, Grace begrudged the truth in her aunt's admonishment. She disliked being scolded by pious old stick-in-the-mud spinster Aunt Cora. The woman spent too much time absorbed in her Bible and not enough time understanding that young people might want to wade in the ocean, sample the cuisine in New York City, or escape dusty Denver once in a while to visit other parts of the country.

But how stupid Grace had been asking about Josephine and Henry! She had known their house had perished. She had witnessed unimaginable destruction on the drive in from the train station and hadn't meant to be hurtful. Grace shivered as she shuttled bloomers, stockings, and dresses to the armoire. She pressed a hand to her midsection; the horror of potentially being without a home hollowed out a pit in her stomach. She didn't know how long it would take to build a house because she had never been without one. She couldn't imagine losing everything, watching it crumble to the ground, so cruelly eaten by fire. Still, her comment had been an innocent oversight, nothing more; she truly hadn't believed it would take so long to rebuild Josephine and Henry's home. Grace shook her head and internally chastised herself. *Maybe Aunt Cora's right. Am I selfish?* With two brothers, Grace wasn't accustomed to sharing much of anything. But she wasn't in Colorado anymore, nor would she be returning any time soon. She vowed to do better.

Grace's gaze skipped around the luxuriously appointed room again. Though Aunt Cora's squat body contrasted with Grace's long, lithe limbs, the bed would be big enough for both of them. Grace sniffed. *It's only a week. Then she'll be gone, and I can have this beautiful room all to myself for the next several months.*

FIVE

L ater that afternoon, Grace stood on the beach, her hand shielding her eyes, awed by the spectacular views of the ocean. Behind her, Henry and James spread two woolen blankets on a smooth stretch of sand set close to the winding road that led up to the Cliff House. Grace and Isabelle removed their shoes and waved at the family, who unpacked baskets full of beverages, fruit, and cheese. Finally, the two cousins set off down the beach, Grace's toes delighting in the softness beneath her feet.

She inhaled the faint scent of brine and reveled in the crisp salt air that washed over her. Two little boys ran by, laughing and churning through the thick sand. Farther out, a few sandpipers wheeled, held aloft by a gentle breeze. Grace could almost picture her new life in California. The climate was so different from the dry Rocky Mountain air that chapped her lips and pinched her skin.

A few minutes later, Grace stopped and gazed into the distance at one of the most beautiful yet imposing structures she had ever seen. The Cliff House rose from its rocky perch, majestic against the blue sky, like a castle in a dream, stark white, with four floors of windows and a square central tower. The pointed turret roofs at the ends of the building enchanted Grace. She imagined that staring out at the ocean from inside one of the turrets might leave her feeling like a princess.

"It's magnificent," she said in awe.

Isabelle giggled. "It really is. It has several parlors and a curio shop, but the most amazing part is the balcony that runs all the way around the fourth floor. You can see the ocean for miles."

Grace remained rooted in place, still overwhelmed by the sheer size of the Cliff House. "It's spectacular but so precarious. How did they build it so that it sits right on the rocks there at the edge of the ocean?"

Isabelle shrugged and continued walking. "I'm not sure. The old Cliff House was much smaller. It burned down and they built this one to replace it. President McKinley and President Roosevelt have visited, along with Cornelius Vanderbilt the Second."

Grace continued up the beach next to Isabelle, excitement building in her chest. Presidents had visited the Cliff House, and soon she would too. "Did they stay overnight?" Grace envisioned herself and her husband-to-be as a married couple waking up to the sight of the ocean and enjoying a stroll on the beach after a lavish breakfast.

Isabelle shook her head. "Sadly no. It's not a hotel."

Grace's spirits sank. "That's too bad."

"You must tell me all about Denver." Isabelle clasped her hands together.

Caught off guard by the abrupt change in topic, Grace frowned. "It's not nearly as nice as this."

She wanted to apologize for her earlier thoughtless comment about Josephine and Henry's home but sensed the time had passed.

"But surely, the mountains must be beautiful. They're so much taller than ours and have more snow in winter," Isabelle continued.

Grace arched her eyebrows. "Yes, they're pretty, but it's so awfully cold."

Isabelle twisted her mouth to one side in silence. As the cousins continued their stroll, Grace wondered why Isabelle was so interested in her life. No one at home was. Not her father or mother or older brother. Her younger brother, Jacob, was the only one in her family who ever bothered to take any interest in her. It was an interest that had saved her in more ways than one.

"But I'm sure there are things to do in the spring after the snow melts," Isabelle said.

Grace smoothed her pale blond hair, pressure building in her chest. Though flattered by Isabelle's interest, Grace found her cousin's relentless attention and zest for life both refreshing and a little disorienting.

"We have Elitch's Zoological Gardens." Grace's face lit up. "It's a nice place to walk, and the park is full of curious animals. The Brown Palace ballroom is also first-rate. I attended a dance there last year."

"Oh," Isabelle replied, her energy retreating like the tide.

Did I say something wrong? Grace pressed her lips together. The last thing she wanted to do was inadvertently offend Isabelle again. "Tell me about your friends." The prospect of visiting the beach and Cliff House often during her stay thrilled Grace. "Do you come here with them or only with your family?"

Isabelle guided Grace over to a couple of boulders set away from the surf. "We only come as a family. I do the usual things at church with a few girls, and there are social events I have to attend with Mother and Josephine. My good friend Violet from school is hosting a tea soon, and we'll go to that. You'll love her."

Grace leaned back against a boulder and shimmied onto it. She shielded her eyes and gazed again at the Cliff House, a smile tugging at her lips as she imagined the opulent interior of the grand building.

"We're lucky, you know." Isabelle carefully perched herself next to Grace and smoothed the boulder's surface with a gentle palm. "The Cliff House survived the disaster with almost no damage. It could've crashed into the sea, but—"

Grace gasped, and Isabelle patted her hand in reassurance. "It's fine, but I'm much more grateful for it. So much was destroyed that I find it more precious than ever. It's the place where I dream."

Grace crinkled her eyes. *Maybe the Cliff House is where I can dream too.*

Isabelle bit her lip as if she wanted to speak, while Grace waited, hopeful in anticipation.

"Maybe I shouldn't be telling you this since I barely know you, but I want to become a nurse." Isabelle leaned forward, her voice conspiratorial. "I've asked Violet to write a letter of character for me for my application to the California Hospital School for Nurses in Los Angeles. I'm nervous I won't be accepted, and Mother *does not* approve. Whenever I bring up going to school, she shoots down the idea."

Isabelle's dejection tugged at Grace. And yet, when Isabelle stared with palpable determination at the ocean, Grace sensed a resolve in her cousin that she longed for but lacked. Grace opened her mouth and then closed it; she so badly wanted to share her own plan with Isabelle, but something told her to remain quiet.

"You're so brave," Grace whispered, though no one else was within earshot. "My father's a doctor, and I don't know how he tends to bleeding and sick people. The sight of blood turns my stomach, and I freeze when I'm in danger. Being a nurse must be very hard."

Grace shivered and wrinkled her nose. Her father treated patients in the Hamiltons' home. Grace had been forced on more than one occasion to clamp her hands over her ears to muffle the screams and howls of the unfortunate souls who expired in pain behind his office door. Afterward, she had peeked through the keyhole in fascination, only to be met by the sight of blood-soaked bandages and the lingering stench of infection. Over time, Grace had wondered about the pale, lifeless bodies laid out in her father's office. She had secretly mourned them despite her father's sometimes coarse and disturbing comments about how it might have been better for everyone if one or two of them passed on.

Isabelle tucked a stray wisp of hair back in place, her face somber. "I'm sure it'll be hard, at least until I get used to it." Isabelle clutched Grace's hand, and Grace jerked in surprise at her cousin's unexpected physical contact. "But can you imagine?" Isabelle gushed. "I'd get to go to a new city and go to school in a proper hospital and meet girls from all over the country. And I'd get to learn about delivering babies and assisting with surgery. It'd be exciting."

It'd be positively dreadful. Grace hoped her feelings of mild revulsion weren't plastered all over her face. *But how marvelous that we both want to go to school and have gone behind our parents' backs to make our dreams come true.*

Isabelle turned toward the family and frowned. "Father's waving for us." Isabelle slid off the boulder, and Grace followed.

On their way up the beach, Grace and Isabelle passed a little boy toddling in the sand, his father trotting after him. The man's wife sat nearby, holding their infant daughter. The woman planted a gentle kiss on the baby's forehead before waving to Grace and Isabelle.

"What about a family?" Grace acknowledged the woman with a quick smile.

Isabelle shrugged. "He'd have to be progressive—the husband, I mean."

Grace scratched her cheek and screwed up her mouth. A man *did* need to be progressive to allow his wife the opportunity of an education. It was yet another reason Grace was grateful for her newly minted fiancé. Unlike her parents, who wouldn't even allow Grace to consider going to school, he hadn't batted an eye when she had revealed that she had been accepted into the kindergarten training course at the California State Normal School's southern campus in Los Angeles.

"It isn't unheard of, you know." Isabelle stepped closer to Grace, her voice thick with barely contained excitement. "Adolph Sutro's daughter Emma is a doctor. Can you imagine? Mr. Sutro owned the Cliff House and was our mayor, but he passed away several years ago. Emma still sometimes visits with her husband. I pointed them out to Josephine once, but she shook her head and told me to stop pestering her with my nonsense."

Isabelle chuckled and rolled her eyes. Grace feigned a laugh, trying to absorb what Isabelle was suggesting. *Does she not want a husband? Would she really give up the chance to be loved and to have children to be a nurse?*

"So, maybe," Isabelle said. "I wouldn't say a family is out of the question, but I want to do this first."

Grace willed herself not to scoff in exasperation. *First?! Good heavens, what man will want her if he doesn't get a say in what she does? This is not a good plan.*

Grace and Isabelle slowed as they approached the family, who sat enjoying their snacks. Grace nearly groaned when she spotted Aunt Cora twisting her hands together in her lap, clearly lamenting something to the others. *That woman wouldn't know fun if it leaped up like a small dog and bit her on her more-than-ample backside.*

Isabelle laid a hand on Grace's arm. The two women stopped and faced the water. "Please don't say anything to Mother about Violet's letter." Isabelle was clearly a woman in need of a confidante. "Mother and Father don't know I have the application, and I'm not sure I can convince Father to let me go even if I'm accepted."

Isabelle's pleading eyes touched Grace in ways she hadn't expected. She recognized in Isabelle a woman like herself, a woman trying to keep secrets so she could live the life she wanted. But while Isabelle might be able to gain the support of one of her parents, Grace wasn't so lucky. Neither of her parents would ever approve of her new fiancé or of her becoming a teacher. Neither Grace nor

Isabelle was in control of what or whom she loved; they were both simply trying to follow their hearts.

"I won't," Grace assured her.

"Margaret? Margaret!" The alarm in Aunt Cora's voice sent Isabelle racing across the sand toward her mother.

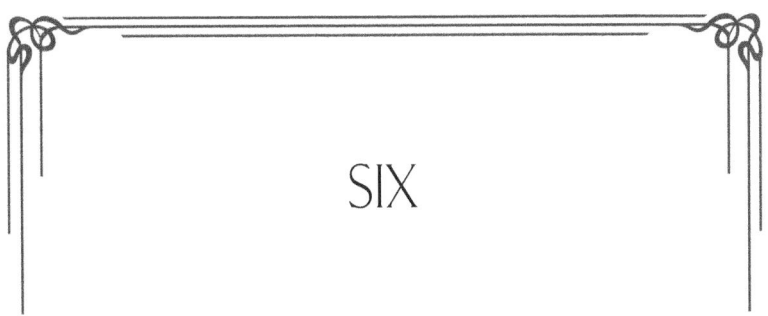

SIX

Isabelle arrived at the blanket to find Margaret unconscious, her arms splayed at her sides. James's face had drained of all color, and he sat trancelike, stroking his wife's hand and whispering to himself. Henry stripped off his coat and tucked it beneath Margaret's head while Cora gently patted Margaret's cheek. Isabelle knelt next to her mother and shot an incredulous glance behind her at Grace. *Why isn't she helping? Oh, that's right. She freezes in the face of danger while I run toward it.*

After one or two agonizing minutes, Margaret mumbled, "Purse, in my purse." Margaret's faint voice could barely be heard above the squawking gulls circling overhead.

"Josephine, why are you being useless!" Isabelle snapped, and pointed at their mother's handbag."

"I, um, yes." Josephine lurched across the blanket, grabbed the small bag, and thrust it toward Isabelle.

Isabelle rummaged in the bottom of the bag until her hand closed around the tin of aspirin that Margaret's doctor had recommended she keep on hand. Margaret had a history of brief dizzy spells, but Dr. Jenkins had assured the family they were nothing serious. Isabelle shook her head and removed two aspirin from the tin. Though she was grateful that Dr. Jenkins had secretly provided the signed physical examination that was required for her nursing school application, Isabelle had begun to doubt his wisdom regarding her mother's health.

"I think it was all the excitement." Cora brushed a gentle palm across Margaret's forehead.

When Margaret blinked, Isabelle sighed in relief. She took Margaret's hand from James and squeezed it. "It's all right now, Mother. You rest for a bit."

Isabelle surveyed the group and returned her attention to her mother. Grace had parked herself next to an equally frozen Josephine. Both of them stared unmoving at Margaret, their eyes brimming with concern. But while Josephine gripped the woolen blanket so tightly that her knuckles had gone white, Grace's face remained still, almost eerily so. That Josephine would have more of a reaction seeing her mother faint was understandable, but Grace's inability to help—despite her earlier explanation for it—struck Isabelle as strangely cold and uncaring.

"It came on so suddenly." Cora searched Isabelle and Josephine's faces, clearly seeking an explanation for what had transpired with Margaret.

How can Josephine sit there and do nothing while a woman who isn't related to our mother comforts her? Bile rose in Isabelle's throat.

Margaret regained her senses a few minutes later and, with help, managed to sit up and lean her head against her husband's shoulder. James kept his arm protectively around her, his face having regained most of its color. Though he often found it difficult to say, Isabelle knew James loved Margaret as if the sun rose and set with her. Isabelle also suspected that he feared Margaret would one day perish from a heart attack, leaving him bereft and alone.

"I have these for you." Isabelle dropped the two aspirin tablets into her mother's trembling hand. Henry hurriedly filled a mug with water and offered it to Margaret. She accepted it with a grateful smile.

What a sweet, helpful man. Isabelle mouthed "thank you" to Henry. *Josephine doesn't appreciate what she has in him.*

Margaret washed down the aspirin and rested her head once

more against James's shoulder. To Isabelle's surprise—James hated public displays of affection—he didn't pull away. Isabelle scanned the beach, a hand resting on her mother's leg. As Isabelle watched couples frolic with their young children, she tried not to think about how quickly her parents seemed to be aging. Maybe her plan to leave San Francisco to attend nursing school was a bad one; who would be there to help her parents once Josephine and Henry moved into their new home? Who would be there as James and Margaret grew frail in their grand house with all its stairs? When the pangs of guilt became too much, Isabelle inhaled a deep, quiet breath and tried to push her fears aside.

"I'm very sorry to have ruined the day," Margaret said.

"No, no," Cora reassured her. "Not at all."

"You didn't ruin anything, Mother. Please rest," Josephine added.

Isabelle pursed her lips at her sister. How typical of Josephine to offer advice now that the crisis had passed.

"We'll sit for a spell and call it a day," Cora said. "We can come back to—"

"Nonsense," Margaret interrupted. "I'm already feeling better, and we need to give you and Grace a proper tour of the Cliff House. Henry, would you fetch me the bowl of cherries?"

Henry handed his mother-in-law the bowl and a napkin, and Cora helped Margaret spread the crisply pressed square cloth across her lap. A sly smile played on Isabelle's lips, her fears receding. Her mother *was* feeling better. They would be touring the Cliff House, albeit at a slower pace than planned, within the hour.

"Now then, you young people take another walk on the beach." Margaret fluttered a hand at Josephine, Grace, and Isabelle. "I'll be fine. I just need to sit a little while longer. No need for more bluster and bother."

Josephine and Grace rose while Isabelle lingered on the blanket. "Are you sure? Do you need more water?"

Margaret crinkled her eyes and patted Isabelle's hand. "That would be nice, but you go on ahead. Thank you again, my dear girl."

Strange. Isabelle held Margaret's mug while Henry refilled it. *She doesn't see the connection between my caring for her and my wanting to care for others. Does she not want me to become a nurse so I can stay home and be her personal maid instead?*

"You're welcome, Mother." Isabelle handed her mother the mug and rose.

Isabelle trotted to catch up with Josephine and Grace, who now tiptoed toward the waves on wet sand.

"Yes, we'll be quite fine. I'm sure Henry, James, and I can manage," Cora called.

SEVEN

Henry discreetly laid his coat aside now that his mother-in-law had finished using it as a pillow. He rolled up his shirtsleeves, helped himself to a few cherries, and silently offered water to Cora, who declined. The woman talked nonstop, never seeming to need to come up for air. He loosened his tie and inhaled the soft breeze that floated in from the water. While he watched Josephine, Isabelle, and Grace stroll down the beach, Cora continued to unspool her endless tale in a grating voice that seesawed between breathless and shrill. She was far too nervous for his liking, and Henry was silently grateful that her stay with the family would be a short one. He suppressed a smile; he pitied the poor person who ended up sitting next to her on her train trip back to Denver.

James motioned for the cheese and crackers plate, and Henry passed it across the blanket to him. Margaret helped herself, and James encouraged Cora to do the same, likely to have a moment's peace.

Cora helped herself to a cracker and, when finished, blotted her mouth with her napkin and continued. "It's been hard for Grace, what with Charles's disappearance and all."

Henry's ears pricked up, and he haltingly turned to face Cora. He had hoped to learn more about the difficult situation with Grace's suitor, but a disappearance? Was Cora about to tell tales about the Denver Hamiltons out of school?

"Yes, we knew something happened but didn't want to press." Margaret straightened, clearly intrigued by the fortuitous revelation.

Henry bit the inside of his cheek to keep from chuckling. He understood all too well from whom Josephine had inherited her love of gossip. Margaret adored it and was a master at carefully questioning someone to reveal what she wanted without appearing overly nosy. A passing cloud blotted out the sun, much like the shadow that crossed Henry's mind. Wherever the conversation was going, he hoped it wouldn't cause Margaret to have another dizzy spell.

Though no one was within earshot, Cora scooted closer to James and Margaret and pressed a hand to her chest. "It was quite frightening. There was a dinner at the house, and I think Grace and Charles had had some type of disagreement beforehand. Three people ended up getting food poisoning. Charles wasn't ill at the party, but no one's heard from him since."

Cora took a sip of water, her eyes sparkling.

"That's terrible," James said. "That cook should've been fired. They did fire her, didn't they?"

Henry rolled his eyes. Always one to start with bravado and bold pronouncements, James played off of Margaret's energy. He sometimes failed, however, to sense the obvious and read the conversation.

"No—they—anyway," Cora blustered, "Charles's friend Benjamin called on Grace regularly after Charles disappeared. The family, they . . . didn't approve."

So the real reason for Grace's visit is revealed. Henry nodded, struggling to keep his expression neutral. *Her parents didn't like her new suitor and sent her away for a cooling-off period.*

Margaret nearly gulped the remaining water from her mug as if trying to keep from blurting out, "Why?" With no one carrying the conversation, the laughter of children floated down the beach and kept the silence from growing too loud.

James dusted a few grains of sand from his trouser leg. "Well, I'm sure it's for the best, but this Benjamin must be one disappointed young man."

Cora shrugged. "Benjamin is apparently older and, how shall I say, *unsuitable*. He has a reputation in Denver for gambling and rabble-rousing. Nothing sinister, of course, just excitement. I hear his business does quite well, though. His family has something to do with the food served at the Brown Palace." Cora jutted out her chin, a triumphant smile spread across her face, and helped herself to an apricot slice and a couple of cherries.

Henry smiled at Cora's name-dropping despite the alarm bells sounding in his head. When he had arrived in San Francisco years ago from Pennsylvania, he had quickly learned how important it was to say the right things to the right people. It had saved Henry in the past, and he guessed Benjamin had also discovered its power. What concerned Henry most was Benjamin's reputation. Gamblers and rabble-rousers were always a little sinister. Henry shifted uncomfortably on the blanket. Benjamin reminded Henry far too much of the local businessmen who had been involved in the underhanded dealings before the quake. Those men either had been shuttled off to jail or, like his father-in-law, had barely escaped indictment.

"I've never met Benjamin." Cora stared down the beach at Josephine, Isabelle, and Grace, who now ambled back toward the family. "Her parents say he suddenly stopped calling. They're not sure if he left town or found someone else to chase. They were hoping, with Charles and Benjamin *both* out of the picture, that Grace might do better in a different environment, where she can, um, make new connections."

James raised his eyebrows, and Henry choked back a snicker. *Poor Grace. Not only is she here to recover from the loss of two suitors, but her parents want her to meet a more appropriate man to boot. That's a tall order for any woman.*

Josephine, Grace, and Isabelle rejoined the group on the blankets, and Isabelle immediately asked Margaret how she was feeling. *So unlike Josephine with her obvious caring.* Henry smiled at Isabelle. *And if Grace's father is a doctor, why didn't she offer to help when Margaret became ill?*

"We found something for you, Aunt Cora." Grace unfurled her fingers to reveal a small ivory shell, its edges smoothed from a lifetime of being caressed by water.

Cora took it and thanked her. Grace asked for the dessert plate and a napkin, and Henry handed both to her. Henry snuck a peek at Grace as she savored her slice of apricot. *If she's grieving, she's doing an excellent job of hiding it. Then again, she's young. I wonder what her plan is?*

Henry ran his fingers through his hair and unfolded his jacket. Internally, he scolded himself for being suspicious of Grace. He was distrustful of new people—anyone who had watched his family be cheated as his had when he was a child would be—but he had learned to keep his suspicions to himself. And Grace was a woman. Not only was it unseemly to suspect women, experience—both in business and in his private life—had taught Henry that women were much more trustworthy than men. If not for James's comment and Cora's story about Grace's suitor, Henry would have probably thought Grace was simply visiting for the summer as a way for her to get to know her cousins.

Unlike his father-in-law, Henry had also mastered the art of reading those around him. In this case, patience would win the day. With careful listening and observation, Henry was confident he could learn more about why Grace Hamilton had really been banished to California.

EIGHT

ater that afternoon, beneath the imposing gray stone archways that faced the dirt road, Grace followed Uncle James and Henry into the Cliff House through the third-floor doors. When Grace stopped to take in her new surroundings, Isabelle almost bumped into her.

"I'm—I'm sorry," Grace stammered, quickly stepping aside to let the others pass.

Waiters dressed in black carried trays of drinks and moved briskly along the wide hall lined with mahogany wainscoting. Chandeliers dotted the ceiling, their light struggling to fill the space with a warm glow. Short passageways dead-ended into closed doors to her left and right, while other narrow corridors led straight into tall windows that cut shafts of light onto the dull walls. Grace had expected airiness and opulence; instead, she was met by dingy, threadbare burgundy carpet and scuffed woodwork.

It's disappointing that it's so old and shabby. Nothing like the outside. Grace wrinkled her nose in distaste, her spirits sinking in disappointment.

"Isn't it wonderful?" Isabelle whispered.

Grace, Isabelle, and Josephine walked three abreast down the main hall.

"It's—I—I hadn't expected it to be so dark, and—"

Behind her, Aunt Cora cleared her throat, and Grace winced. *She thinks I'm being selfish and ungrateful again.* "Yes, it's grand. I'm looking forward to seeing the ocean from the balcony," Grace said quickly.

Grace's assessment of "grand" had been honest; the Cliff House was cavernous. As the party passed several more corridors, Grace tried to imagine how luxurious the carpet and woodwork had been when the building had first opened. *The Cliff House is like Isabelle and me. On the outside, we're beautiful, but on the inside, we hide the tattered secrets of our hearts behind closed doors.* Uncle James led the group past the heavily frosted glass doors of the main barroom and up the stairs to the fourth floor. They exited through a side door onto the balcony.

Warm air caressed Grace's cheeks, and she squealed and pointed to where she, Isabelle, and Josephine had recently strolled on the beach. Isabelle motioned to Grace, and when they rounded the turret at the end of the building, Grace gasped. The Pacific spread out before her; the light glinted off of the water as far as the eye could see.

"Oh, I could stand here all day." She clutched Isabelle's arm.

Isabelle squeezed Grace's hand, and they followed the family to the balcony parapet. "Now, do you see why I come here to do all my dreaming?" Isabelle asked.

Grace had never seen anything so breathtaking. Not even the grandeur of the Rockies, capped with their lacy bonnets of snow and stands of fringed pines, could compete with the views from the Cliff House. Ships inched by in the distance, waves lapped against nearby rocks, and birds whirled overhead. *This is what it feels like to be free.* Every cell in Grace's body buzzed with excitement.

Grace stepped closer to the balcony parapet, thoughts of her fiancé pushing their way to the front of her mind. When she and Frank visited San Francisco from Los Angeles, he would need to bring her here so she could gaze at the ocean. She closed her eyes and basked in the moist, warm air, soft on her skin. *Thank God I won't be in Denver this winter.*

A sharp pinch on her arm shattered her reverie, and she tried to pull away.

"You really must pay better attention, girl," Aunt Cora hissed, then spun Grace around to face a man and his wife, who had stopped to chat with the family.

"Graham, you must meet my niece and her aunt," Uncle James said.

Grace plastered on a pleasing smile, struggling to wiggle out of Aunt Cora's pincerlike grasp.

"Welcome, ladies," Graham said.

He's a wealthy man with flair. Grace's cheeks warmed, and her stomach fluttered. Though Graham reminded Grace of her father with his lanky build, angular face, and thick shock of chestnut hair, his manner was completely different. Where her father was cold, Graham radiated warmth, almost too much of it. His russet silk cravat was tied to perfection, and the gold signet ring on his left pinkie accented his French knot cufflinks.

"Nice to meet you, sir." Grace extended her hand, and Graham shook it.

Grace's clear and steady voice was a product of practice. Having been schooled in the art of social graces by her exacting mother, Grace now put those skills to work to impress Graham and soothe Aunt Cora. Graham was clearly a powerful man and not one to be ignored. His intense brown eyes unnerved Grace, and she quickly averted her gaze to the woman next to him.

Grace next met Rosaline, Graham's curiously squat wife. Dressed in layers of peach cotton, Rosaline waddled up and shook Grace's hand with such vigor that she almost had to brace herself against the thick parapet. *What an interesting couple. I would have never pictured him with someone like her.*

Aunt Margaret, Rosaline, and Aunt Cora broke from the group, leaving Isabelle and Grace alone at the parapet. Grace was about to take in the spectacular ocean view again when she caught Josephine smiling at Graham in a way that felt overly familiar. Moments later, Josephine laughed and briefly laid a hand on Graham's arm. Henry noticed but did nothing, and the entire event happened so fast that Aunt Margaret, Uncle James, Aunt Cora, and Rosaline hadn't seen it. *That was improper.* Grace instinctively touched her fingers to her lips. *Maybe decorum is different in California than it is in Colorado, but Mother wouldn't have approved.*

"It was nice to meet you, dear." Rosaline had materialized at Grace's side. "We hope to see you here with your family again."

Grace quickly pulled herself together. "Thank you, ma'am. It was nice to meet you too. I'm sure I'll see you soon."

Graham tipped his hat to Grace, his smoldering stare causing her stomach to flip. Her cheeks flushed, and it was all she could do not to giggle like a schoolgirl. *Does he flirt with everyone? And how does he get away with it without anyone noticing or saying anything?*

Rosaline waved and took Graham's arm, and the couple strolled away.

NINE

Isabelle remained with Grace and basked in the warmth of the late-afternoon sun. Josephine joined them in silence, her cheeks flushed, her hand absentmindedly gliding over the hair on the left side of her head. The ocean lapped against the rocks, sending a cool breeze wafting up from below.

"Who is he?" Grace asked, her voice filled with undeniable intrigue.

Isabelle furrowed her brow. Josephine patted her cheeks and inhaled audibly as if trying to gather herself.

"That's Graham McCormick," Isabelle said. "He's one of Father's best friends and business associates."

Grace licked her lips as if wanting to ask more.

"Why?" Isabelle ventured.

Josephine haltingly turned to Isabelle, as if she had committed a crime by pressing Grace with a question.

"I—nothing," Grace said. "He's—he has a certain presence."

A nervous laugh bubbled from Josephine, and she clamped a hand over her mouth. Isabelle chuckled, confused by her sister's reaction.

"Rosaline has a presence, too," Josephine whispered, and pointed into the distance to where two seals lurched onto Seal Rocks.

Isabelle gasped and swatted Josephine's shoulder. "Don't say that. She's always been kind to us."

Josephine shrugged and waggled her eyebrows. Isabelle giggled and Grace snickered before pressing her lips together as if trying to keep from laughing out loud. Isabelle returned her attention to the seals. Josephine and Grace were right; Rosaline and her husband both had *presence*. Standing near Graham sometimes made Isabelle's stomach flutter, not because she was attracted to him, but because he had an innate ability to make her feel noticed and appreciated in ways she had never experienced. She had found the sensation pleasurable and flattering and suspected that Josephine had felt the same.

"Ladies, we should go in," James said, motioning to Isabelle, Grace, and Josephine from where he stood a few yards away with Henry, Cora, and Margaret.

Isabelle and Grace crossed the balcony behind Josephine, who wrapped her fingers into the crook of Henry's arm. Once inside, the family walked up the narrow hall and turned left. James pulled open an enormous wooden door, and the family stepped inside the main parlor.

Groups of leather chairs sat clustered around oval mahogany tables, and waiters wandered past on the lookout for empty glasses. The water views through the tall picture windows made Isabelle feel like she was a passenger on a luxurious ocean liner far out at sea. Cigar smoke and the sound of men's conversation permeated the space. When James and Henry excused themselves, Margaret and Isabelle led Josephine, Grace, and Cora across the parlor to a door set into the far right rear corner of the room. Isabelle opened the door to allow the other women inside and closed the door behind her.

"This is—this is *very* nice," Grace said. "And again, with the ocean views."

Low-backed chairs and Georgian-style settees upholstered in rich tapestries set atop vibrant oriental rugs dotted the sunlit women's parlor. Fine bone china tea services graced the tables, and a few ladies in plumage-adorned hats turned in Isabelle's direction before continuing their conversations. Given that the parlor was located in one of the Cliff House's four turrets and only frequented by women, Isabelle was unsurprised that Grace found it charming.

Isabelle, Josephine, and Cora followed Grace toward the curved wall of windows that faced the ocean. Margaret wandered away to greet an acquaintance across the room.

"Quite civilized." Cora stood at a window and admired the dazzling light that sparkled on the water.

Isabelle and Josephine flanked Grace and gazed at the spectacular view.

"This is the best room in the Cliff House," Josephine said. "It's where all the action takes place, and the things we learn here are *always* interesting."

Isabelle rolled her eyes. Josephine reached behind Grace and swatted her sister's arm.

"What you learn is that they gossip and talk about the weather too much," Isabelle scoffed.

Josephine huffed out a sigh and leaned closer to Grace. "My sister abhors my love of gossip and thinks me shallow, but listening to Harriet has its uses. It keeps me up to date on—how shall I say—current events. I have my own causes, though, like the Protestant Orphan Asylum. Doesn't that word 'asylum' have the most awful ring to it?"

Grace nodded, and Josephine rushed on. "It was damaged during the quake, but thankfully the fire didn't reach it. All the children were able to return by the beginning of this year."

Josephine quirked a brow at Isabelle, then returned her attention to Grace. "Rest assured, I'm not the social climber my sister makes me out to be. You'll enjoy the parlor and its company."

Josephine winked at Grace, who smiled.

"Mother's motioning for us." Isabelle painted on a pleasing smile, while bracing herself for what was bound to be yet another round of Harriet's interminable tattling.

Josephine acknowledged her mother with a quick wave, then leaned closer to Grace. "You'll like Maude, Harriet's daughter. There really is no hope for her. She looks way too much like a mud fence, but—"

"Josephine, that's terrible." Isabelle frowned hard at her sister.

"She's pleasant and about your age," Josephine continued. "And it never hurts to know anyone related to Harriet."

The cousins and Cora crossed the room, Josephine in the lead. They met Margaret, who stood alongside an elegant woman. Josephine introduced Harriet Wickham and her daughter, Maude, to Cora and Grace. Maude stood, flat chested and narrow as a barn board, slightly behind her mother, much like a small child. Dressed in a sky-blue ensemble that highlighted her sallow cheeks and made her mousy brown hair appear dull, she greeted Cora and Grace in a quiet voice. Harriet, in contrast to her daughter, wore a soft cream-colored dress that accentuated her ample bosom. Her flawless skin, accentuated by her glossy chocolate-brown pompadour, made her appear younger than her actual age.

"Welcome." Harriet took one of Grace's hands in hers. "How nice to meet you."

Isabelle suppressed a sigh. Harriet appraised Grace as she did all women, her hazel eyes flicking over Grace once as if to size her up. Harriet was the wife of a prominent lawyer and had the most connections of any of those who frequented the women's parlor. She also had the inside track on all the most salacious and sensational gossip, which Isabelle guessed came from living with a husband who played a little too fast and loose with the privacy he had promised his clients. Though Harriet obviously savored telling tales about others—a habit Isabelle found repugnant—she at least had the self-restraint to be discreet by not naming names.

"Thank you, Harriet." Grace's remarkably confident voice surprised Isabelle. "I'm thrilled to be here. The parlor is so pretty, and the views, my goodness. We have mountains near Denver, but they're not as beautiful as your ocean."

Isabelle tilted her head, bemused by Grace's flattery of Harriet.

"And this is Charlotte Gordon." Isabelle introduced Cora and Grace to one of her closest friends. The young woman, radiant today in a rich plum-colored dress, was almost as stunning a beauty as Josephine.

"Hello." Bubbling with eagerness, Charlotte shook Cora's and Grace's hands. "It's so good to meet you both. It's been so long since I've been able to mix with people. We should do tea while you're here."

"We'd like that, thank you," Grace said.

"Would you like to sit, Grace, Cora? Do you have time?" Harriet motioned toward a couple of chairs behind her.

"Yes, let's take a moment," Margaret said.

Chairs were pulled closer to Harriet, Maude, and the others, and Cora and Grace sat down.

"We'll join you in a bit," Josephine assured her mother, then laid a hand on Isabelle's arm and led her away.

At the window, Isabelle stood next to her sister in silent anticipation. She and Josephine had less in common than they once had because of their differing views on women's roles in society. And since Josephine had married, she usually confided in their mother, not Isabelle. Given Josephine's earlier judgmental comments about Rosaline and Maude, Isabelle feared what Josephine might say next.

"What do you think of her?" Josephine whispered.

Isabelle stared out at the ocean, willing herself not to peek at her cousin across the room. Grace had been in San Francisco only a few hours, but she had made an impression.

"I'm not sure yet, but she seems nice enough," Isabelle said. "She was a little distant when we talked on the beach, but she doesn't know me, or any of us, really. I'm hoping she'll warm up to everyone once she's been here a bit longer."

Josephine threw a glance over her shoulder to where Grace, Cora, and the other ladies sat enjoying a cup of tea.

"There's something going on with her." The gleam in Josephine's eyes unnerved Isabelle. She opened her mouth to protest, then closed it. *Of course there's something going on. Father told us it had to do with a suitor. What does Josephine know that I don't?*

"I like her, and her buttoned-up act is admirable, but I'm *sure* there's more to her being here than what we were told." Josephine clasped Isabelle's arm, and Isabelle startled. "And who knows what stories Cora told while the three of us were walking on the beach? I must remember to ask Henry what she said while we were away."

Isabelle shook her head and extracted her arm from her sister's grasp. "You and your wheedling. You were the one who said we needed to make sure Grace has a pleasant time while she's here. Being suspicious of her doesn't help us do that."

A toothy, devilish grin spread across Josephine's face. "At least she seems interested in the right things, unlike you."

Isabelle stuck her tongue out at Josephine and they both giggled. Josephine's implication was that Grace was more like herself instead of Isabelle. Grace appeared to be yet another proper young woman who wanted what all young women were supposed to want: a husband, a home, and children. But was Josephine right?

Isabelle stared at Grace. A reserved yet pleasant expression had made itself at home on her cousin's face. Isabelle wondered if it was sincere or a mask Grace wore, given the sorrow she had probably endured with her suitor. Isabelle's spirits sank; she had hoped that Grace wouldn't be like so many of her other conventional and unimaginative friends, but so far, that was exactly who Grace was. Isabelle wondered if time, patience, and a little trust might help Grace reveal more about herself. Only then would Isabelle be able to tell if she or Josephine had been right about their cousin.

A movement out of the corner of her eye caught Isabelle's attention. "Father's at the door motioning for us."

Isabelle and Josephine rejoined the circle of women seated around Harriet.

"Yes, if you'll excuse us," Margaret said, and rose, as did Grace and Cora. "We'll be seeing you all again very soon, I'm sure."

Isabelle dutifully followed the other women in her family out of the women's parlor. As she slowly closed the door, her gaze lingered on Harriet. It wasn't that Isabelle disliked the woman; it was that she had no stomach for gossip or pretending. She resented having to sit and feign a smile while those around her babbled on about the trivial and mundane. Sometimes Isabelle wanted to scream; listening to Harriet was an enormous waste of time.

Yet, begrudgingly, Isabelle needed Harriet for all the reasons Josephine didn't. Isabelle needed the ladies in the women's parlor with their elegant hats and fine dresses because, cruelly, they held the key to her success. If she and the Red Cross were to do good in the world, Isabelle would eventually have to learn to appeal to those who had the means to support those dreams. She sighed and crossed the main parlor close at her father's heels. *Maybe when I get into school, they'll take me seriously.*

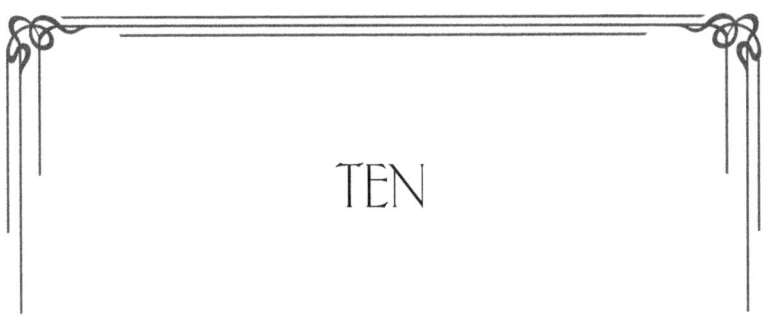

TEN

Grace sat next to Isabelle beneath the canopied top of Henry's Buick, which putted toward home. Uncle James and Aunt Margaret had insisted that Aunt Cora ride with them, leaving Grace alone with those closer to her age. The humidity that tinged the spring breeze had a chilly edge that Grace wasn't accustomed to, and the air moved a little too freely inside the covered car. Grace rested her hand on her hat, fearing she might lose it despite it being pinned to her head in at least six places.

Josephine had been right. The women's parlor was the nicest room in the Cliff House, at least that Grace had visited. Despite the spectacular water views, the parlor reminded her of some of the homes she frequented with her mother when they called on friends in their social circle. The carpets were relatively clean, the tables polished, and the chairs and sofas hadn't been subjected to cigar smoke or stained by unfortunate whiskey and brandy spills.

I hope there's more than gossip. Grace stifled a sigh. *I'd like to meet people and explore the city.* While Grace usually enjoyed learning about the latest engagement or impending new arrival, she was disappointed by what was rarely discussed during social calls. Only one other girl in Grace's circle had ever gone to college. When the girl had made her announcement, the other women in the room, including Grace's mother, had remained still as stones. The roar of their silent judgment and disapproval had only amplified the clopping horses' hooves that passed by outside on the street and the sudden crash of a tray somewhere deep within a kitchen on the main floor below. Grace smiled to herself. *The Cliff House is the perfect place, but I don't regret not being able to announce my engagement there.*

"I forgot to ask you," Isabelle said, startling Grace from her thoughts. "How did you like riding the train? Did you see anything interesting on the way here?"

A sly grin formed on Grace's face. Coming to California with the man who had saved her from Charles had been so easy. "Oh yes. The country was beautiful, especially when we got to the Sierras."

Grace and Aunt Cora had disembarked from the train in Cheyenne and boarded the Overland Limited bound for San Francisco. Benjamin Franklin Buchanan, dapper in his chocolate-brown suit and matching bowler hat, had boarded the train at the same time. When he had strolled up the aisle and tipped his hat to Grace and Aunt Cora, Grace's heart had almost leaped out of her chest.

"I'm sure it's a fun way to travel," Isabelle continued. "Have you been anywhere else?"

Grace shook her head and shifted in her seat, her pulse thrumming. "No, but maybe one day."

That day would come much sooner than any of them might guess.

With Charles nowhere to be found, Ben had called on Grace several times, impressing her with his simple charm and sense of humor. He had promised that if she married him, she would never lack adventure, money, or freedom. He had treated her to fine meals at the Brown Palace and strolls in Elitch's Zoological Gardens. His whispered dreams of travels to California and New York had often filled her ears as they bid each other good night. The prospect of those travels made Grace feel like she was floating off of her front porch and into the starlit sky. Ben had also stunned her by approving of her plan to become a teacher. He fully supported her going to school as long as she was willing to give up teaching when they had children.

Thankfully, Aunt Cora had never been formally introduced to Ben. Still, Grace had worried about how she would introduce her California relatives to him without risking Aunt Margaret and Uncle James's alerting her family to his presence. Grace's parents disapproved of Ben. He was a little older, a little wild, and unbeknownst to most, divorced. To solve the problem, Grace had begun to call him Frank, a shortened version of his middle name, Franklin. In their correspondence, he had agreed to go by that name when he made contacts in California.

Frank was from a well-to-do Kansas City family who sold beef cattle. His brothers had asked him to move to Cheyenne to be closer to the country's main rail line shortly after Grace's near-disastrous debacle with Charles. With one of Grace's friends also living in Cheyenne, it had been easy to write to Frank once he had left Denver. Grace's mother hadn't even asked to see the envelopes; Grace had simply handed them to the maid to add to the post. Grace and Frank had agreed to write to one another once they were in California, and Grace had given him her aunt and uncle's address before leaving Denver. Frank was staying at his sister and brother-in-law's house, and Grace had agreed to send letters to him in care of her. Grace hadn't met the Hamiltons' housemaid yet but was confident a few extra dimes could convince her to send and collect Grace's mail privately.

When the car rounded another corner and hit a bump, Grace wrinkled her nose, remembering Aunt Cora's admonishment about being selfish. "I've been remiss. Have you been anywhere by train?" Grace asked Isabelle.

"No. Mother, Josephine, and I want to, but we can never seem to steal Father away from work." Isabelle's tone was heavy with disappointment.

Josephine turned in her front seat. "Henry and I were thinking of going to Chicago, but then the quake happened."

"Oh, that would be such fun," Grace enthused. She had always wanted to visit Lake Michigan and Riverview Park with its merry-go-round and arcade.

Grace wanted to ask Josephine if she and Henry still planned to take their trip, but she didn't want to pry. Outwardly, Josephine and Henry appeared content with each other, but the casual way that Josephine had smiled at Graham and her quick touch of his arm still didn't sit quite right. *Did I ever look at Charles that way?* For a brief second, pangs of sadness tugged at Grace. She had loved Charles once, or at least believed she had. That thought was quickly replaced by one that made her pulse race. *I must not look at Frank the way that Josephine looked at Graham. That would ruin everything!*

The car now chugged up a hill, and Grace stared at the floor, wanting to avoid the same shells of burned-out homes she had witnessed on the drive in from the train station. Grace was confident that whatever she had seen between Josephine and Graham was harmless, but she understood the allure. The man's gaze had possessed enough heat to melt the buttons off of the front of her dress, and wasn't that one of the reasons she liked Frank? He was a little daring, and his smoldering stare sometimes made her heart skip a beat.

Warmth pooled in Grace's stomach. Unlike the precarious Cliff House, her dreams of being with Frank and becoming a teacher were built on solid ground. Grace needed to write to him soon and tell him about the breathtaking palace that overlooked the sea. More important, she needed to figure out how to see him again.

ELEVEN

The next morning, Grace joined her family for breakfast in the dining room and stifled a yawn. Outside, the clouds were lifting and light streamed through the windows. It glinted off of the dark wainscoting that ringed the room and highlighted the sage-green walls. Aunt Cora had parked herself in the middle of the bed and snored the entire night. Selfish or not, Grace had tried to get what fitful sleep she could feeling as if she were perched on the edge of a cliff. She wouldn't miss Aunt Cora when she boarded the train bound for Denver next week.

Eleanor bustled into the dining room, her white pinafore gleaming against her black dress. She offered Grace a cup of steaming coffee, which she gratefully accepted. The scent of sausage wafted over from the buffet, and plates of ham slices, potato patties, eggs, toast, and various preserves tempted Grace. Having downed a few sips of coffee, she left the table, helped herself to a sausage patty and a potato patty, and returned to her seat.

"Says here the bubonic plague has returned." Uncle James spoke from behind his newspaper at the head of the table. "Not surprised given the mess this town's still in."

Aunt Margaret, who sat across from Grace along with Henry and Josephine, let out a disgruntled sigh.

Her husband lowered his paper and leveled an amused stare at his wife. "We're not going to die, dear. It comes and goes, and I'm sure—"

"I'm sure you'll forgive me for being alarmed, but that's a serious illness, and people *will* die. I'm also sure it needn't be discussed at the breakfast table." Aunt Margaret's sharp eyes held her husband's gaze.

Uncle James shook his head and raised his paper. Grace bit her lip to keep from giggling. *How funny they are! Mother and Father, with their stifling seriousness, would never speak to each other like that. I'm going to have such a grand time here once Aunt Cora leaves.*

"Chances are, we'll be fine, Mother. But it *is* important." Isabelle scooted her piece of ham around on her plate, her knife sawing away. "It's one more thing the Red Cross and the hospitals will have to watch for, and the nurses—"

"Let's have no more talk of nurses or illness this morning, please," Aunt Margaret admonished Isabelle. "There are more appropriate topics to discuss."

Isabelle hung her head, and Grace's heart went out to her cousin. *She's not appreciated for what she wants to do either.* Grace quietly sipped her coffee and cut her sausage patty and potato patty into manageable bites. *At least her parents aren't outright mean. Mine only see me as someone to be married off.*

Isabelle laid a hand on Grace's arm, and she startled.

"The Red Cross tea at Violet's is coming up soon, and *everyone* will be there. I think you'll like Violet." Isabelle raised her eyebrows at her mother, who shot her an annoyed stare.

Grace, now partially revived from her groggy night's sleep thanks to the coffee, lively conversation, and delicious food, smiled. "That sounds fun. I'd like to meet your friends and see the city while I'm here."

A warning glance from Aunt Cora silenced Grace. Chastened, she returned her attention to her potato patty.

"It's generous of you to donate to these causes," Aunt Cora said to Isabelle, before stuffing an oversized bite of potato patty into her mouth. She hadn't quite finished chewing when she spoke again. "Will there be a collection?"

At the mention of a collection, Grace paused midchew, frustration tinged with doom descending over her. Donating to the Red Cross was an opportunity to make a good impression on Isabelle and her family's social circle, but Grace had little money. Before her trip, she had nearly drowned in guilt when she had lifted several coins from her mother's purse. But dropping a few quarters and dimes into an offering plate was out of the question. She wanted to donate several *dollars* but had none. Her parents had sent the allowance for her trip with Aunt Cora, but Grace wouldn't receive it until her aunt left. Grace would also need to budget carefully, which she hated; she wanted to leave a generous donation and have plenty of money to buy at least one or two dresses before she and Frank left San Francisco.

Grace ground through a bite of sausage, fuming in silence. Her lack of money highlighted the recurring problem she and so many other young women had. Her parents treated her like a child and didn't trust her with anything more than a pittance. And with two brothers, she would inherit nothing. *This is why I need Frank.* She straightened in her chair. *He has plenty of money, and once we're married, there'll be no risk of me being seen as a pauper or a tightfisted miser like my father. I'll also be making my own money once I finish school and am teaching.*

"Have you read it?"

Isabelle's question jolted Grace back to the present. Grace dabbed her mouth with her napkin, her cheeks flushed. "I—I'm sorry, I wasn't quite following, can you—"

"Have you read *The House of Mirth*?" Isabelle repeated, seemingly undisturbed by Grace's lack of attention.

"I—no." Grace sipped her coffee.

Across the table, Henry raised his hands like a minister about to begin preaching from a pulpit. "You must," he insisted. "The parties, the financial intrigue, and the way Edith handles the shocking ending all make for quite a good story."

Isabelle beamed and finished her bite of ham. "Henry, don't ruin it," she chided him. "I haven't read it yet."

Henry waved a hand at her. "I have a copy in my briefcase that I can leave for you in the study. Really, Isa, you'll love it."

Grace grinned. *Isa, what a charming pet name. And how curious of Henry to offer her a book. I doubt Josephine cares a whit about reading.*

Isabelle silently clapped her hands while Josephine gazed at Henry with polite adoration.

He's kind and devoted to his wife. Grace smothered a smug smile behind her napkin. *I'm lucky that Frank is kind, devoted, and also interesting.*

"Well then, my boy." Uncle James folded his newspaper and tossed it onto the table next to his empty plate. "Should we be off then?"

Henry slurped down the last of his coffee and kissed Josephine on the cheek. He rose from the table and scooted in his chair.

"Ladies, have a wonderful day." He nodded to the women at the table and followed his father-in-law out of the room.

With breakfast finished and the men off to work, Grace followed Isabelle and Aunt Cora into the foyer. Isabelle and Aunt Cora ascended the stairs, but Josephine surprised Grace by pulling her aside.

"I know your time here must feel terribly tedious," Josephine whispered.

Grace checked the landing midway up the stairs, concerned

that Aunt Cora might have overheard Josephine, but Isabelle and Aunt Cora had already disappeared.

Grace turned her head askance, alarmed that she had given off that air. "I—no, not at all. The walk on the beach, the time on the Cliff House balcony. I hope I haven't given you that impression."

Josephine patted her arm. "You haven't, but my sister can be a bother, and her interests aren't quite the same as ours."

Grace tilted her head in curiosity.

"Isabelle and I are going shopping for new dresses this afternoon, and you're to come too." Josephine leaned closer, her voice returning to a whisper. "We've convinced Mother to look after Cora, so it'll only be the three of us."

Grace pressed a palm to her chest, her emotions a tangle of relief tainted with unfortunate embarrassment. "Thank you so much. I want to see more of the city while I'm here, and I'd love to come. But I—I don't have any—"

Josephine flashed a brilliant smile, her beauty accentuated by her perfect teeth. That smile added to the already finely crafted, confident yet feminine allure that Grace hoped to emulate.

"We'll take care of it," Josephine said with a wink.

Grace's heart thrilled; Josephine understood the plight of an unmarried woman. Luckily for Josephine, *her* father didn't protest every time she wanted a new hair comb or pair of gloves and understood the importance of not showing up to every social function wearing the same rotation of dresses. Grace stepped toward the stairs but stopped when Josephine laid a hand on her shoulder.

"I'm sorry about your beau in Denver. I don't know what difficult situation you went through, but I understand how hard it is not to get what you want—I mean, to be separated from someone you want."

Grace swallowed hard and averted her eyes to a spot on the white marble floor. *What have Mother and Father and Aunt Cora told Uncle James and Aunt Margaret?* Grace's heart pounded. *How much does Josephine know about Charles? And what does she mean she knows how hard it is to be separated from someone you want?*

Grace contemplated a sliver of gray veining running through the marble, the thought hitting her much like a bolt of lightning. This was her chance to tell her story how she wanted it to be told.

"Sadly, yes, he disappeared." Grace's eyes met Josephine's, her voice thick with practiced sorrow. "It was all quite awful, and I've wondered so many times if he's passed away. The not knowing has been . . . well, you can imagine." Grace stared at the marble floor again for effect. "But after some soul searching, I suppose we weren't meant to be together."

The pall that fell over Josephine's face was the exact reaction for which Grace had hoped. She had delivered a stunning performance with the right amount of grief and no melodramatic tears.

"Oh, I—I didn't know he'd disappeared. That *is* awful." Josephine stepped back, her face still ashen.

But Frank hasn't disappeared, even though Mother and Father think he has. Grace forced a closed-mouthed smile from her face as she stepped onto the first stair. "Thank you again for your kind thoughts. And thank you for inviting me to go shopping. I'm looking forward to it."

TWELVE

Beneath the warm midafternoon sun, George helped Grace, Isabelle, and Josephine out of the car at the corner of Van Ness Avenue and Bush Street, a few blocks from Walters Dress Shop. Grace followed closely at Josephine's elbow as the two made their way up Van Ness, with Isabelle trailing behind. Grace appreciated the gentle breeze that smelled like the sea; it spirited away the exhaust from the trucks as they belched along the street. Despite the sobering walk past cleared lots and those still piled with stray bricks and ash, Grace couldn't help but notice how quickly San Francisco had recovered. New structures rose from the ground, bags of cement lay strewn across building sites, and the sound of hammering rang out from every direction. The scene reminded Grace of a beehive.

"If you don't mind my asking, how long have you and Henry been married?" Grace asked Josephine.

A broad smile spread across Josephine's face; she clearly loved her husband and felt a sense of pride in him. "Only about two years," she said. "He's such a good man and is ever so sweet and devoted. I know most wives would probably say that about their husbands to be polite, but with Henry, it's true. Some women might find him dull, but I've seen much worse. It makes me love him that much more."

When Josephine arched her eyebrows and shot Grace a "men can be such scoundrels" look, Grace's eyes widened in wary surprise.

"Beware the adventurous ones," Josephine warned. "They always do something naughty and leave you heartbroken."

The three women stopped at the next corner, waited for a few trucks to pass, and continued across the street.

Grace shivered beneath the bright sun, suspicion seeping into her mind. *Frank's one of the adventurous ones. Will he do something naughty? Would he come all the way to California under the guise of marrying me, only to jilt me and run off with someone else?*

She smoothed a hand over her hair and forced the thought away.

"Of course," Josephine continued, "there are women who have both."

Grace frowned in confusion.

"They have their little adventures but don't have to take care of them at home."

Grace's eyes flew open. She inhaled sharply, then clamped her mouth shut. *Women have affairs? But that's outrageous! Only men have— Oh, yes, men have the affairs, but it takes two to have a tryst.* Grace had never considered how a woman might benefit from such an arrangement.

"Oh—*oh.*" She glanced behind her, fearing that Isabelle might have been eavesdropping. "That's very . . . scandalous."

"Only if you get caught." Josephine winked and grinned.

Grace continued up the sidewalk in stunned silence. *Is Josephine naughty? No, she certainly isn't involved in anything like that. She just went on about how sweet Henry is. I'm sure it's only gossip she's heard at the Cliff House.*

Josephine stopped without warning in front of an eight-paneled black-painted door inset with glass. "Isa, are you coming?"

"Yes." Isabelle hurried to catch up.

Josephine opened the door, and they all stepped inside Walters Dress Shop. The store's copper-colored tin ceiling and polished oak floor gleamed, and only a few cracks—unfortunate remnants from

A Season at the Cliff House

the quake—still ran down one whitewashed wall. Grace wandered up the center aisle toward a long, wide wooden counter suitable for cutting fabric. Along the way, she admired the ready-made satin dresses hanging on racks dotted throughout the store. The displays of hats, gloves, and a small selection of finely beaded purses also offered plenty of temptation.

"Mrs. Rothwell, so good to see you again." A tall, spindly man sporting a pencil mustache and wearing a crisp black suit greeted them. "And, Miss Isabelle, you're looking lovely as always."

"Thank you." Isabelle's tone told Grace that accepting this man's praise was part of the game.

"And who do we have with us today?" His eyes swept over Grace. She imagined he was already sizing up what color and dress style would look best on her.

Grace's cheeks warmed from his attention. "I'm Grace Hamilton, sir, a relative from Denver."

The man's eyes absorbed Grace from head to toe once more. "Visiting from the Rockies. How nice to have you with us."

"Yes, we're excited to have her here, Mr. Walters. We'd like to see any new fabrics you have, and then we'll make our choices," Josephine said.

"Of course." He turned on his heel, and the ladies followed him toward the back left-hand corner of the store.

Josephine leaned closer to Grace and spoke in a low voice. "Choose whatever fabric and style you like. Isa and I are getting new satin dresses for the season, and Father has promised not to grouse about the bill."

Grace's spirits lifted, and she nearly danced a jig in delight. *How fun it is to shop for something new without fear of being scolded when I get home.*

The women browsed a few racks full of the latest dress styles, then examined several bolts of satin in the newest fashionable shades. Grace fingered the collar of an emerald-colored gown, her thoughts returning to her earlier conversation with Josephine. *Frank travels a lot on business. What if he has an affair after we're married? Could I put up with knowing he had someone on the side, possibly in more than one city?* Heat prickled on her neck, and Grace's purse fell to the floor with a plop. She quickly retrieved it, her cheeks aflame. *I guess that's a no. I must make sure that doesn't happen; no amount of money is worth having an unfaithful man.*

Moments later, a scream and the sound of crashing metal ripped through the shop. Grace froze in fear.

Isabelle flung the sapphire-blue dress she was holding onto the floor. She almost ran down Mr. Walters as they raced behind the counter and disappeared behind tall, thick curtains into a cramped rear storeroom. On the floor, beneath a pile of heavy bolts of rose, dusty blue, and cream-colored silk and satin, a rail-thin shopgirl not much younger than Isabelle writhed and wailed. Tears streamed down the girl's face, her right forearm bent at an unnatural angle.

Mr. Walters and Isabelle began to chuck bolts of fabric off of the girl like logs. "Try to hold still. We'll have you out from under there soon," Isabelle said, her pulse racing.

With the bolts finally flung aside, the shopgirl struggled to sit up on the concrete floor. She whimpered and clutched her arm, her face twisted into a grimace. Isabelle and Mr. Walters knelt beside her.

"I've told you," he hissed at the girl. "You mustn't try to reach the back bolts without help."

The girl cowered much as a dog would beneath the wrathful words of its owner. "I'm sorry, sir," the girl sobbed. "I just thought the ladies might want to see the new bolt that arrived a few days ago."

The girl tried to move her arm and cried out in pain.

"It's fractured, I'm certain." Isabelle narrowed her eyes at Mr.

Walters, anger bubbling within her. "I need a magazine, a long scrap of cloth, and three shorter pieces of cloth to set the arm. Can you get those for me, please?"

Still crouched next to Isabelle, Mr. Walters drew back as if shocked. He opened his mouth to say something, but Isabelle beat him to it.

"Mr. Walters." Her tone was that of a drill sergeant. "I need to set her arm *now*. Please go fetch the strips of cloth."

"Yes, I—there must be, I'll find—" Mr. Walters jumped up and scurried to a worktable and then a desk, tossing aside vibrantly colored scraps of fabric as he went.

Isabelle comforted the shopgirl, barely able to hide the immense feeling of satisfaction that coursed through her. Not only was she helping much as a nurse would, she had also put Mr. Walters in his place for his coarse treatment of the girl. Isabelle pressed her lips together to smother a smile. *He's not used to being bossed around by a woman. The last thing he wants is me babbling to all my friends that the owner of Walters Dress Shop was terribly cruel to his seamstress, who had just broken her arm.*

Mr. Walters returned moments later and handed Isabelle a magazine and four strips of satin. Isabelle bent the magazine into a U shape, cradled the girl's broken arm in it, secured it with three strips of pink satin, and tied the arm at a ninety-degree angle to the girl's shoulder with a strip of red satin. The girl continued to sob but finally managed a thank-you to Isabelle.

"Let's take you out front so you can be ready when the ambulance arrives." Isabelle helped the shopgirl up.

Mr. Walters offered no assistance and instead smoothed his mustache. He led the ladies out of the stockroom with nary a glance over his shoulder, Isabelle trailing behind him, her arm wrapped around the shopgirl's waist. Once behind the counter, Isabelle helped the shopgirl ease herself onto a short stool.

"I'll be right back," Isabelle reassured her.

BROOKE L. DAVIS

Isabelle clutched Mr. Walters's arm and hurried him toward the phone at the far end of the counter. She shushed him along the way as he grunted low sounds of protest. The man was obviously not used to being pushed around in his own store. At the end of the counter, Isabelle stopped and glared at him, her back to the shopgirl.

"Call the Park Emergency Aid Station," Isabelle insisted in a whisper. "They'll take care of her for free and send her to the general hospital. Does she sew with her right hand? And is she one of your best seamstresses?"

Isabelle quirked an eyebrow at Mr. Walters, wondering if he would be smart enough to grasp her insinuation or caring enough to do the right thing. *The shopgirl certainly doesn't have the money to go to a private hospital for care, and she won't be sewing any time soon with a broken arm. Better to send her to the Park station first, so the arm has a good chance of being set quickly.*

Mr. Walters's eyes bulged. Isabelle smiled at him, relief settling over her. Despite his tongue lashing of the girl in the back room, losing a talented seamstress would be bad for business. The accident had forced him to make the right decision.

"I—yes, let me." Mr. Walters hustled to the telephone and dialed.

Isabelle returned to the shopgirl, whose face continued to contort in pain.

"They'll set it properly at the emergency hospital, and it'll heal up fine," Isabelle whispered to her.

Josephine cast her eyes skyward, Grace standing stock-still beside her.

Isabelle shook her head in disgust at her sister and rubbed the shopgirl's shoulder. *At least I was here.* Isabelle shuddered. *Who knows what would've become of her if I hadn't been.*

"Thank you, miss." The girl's large brown eyes shone with tears. "It isn't quite as bad, but it still hurts a lot."

"You're welcome," Isabelle said. "I helped others when we lived in the park last year and have read some on how to treat broken bones. I want to become a nurse."

The girl adjusted her arm and winced. "You'd be a fine one, miss. Never a bit of panic in you. I'd not ever have thought to tie it up like this."

Several minutes later, a black horse-drawn emergency ambulance arrived, and the driver leaped down from the seat. Isabelle and Mr. Walters helped the man usher the girl out the door and into the back of the ambulance.

THIRTEEN

From the dress shop window, Grace watched the ambulance roll away from the curb, her fear fading like the sound of the horses' clattering hooves. She hung the dress Isabelle had discarded back on the rack and calmed her shaken nerves by admiring a nearby burgundy dress. *How awful to be working-class.* Grace fingered the ornate black lace set into the bodice of the dress. *At least I'll be married and can choose to be a teacher. I can't imagine having to work to live.*

Mr. Walters hustled back into the store and smoothed his hair. "I apologize, ladies. She's a hard worker, and heaven knows she needs the money now that her father's gone, but sometimes . . . "

"I was happy to help," Isabelle assured Mr. Walters before wandering back through the racks of dresses.

"Yes, Miss Isabelle, I'm quite grateful. I wouldn't have known how to set the arm like that and secure the shoulder. Still, I'm sorry her carelessness ruined your day."

Josephine raised a demure hand, no doubt trying to ease Mr. Walters's concerns.

Isabelle shrugged and returned to the sapphire-colored dress she had been holding before the shopgirl's accident.

She's so eager to help and enjoys the admiration despite shrugging it off as nothing. Grace removed the burgundy gown from the hanger and held it against herself. *Maybe that's why she wants to become a nurse. She doesn't get attention at home because her notions aren't accepted. At a hospital, patients will appreciate and praise her.*

Grace bit her lip, a familiar wave of discouragement sweeping over her. She understood Isabelle's frustration. Grace's parents had done nothing but dismiss her idea of going to normal school to become a teacher, so much so that they had finally outright forbidden her to talk about it. At least with Frank, Grace felt she had a confidante and co-conspirator.

With dress orders placed—Grace had opted for the burgundy satin with the black lace insert—the three ladies rode in silence in the backseat of the Winton as George navigated around cable cars, automobiles, and horse-drawn carriages on the hilly ride home. *What an afternoon. It was such fun to be away from stuffy Aunt Cora.* Grace closed her eyes to avoid viewing the charred remains of burned-out homes. *Other than that awful business with the shopgirl, the outing was a great success. I can't wait to show off my new dress. Maybe it'll arrive in time to wear to something at the Cliff House.*

Grace licked her lips and smiled, a delicious thought forming in her mind. *Maybe I'll be wearing it when I see Frank.*

As evening shadows crept across the front yard and the clouds melted into a confection of peach and gold, Grace crossed the foyer on the way to the downstairs lavatory, only to be met by a young maid in a long black dress covered with a crisp white pinafore. The maid reminded Grace of the girl who had broken her arm earlier at the dress shop: timid, thin, subservient.

"This came for you today, miss." The maid handed Grace a letter.

Grace's pulse quickened, and she clutched the letter to her chest. She glanced behind her to see if anyone had seen their exchange, but by the time she had reassured herself that no one had, the maid had disappeared. With her aunts deep in conversation in the sitting room, Grace hurried upstairs and into the bedroom she shared with Aunt Cora. She closed the door, her heart pounding, and walked to the window. She noted the Cheyenne return address and tore open the envelope.

> *Dear Grace,*
>
> *I've settled in with Mary and Harlan, and on my first day here, won ten dollers in a card game. Can you believe that luck? There is all sorts of entertanement here for a man, and I think we'll be rightly happy living in California.*
>
> *Before I left Wyoming, my brothers in Kansas City gave me the name of a man who might be able to introduce me to local people, and I have a meeting with him this week to talk cattle. He isn't in the restraunt bisness but sounded like a mighty big-time fella on the phone. I'm hopeful I can get him to sine a contract to get a trainload of hoofs rolling west soon. I see big opporunitees here Grace. With Los Angeles booming with oil and San Francisco rebilding, people are going to want to eat steak to celebrate!*
>
> *Have you ben to the oshun? I can see it from my window at Marys but haven't walked on the sand yet. Just seeing that blue made me glad to know I won't be spending any more winters in windy cold Cheyenne.*
>
> *It's hard to be apart from you and I know you feel the same about me. I don't know when I can see you, but I'll write agen when I'm able. Write and let me know how you're getting along with yer family.*
> *Frank*

Grace folded the letter and gazed down into the narrow yard.

Though Frank might not have been the world's best speller, he was ambitious. And like him, Grace wanted to *be* somebody. Mostly, she wanted to *marry* somebody and have a life of her own, away from her uncaring and overly strict parents. Her thoughts wandered to Graham's wife, Rosaline, whom she had met at the Cliff House. *Now, there's a woman who married somebody.*

Plodding footsteps that could only belong to Aunt Cora sounded in the hall. Grace hurried to the armoire and stashed the letter under a pile of chemises. She had just jammed the drawer shut when the bedroom door opened.

"Dinner's ready, dear," Aunt Cora said. "Didn't you hear us call?"

"I—no, I'm sorry, I didn't." Grace joined her aunt in the hall.

FOURTEEN

That evening, Isabelle sat in her usual place at the dining table, Grace to her immediate left and Cora one place farther down. Across the table, Henry scooted a large bowl of steaming mashed potatoes toward Isabelle. Nearly ready to burst, she beamed at him. She couldn't wait to share the story of how she had helped the girl at Walters Dress Shop.

"Father, did you have a good day?" Isabelle hoped he would answer quickly and return the favor by asking her the same.

"Hmm." James's brow creased. A thick piece of roast beef was threatening to wiggle its way out from between his knife and the serving fork.

That's a good enough answer. Isabelle straightened in her chair. "I set a broken arm today." She held her head high in triumph and waited for what would undoubtedly be more questions from her father.

"Just a moment," James said.

Isabelle's shoulders slumped. *I should've known he wouldn't have heard me.* Her father had a man's typically singularly focused mind. Isabelle half believed that if their house had caught fire as so many others had on that fateful morning when the earth shook, he might have only escaped with his trousers and not his shoes.

Sitting next to Henry, Josephine rolled her eyes, and Isabelle stuck her tongue out at her sister.

"Girls." Margaret's disapproving tone was the same one she

had used when Isabelle and Josephine were little and delighted in tormenting each other.

"What's this? What's going on?" James finally landed the slab of meat onto his plate, splashing a few drops of melted butter onto the white tablecloth.

"I set a broken arm today," Isabelle repeated, barely able to contain her excitement.

"What she did was stick a girl's arm in a magazine and tie it up with ribbons." Josephine motioned for Cora to pass the basket of rolls.

"Well, *you* did nothing to help," Isabelle shot back.

James cleared his throat from where he sat at the end of the table. He cut his slab of roast beef and piled a piece onto the back of his fork. Isabelle pressed her fingernails into her palm and made a fist under the table. She hurriedly took a bite of mashed potatoes to keep from saying anything further. *Why does my family pretend like bad things don't happen?* Hadn't they all survived smoke inhalation from living outdoors in the aftermath of the great fire? Hadn't they seen bedraggled people with open wounds and puckering burns wandering the streets for days?

"I just—" Isabelle sighed in exasperation and stared at her plate to avoid a glare of reprimand from her mother. "I couldn't stand there and do nothing. I read books, Father. I knew what to do. You wouldn't let me apply to the University of California diploma program for nurses here, which, by the way, is accepting new students again since the hospital's been rebuilt. It's not quite as good as the program in Los Angeles, but—"

Margaret choked on a sip of wine and coughed. "What program in Los Angeles?" she squeaked. "How do you even know of such a thing?"

Isabelle surveyed her family, a smug grin tugging at the corners of her mouth. *I have their attention now.* She had expected her mother's dismay at the mention of the nursing program in Los Angeles, but what pleased Isabelle most was that Margaret's alarm had served another purpose. It had forced James to finally afford Isabelle the serious attention for which she so often yearned.

"I read the newspaper, Mother." Isabelle loaded her fork with another helping of mashed potatoes. "There was a notice."

Before Margaret could reply, Josephine spoke. "How could you even get in?"

Refusing to be provoked, Isabelle aimed a coquettish smile at Josephine. Isabelle had made her point, most of all, for her father's benefit. She believed that if she kept pushing, gently yet consistently, he might allow her to attend school should she be accepted.

"Yes, then," James said, sipping his wine. "We all have our little passions. As long as helping that girl didn't put you in danger, I'm sure what you did was appreciated."

It's better than doing nothing and only watching, like Josephine and Grace. Isabelle pulled a face.

Margaret started an uninteresting new thread of conversation with Grace and Cora, forcing Isabelle's thoughts toward the outrageous plan she had set in motion. If caught, she feared, her entire world would crumble and burn, much as the city had a year ago.

The application to attend the California Hospital School for Nurses training program in Los Angeles required two letters of character, a physical examination signed by a doctor, and a photograph if the applicant could not apply in person. Isabelle had cut an image of herself out of a family photograph she kept in her room. She had also assured Dr. Jenkins and her Sunday school leader—a secretly progressive woman she trusted—that her father approved of her applying. Her last letter of character would come from Violet Gilchrist. As Isabelle's best friend, Violet could be counted upon to speak glowingly about Isabelle's actions after the quake and her continued interest in and support of the Red Cross.

The letter of character from her Sunday school teacher and her signed physical exam had been received; her letter from Violet had not. With one missing piece left in the puzzle, Isabelle struggled to remain patient. Given the day's events, she was more confident than ever that she was meant to be a nurse, but she hated feeling silenced by those who refused to see the good she could accomplish.

Thwarted in her attempt to rouse enthusiasm from anyone in her family, Isabelle finished her roast beef and quietly helped herself to a generous spoonful of chocolate custard. She savored the rich dessert, resigned to celebrating her triumph alone. Her knowledge and quick action, paired with medical care from the Park Emergency Aid Station and the general hospital, would give the shopgirl's arm the best chance to heal properly. *And she thanked me.* Isabelle licked a bit of custard from her lips. *For now, that'll have to be enough.*

After dinner, Isabelle, Margaret, and Josephine gathered in the sitting room and slowly pulled their needles back and forth through their needlepoint canvases. Grace and Cora joined them, Grace with a small needlepoint piece and Cora with her knitting.

Eleanor served coffee, and amidst the chatting, Isabelle admired Grace's even stitches, which would eventually bring a deep-red rose to life. *I'll never be able to sew like that, and I don't want to.* Isabelle sighed inwardly. *Sewing's so terribly tiresome.* The scene reminded Isabelle of when she and Josephine were little girls. Josephine's uniform stitches were always pulled with the same tautness, which made the canvas spring to life, a picture painted in wool. Unfortunately, Isabelle's uneven stitches and occasional knots had failed to produce the same effect.

Isabelle checked the clock, which read quarter to nine. Josephine and Grace both stitched away, quiet contentment etched on their faces. *I will not be like my sister and cousin.* Isabelle nearly growled at her twisted strand of wool. *Father's right. Each of us has our passions, and the sooner I can apply to nursing school, the sooner I can start following mine.*

FIFTEEN

A few days later, Isabelle sat with a cup of tea opposite Grace in an oversized wing chair in Charlotte Gordon's sitting room. In the far corner, fragrant roses unfurled themselves in a vase, two buds stubbornly refusing to open. They reminded Isabelle of how impatient she was to apply to nursing school. Several heavy oil paintings depicting ferns, palm trees, and sea life hung within the outlines of the floor-to-ceiling Edwardian paneling. The late-morning sun streamed through two windows flanked by moss-colored velvet curtains and warmed the women. The soothing green and cream color palette was reminiscent of a conservatory; all that was missing was the glass ceiling and a tangle of hanging plants.

"I'm thrilled you could come." Charlotte offered Grace and Isabelle a selection of sugar wafers from a silver-plated tray.

Grace accepted one, but Isabelle declined.

"It's hard for me to get out, as you know, Isa." Charlotte tucked a tendril of onyx hair back in place. "And I love having new people to talk to."

Charlotte's pointed comment caused Grace to smile so widely that her teeth showed. "I—thank you." Grace covered her mouth with her hand, her sugar wafer not fully finished.

"Now then, Isabelle, you *must* update me on how things are going with your nursing adventure," Charlotte prompted in a conspiratorial tone.

Isabelle grinned and sat her teacup back in its saucer on the oval coffee table in front of her. Grace leaned forward in her chair, her eyes widening.

"Well, I'm still missing one letter from Violet, and then I can apply." Isabelle's hands were clasped so tightly together in her lap that her fingers ached. "I think it's going to boil down to convincing Father. There's no tuition because I'd be working at the hospital and living in the Nurses' Home, but I'd still need money for books and sundries. And even though the program takes three years to complete, I could come home during the summers." Isabelle rolled her eyes and took another sip of tea. "Mother's so overly dramatic about it; you'd think I was planning to run off to Guam for the rest of my life."

Charlotte and Grace laughed.

Isabelle slumped back into her chair. "I've decided that if I get accepted, and Mother and Father don't approve, I'm going anyway."

Grace sobered, in contrast to Charlotte, who gaped, her expression one of barely concealed glee.

"I'll sell the jewelry I inherited from Grandma Rudolph. I'll live in a boardinghouse and work as a telephone operator. I'll even stand on a box and recite poetry on a street corner to pay for books," Isabelle said.

Charlotte burst into giggles. When Grace choked on her tea, Charlotte handed her a napkin.

"I *am* going to be a nurse!" Isabelle pronounced.

Charlotte clapped her hands quietly and bounced up and down in her chair. "Yes, yes, you must do it!" she breathed.

Isabelle picked up her teacup and toasted Grace and Charlotte. "It's all I have. Heaven knows I can't dance or play the piano or sew or sing for my supper."

Charlotte cackled, but Grace coughed again.

"I'm sorry, Grace." Isabelle patted her cousin's leg. "I hope I'm not offending you by speaking so plainly."

"No," she squeaked, napkin over her mouth, her coughs

refusing to subside. Grace sipped more tea and coughed again. "Not at all. I appreciate it. Mother and Father won't let me—"

Grace fell silent and lowered her head, her cheeks flushed. Isabelle held her breath in anticipation. *Does Grace want to go to school? She seems like Josephine with her proper ways, but maybe she's more like me than I know. Does she have a secret dream too?*

Charlotte topped off Grace's cup of tea, then calmly refilled her own.

"I know it's not my place to pry." Charlotte's kind eyes belied her curiosity. "But please continue, Grace. Nothing said in this room ever leaves it."

A knowing look passed between Isabelle and Charlotte. Isabelle had cried more than a few tears in Charlotte's sitting room, having poured her heart out to her friend when Margaret had prevented her from applying to the local University of California diploma program before the disaster.

"Is there something you'd like to do to help others, perhaps?" Charlotte ventured.

Isabelle sat in rapt suspense. *She is like me, and there is something she wants to do! Why won't she tell us?*

Grace smiled weakly and sipped her tea.

"I'd very much like to be a kindergarten teacher," she whispered.

The way Grace retreated into her chair after her revelation made Isabelle wonder if her cousin was relieved to have shared her secret or filled with shame for admitting it, let alone wanting it in the first place.

Charlotte blotted her mouth with her napkin. "That's wonderful. It's so important for children to be educated, especially little girls." Charlotte slanted her eyes toward Isabelle, her expression one of hesitation. Isabelle dipped her chin, eager for Charlotte to continue.

"You know," Charlotte said, "I had scarlet fever when I was two. It damaged my heart, which is why I'm unable to pursue the things that you—that most other young women—can. It's why

I'm so passionate about helping my friends. Without the tutors my parents hired when I was young, I would've been so far behind in my education. I couldn't go to school with other children until I was ten." Charlotte raised her eyebrows at Grace.

"Oh." Grace stared at her teacup, clearly moved by Charlotte's plight. "I didn't know about your heart. I'm sorry to hear about that."

Charlotte gazed out the window wistfully. A lump rose in Isabelle's throat. *I can't imagine how envious she must be.* Isabelle tried but failed to swallow the lump. *She and Violet have always been my closest friends; I don't sense Grace has many of those.*

"So tell us." Charlotte laid two wafers on her saucer. "Tell us how we can help you become a kindergarten teacher."

Grace chewed on her lip. For a moment, Isabelle feared her cousin would demur and decline Charlotte's offer. *Please don't,* she prayed.

"I would—it—" Grace sputtered, and clamped her mouth shut. Isabelle squirmed in anticipation.

"There's a program in Los Angeles," Grace said. "It's two years long, but I have no way of going, no money."

Cowed by what Isabelle imagined was unnecessary shame and sadness, Grace lowered her head again and sipped her tea. Isabelle bit her tongue to keep from interrupting.

"If I were married or had family in Los Angeles, then maybe I could go." Grace's voice was thick with discouragement. "But without a home, I'd have to board with a family. I'd have to pay to stay with them and extend my time in school if I had to work off my debt by doing domestic chores. Mother and Father don't approve, and without a husband, I couldn't dream of—"

"But what if that's not true?" Isabelle interjected, unable to remain quiet any longer. "I've seen your needlepoint. It's perfect and makes my canvas look like piles of knots tied by scatterbrained mice."

Charlotte almost blew tea through her nose, and even Grace twittered a laugh.

Isabelle waved her hand and continued. "What I'm curious about are your other talents. Can you sing? Dance? Play the trumpet?"

Charlotte howled with laughter, but Grace's eyes grew glassy. When Grace laid a hand over her mouth as if she might cry, Isabelle sprang forward in her chair, regretting her comments.

"Grace, I apologize," Isabelle said. "I'm not trying to make light; I'm simply trying to help. Teachers are important, and if you want to be one, you can. And without a husband."

It was all Isabelle could do not to groan when Grace shook her head. *Why is she giving up so easily? Does she think so little of herself that she believes she has nothing to offer?*

"In all seriousness, can you sing or dance?" Isabelle pressed.

Grace sniffed and licked her lips. "I can play the piano. I love to play and I have to know how to graduate as a teacher. I can also sing, and when I was little, I loved sketching things, especially animals."

When Isabelle mashed her palms onto her cheeks, Charlotte giggled.

"I'm so envious!" Isabelle exclaimed. "Sewing, piano, singing, *and* drawing? You don't know how lucky you are."

"I could never teach them outside of a classroom." Grace's voice had gone quiet. "I could never ask people to pay me for—"

"Why not?" Isabelle asked.

Grace remained quiet, much to Isabelle's consternation. *Why is she so weak? She has so many ways to help herself achieve her dream. Why is she waiting for some man to come along and save her when she could give piano or singing lessons?*

As the silence in the room grew deafening, Isabelle wrestled with why her cousin would willingly choose to have her life dictated by her parents or a husband instead of being clever enough to dictate it herself.

"Thank you, Grace," Charlotte said, finally breaking the awkward impasse. "It was very brave of you to share. Regardless of how you get there, I hope you're able to become a teacher one day. Please know I'm willing to help you if I can."

Isabelle ground through a sugar wafer, her frustration refusing to cool. Leave it to Charlotte to say the right thing and comfort Grace when all Isabelle wanted to do was goad her. Despite Grace's bewildering number of options to bring in extra money—all of which Isabelle envied more than she wanted to admit—Grace was choosing to be another submissive young woman by not taking charge of her future. *She's never going to be a teacher; she doesn't want it badly enough.* Isabelle stared out the window while Charlotte and Grace chatted about a frivolous detail on Charlotte's dress. *But I'll be a nurse, even if I have to recite poetry and live under a pier.*

Grace sat next to Isabelle in silence on the ride home from tea. As the car strained forward on its climb up the hill, Grace's mind strained with it. She had bared her soul to Charlotte and Isabelle, astonished and heartened by their encouragement and acceptance.

Though not offended, Grace found herself out of sorts. Between how Isabelle and Josephine teased each other and the way Charlotte and Isabelle used Charlotte's sitting room as some sort of clandestine headquarters to plot Isabelle's great escape from San Francisco, Grace wanted to scream and hug her cousin and new friend simultaneously. Grace had obviously missed out on a great deal of conniving female conversation by sitting quietly and obediently in the houses of her proper female friends in Denver. She had desperately wanted to unburden herself to Charlotte and Isabelle, to regale them with romantic tales of how Frank had proposed and how she would soon be living in Los Angeles and attending school, all while being happily married. But much like when she had arrived in San Francisco, something had told Grace not to breathe a word of her plan until she had gone through with it. While she delighted in her newfound freedom and the opportunity to share her dreams, getting comfortable with how Isabelle, Josephine, and Charlotte interacted with one another would take some time.

Grace's pulse thrummed faster, her fingers stroking her pearl teardrop earrings. Isabelle's offhand comment about selling inherited jewelry to pay for school supplies had surprised Grace so completely that it had brought on a coughing fit of epic proportions, mainly because Grace hadn't thought of it herself. And Isabelle's insistence that Grace use her *talents* to earn money to pay for school? The idea was preposterous, though it thrilled—and frightened—her to her core. *I have inherited jewelry, too, but could I bring myself to sell it? Could I teach piano or voice lessons to earn money?* Grace had never considered that she might have valuable expertise other than what she would need as a teacher. Hadn't she been led to believe that the only aptitudes she needed, or that would be recognized, involved securing a husband, creating a beautiful and loving home, and entertaining those in her social circle?

The car belched, its engine still struggling, and Grace's thoughts turned to Charlotte. Her poignant story about enduring scarlet fever, which had left her with a permanently damaged heart, had touched Grace. She, too, had a heart that sometimes struggled, especially in Denver's thin air. That, along with her mysteriously growing lack of appetite, had convinced her father to prescribe a stimulant so potent that, in large doses, it could kill a man. Fortunately, the one-sixtieth-grain tablets Grace took were minuscule enough to stimulate her heart and appetite but do nothing more. With her heart remaining stable at sea level, she hadn't needed any of her medication, and the bottle remained tucked safely in her train case. The hearty food along with the relaxed and amusing mealtime conversations had done wonders for her appetite.

George parked the car by the curb, and Grace turned to Isabelle. "Thank you for this morning. It was kind of you and Charlotte to listen. I appreciate it more than you know."

Isabelle offered a closed-mouthed smile. "I'm glad. I'm sure we'll see her again soon."

George helped Grace out of the car, and she thanked him. On her way up the front steps, she exhaled a silent sigh of relief. She had revealed as much as she could and more than she had intended to Isabelle and Charlotte. *I must remember to keep my mouth shut in the future. I can't risk another slip that might ruin my plan to be with Frank.*

SIXTEEN

Having placed their lunch orders, Henry, his father-in-law, and Graham McCormick sat at a table near the back of the Fairmont Hotel dining room on a Tuesday. Around them, couples held quiet conversations, and sunlight glittered off the gold gilt filigree that adorned the stark white-paneled walls. Henry suppressed a smile. With its ostentatious glow, the space conjured up the image of a glorified reception room one might find oneself in while waiting to be called before Saint Peter at the pearly gates.

Henry settled into his comfortable seat surrounded by familiar company and the alluring scents of tournedos of beef and roast squab in demi-glace. He usually enjoyed lunches with James and his business associates, although they were infrequent. Today, however, Graham had joined them, and Henry was already dreading the man's latest scheme.

"I have someone new in mind for this." Graham's comment jolted Henry back to the present. He had been distracted by the scrumptious-looking piece of triple chocolate cake that a waiter had delivered to a man across the room.

"Mmm." James fiddled with the end of his unlit cigar. "You should bring him around. What's his name?"

Henry knew the man's name didn't interest James. Instead, the concern was more of a three-part "what's his name, where's he from, and is he willing to do what we ask without problems" question all rolled into one.

"Frank Buchanan." Graham leaned back in his chair and crossed his legs. "His family owns a beef outfit in Kansas City. Frank runs the western business out of Cheyenne."

James finally lit his cigar, the end glowing red. "Good, good." James undid one of his suit vest buttons, and Henry winced. The stress of the last year, paired with Eleanor's superb cooking, had conspired to severely test the garment's seams. "Invite him to an afternoon meeting then," James said to Graham. "Let's do it at the Cliff House. Season's getting short, and Henry and I can bring the girls for lunch. You've met Grace, right, Graham?"

The sly smile that creased Graham's face made Henry swallow in disgust. Henry suspected Graham had at least one, if not two, mistresses. Henry also didn't appreciate the prospect of the lascivious thoughts that were likely slinking through Graham's mind about Grace.

"Yes, we did," Graham said. "Cora, too, I believe? An aunt?"

"Yes, long-winded woman, unfortunately—Cora, not Grace. Believe it'd be best to take Grace back to the gingerbread palace. She seems to have had an out with a suitor in Denver, poor child, and the family didn't approve of her most recent fellow. We want her to enjoy herself while she's here." James puffed on his cigar.

An out? Henry struggled to keep his mouth from gaping open. *Her suitor disappeared!*

"Well, her new fellow should've been more creative." Graham winked at James.

The tendons in Henry's neck tightened, and he worked his jaw. *The word isn't "creative"; it's "discreet."*

It was well-known to Henry and a few select others that James, too, had a mistress. Henry didn't know who she was, nor did he want to, but there were nights when James came home late from the office. He suspected Margaret knew, but he wasn't certain. The entire enterprise struck Henry as not only immoral but also dangerous and exhausting on a number of levels. He couldn't imagine all the mental and logistical gymnastics it took to manage someone on the side, despite the enjoyment one might derive from the physical encounters.

"I'm not sure that's the answer." James laid his cigar in a nearby ashtray. A waiter brought the men their meals. "But I'd like to meet this Frank. We need some new faces around here."

Henry rubbed his hands together and eyed his hot turkey sandwich and asparagus tips. He ordered the same thing every time he lunched at the Fairmont. It wasn't the most novel behavior, but the hot turkey reminded him of home.

As Henry took a large bite of his sandwich and the tang of the mushroom sauce mixed with the delectable tender meat, his mind wandered to his childhood. His father had worked as a laborer in the shipyards in Philadelphia, and by the time Henry was ten, he had nearly beaten Henry's mother to death before drinking himself into an early grave. With work scarce and two boys to feed, his mother had moved them in with her older sister and brother-in-law. His mother had taken in mending and laundry to help earn money, but the damage had been done physically and emotionally. She had died two years later.

Henry had often lain awake in his aunt and uncle's cramped attic and promised himself he would not become his father. He wanted an education, and thanks to his aunt and uncle's encouragement, he excelled at math. By the time he was in high school, he was keeping the books for his uncle's prosperous mercantile business. Schooling followed at the University of Pennsylvania, and he came west. Through honesty, hard work, and loyalty, he had finally escaped the shadow of his family and become successful.

Henry's brother, however, had embraced other ambitions and fallen into a life of petty theft before moving into the dark world of organized crime. Henry had watched his brother's descent with sorrow, often feeling helpless to save him. Henry shivered and took a sip of iced tea. He had bailed his brother out of jail three

times before he had boarded a train to California. His brother had
promised that each time was the last, but Henry had known better.
His brother's muscular build was perfect for being a tough. He also
enjoyed occasional rounds of fisticuffs, which sometimes left him
with a black eye and bloodied knuckles. Their mother had never
praised him, and their aunt and uncle had found him troublesome
and willful. With a police record haunting him and the crime bosses
paying well, Henry knew his brother would never move beyond the
life he had created for himself.

James and Graham both chuckled, possibly having shared an
inside joke. Henry wiped his mouth with his napkin and returned
his attention to their conversation.

"Of course, of course." Graham sipped his wine. "The money
won't be the problem; it never was. It was that people ran their
mouths when they should've been running their businesses. I can
always arrange the payments. The records, though, will be more of
a challenge."

Henry's stomach clenched, and he struggled to swallow the
bite of partially chewed sandwich that now sat like a ball of slime
in his mouth. Whatever Graham was suggesting reeked of old San
Francisco. Bribes and payoffs were the exact things that had nearly
landed James in jail, yet he behaved like the authorities had never
questioned him. Unlike Abe Ruef, who had finally admitted he was
guilty of corruption only a few days ago, James had survived the
scandal mostly unscathed. The close call with the law had almost
been more than Henry's nerves could bear.

Henry took another sip of tea and pushed a few asparagus
spears around his plate. He knitted his brow and internally scolded
himself. *I promised myself I wouldn't do anything illegal when I
came to California. Since I've been here, all I've done is book some
highly questionable accounting entries for my father-in-law and be*

present when he suggests making deals under the table. I wish James and Graham could see that everyone should be able to work hard and prosper as I did and not be swindled.

James and Graham toasted their newly hatched plan, Henry painting on a believable smile for their benefit. James would try to shield him as best he could by only providing barebones details, but a sinking feeling settled over Henry.

The men were heading back into the lion's den.

Why do I put up with this? Henry forked the last bite of now-mushy asparagus into his mouth. *Oh yes, because this job provides the life that Josephine and I deserve. I love that woman as if there's no tomorrow, and she loves me too.*

Henry's heart had almost seized to a complete stop the day he had met Josephine. She, Margaret, and Isabelle had boarded the cable car on which he was riding. When they had arrived at their stop and stepped off the car, Henry had swiftly lifted Josephine off the ground and into his arms. A carriage, pulled by a spooked horse, had suddenly careened dangerously close to the cable car and had nearly collided with her. Without Henry's heroic gesture, she would have certainly been injured or even killed. Afterward, a shaken Josephine had thanked him and lingered longer than expected in his embrace. A hysterical Margaret had hugged him three times amidst her tears and invited him to dinner.

Two weeks after that meal, James had hired Henry and unexpectedly invited him to the house to discuss a tax situation. Josephine—stunning in an aquamarine ensemble that set off her jet-black hair and almond-shaped eyes—had appeared in the foyer shortly after Henry had stepped through the front door. When James had again arranged for Henry and Josephine to be in each other's presence, Henry had learned about the positive power of proximity. With so much of his young life spent trying to escape his dangerous father, he had only begun to get a taste of what a good influence meant with his aunt and uncle in Pennsylvania. James had welcomed Henry into the family like the son he had never had. Or like the son, Daniel, who had died before Henry could meet him.

With their meals finished and cigars extinguished, James paid the check, and the men strolled out of the restaurant and through the expansive hotel lobby.

"Bring this Frank Buchanan out to the Cliff House, Graham." James clapped his friend on the back. "Call the office with the details. We can impress him and talk business at the same time."

When Henry and James parted ways with Graham on the sidewalk, Henry exhaled a silent sigh of relief. He didn't want to be involved in any more illegal dealings with his father-in-law, but what could he do? He and Josephine's new home would be finished within the next several months; James had paid to have it rebuilt. Henry was a competent and trustworthy accountant and could find another job, but he didn't want to appear disloyal. Much like trying to figure out what was going on with Grace, the situation with Graham, Frank, and James required patience. Unfortunately, Henry wasn't sure how much more of that he had.

SEVENTEEN

The morning of the Red Cross tea, a butler ushered Isabelle, Josephine, Margaret, and Grace into Violet Gilchrist's sitting room. The late-morning sun shone through the tall windows, each adorned with thick panels of peach velvet gathered behind Georgian rope-style tiebacks. A large bowl of similarly colored punch and trays of brownies and slices of almond cake sat on a table in front of the floor-to-ceiling bookcases. Several young women, most of whom Isabelle knew, mingled in groups while their mothers and other city matrons chatted near an unlit fireplace framed by an ornately carved mantel.

Isabelle stood near the table full of tempting refreshments and rubbed her hands together. George had taken Cora to the train station after breakfast. Isabelle had bitten her tongue to smother a giggle when Grace had hugged her aunt and bid her farewell. Grace's luminous smile perfectly expressed the sentiments of others in the household: Cora meant well, but her staunch beliefs and silent judgment would not be missed.

Isabelle and Grace helped themselves to brownies. With Cora gone, Isabelle hoped Grace could finally find comfort in the company of the Hamiltons' social circle. Because of either the mysterious situation with her suitor or the discouragement she most likely felt about her teaching prospects, Isabelle sensed Grace wasn't enjoying herself in San Francisco. She was simply biding her time until she returned to Denver.

Isabelle glanced around the room and finally spotted Violet, dressed today in a most unfortunate shade of mustard. *Judging is wrong, but at least I know what colors look nice on me.* Isabelle sipped her punch. *That yellow dress makes her look like a stained rag.* Isabelle gazed at Violet's dishwater-brown hair and eyes set a little too far apart. Isabelle recalled what Margaret had once said about Violet: "She isn't pretty, but she has pretty ways." Isabelle had agreed.

Violet smiled, her overbite dominating her face, and motioned for Isabelle to join her. Isabelle bit the inside of her lip to smother a snicker. *I shouldn't make fun because she's such a good friend, but she'd never be allowed into nursing school.*

The California Hospital School for Nurses Annual Announcement stated that "applicants should have their teeth examined and put in good condition before entering school." Isabelle remembered the passage—she had almost memorized the entire six-page announcement—and had immediately thought of Violet.

Isabelle pressed a hand to Grace's arm and the two women crossed the room to where Violet stood near the fireplace.

"It's so nice to meet you, Grace." Violet offered the two women glasses of punch. "Are you involved with the Red Cross in Denver?"

Grace sipped her punch and shook her head. "But my father's a doctor, and I know how important their work is."

"Isn't it, though?" Violet ushered Isabelle and Grace toward chairs at the end of the refreshments table, where they all took their seats. "We can't be directly involved—except for maybe you, Isa—but there's so much we can do to help."

"I'm sure," Grace agreed. "And you're right. Isabelle's *directly* involved. She helped a girl with a broken arm last week."

Violet gasped.

"I'll tell you about it another time." Isabelle straightened in her chair, proud memories of helping the shopgirl mingling with the warmth that spread through her. *It was kind of Grace to praise me.*

"They saved so many lives last spring," Violet continued, her urgent voice pitched low. "It's the least we can do to support them as the city continues to recover."

Moments later, Josephine materialized and parked herself with a muffled thud in a nearby chair. "I apologize for intruding on your little group, Violet. Thank you for inviting us. Mother's being fretful about the plague and Cora going back to Denver alone, and she swears that with the weight Father's gained, he'll drop dead of a heart attack soon. I simply couldn't take any more of her worrying."

Isabelle, Grace, and Violet laughed.

"Let's talk about something more pleasant, shall we?" Josephine suggested.

Violet raised a forefinger, still chewing on her brownie. Once finished, she spoke. "I may need some help planning the fall gala. It wouldn't be much, just a bit of time here and there."

Violet popped another oversized bite of brownie into her mouth, and Isabelle gaped at her in astonishment. Despite her progressive leanings, Violet usually remained dignified. Today felt different for some reason.

Grace leaned forward and wiped her mouth with her napkin. "I could help you."

Isabelle turned to her cousin in surprise. "Would you? We could do it together if you'd like, and—"

"Don't ask her to do that, Isabelle," Josephine protested. "She isn't staying."

Josephine turned to Grace. "Please don't feel you need to do anything. You're our guest and—"

"Helping plan an event sounds fun." Grace stared at Violet expectantly.

Maybe she can do things on her own. Isabelle's spirits rose. She wanted to believe that Grace's involvement with the Red Cross gala would be a harbinger of her working up the courage to apply to teaching school.

Violet clasped her hands together and beamed, her prominent front teeth on full display. "Thank you so much, Grace. With my engagement party coming up and a wedding to plan, I'd be thrilled if you could help, even if you're only here for a short time."

"I'd be happy to." In her excitement, Grace set her saucer and punch cup down on the nearby table so quickly they clattered. Her cheeks burned, and she pushed the saucer away from the edge of the table. *What luck! Violet's a soon-to-be bride too. She's the perfect person to help me learn about the latest flowers and dress styles.* "How wonderful for you. Congratulations," Grace said.

The smile fell from Grace's face when she spied Isabelle. Her cousin's energetic and engaging expression had vanished, replaced by a sidelong gaze of polite curiosity. Grace tugged at the high collar of her dress; the temperature in the room had risen at least ten degrees in the last few seconds. *This isn't the reaction of someone who's lost a suitor. I'm not sure how much Isabelle knows, and I can't ask Violet too many questions about her wedding without raising suspicion.*

"When are you getting married?" Grace asked, her voice still a little too animated.

Much to Grace's delight, Violet launched into the specifics of her wedding, from location to flower vendors, to how honored she was to be wearing her mother's wedding dress. At some point during the conversation, Josephine and Isabelle excused themselves, but Grace barely noticed. She was already having trouble remembering everything Violet was saying. Not only did she lack a pencil and paper to take notes, but the taking of said notes would also have been rude and suspicious. Grace would simply have to tuck away what she could remember until she could get home and scribble it all down.

Conversation and the clinking of punch glasses filtered throughout the room, and Grace found herself swept up in Violet's wedding excitement. An engagement party had been planned, "and you really must come," Violet insisted. The couple would be married early the next year. Grace could almost see herself in the ensemble Violet described: the white gown with lace sleeves, the bouquet of lavender lilies, the short string of pearls gifted to her by her grandmother. Every woman in Violet's family had worn those pearls on their wedding day. Grace's eyes grew moist when Violet spoke of how meaningful it would be to carry on that tradition.

"I can't tell you how much I love him," Violet admitted. "I'm sure we'll be very happy together."

"It's a wonderful feeling, isn't it?" Grace pressed her lips together into a sly grin.

Violet giggled, her eyes sparkling. "It really is."

Violet excused herself, leaving Grace alone. She savored a few bites of almond cake, wondering if she had ever felt about Charles the way Violet felt about her fiancé. One of the challenges Grace had faced earlier in the year had been feigning heartbreak over Charles's disappearance. She had lived in quiet desperation for weeks after he had vanished, hating herself for hoping he would never return, yet fearing he would. She had thought she loved him, but given his behavior, those feelings had been shattered so quickly she wasn't sure. *But I love Frank. He isn't like Charles. He rescued me, and my heart's telling me the truth this time.*

Grace accidentally choked on a sip of punch, coughed, and sat her cup and saucer back on the table. She wiped her mouth with her napkin and spotted Josephine and Aunt Margaret chatting with a few of the older ladies near the far window. *When Frank and I are together, this will be my life, along with my students.* She popped the last bite of almond cake into her mouth in satisfaction.

Grace relaxed into her chair, anticipation swelling in her chest. Collecting money for charity meant that she would meet other women and their husbands. Once married, Grace would have her work and be part of a brand-new social circle. Except in Los Angeles, she would be the hostess; she would be the one leaving generous donations, and best of all, she would have earned her money doing something she loved.

A few minutes later, Isabelle rejoined Grace on a nearby chair. "Are you having a good time?"

"I am," Grace said. "You were right. I like Violet. I know I won't be here for all of the fall season, but I'm excited to help with the gala."

Isabelle finished her punch. "I'm excited you want to help. It's going to be such fun."

Grace picked up her cup and observed the women in the room. *This is going to be easy. By the time I leave San Francisco, I'll have my wedding planned and a new group of friends to visit during my summers off from teaching. Coming on this trip was the best thing Mother and Father ever made me do.*

After dinner that evening, Grace and Isabelle sat in the sitting room, Grace with her needlepoint and Isabelle with her nose in a book. As the soft lamplight glowed and the clock ticked on the mantel, Grace recalled her day.

Before leaving for the train station, Aunt Cora had left Grace the allowance from her parents. With money now secured, Grace had been able to lay an entire dollar and a half onto the Red Cross collection plate at Violet's. She had stood to the side of the plate instead of directly in front of it so others could watch her donate *real money*. Her miserly father would never have donated in such a way, but she had watched her brothers and Charles do it. Grace liked how men handled money; they tossed it into a donation plate or onto a table to pay a dinner check as if they had a hoard of it and weren't parting with anything valuable. *They're confident or they're pretending, and if they're pretending, their act is very convincing.* Grace smiled to herself.

Grace hadn't tossed her bill and coins onto the plate, but she had had her money ready. She didn't want to look stingy by doling it out. Her chest had swelled when she had laid the two quarters atop the crisp dollar bill and breezed from the table. Violet's approving smile and almost imperceptible nod had assured Grace that she—and her money—had been noticed and appreciated.

Grace pulled another strand of pale green wool from the hank and threaded her needle. *I should write to Father and ask him for a Red Cross donation.* Grace bit her tongue to stifle a giggle. *It's the least he can do, given that he won't support my attending school. And if he thinks I've told people he'd be happy to contribute, he won't want to look too tightfisted.* She chewed on her lip, plotting how she would request twenty-five dollars. *No, I'll ask for fifty.*

Isabelle sat absorbed in her book. Her reading reminded Grace of an exchange during dinner between Isabelle and Henry earlier that evening. There had been a joke that Isabelle and Henry had shared that no one else had seemed to get. Grace had found it odd; she had no idea what it referenced, and Josephine had reacted with benign ignorance.

Henry and Isabelle struck Grace as intellectually suited to one another, much more so than Henry and Josephine. Not only had there been the joke, but Henry had handed Isabelle a book before dinner. She had eaten the entire meal with her napkin draped over it in her lap. *She should've put it on the floor.* Grace paused to consider Isabelle's breach of etiquette, then pulled her needle through the canvas. *Maybe that's another familiar and casual thing they do, but he shouldn't have brought the book to her in the dining room. Honestly, he shouldn't be bringing books to her at all.*

Grace secured the loose end of green wool to the back of the canvas with a few stitches, recalling what Josephine had said during their afternoon of dress shopping. She and Henry had only been married for two years. Isabelle would have been nineteen when her sister married. Assuming that Josephine and Henry had courted and been engaged for six months to a year before they wed, Isabelle would have been a little too young to be considered "available," but not by much. Grace shook her head. *Isabelle probably struck him as uninterested, given how intent she is on becoming a nurse. And Henry loves Josephine; she's elegant and charming and adores him. What man wouldn't want that?*

Grace continued her stitching, her thoughts turning to Frank. She had seen the life she could have in California today at Violet's, and liked it. If she was honest, she loved it. *But will Frank be able to give it to me, or should I set my sights higher?* She stopped midstitch and considered the brightly colored glass panes in the shade of the Tiffany lamp that cast its light onto Isabelle and her book. Grace's pulse ticked faster. *No, I probably shouldn't. He's Jacob's friend, and if it weren't for Frank and Jacob . . .* A shiver shimmied up Grace's spine.

Frank thought he knew everything about what had transpired between her and Charles; Grace knew otherwise. Frank and her younger brother, Jacob, had saved her from Charles that night. If she left Frank, he could either reveal the truth or spread lies so damaging she might never find herself married, or at least not married to someone who could give her the life she wanted and deserved. *Now is not the time for doubt. Now is the time for patience. We've come this far, and I love him. I can't be distracted or discouraged before our new life in Los Angeles begins.*

Isabelle placed her bookmark between two pages and rose. "I'm going up."

Grace motioned for her to wait, then rolled up her needlepoint canvas and stuffed it into the carpetbag on the floor next to her chair. "I'll join you."

The two women ascended the stairs, Grace's gaze lingering on the foyer below. The gleaming white marble floor, the mahogany credenza with its vase full of roses and lilies, and the pale floral-patterned wallpaper surrounded her in familial comfort and warmth. This was the life for which she was meant. *I can't wait to have a home like this with Frank. It's only a matter of time.*

EIGHTEEN

The Thursday after Violet's Red Cross tea found Grace and her family relaxing in the main dining room of the Cliff House after lunch. Uncle James had secured a table near the window and insisted that Grace sit facing the ocean. She sipped her tea and appreciated her uncle's thoughtful gesture. The views of the undulating water, the white table linens and bone china, and the sparkling crystal threatened to transport her to another world. A meal of delicious roast chicken, tomato and romaine salad, and a slice of chocolate mousse cake had left her wanting to walk out onto the beach, lie down, and drift off to sleep.

"James, Margaret, so good to see you again." A man's rich, deep voice startled Grace from behind.

She turned in her chair and almost dropped her teacup.

Graham McCormick approached the table, followed closely by Benjamin Franklin Buchanan, a confident smile plastered across Frank's face. Grace flushed, her heart fluttering like a wild bird trying to escape its cage. She gripped her chair arms so tightly that her fingernails hurt. The collar of her navy dress became more constricting, given how warm the room had become. She composed herself as best she could, her foot tapping the carpet under the table.

Uncle James rose from his chair.

"This is Frank Buchanan," Graham said, introducing Frank to Uncle James, and the men shook hands.

"Good to meet you, Frank," Uncle James boomed. "I hear you're new in town."

"I am, and I'm pleased to meet you," Frank said. "Looking forward to helping this city get back on its feet."

Frank's cordial yet restrained tone impressed Grace. *Good, Frank, very good.*

"Yes, we'll be off in a moment to talk about that, but first, I'd like you to meet my family," Uncle James said.

Introductions followed, and by the time it was Grace's turn to meet Frank, she had recovered most of her senses, though her pulse still raced. She greeted Mr. Buchanan as she would have any other unknown man of class, and was relieved when he dipped his head toward her in much the same way he had to Isabelle and Josephine. *How am I looking at him?* Grace longed to emulate Josephine. The picture of proper behavior today with her neutral yet attentive expression, Josephine was expertly splitting her attention between her father, her husband, and Graham.

Graham, Uncle James, and Frank talked for a few moments, then excused themselves from the table, along with Henry. The ladies returned to their seats, and Grace willed herself to wait until the door across the dining room had closed behind the gentlemen before speaking.

"Where are they going?" Grace crinkled her eyes. She had wanted to sound nonchalant but had failed thanks to being flustered by Frank's surprise appearance.

Josephine finished a sip of tea. "Downstairs. All of those doors you see in the corridors lead to sitting rooms. Men conduct private business there, and people also eat and do other things."

With her foot still pattering away on the carpet, Grace scooped her remaining cake crumbs onto her fork and ate them, a sense of relief enveloping her. Now that Frank had been introduced, Grace could ask her uncle about him from time to time without suspicion. She would have to do it discreetly, of course—no woman ever cared about or was allowed into a man's inner sanctum, better known as "work"—but Grace had paid attention when her mother skillfully wheedled information out of her father. *If I play this right, I can see Frank again. I can suggest we invite him to social events since he's new in town, and that won't be thought of as untoward.* Grace swallowed a giggle. Frank was now part of her circle, and much like a cowboy tending a string of cattle on their way to a mountain stream for a long drink, she had no intention of letting him wander away from the herd.

Ten minutes later, Grace followed her cousins and aunt into the women's parlor. Sunlight cut rectangles onto the wood floor and brightened the vibrant burgundy and navy oriental rugs. Harriet held court in her usual high-backed chair in the far corner of the parlor. Dressed in aubergine, she acknowledged Aunt Margaret, then continued speaking without skipping a beat.

"We must join them, Mother," Josephine whispered, heading toward the group of ladies who sat in a circle of closely spaced chairs around Harriet.

Grace stopped short, unsure of whom she should follow. She sensed Harriet was deep into a scandalous tale that Josephine didn't want to miss, but Grace didn't want to be impolite. Thankfully, Aunt Margaret saved the day and led Grace and Isabelle across the room to where Harriet sat. While enough chairs were available for Josephine, Isabelle, and Aunt Margaret, Grace ended up relegated next to Maude on a nearby love seat. Grace smiled in surprise; Maude did *not* look like a mud fence today. Her fresh and stylish coral-colored dress, complete with pink sash, highlighted her milky skin. Maude scooted over so Grace could sit down next to her. Josephine gently yet firmly shifted a bemused Isabelle toward a different chair so she could have a better view of Harriet.

"And I've discovered something else about a certain businessman who shall remain nameless," Harriet said, her breathy voice enthralling Grace. "Not that you'll need to do much guessing. He comes here regularly and is well-known in landed circles."

Josephine quietly cleared her throat, and Grace cut her eyes toward her cousin in suspicion. Was Josephine nervous? About to say something? Josephine clutched her hands together in her lap, her attention locked on Harriet. Uncle James was a real estate man. Was Harriet talking about him? Aunt Margaret leaned forward in her chair, and Josephine licked her lips. Harriet had them hooked; even Grace wanted Harriet to name names.

"He has not one but *two* tarts on the side," Harriet finally revealed.

Her pronouncement elicited a few strangled gasps from the group. Josephine shifted in her chair and nervously stroked the buttons on her cuff.

"Of course, I'm not sure who they are, but it certainly was news. He's had the one for quite some time. I'm not sure if his roly-poly at home knows—"

A burst of snickers and giggles erupted from the group, and Grace swallowed hard, an ominous sense rising within her. Was Harriet talking about Graham McCormick? Isabelle had said that Graham was one of Uncle James's best friends and business associates. Was he also a real estate man? Regardless, Rosaline was certainly the epitome of roly-poly.

"But to have another one is . . ." Harriet quirked an eyebrow and tutted, raising her teacup to her lips with a dainty hand.

Josephine shifted in her chair again and smoothed a palm over her cheek. Grace sipped her tea, her mind reeling as she tried to convince herself that nothing was going on between her eldest cousin and Graham McCormick. Moments later, Josephine whispered something to her mother and slipped out of the parlor.

A full forty minutes passed and Josephine still hadn't returned to the women's parlor. During that time, Grace and Maude had enjoyed a quiet, yet pleasant, conversation. They had not only talked about the weather, but also about sewing. Maude had completed her first needlepoint project—a Christmas stocking—at age six, as had Grace. Grace had also learned that Maude appreciated fine food, dancing, and attending the occasional orchestra concert.

"I attended a dance at the Palace Hotel before the fires took it." Maude's sorrowful voice saddened Grace. "The sculptures on the Conservatory Floor were so beautiful."

Grace laid a comforting hand on Maude's arm. Grace struggled to understand how devastating the quake and fires had been. Though she genuinely pitied those who had lost their homes, repeated mentions of the destruction were wearing thin. *Buildings are going up everywhere, and it's been over a year. Why can't people move on?*

Despite Maude's apparent shortcomings in the looks department and the shadow that the quake had left on her and evidently everyone else's psyche, Grace liked her. Maude and Harriet weren't so different from the women in Grace's mother's circle. Denver had worse winters, and the occasional dusty cattle drive through the streets of downtown, but women in both cities still appreciated the finer things in life, including a bit of gossip.

Having imbibed too much tea, Grace asked Maude for directions to the lavatory and excused herself. Isabelle followed her out the door and across the main parlor.

"I'm about to die of boredom in there," Isabelle whispered, following close at Grace's heels. "All the empty gossip and women sitting around looking like flowers in a bouquet."

Grace giggled.

"What? What's funny?" Isabelle pressed, following Grace into the lavatory.

"I've never heard women described that way."

Isabelle disappeared into a bathroom stall and bumped the door shut. "Well, that's how it feels. And by the way, where's Josephine? I saw her sneak out and figured she'd be in here. Where on earth could she have gone?"

Several minutes later, Isabelle and Grace rejoined Maude and the other women. Josephine reappeared moments later and took her seat. "Did I miss anything?" she whispered to Maude.

Grace swept her eyes over Josephine and cocked her head. Maude assured Josephine that she hadn't missed anything, but Grace undoubtedly had. Josephine's hair was undisturbed, but she had certainly done something. Josephine smoothed the skirt of her dress, her attention focused on Harriet. Grace eased back on the love seat and noticed the wrinkles on the back of Josephine's dress. Josephine had done a superb job of smoothing the skirt portion under her, as all women did when they sat down, but the creases that remained in the fabric made it look as if it had been compressed, much like an accordion.

Why is she rumpled? Grace crinkled her eyes. *And there's a hint of something else. Maybe it's her perfume, but it's mixed with an unfamiliar smell I don't recognize.*

Several women laughed, and Grace returned her attention to Harriet.

"He won't be doing *that* anymore." Harriet raised an eyebrow.

The women laughed again, though Grace had no idea what juicy piece of gossip had been served. Surprisingly, she found she didn't care. What shocked her most was her appalling sense that Josephine might be Graham McCormick's—or some other man's— tart. Grace fidgeted on the love seat and stared out the window toward the rolling ocean in the distance. She hated assuming the worst about Josephine, but how could she not? Josephine had joked about women having adventures but not having to take care of them at home the day the cousins had first visited Walters Dress

Shop. Grace had dismissed the comment but now found it telling. Graham was alluring, but if caught, Josephine would pay the ultimate price. Her reputation would be ruined, and the scandal would devastate her family. Her dalliance might also compromise her father's business. Worse, it would destroy Henry and probably end her marriage.

Grace took another sip from her cup and wrinkled her nose; her tea had gone cold. Josephine would be a fool to become entangled with another man. Graham might leave Rosaline for Josephine, but Grace doubted it. And Henry loved Josephine. He loved her in the ways Frank loved Grace. How Josephine could so carelessly disrespect their love and her marriage vows was unfathomable.

Josephine retrieved her teacup and saucer from her mother and took a long sip. "I told you," Josephine said, winking at Grace, her demeanor so changed from when Harriet had shared her earlier delectable morsel of gossip. "The Cliff House is the best. It's where all the action takes place."

NINETEEN

Henry relaxed into a leather armchair in one of the small sitting rooms that lined the corridors on the third floor of the Cliff House. The corner fireplace wasn't lit, but the sun brightened the space. Henry sipped his drink and drummed his fingers on the chair arm; all the sitting rooms were much the same. A few chairs, a small wooden table, and a long roll-armed chaise allowed families and business parties to enjoy private meals and conversation with views of the ocean. Henry shifted uncomfortably and crossed his legs. He had been in numerous sitting rooms over the years with his father-in-law and knew they weren't only used for business meetings and family gatherings. The Cliff House had once had a reputation that poor departed Adolph Sutro had tried and mostly succeeded in cleaning up, but waiters still always knocked before entering a sitting room to give those within time to make themselves decent.

James sat across from Henry, and Frank sat to his right. Graham, however, had pulled a mysterious disappearing act after he had ushered the men into the room. He had now been absent for more than half an hour. Henry had strong suspicions about where Graham went and what he did during these absences, but he also knew the man would return, eventually.

Suddenly, the door jerked open, and Graham strode in. He thumped the door closed and ran his fingers through his hair.

"I apologize, gentlemen," Graham said, as if trying to catch his breath. "That diversion turned out to be a little more taxing than I'd expected. Lost all track of time. Where are we?"

Graham settled into the chair next to James, removed a cigar from his pocket, and lit it.

"Frank was telling us about some of his contracts in Denver. Was it with the Brown Palace and the Oxford, you said?" James smoothed the front of his vest.

"Yes, and the Cliff House in Manitou Springs. We have some of the finest beef in the west." He winked at James, whose expression remained unchanged. "San Francisco, Los Angeles, and maybe even Seattle are all markets we'd like to be in."

Graham settled further into his chair and inhaled a deep draw on his cigar. The redness had receded from his face but lingered on his neck. *Why is he so winded? Did he run down the hall to get here?* Henry raised his eyebrows. *Then again, maybe I don't want to know.*

"Have you had the beef here?" Graham asked.

Frank stroked the corners of his mouth with a thumb and forefinger. "No. I haven't had the chance yet. I'm sure it's good. Of course, I'm always going to like ours better. Visiting some of the local restaurants and learning about new opportunities is what I'm here for."

How familiar this act is. Henry bit his lip to keep from rolling his eyes. The man reminded him of a few vendors who sold their wares to his uncle at his mercantile store in Pennsylvania. *He's cagey and a bit of a braggart. He'll fit in here if he doesn't overplay his hand. And saying he hasn't had dinner here yet was smart; he's hoping they'll ask him back and pick up the check.*

"New opportunities are what this town is about, my man." James tapped his cigar into the standing bronze ashtray and shot a sly grin at Frank and Graham. "There are always opportunities on the horizon if you know the right people. Of course, there aren't as many opportunities as there used to be."

James and Graham chuckled, exchanging knowing smiles.

"But things crop up, much like all the new buildings," James continued.

Yet another sick reference to corruption. Henry's lunch turned uneasily in his stomach. *I wonder if Josephine would move to Los Angeles if I got a job there. She'd like the weather and the atmosphere. Oil's booming, and companies would pay a good accountant well. I should call a few of the contacts I have at the office.*

Graham scooted forward in his chair and stared at the tiepin on Frank's necktie. "That's quite the decoration. Is that a steer in the middle?"

Frank touched the pin. "It is. Belonged to my father, who started the company."

Henry appreciated the pride in Frank's voice, but what caught his attention was Frank's hand as it held the necktie at an angle so the men could better view the pin. *His fingers look like my brother's.* Henry's spine stiffened, and his nerves tensed. *His forefinger's slightly crooked because someone has broken it before, and his knuckles are a little big. He may dress like a businessman, but he's been in his share of scrapes.*

Henry forced himself to ease forward in his chair long enough to admire the pin and peek at Frank's other hand. *He did have an unusually firm handshake upstairs. And come to think of it, his hand was also a little rough, not soft like the hands of men who work in offices.*

"Tell us a little more about how this operation would work," Graham prompted Frank. "The shipping and all. Kansas City and even Cheyenne are quite a distance."

As Frank discussed the finer points of shipping live beef to California from Missouri and Wyoming, Henry feigned attention and quietly examined the man that was Frank Buchanan. Frank had done a remarkable job of cleaning himself up. His brown suit fit well, but the coat was a little too snug around his biceps. Henry angled his body more toward Frank, unable to shake a growing sense of unease. *I doubt Cheyenne has a boxing club like the one here that was destroyed during the fires. He's a bit of a rounder, and his muscles have been gained through other, less "sanctioned" physical activities.*

Frank's brown derby hat perched on the side table and his matching polished brown patent leather shoes were of quality. The gold watch chain, the crimson necktie, and the close shave completed the look, but something in Henry's gut gave him pause. *He has Graham and James fooled, but he's dangerous. I'll need to watch him.*

At a lull in the conversation, James removed his pocket watch from his vest and sat forward with a start. "How time does fly." He stubbed out his cigar and hoisted himself out of his chair. "Henry, we must be getting back."

Graham mashed out his cigar, tugged his suit coat lapels, and rose along with Henry and Frank. James motioned the men toward the door, and they exited into the corridor that led back to the main hall.

"We'll be in touch, Frank," Graham said, clapping the man on the back. "Not only about the beef, but about the real estate deal I mentioned when we first met. How long will you be in town?"

Frank donned his hat and dipped his chin. "Several more weeks, if not longer."

James and Henry shook Frank's hand in turn and bid him and Graham farewell. Henry and James walked up the hall toward the stairwell, the wheels in Henry's mind spinning. Graham and James were planning on helping Frank expand his family's beef business, along with trying to rope him into a real estate deal. Henry's stomach turned again. That deal could lead to more scrutiny from the authorities and potentially a stint in jail, neither of which interested Henry in the least. *The sooner I can find my way out of this, the better.* Henry shivered and followed James up the stairs to collect the Hamilton ladies from the women's parlor.

TWENTY

As evening shadows fell across the backyard and the sun sank behind glowing yellow ochre clouds, Isabelle locked her bedroom door and opened her window. It was the second of June and the day had been unusually warm. The air had grown stagnant in her room and she welcomed the cool breeze that ruffled her curtains. She had finally received the letter of character from Violet yesterday, thanks to bribing the maid, Sarah, to help her in her secret quest to attend nursing school. Isabelle clasped her hands together and paced in front of her bed, gazing at the items on the pale pink coverlet. The signed physical from Dr. Jenkins and the photo of herself were there, along with both letters of character. Isabelle perched on the edge of the bed and reviewed her application one last time to be sure it was complete. There was no fee to apply to nursing school because the young women selected weren't automatically admitted. If, at the end of two months, Isabelle showed "an aptitude for the work and general fitness"— words she had again memorized from the nursing school's annual announcement—she would be formally accepted into the nurses' training program.

"They have to let me in," she whispered to herself. "I'll show them I have more aptitude and fitness than anyone they've ever seen."

She gathered the items and carefully tucked them into an envelope she had stolen from her father's study. She sealed the stamped and addressed envelope and stared at it with an irrepressible smile.

Someone tried the doorknob, and Isabelle hopped off of her bed with a start.

"Isabelle? Why is the door—"

"We have plenty of time, Mother. I'll be out in a few minutes." Isabelle shook her head, annoyed at being interrupted.

Violet's engagement party started in less than half an hour, and the family was busy readying themselves for the event.

Isabelle stuffed the envelope under her pillow, examined herself in her dressing mirror one final time, and smoothed her rose-colored gown. She fingered the pearl choker at her neck and ran both hands along the sides of her pompadour. While elated for Violet, Isabelle was not looking forward to an evening of listening to her peers talk about courtships, weddings, and babies. *All of this pretending and society mingling is almost over. Once I'm in nursing school, my life can finally begin.*

Isabelle left her room and crept downstairs. She said a quick prayer before entering the kitchen, hoping Eleanor wouldn't be parked at her usual spot in front of the sink. With no sign of Eleanor, Isabelle had only a few moments to execute her plan.

"Sarah?" Isabelle whispered as loudly as she dared.

The young maid stepped out of the pantry. "Yes, miss?"

"There's an envelope under my pillow. Get it once we leave and make sure it goes out tomorrow. I'll pay you in the morning."

"I will." Sarah's eyes gleamed. "Thank you, miss."

Isabelle smiled reassuringly at the girl; she was a new maid and had undoubtedly been instructed to always formally address anyone in the household. "Please call me Isabelle, and thank you for helping me."

Sarah beamed and disappeared back into the pantry.

Isabelle hurried out of the kitchen, her head held high. *Now it's done.* She calmly walked up the hall to wait for her family in the foyer.

Grace examined herself in her dressing table mirror, finished tying the deep-purple bow on her ivory dress, and smoothed the lace cuffs on both wrists. Tonight was an important evening. She would see Violet again and meet more people that she and Frank might call on when Frank had established his business in California. Something gently scraped across the floor behind her, and she turned. Someone had pushed an envelope underneath her door.

It's from Frank. She hurried across the room, her heart pounding. *He wants me to know how excited he was to see me.*

She returned to her dressing table, sat down, and tore open the envelope. Removing the letter, she began to read.

> *Dear Grace,*
>
> *I've met a good many bisness men here and have already sined a contract with one. Graham McCormick has the inside rail on all kinds of deals. He asked if I wanted in on a real estate adventure that he and a few uther men are working on, and it'd mean I cud open my own restraunt! Can you imagin? Bringing the hoofs into town and getting to eat for free too.*
>
> *Sum of Graham's friends have invited me to cards and pool and I know I can win more munny there. These boys play a good game, but they don't know how we play cards back in Wyoming. I have sum tricks to lay on them that they've not seen yet.*
>
> *Graham has invited me to the Cliff House to meet the head cook and I'm xcited for it. To have our beef served at a place as fine as that would make my brothers green around the gills with envy. Sumtimes I think they*

keep me stuck out west becuz they don't think I'm good at bisness. I'll show them! I'll have our beef in every restraunt in this town within the yeer!

You looked so pretty the uther day at the Cliff House and it makes me want to see you agen and be with you real soon. It was all I cud do not to kiss yer hand and take you for a spin on the balcony so we cud look at the oshun together. I admit that I'm a mite jelus knowing that you're going to meet uther men at parties. It raises my blood and I'm not proud of that.

I'll write agen when I have more newz or when I win more munny at cards.

Frank

Grace tapped a forefinger on her lips and pulled her mouth to one side. She returned the letter to its envelope and stuffed it into the armoire drawer next to the other letter Frank had sent. *He sure is playing a lot of cards. Maybe some of the rumors about him in Denver were true.*

A knock sounded on the door, and Grace jumped.

"Grace? Are you about ready, dear?"

"Yes, Aunt Margaret." Grace checked herself in the dressing table mirror once more, removed a dime from her change purse, and placed it on the bedside table nearest the window. She had promised to pay Sarah each time the maid delivered a letter.

Grace gnawed on her lip, the last line of Frank's letter lingering in her mind. She *would* meet other men at parties. She had only been in San Francisco a month but had already agreed to help with the Red Cross gala. There would certainly be men there, as there would be at Violet's engagement party this evening. *But am I excited to meet those men to help Frank?* Grace crinkled her eyes, her emotions a tangle of uncertainty and promise. That Frank was jealous of her meeting other men also gave Grace pause. *I didn't know he was the jealous type.* Grace walked to her door and stopped, her hand poised over the knob, a sinking feeling descending over her. It was the same feeling of self-doubt that had tried to worm its way into her mind and heart after she had arrived in California. She closed her eyes and tried to breathe away her unease. *I'm sure once we're together, he'll be fine.*

Grace left her room and started down the stairs. On the landing, she gazed into the foyer and smiled at Isabelle. There would be no more thoughts of Frank. Grace would meet other men at Violet's engagement party, but that wouldn't matter. What *would* matter was the opportunity to glean more information from Violet about how to plan the perfect wedding. Grace carefully descended the remaining stairs, eager for the evening to begin. *There's no harm in getting to know other people. I'll enjoy myself and not worry another minute about Frank.*

TWENTY-ONE

L ess than an hour later, Grace followed Isabelle into Violet Gilchrist's glittering foyer. To her left, the sitting room that had hosted the Red Cross tea had been transformed into an intimately lit space with a buffet laden with shrimp, crabmeat, fruit, and assorted wines. Soft lighting bathed the room in a warm glow, and several couples stood by the unlit fireplace, the lamplight reflecting off the rich jewel tones of the ladies' dresses. Uncle James, Aunt Margaret, Josephine, and Henry wandered farther into the house, having spotted some friends. Grace followed Isabelle up a long hall that led out onto an expansive patio. A mixture of women draped in all shades of gathered satin mingled with sharply dressed men alongside another giant buffet heaped with warm bread and fresh roast beef.

"There you are." Violet floated toward Grace in a cloud of lilac, a tall, clean-cut man with sandy blond hair in tow. "Grace, this is William, my fiancé." Grace greeted William and shook his hand. She nearly giggled when he spoke; the register of his voice was about an octave higher than she had expected.

Violet sent William off to fetch glasses of punch for Grace and Isabelle.

"Isn't he handsome?" Violet gushed. "Now, I don't mean to be curt, but I must go. Mother's motioning, and I think a senator friend and his wife have just arrived."

Though she painted on a false smile for Violet's benefit, Grace's heart sank. There would be no time to talk to Violet about wedding plans; she would be too busy mingling with her guests.

William reappeared, and Grace and Isabelle thanked him for their glasses of punch.

"How are you?" Isabelle asked William, his eyes searching the crowded patio for Violet. "You start your last year at Stanford this fall, right?"

William turned to Isabelle, his face the picture of surprise. "I will. Senior year of law school and then on to work with my father's firm."

Grace gazed up at the faint stars that twinkled in the inky sky. Frank wasn't a lawyer, but he, too, had taken his place in his family's business. Grace could relate to how proud Violet must have felt about marrying a man who was carrying on a legacy of success.

"There she is, bringing someone else for you to meet, I see." William tilted his head toward Violet, who threaded her way across the room. "He's from Los Angeles," William continued, his voice pitched low. "The family's very influential in the oil business, from what I hear."

Grace clutched her punch cup with both hands. *How surprising and fortuitous to meet someone from Los Angeles.*

Violet approached, a tall and unexpectedly handsome man at her side. His classically chiseled face, musky cologne, tailored black suit, and sapphire-blue tie gave off the impression of a polished and proper gentleman.

Violet introduced Grace and Isabelle to Andrew Kepler. Grace steadied herself when he spoke; his rich baritone voice washed over her like honey. Andrew shook Isabelle's and Grace's hands in turn.

"It's good to meet you, sir," Grace said.

"Please, call me Andrew."

"William says you're from Los Angeles," Isabelle said. "I may be going there this fall and would love to hear a little about it if you have a few minutes."

That's a great idea. Andrew would make an excellent contact for Frank's business. Grace stepped closer to Isabelle.

"Yes, of course." Andrew motioned for Grace and Isabelle to join him at a nearby table.

As Andrew regaled Isabelle with tales about the skyscraping Continental Building, the ancient La Brea Tar Pits, and the city's rapid growth, heat pooled in Grace's stomach. Andrew would make a good contact for Frank's business, but Grace found herself unnerved by how he made her feel. *I get it now. I understand how other women find themselves in trouble.* Grace had been shocked and filled with pity when a school friend who had agreed to sleep with her beau out of wedlock had become pregnant. *It was a disaster of the highest order, and I'd never do it, but I now know the feeling that inevitably doomed her.*

Andrew had returned his attention to Grace and had asked her a question, which, per usual, she hadn't heard. Her cheeks flushed, and she was about to ask him to repeat himself when crashing glass and the thwack of wood shattered the evening.

Isabelle whirled toward the commotion. When James drew back and Henry sank behind a crowd of onlookers, she shot out of her chair so fast it tipped over and fell with a thud behind her.

"Mother!" She rushed from the table, pushing her way through the crowd.

Margaret lay on the concrete patio, her chair overturned, shards of a broken champagne glass scattered beside her.

"She's fainted," Isabelle announced, the crowd pressing closer. "Can you move—"

"Everyone, please take a few steps back. She needs some air." Andrew had suddenly materialized at Isabelle's side. To her relief, those around her heeded his order.

Henry stripped off his coat and gently placed it beneath his mother-in-law's head.

"I have the aspirin for her." Crouched beside Isabelle, Grace turned toward her cousin on the balls of her feet.

Thank heavens she didn't freeze this time. Isabelle quietly thanked Grace.

"Here's some water, too." Andrew had commandeered someone's glass and handed it down to Grace.

Isabelle clutched her mother's hand, her nerves jangling as agonizing seconds ticked away, Margaret still unconscious. Isabelle's breathing grew shallow, and she said a silent prayer. She feared that one day her mother would faint and never awaken. Finally, Margaret blinked at Isabelle.

"What has, where am I . . . ," Margaret mumbled. "Did I do it again, dear?"

Isabelle blew out her cheeks, her dismay subsiding. "Yes, Mother, but you're fine now. Please rest."

Isabelle and Henry sat on the concrete near Margaret. James and Andrew drew a few chairs away, other guests milling about, still staring and whispering in concern. Finally, Margaret hoisted herself up with the aid of her son-in-law and youngest daughter. She perched on a chair, downed her aspirin, and clutched her water glass with trembling hands.

With Margaret revived, guests gathered again in circles of conversation. Several more minutes passed, and Margaret shooed Isabelle away, assuring her she had fully recovered. Reluctant to leave her mother, Isabelle finally sought out Andrew. She thanked him as he stood with Grace near an overflowing planter of greenery at the edge of the patio.

"Nothing at all," he assured her. "Always frightening to see a lady do that. Good of you both to help her so quickly."

"Yes, thank you, Grace," Isabelle said, her voice sincere. *At least she didn't react like Father and Josephine, who did nothing—yet again—like useless, scared children.*

Isabelle excused herself and stepped into the yard. She stared up at the sky, the stars hidden behind the clouds, and then back at the guests. They sipped their punch and champagne and helped themselves to roast beef and crabmeat cocktail as if nothing had happened. As Isabelle gazed up into the dark ocean of the sky, tendrils of fear gripped the edges of her mind. *Is Mother's heart getting worse?* Isabelle sniffed and fretted her hands together, struggling to push the thought away. Isabelle wanted to believe her mother's fainting spell had been brought on by a corset laced too tightly or imbibing too much champagne. *That's what it has to be. Though we don't agree on everything, I love her and can't bear the thought of being without her.*

TWENTY-TWO

At home after the party, Grace joined the other women in the sitting room for an evening cup of tea. Aunt Margaret insisted she didn't need to turn in yet and waved Henry and Uncle James off to the study.

"That was such fun." Grace sat at the end of the settee near one of the colorful Tiffany lamps, Josephine to her left.

Other than the part when Aunt Margaret fainted, Violet's engagement party had been splendid. It had also been bittersweet, serving as a painful reminder to Grace that she would never get to throw a party to celebrate her engagement to Frank.

"Yes," Aunt Margaret concurred, settling herself into an overstuffed armchair. "Violet and William are a good match. I'm not sure how she caught him, but he seems quite fond of her."

Aunt Margaret sat her teacup and saucer on the table next to her. "Speaking of fond, who was that man you were talking to, Isa? I meant to thank him for helping with my episode, but I believe he'd already gone by the time we left."

Grace suppressed a smile. Her aunt meant well by trying to steer her youngest daughter toward an eligible, well-to-do bachelor. But unlike Grace, who understood the value of a husband, Isabelle had prodded Andrew like he was a college professor. The only reason she had spoken to him for so long was so that she could learn more about Los Angeles.

"That was Andrew Kepler." Isabelle's nonchalant tone told

Grace that Isabelle wasn't attracted to him. "I thanked him for helping you."

"Good, good," Aunt Margaret said. "He looked interested in you, or at least put up a good show."

Josephine snickered and leaned closer to Grace. "This is the part of the evening where Mother tries to play matchmaker."

"I'm not trying to play matchmaker," Aunt Margaret said, tsking at Josephine. "I simply want to make sure that—"

"But I am interested in him, Mother." Isabelle winked at Josephine, who took a sip of tea. "He's a rich, handsome oilman who lives in *Los Angeles*. You'll be thrilled to know that we're a perfect match. With him, I could accomplish your goal and mine. I could get married *and* go to school."

Josephine blew tea through her nose, and Grace accidentally blurted out a laugh. *What an outrageously funny yet disrespectful thing to say!* With no sisters, Grace hadn't quite grown accustomed to Isabelle and Josephine's playful teasing. Amidst a coughing fit, Josephine groped around for something with which to wipe her face, and Grace quickly handed her a napkin.

Aunt Margaret protested with an indignant snort. "I'm only thinking of your future, Isa, and I thought he might be an interesting gentleman to get to know. And you *must* get this schooling idea out of your head. There's no need to run off to Los Angeles when you can find a perfectly nice man here and also be involved in your causes. Besides, this Andrew looked a little older, and I'm not sure that's the best match for—"

"Trust me, Mother," Josephine interjected. "Any man who ends up with Isa will need to be a little older."

"What? Why do you say that?" Isabelle stuck her tongue out at her sister.

Before Grace could stop herself, she laughed with more heartiness than she had in a very long time. *Isabelle's condemning the very thing I'm going to do, but I can't be angry with her because she and Josephine and Aunt Margaret poke at each other in the most hilarious way. Father and Mother would've banished me to my room for a month if I'd spoken to Mother like Josephine and Isabelle just did to Aunt Margaret.*

"You're the one who wants to save the world." Josephine raised a hand in surrender to Isabelle. "Someone older will have the experience and means to show it to you and foot the bill. But he'll have to have stamina, what with you running around being Saint Isabelle."

Isabelle stuck her tongue out again at her sister, Josephine wrinkling her nose in gleeful delight.

They get funnier by the minute! Grace snickered. *Josephine's right, though. Isabelle will need someone a little older and wiser, and he'll certainly need stamina.*

"Did you meet Andrew, Josephine? You or Henry?" Grace clutched her teacup, her voice more eager than she would have liked.

Josephine shook her head. "No, I didn't, but I don't know about Henry."

Aunt Margaret took a sip of tea. "Let's change the subject, shall we?"

Isabelle pulled a face at Josephine, who refused to be goaded into a response.

"I talked to Violet about her wedding at the Red Cross tea, and she said she's going to use lilies and roses in her bouquet," Grace said. "They should look perfect with the gown she described."

Isabelle shot a "they're all hopeless" glance at the ceiling, and Grace dismissed her with a wave and a grin. Josephine and Aunt Margaret launched into an animated conversation about what else they had learned from Violet's mother earlier in the evening about Violet's wedding. As the women continued to talk, Grace wanted to relax further into the settee but couldn't. Meeting Andrew, helping with Aunt Margaret's fainting crisis, and Isabelle and Josephine's good-natured sparring had launched Grace on a wild emotional ride that would take more than a cup of tea and a good night's sleep from which to recover. What unsettled her most, however, was Frank's letter. *I'm going to meet other men, and there's nothing he can do about that. I must write back and assure him there's no need to be jealous.*

Later that night, Isabelle and Grace sat alone in the sitting room. Isabelle settled deeper into her chair, her legs tucked under her, and stared out the window at the stars that winked behind the clouds. She silently congratulated herself on a superbly successful round of "Let's Tease Mother," a faint smile playing on her lips.

"So, you really don't think you can have a husband and be a nurse?" Grace's question roused Isabelle from her self-satisfied thoughts.

"I don't know," she admitted. "It's not so much that I'm uninterested; it's that I'm more interested in becoming a nurse first. It's the order of things, I . . ."

She waved her hand and shifted in her chair. *Why is she asking me this? Is she on Mother and Josephine's side?*

"I don't mean to be critical," Grace assured her, "and I think it's very brave, but Andrew did seem awfully nice. And he was quick to help when your mother had her fainting spell."

Isabelle tilted her head to one side. Grace was right; Andrew had taken charge of the situation with a determined calm that Isabelle found appealing.

Grace leaned forward in her chair. "And he lives in Los Angeles," she whispered.

The two young women giggled like conspiring children.

Why can't I have a husband and a job? Isabelle wondered in seriousness for the first time. *Emma Sutro Merritt became a doctor and also got married. Why can't I be a nurse and have a man who loves me?*

"That's true," Isabelle said. "I know I'm supposed to want to get married first, but I don't. I don't want to risk having a child and never being able to do what I love because I have to be at home. Life can change so quickly."

Isabelle crinkled her eyes. Images of the fires and sudden devastation left behind by the earthquake were still scorched in her memory. Even though San Francisco was rising from its knees, the toll the disaster had taken on the psyche of those who had survived was impossible to explain to someone who hadn't lived through the horror.

"I need to do this first, even if it means doing it on my own. I'm so passionate about helping others. I don't want anything or anyone to get in the way."

Grace nodded, though Isabelle doubted her cousin was being anything more than polite.

Isabelle absentmindedly twisted a strand of hair, her thoughts floating back to Andrew. He was handsome and friendly, and had helped Margaret, but Isabelle wasn't attracted to him in *that* way. But what if she was attracted to someone? She had been so busy convincing herself and her obstinate mother that she wanted to focus on school that she had completely shut out the possibility of having a husband. She chewed on her lip as the door of possibility opened a crack. *Could I go to school and get married?* The same line she had used to tease her mother no longer seemed so far-fetched.

Isabelle pushed the thought aside and unfolded herself from her chair. "I'm going up."

Grace rose, and Isabelle motioned for her to go ahead. As Isabelle walked out of the sitting room, hope bloomed within her. She turned and gazed once more at the starry sky. *I'll go to school first, then worry about a man.*

TWENTY-THREE

Sitting at his desk, Henry closed his accounting ledger and grabbed his notebook and pencil. After the quake, Hamilton Holdings had been hastily pulled back together and rehomed on the second floor of an unscathed building on Fillmore Street. James and Henry shared a large south-facing office, and the sunlight streaming through the windows highlighted the maddening amount of dust that had been impossible to eradicate, given the surrounding destruction. A few weeks had passed since the two men had met Frank Buchanan, and today, Henry and James were meeting to discuss the details of a new real estate deal.

While horns honked and people bustled by on the street below, Henry dragged his wooden chair across the room and sat down in front of James's enormous oak desk. *With papers strewn about like they've been shot out of a cannon, no wonder he can't find anything.* James sat behind his desk, puffing on a cigar. Henry shook his head. Only a couple of square inches of wood remained visible beneath the mountains of documents.

"I'm about to call another meeting with Graham. Going to have him bring Frank along this time." James rummaged through a stack of paper in front of him to no avail and finally grinned. "Nothing is ever lost, my boy, only 'temporarily misplaced.'"

Henry laughed. Despite desperately wanting to wipe the desk clean with a swift sweep of his arm, Henry waited patiently and with barely concealed amusement while James performed his usual dog-dig through various piles.

"What do you think of him?" James plucked a document from the morass and held it up as if he had struck gold.

Henry furrowed his brow. "Frank?"

"Mmm," James said, examining the page.

Henry paused to consider his response. He didn't trust Frank but didn't want to tell James why. *The hands.* Henry's stomach clenched, and he straightened in his chair. Frank's slightly bent finger and enlarged knuckles had been the giveaway that he wasn't all he claimed to be.

"Tough to tell after one meeting," Henry said. "I'd like to get to know him better before I judge, but he's a confident businessman. Buchanan Beef's been around a long time. Honestly, I'm surprised they haven't tried to get into this market before now."

James leaned back in his chair, and Henry held his breath; one of the buttons on James's vest was straining so hard Henry feared it might pop off, fly across the desk, and put out his eye.

"Agreed." James picked up his cigar and puffed on it. "Makes me a little suspicious, especially with the state the city's in. But you're right; it's tough to tell after one meeting." James lurched forward, waving the piece of paper in his hand. "I still think he's worth having around, at least until we learn more about him. Graham's going to make that happen. Now, here's what I have in mind."

The real estate deal James and Graham were plotting caused Henry to sink into his chair slowly. It involved "extended and plot-widening" survey lines, "persuasive strategy meetings" with current landowners, and "aggressive" construction timelines. Though James hadn't revealed too much, Henry understood the plan's implications. James and Graham, along with many of their friends, were taking a different and somewhat more benign tack on corruption. Nonetheless, what they were planning was illegal. *This is doomed, and I do not want to be part of it.* Henry nodded as he tried to keep his emotions from betraying him.

With city hall and all of its real estate records destroyed, the inevitable scramble to be king of the hill—sometimes literally—had begun nearly as soon as the fires had been extinguished. With their substantial resources, James and Graham had had no trouble tiptoeing and then leaping back into the sea of land speculation. They would no doubt encourage others to "extend and widen" plots and "persuade" landowners with fat envelopes passed under the table or through strongarm tactics much like those Henry's brother engaged in back in Pennsylvania.

Silence could always be purchased with cash or by far more nefarious means.

When James had finished the list of what he needed Henry to do, he sat back and stared out the window, the sun blazing in the late-afternoon sky. Henry started to rise to return to his desk, but James spoke.

"I'm concerned about Margaret." James stubbed out his cigar, smoke lingering as it dissipated.

A sense of foreboding forced Henry back into his chair.

"Afraid she may leave me one of these days."

Has Margaret discovered James's affair? Is she planning to leave him? That could be the case, but where would she go? Henry wrinkled his nose at the odious idea of infidelity. *Dear Lord, what if she wants to move in with Josephine and me, eventually? That can't happen!*

The women in Henry's life—his mother, aunt, wife, sister-in-law, and mother-in-law—had always been shining lights of truth and comfort to him as he navigated the rough waves churned up by the sometimes unscrupulous businessmen in San Francisco. Henry sniffed and bit the inside of his cheek; he couldn't imagine how devastated he would be if Josephine were ever unfaithful. But Josephine would never betray him; she couldn't. Her social calendar kept her busy, and she never frequented any place where she could be alone with another man.

"I don't believe the doctor when he says Margaret's ticker's fine." James eyed Henry grimly.

Henry wiped the edges of his mouth with his thumb and forefinger. *He thinks she's going to die of a heart attack, and he could be right.* Henry usually stayed quiet during sensitive conversations because he never knew what to say. This, however, was not the time for silence. James needed encouragement, no matter how awkward it might be.

"It was when she—" Henry sputtered, then gathered himself. "Her episodes on the beach and at the engagement party are worrying."

When James's eyes grew large, Henry quickly tried to comfort his father-in-law.

"I wrote most of it off to excitement, though." Henry tried to sound upbeat. "And she gets back into fighting form quickly once she takes her aspirin. That's a good sign."

James tilted his head from side to side.

At least he's considering my opinion, even if she is one massive jolt away from leaving us. A lump rose in Henry's throat, and he tried to swallow it. He did not want to think about Margaret dying. She was like a surrogate mother to him and kept James steady. Henry couldn't fathom how adrift the family would be without her.

"I think Grace is finally enjoying herself." James returned his attention to a stack of paper. "Saw her smiling quite a bit at the engagement party, especially around that Andrew fellow. Not my business, and I don't know the man, but they'd make a fine pair. Wish we could get Isabelle to take an interest in someone like that."

Henry considered his endearing, enthusiastic, and determined sister-in-law, a warm smile slowly spreading across his face. "Yes, well, Isabelle does have other ambitions. No offense to Josephine, but Isabelle's helped Margaret a lot lately, and apparently that poor girl at the dress shop too."

James gathered several sheets of paper together and tapped them on the desk. "You're right about her ambition. Between you and me, I admire Isabelle's spirit. I can't say that in front of Margaret, but Isa reminds me of myself. If the hospital hadn't fallen to dust, I'd have paid for her to attend nursing school. They've rebuilt the place now, but I have no idea if the program has restarted. If she was ever accepted into school, we might have to revive Margaret again and soothe some hurt feelings, but Isa would make a good nurse. No harm in giving her a chance to prove it." James dipped his chin and winked.

A stunned Henry remained rooted in his chair. *James would support Isabelle in going to school?! Never in all my life would I have expected that revelation.* Henry finally rose and returned himself and his chair to his desk. James sat ratting through yet another pile of paper, a scowl on his face, undoubtedly searching for yet another temporarily misplaced document.

Isabelle had mentioned that the nursing program at the hospital on Parnassus Avenue had restarted. James had apparently not been paying attention when she had announced that during the dinner where she had revealed she had set the shopgirl's broken arm. *So why won't James say it's all right for her to apply to nursing school in Los Angeles?*

"Henry," James said, absentmindedly continuing his paper shuffling, "remind me to ask Eleanor to buy Margaret some flowers when I get home. I want to surprise her."

Henry scribbled a note in his notebook. As he closed the leather-bound volume, he froze. *Margaret's the reason James won't tell Isabelle he'd support her going to nursing school. Isabelle would move away, and then who'd be left to help him if something happened to Margaret? James wouldn't be able to handle her care, what with work.*

And Josephine and I will eventually move into our new home and won't be there to help either.

Henry cleared his throat, picked up a stack of invoices, and opened his accounting ledger. How sad for Isabelle. Henry's heart went out to his sister-in-law. *I must escape this business, but she's trapped, even more so than I am. For her sake, I hope she finds a way out of her situation too.*

TWENTY-FOUR

Grace had arrived home to a letter poking out from under the edge of her pillow. Having locked her bedroom door, she now sat at her dressing table, the warm afternoon breeze ruffling the curtains. A few sparrows chirped outside the window, their joy mirroring Grace's emotions. *Frank must be doing well. He's already written twice, and I've been so poor in replying.*

Grace opened the letter and began to read.

> *Dear Grace,*
>
> *Graham took me to more meetings this week, and I have two more sined contracts. More hoofs on the move! He also talked about meeting with yer unkel about real estate. Graham sure is a fast mover. He says with everyone out of the way and the records burnt down, he and yer unkel can help me get a peece of land for my restraunt without any truble.*
>
> *Graham also wants me to meet a few men that used to be on the Committee of Fifty. I think these boys were the big-timers before the quake. Sum of them didn't quite dodge the law fast enuf and went to jail, but uthers are still around. If I can get in with them like I am with sum of the boys in Cheyenne, we'll have it made.*
>
> *You just wait Grace. I'll buy you the biggest new*

house up on one of those hills in Los Angeles and we'll be at the top of California sosiety in no time.

I'm trying not to be hurt, but you haven't ritten to me. I know you have to play sly with yer family so I hope you can pleez write soon.

Frank

With a trembling hand, Grace set the letter aside and rose from her chair. The birds who had sung so happily outside were gone; all that remained was silence. Tears sprang to her eyes, and she laid a palm over her mouth, her stomach tightening. She hurried onto her bed, curled into a ball, and cried as quietly as she could. *This was all a mistake.* She clamped her eyes shut and muffled her sobs into her pillow. *Frank isn't an honorable man; he's a crook. Coming to San Francisco with him was a terrible idea. Why am I such a poor judge of character when it comes to men?* Grace wiped the tears from her cheeks, the dreadful truth descending over her like a blanket of shame. *I came with him because I wanted out of Denver so badly, and he saved me.*

Grace sobbed, her illusions and the romantic ideal of Frank Buchanan melting away. What did she know about Frank besides what Jacob had told her? Frank had only called on her a few times, and he had behaved well enough to pass for a gentleman. She had assumed he was an honest card player and businessman. And she had liked and even welcomed his daring approach to life. But Frank's true colors had been revealed; he was a swindler in both cards and business, facts that now forced Grace to make yet another heart-wrenching decision.

I have to break our engagement.

Grace's shoulders shook as she wept; everything was ruined. She shuddered when she imagined telling Frank she no longer wanted to be his wife. She feared his angry response and all of the ways that he could damage her. Grace also couldn't imagine losing her place in the kindergarten training course at the California State Normal School. She had worked hard to apply in secret and, unlike Isabelle, had already been accepted. *I want to be like Isabelle and go to school, but how will I ever pay for room and board? I don't want to go home, but I can't stay here. Who can help—?*

Grace sat bolt upright, her spirits soaring, tears still leaking down her cheeks.

Andrew.

She dismissed the idea as quickly as it had hit her and collapsed back onto the bed. *What if I'm making another mistake?* She chewed on her lip. *What if Andrew's a crook too? Are all men deceitful?* A pulling sensation in her chest told her no. All men weren't like Frank or Charles, or even Graham. Henry and Andrew had been nothing but kind, polite, and caring—all qualities Grace thought she had found in Charles and Frank.

"I hate doubting myself," Grace muttered to no one. "Men don't; if they do, they don't show it, so neither will I."

Grace blotted her tears with her sleeve and closed her eyes. *If I can't trust myself, I can't trust anyone else. I need to do this alone.* Menacing shadows of doubt crept back over Grace and her tears returned. Moving to Los Angeles as a single woman frightened her. She didn't know anyone there, and it meant abandoning her family. Jacob and her handful of friends wouldn't be around to help her if something went wrong.

Could she do it?

Grace wiped the tears from her cheeks with the back of her hand and willed herself to be brave. So many new plans had to be made. In the meantime, she had to keep up her ruse with Frank. Recalling the girl at Walters Dress Shop, Grace sniffled. She had pitied the shopgirl for being working-class. She had pitied her for having to work instead of working because it was a choice. *And now I'm just like her.* Grace grimaced.

She rose, grabbed her handkerchief from her dressing table,

resettled herself onto her bed, and blew her nose. She tried to calm her frayed nerves by taking a few deep breaths, but the pain that gripped her wouldn't subside. Unlike Isabelle, Grace wanted a husband and love. She wanted a man like Henry Rothwell or Andrew Kepler, but discouragement clung to her. *This is how the quake survivors must feel.* She stared out the window into Lafayette Park, the ghostly vision of tents wavering for a moment before her eyes, the pall of the destruction hovering close to the surface of memory. *My heart may not be ready to let go of the hurt, but I have to do something.*

Grace sat up and brushed a few more tears from her cheeks, the true meaning of Frank's words sinking deep within her. *With everyone out of the way and the records burnt down.* Grace secretly loved sensational stories and, over the past year, had often disappeared with her father's day-old newspapers. She had inhaled the articles about the 1906 corruption trials in San Francisco. She had read about the group of influential local businessmen known as the Committee of Fifty. While many had escaped punishment, some had ended up in jail.

Her throat went dry, the puzzle pieces finally snapping together. Graham and her uncle James were members of the committee. They had escaped the fires and the risk of imprisonment unscathed but were now trying to reestablish themselves, legally and illegally. *How much easier that'll be without documents.* Grace's gaze landed on Frank's letter, which sat on her dressing table.

How can I let him go without him knowing?

Grace pushed herself up onto her elbows and stared into the brilliant blue sky. *I don't know if I can see it through, but if there's anyone who can help me figure out how to strike out on my own, it's Isabelle.*

Grace rose from her bed and retrieved two envelopes and two sheets of paper from her train case. She returned to her dressing table and quickly scribbled off a missive to her younger brother, Jacob, asking for money. He was a good friend of Frank's—knowledge that suddenly did not endear Jacob to her—and would help. He would send her money, thinking it was for dresses or souvenirs. *This is the last time I ask for money from a man!* She signed her name with an emphatic flourish.

Grace lingered at her dressing table and wiped away a tear, pen poised over the second crisp blank piece of stationery. She needed to write to Frank as if nothing between them had changed. She would say how much she missed him and looked forward to seeing him again. She would also praise him for securing more beef contracts and promising her a grand home in Los Angeles.

She finished her letter to Frank and tucked it alongside the one to Jacob on the side table next to her bed. Tomorrow, she would leave both letters under her pillow along with a dime for Sarah.

Grace rose and walked to the window. Salmon-colored clouds streaked the sky, the sun beginning to set. Grace shivered and swallowed hard. The colors brought to mind a slowly spreading fire. San Francisco had burned like Grace's dreams of love and the perfect life with Frank now did. Much like the city had risen again, Grace vowed to salvage her dream of becoming a teacher. Try as she might, she couldn't help but tap her toe on the floor and keep time with a forefinger on the window casing. *Like Frank, I'm playing with the big boys now, but the stakes are higher because I'm a woman.* Grace narrowed her eyes and clenched her jaw in steely resolve. *This is the most important game of my life, and I will not lose.*

TWENTY-FIVE

On a Thursday afternoon, Grace, Isabelle, Aunt Margaret, Harriet, and Maude sat together with a few of their friends in the Cliff House women's parlor enjoying tea. Josephine had excused herself almost as soon as the Hamilton ladies had arrived. Outside, the gray ocean lapped against the sand, the afternoon fog rolling in as it did each day. The sounds of quiet conversation and the tinkling of spoons played around Grace, and a few seagulls circled and dove toward the rough water.

"We'd hoped to walk on the beach today, but this weather certainly isn't cooperating," Aunt Margaret said, shaking her head.

Grace, who once again sat next to Maude on the settee, agreed.

Thanks to a surprisingly engaging conversation with Maude, Grace barely noticed Josephine's return to the parlor later that hour. Despite Maude's social awkwardness and even worse taste in dresses—the shade of purple she was wearing today had the unfortunate effect of highlighting her ghostly pale skin—she had yet again proven to be an excellent conversationalist. She had even revealed an interesting tidbit about Isabelle and the Red Cross.

"So she asked these ladies to donate?" Grace clarified, her voice hushed.

Maude lowered her head and motioned for Grace to scoot closer on the settee.

"She did, but she was so boisterous that it came off as unseemly. Mother nearly choked on her coffee cake." Maude giggled and laid a hand over her mouth. "Margaret's face turned the same shade of red as the rug. I think the entire scene left Isabelle feeling hurt and discouraged; she's never asked for donations again."

Grace forked in a bite of white cake, an idea forming in her mind.

"Mother said Isabelle should've never asked the ladies to donate here. She should've waited until she was at an official gathering for the cause," Maude continued. "I've heard some of the women speak approvingly of you. Are you helping Isabelle and Josephine with their charity work? I can have Mother put in a good word for you if you are."

Maude's expression was one of "what do you think of that plan."

Grace sat quietly, struggling to remember Josephine's chosen charity. *The orphanage.* She blotted her mouth with her napkin. *Maude may look like a nicely dressed ghost, but she's a helpful ghost. Maybe it's because she's always stuck with her mother, poor thing. I certainly can relate.*

"I—yes, I'd appreciate that. Thank you," Grace whispered, still struck by Maude's kindness.

I'm not surprised Isabelle blundered the fundraising, but it's certainly something I can help her with. It'll also allow me to practice how to ask for money politely. Grace had mastered the fine art of securing donations, given that she and her mother supported the Denver Ladies' Relief Society and the Orphans' Home. Grace took another bite of cake, the frosting suddenly losing its sweetness. A growing sense of unease pressed around the edges of her mind. To ask for money for herself would be an entirely new and nerve-racking endeavor. *I'll have to learn to do it if I'm to offer piano, voice, or art lessons to children to help pay for school.*

Forty minutes later, the Hamilton women descended to the third floor of the Cliff House. They loitered outside the main barroom, the dim chandeliers struggling to illuminate the otherwise gloomy hall.

"Ladies." A deep voice startled Grace from behind, and she whirled around.

Much to her delight, the voice belonged to Andrew Kepler.

"Grace and . . . Isabelle, was it?" Andrew shook each of their hands in turn.

Andrew introduced himself to Josephine and Aunt Margaret. Grace's heart sank as Aunt Margaret thanked Andrew for his help during her episode at Violet's engagement party. *How I wish I could get to know him better, but I simply can't risk another betrayal.* Grace tried her best not to be distracted by Andrew's deep voice as he talked to her aunt and cousins with polite ease. He wasn't flirting, but his calm yet confident demeanor somehow disarmed them. Even Aunt Margaret dropped her usual proper, stilted replies and warmed to him.

"There they are." Another voice surprised Grace, and she turned to her left.

Uncle James, Graham, and Frank had emerged from the main barroom and were walking straight toward her. Grace painted on a pleasant smile, a sense of wariness worming its way through her chest. Grace had caught Frank's jealousy before he had wiped it from his face. The narrowed eyes, the flared nostrils, and the pursed lips had all made her pulse pound in fear. *Does he think I'm mooning over Andrew?* Frank grew closer, and Grace almost stepped back. *I wasn't, was I?* She smoothed a hand over her cheek.

Grace greeted Graham, then faced Frank. "Hello, Mr. Buchanan. It's good to see you again." Grace's brilliant smile and intense gaze seemed to flummox Frank.

The barely concealed look of suspicion fell from his face,

replaced by one of flattering surprise. "I, um, hello, yes, Grace, is it?" Frank stammered. "It's good to see you, too."

That did the trick. Grace wanted to smirk in triumph. *Men are so easily swayed.*

Andrew introduced himself to Graham and Frank. Andrew was not only a little taller than Frank, but also a hair broader across the shoulders. While the men stood across from each other and traded pleasantries, Grace wondered if Frank was sizing up Andrew as personal and professional competition.

Andrew finally spoke to Uncle James, who greeted him with a hearty clap on the back. "Thank you again, my boy, for helping my dear wife. Don't make yourself scarce. We need more fine men like you around here."

Unable to keep from worrying a fold in her skirt between her fingers, Grace tried to emulate Josephine, who was expertly splitting her attention between Andrew, Frank, and Uncle James. Grace nodded correctly to acknowledge Frank and Graham as they left together and to Andrew before he disappeared back up the hall and into the main dining room.

As the family walked toward the enormous doors that opened out onto the covered walkway, Grace laid a shaky palm over her chest in relief.

"We should invite Andrew to your party." Aunt Margaret tucked her hand into the crook of Uncle James's elbow.

Grace picked up her pace, making sure she didn't step on Henry's heels. *What party?*

"Hmmm," James said.

"I think you should, Father." Josephine strolled alongside Henry.

Isabelle pulled a face and swatted Josephine's backside. Josephine lurched forward and squealed. Surprised by her cousins' unladylike behavior in public, Grace laughed before she could stop herself. *Yes, someone should invite Andrew to a party. Uncle James and Aunt Margaret are fooling themselves if they think he likes Isabelle, but it'd give Isabelle and me a chance to talk to him more about Los Angeles.*

TWENTY-SIX

s the faint midmorning sun illuminated the lush white roses along the back fence, Isabelle left her bedroom and walked down the hall. She knocked on Josephine's door and popped her head inside.

"Josephine, can I borrow—"

Isabelle closed the door and hurried across the room to the bed.

"What's wrong?" Isabelle sat down next to her sister.

Josephine lay on her back, a palm resting on her stomach. Her eyes brimmed with tears, a few escaping down her cheek. Concern welled within Isabelle; Josephine's pallor was tinged with an unnatural green tint. Josephine worked her jaw, her gaze landing on a photo of herself, Isabelle, and Daniel taken when they were children.

"Nothing," Josephine croaked through a sob. "I'm not feeling well. It might've been the eggs."

"But you're crying," Isabelle said. "Eggs don't make people cry."

Josephine pressed a hand gently to her chest and winced. She rolled toward Isabelle, her breaths deep and long. Isabelle recognized the symptoms of nausea; she feared her sister might lose her breakfast all over the beautiful lavender bedspread. A few moments later, Isabelle gasped and sat back in astonished surprise. Breakfast wasn't making Josephine sick. Isabelle had enjoyed a hearty helping of the same eggs less than an hour ago with no ill consequences. Something else was making Josephine's chest sore and her face sallow. It was something tiny and precious and would be welcomed with much fanfare and open arms.

"Are you pregnant?" Isabelle whispered, almost unable to contain her excitement.

Josephine stared up at Isabelle, her eyes full of sorrow instead of joy. The smile fell from Isabelle's face.

"I think so, but please don't tell anyone," Josephine begged. "All my fun is over now, and I have no one to blame but myself."

"I won't," Isabelle assured her sister.

What does she mean her fun is over? And why isn't she more excited? Isabelle couldn't imagine how terrible morning sickness made one feel, but despite it, Josephine should have at least been happy for Henry. Her parents would be overjoyed. Margaret had tried her best not to drop hints about grandchildren in Henry and Josephine's company, but Isabelle knew her mother longed for one. Isabelle's chest tightened to the point she feared it might burst. Her niece or nephew would grow up with parents who loved it and grandparents who would do nothing but spoil it rotten. Isabelle wanted to rush downstairs and share the news with their mother and Grace.

Josephine eased herself up and scooted back, her tears still gleaming.

Isabelle stuffed a pillow behind her sister's head. "I don't—I don't under—"

Josephine silenced her with a wave of her hand. She swiped her handkerchief from her side table, blew her nose, and dabbed tears from her cheeks. "I have so much to do."

Isabelle remained on the bed, still puzzled by Josephine's melancholy reaction.

"I have to get the sickness under control and speak to Henry. And no one can say a word until I've seen the doctor." Josephine stared hard at Isabelle.

"No, of course we won't say anything."

Isabelle worried a thick fold of her skirt between her fingers and bit her tongue. Keeping Josephine's condition a secret threatened to be almost as hard as not telling her family that she had applied to nursing school. As a mother-to-be, Josephine should be the one to announce her pregnancy, but Isabelle was at a loss as to why her sister wouldn't want to share her news immediately.

Josephine sniffled and wiped her nose. "Henry and I want children, we do. But it's so soon and I hadn't planned on . . . Mother always scolded me and said that pride cometh before a fall. She was right."

Isabelle forced herself to maintain a neutral expression, her mind spinning. Though she hadn't been intimate with a man, more than a few married women in her and Josephine's circle had found themselves pregnant despite their best efforts. Those women, at least outwardly, had still expressed resigned happiness. For Josephine to find herself in the same predicament didn't surprise Isabelle. What gave her pause was Josephine's comment about pride. There was no shame in a woman wanting to have intimate relations with her husband. How Josephine considered herself fallen was beyond Isabelle.

Josephine sat up farther and adjusted the pillow behind her. She and Isabelle chuckled when her stomach rumbled.

"Please don't say anything," Josephine reiterated. "Ask Sarah to bring up some tea and a piece of toast, and tell Mother I'll be down soon."

Isabelle hopped off of the bed and strode away. "Yes, I'll do it now."

"Isa, *slow down*," Josephine scolded her sister. "You'll make everyone suspicious."

Isabelle jerked to a crawl. When she reached the door, she turned back to Josephine.

"I'll let Sarah know. And I won't tell a soul, I promise." Isabelle left the room and clicked the door closed behind her.

TWENTY-SEVEN

L ater that afternoon, Isabelle sat in rapt attention between her mother and Grace in Violet Gilchrist's sitting room. Midday light made the drapes shine like fresh peaches and reflected off the burgundy and evergreen book spines that lined the floor-to-ceiling bookcases. Mrs. Katharine Felton—or Kitty, as she was known to her friends—was speaking to the ladies in Violet's circle and some of those who frequented the Cliff House women's parlor. As the director of Associated Charities, and one of only two women on the Committee of Fifty, Mrs. Felton, a bespectacled woman with a heart-shaped face, serious eyes, and a determined intellect, was the woman Isabelle most admired.

Today, Kitty was updating the ladies on the progress the committee was making with social services and solutions for those still recovering from being displaced by the earthquake and fires. When she finished, a polite round of applause followed, and the ladies broke into groups to enjoy punch, tea, and cake.

Kitty joined Violet and her mother near one of the tall windows that overlooked the manicured front lawn. Violet discreetly motioned to Isabelle to join them. *I can't believe I'm going to meet her.* Isabelle nearly burst out of her seat. *If I could only tell her I was going to be a nurse, that'd be even better.*

Isabelle tried not to push her way across the room but accidentally collided with Maude in her excitement. She apologized without even a glance in Maude's direction. Isabelle smoothed her dress, her heart thundering in her chest, and joined Violet.

"This is the person I was talking about, Mrs. Felton," Violet said, introducing Isabelle.

"So nice to meet you." Kitty shook Isabelle's hand. "Violet's been telling me about all the work you've done for the Red Cross."

Though she wanted to sound polished and dignified, the delight of meeting her heroine got the best of Isabelle. "I'm so happy to be doing it. There's still so much to be done, and I wish I could be more involved," she gushed.

Mrs. Felton smiled, a gleam in her eye. "That's wonderful. I'll keep you in mind if we bring any new initiatives to the table. We're always grateful to have enthusiastic people involved in our cause."

Mrs. Felton returned her attention to Violet's mother, and Isabelle twisted her hands together, struggling to remain quiet. She wanted to ask Mrs. Felton so many questions, but now was not the time. With a room full of women with whom to mingle, Isabelle couldn't exactly pull the woman aside for a lengthy conversation. Moments later, Margaret and Grace materialized at Isabelle's side.

"Mrs. Felton," Violet interjected. "This is Margaret and Grace Hamilton. Grace is also helping me plan the gala."

Grace shook Mrs. Felton's hand. "Yes, I'm helping Violet and Isabelle while I'm visiting. My father's a doctor in Denver, and I know how important your work is."

Grace's calm, confident tone made her sound like she had been involved in philanthropy all of her life. Isabelle's cheeks burned; she had no way of knowing what causes Grace supported in Denver. *It's my fault; I've never asked her.* Grace's mention of her father being a doctor, however, perturbed Isabelle. *Why does she always bring that up?*

"That's very kind," Mrs. Felton said. "We need more people like you who're willing to help. I'd love to talk to both of you about getting something together for later on in . . ."

Isabelle's eyes widened in stunned horror, and her chin began to tremble. Kitty addressed only Violet and Grace about the gala. Isabelle felt her mother's hand on her arm but pulled away and slowly walked to the refreshments table near the entrance to the sitting room. Isabelle helped herself to a cup of punch and wandered over to one of the bookcases. She fought back tears and pretended to read the titles of several leather-bound volumes, desperately trying to understand why Violet—one of her best friends—and Grace hadn't insisted she be part of the gala conversation with Mrs. Felton. *It's not Kitty's fault.* Isabelle sniffled. *She doesn't know me, but it's hurtful that Violet and Grace shunned me. What did I do wrong? Nothing.*

The answer pained Isabelle more than the question. She continued to peruse the books and swiped away a stray tear. *I don't want to cry like a pouting child, but why doesn't anyone appreciate me? Josephine didn't thank me when I helped her this morning. Mother and Father take me for granted, and Violet didn't insist that I stay when Mrs. Felton began talking about a Red Cross event even though I'm the one who cares the most about what happens to others.*

Isabelle cast a wounded glance over her shoulder at Violet and Grace. They remained engrossed in conversation with Mrs. Felton. *I might as well be one of these books.* Isabelle returned her attention to the titles on the shelves. *No one would miss me if I were gone.*

When Isabelle, Grace, and Margaret returned home, Isabelle retreated to her bedroom. She indeed felt like a petulant child, but the events of the morning had festered, making it impossible to pretend that nothing was wrong. By the time the mail arrived, she could no longer keep herself locked away. She stepped into the hall just as Sarah slipped an envelope under Grace's door.

Sarah rose with a start, her face pleading, much like a child caught doing something naughty. "I—I'm sorry, miss, please don't tell—"

"Come," Isabelle said, motioning to Sarah.

Once inside her room, Isabelle closed the door and paused. *I know what I expect in the mail, but who is Grace getting secret letters from?* "Don't worry. I won't tell anyone what you're doing. You're helping me too." Isabelle reassured the clearly shaken maid. "Have you seen anything for me? I feel like it's been forever since I mailed my application."

Sarah shook her head, her expression solemn. "No, I haven't seen anything, and I check for you first. I put the letters for you and Miss Grace in my pocket before I take the mail to your mother."

Isabelle sighed in irritation and stalked over to the open window. *Why isn't it here? And how long has Grace been getting letters? How bold of her. Maybe they're about school, but then again, how would the school have this address?* Isabelle shook her head, her thoughts returning to the problem at hand. *I must get out of this house, and I can't unless the slowpokes in Los Angeles make their darn decision!*

Isabelle turned from the window to find Sarah fidgeting in the middle of the room.

Isabelle held up her hands. "I'm sorry, you can go. Thank you for watching for anything that comes for me."

Sarah left the room like a mouse scurrying away into a hidey-hole. Isabelle pressed her hands against her temples and paced in front of the window.

"It's coming," she whispered, gazing at the golden rays of sunlight that filtered over the bay in the distance. "The letter's coming, and I'm going to be accepted. Just be patient."

Finally, Isabelle flopped onto her bed. What had promised to be an exciting day had turned into an exhausting exercise in dejection. *The letter will come, and when it does, I'll go to Los Angeles, even if I have to walk there!*

TWENTY-EIGHT

When the letter had appeared under her locked door, Grace had hurriedly tiptoed across her room and retrieved it. *I hope Frank isn't too angry about Andrew.* She opened the envelope. *Aunt Cora may be a pious, persnickety old bird, but she was right; I need to pay better attention to what's happening around me.* Grace hopped onto her bed and gathered her feet under her as she unfolded the single sheet of paper.

> *Dear Grace,*
>
> *I'm that much closer to getting you that big house I promised. I won a good pile of munny off Graham and a couple of his friends this past week. Graham's face turned the color of rare steak and he brissled up like an angry porcupine, but he finally handed over the cash. I don't think these boys were ready for that much loozing and it has stuck in their craws a good bit.*
>
> *I have three more sined contracts and my brothers even sent a telegram spouting off about how happy they are to finally have the bisness break into the market here. I'm hoping to go to the Cliff House agen soon. Me beeting Graham in cards may shut that train down at the stayshun, but I think he's a man of his word and I'll get to meet the Cliff House head cook and try a bit of their beef one of these days.*

I look eagerly toward the day we can be tagether for good Grace. When I saw you at the Cliff House talking to that puffed up Andrew fellow, I wanted to throw him in the oshun. I'm not proud of that as I wrote before but I don't like seeing you talk to uther men. I hope you're not reconsidering our plan. I helped you out of that scrape with Charles and all this time I've thought yer heart was mine. I hope I've not ben rong becuz I can't bare the thought of living without you.

I shud have enuf munny for us to make a start soon and I'll call on you then.

Frank

Grace tossed the letter aside, her heart hammering in her chest. *He's going to show up at our door and cause a scene. I can't allow that to happen.*

Grace rose and walked to the armoire. She retrieved a sheet of stationery and an envelope from her train case, sat down at her dressing table, and considered her response to Frank.

"He simply can't come here, but what do I do?" Grace muttered. She tapped a fingernail on the table and racked her brain for a solution. Rough waves of grief tinged with desperation buffeted her. She couldn't marry Frank and had no intention of ever telling anyone what had happened with Charles.

What do I do? What do I do?

Her stomach dropped, and she slowly turned toward the armoire. *That's diabolical!* But it would work. Grace swallowed hard, her mouth pulling down as she grimaced. She rose and willed herself back to the armoire. She opened the door, crouched down, and thrust her hand inside her train case. When her fingers brushed the smooth glass bottle in the bottom of the case, she clamped her eyes closed.

This is the answer.

Grace settled onto the floor with a thump, shame enveloping her like the cloud that passed in front of the sun outside. The most dreadful and eternally damning plot formed in her mind, and tears filled her eyes. Despite still mourning the loss of Frank and her dream of being married, she couldn't risk him arriving at her aunt and uncle's doorstep. She couldn't risk him spreading lies about what he believed had happened between her and Charles the night he and Jacob had saved her. Though she ached for the man she had thought she knew, her plan would tie up loose ends and give her a fresh start. But could she go through with it? When the time came, would she be able to do what was needed to end her relationship with Frank?

Grace shivered and removed the glass bottle from her train case. She turned it over in her hand, talons of fear piercing her heart. What she was considering meant eternal damnation and the irredeemable loss of her soul. She recalled the wails of the few patients her father had been unable to save. *If I do this, will my soul scream for mercy after I die?* Grace inhaled a ragged breath, warring with her emotions. It might, but it was a risk she was willing to take. She had come too far to turn back; she would not return to Colorado, she would not remain trapped in a dangerous relationship, and she would not give up her place at school.

Finally she placed the bottle back in her train case, rose, and closed the door to the armoire. *I am not an evil woman for wanting to protect myself.* She clenched her jaw. *And I will not let Frank be an angry bull who stands in my way. I'll clear him from the new train track I'm on like a cowcatcher on a locomotive.*

Deeply mortified and shaken by what she was considering, Grace returned to her dressing table. She narrowed her eyes, wiped away a few lingering tears, and picked up her pen.

> *Dear Frank,*
> *I'm very proud of all the fine work you're doing to get*

your business established here. Congratulations on your recent contracts and for winning at cards. I'm so lucky to have a man of many talents.

I'm excited that you may have enough money for us to make a proper start soon. Because I know you respect and want to please me, please do me the favor of writing before you call in person. I'll need time to gather my things and thank my family, who have been so kind to let me stay with them this summer.

I must admit that I'm a little hurt by you thinking I'd reconsider our plan. Andrew Kepler is simply one of my uncle's business associates. It would've been rude of me not to greet him as I did you that day in the Cliff House hall. Please forgive me if I came off as anything but the proper young woman you intend to marry.

Know that I think of you often and can barely wait to see you again.

Grace

Grace sealed the letter and slumped back in her chair. "Why do women have to apologize for things they did that weren't wrong?"

She stowed the letter alongside yet another dime in her side table. She stood at the window and inhaled the warm breeze, evening light beginning to cast shadows across the lawn. Grace wrinkled her nose when she envisioned Frank arriving at the front door and announcing that he was her fiancé, there to collect her. *That simply can't happen.* She stared at the armoire, her train case still tucked safely inside. *I must figure out a way to hold him off until I can work up the nerve to carry out the rest of my plan.*

TWENTY-NINE

Less than a week had passed since Grace had mailed her letter to Frank, and she and her family now lounged on plaid woolen blankets on the beach near the Cliff House. Wide-brimmed hats and umbrellas were the order of the day, the hot sun shooting sparkles off the water. The joyful sounds of small children filled the air, a few frolicking near their parents about twenty yards away.

Isabelle had excused herself for a walk on the sand, and Josephine and Henry sat together helping themselves to strawberries and cheese. Grace, Aunt Margaret, and Uncle James sat quietly and watched in contented amusement as children played nearby. A little girl, so young she still toddled, knelt and picked up a shell. When she offered it to her father with a gummy grin, he hoisted her up, and she laid her head on his chest. *Such a perfect day.* Grace smiled.

"Ho there." Uncle James's voice boomed so suddenly that Grace nearly dropped her plate of crackers and cheese slices. "Isabelle's landed a big fish."

Josephine laughed, and Grace furrowed her brow in confusion. Uncle James pointed toward the Cliff House. Isabelle, Andrew, and Charlotte appeared in the distance, ambling toward the family. A wide grin spread across Grace's face. Everyone rose from the blankets, only to turn in alarm toward a shout down the beach. A man rushed out into the shallow surf. His child had been caught by a wave and had fallen but was unharmed. As the father carried the child back to its mother, Grace inhaled sharply. *People could be watching me. Is Frank around?* Her pulse raced as she quickly surveyed her surroundings. With no sign of Frank, Grace exhaled a shaky breath and returned her attention to Andrew and Charlotte.

"Hello, Mr. Kepler." Uncle James strode barefoot onto the sand and shook Andrew's hand. "Good to see you. Who do we have here?"

The young woman at Andrew's side stepped forward and offered her hand to Uncle James. "I'm Charlotte Gordon, sir, Andrew's cousin."

Uncle James introduced himself and then snapped his fingers. "Yes, yes. Isabelle's mentioned you before. Nice to finally meet you in person. You had tea with the girls a little while back, is that right?"

"Yes, and we must do it again soon, so please save some time for me." Charlotte winked at Isabelle.

"We'd love to join you again for tea." Isabelle beamed.

Uncle James motioned to the blankets spread with food and drink. "Would you like to join us?"

Andrew shook his head and tucked Charlotte's hand into the crook of his elbow. "I'm sorry, but we can't; my aunt and uncle are waiting."

"Well then, maybe another time." Uncle James cut his eyes from Andrew to Isabelle. "I'm sure we'll see you again before you leave town."

Grace bit the inside of her lip to stifle a giggle. Her uncle was clearly angling for Andrew to spend more time with Isabelle. *He's subtler than Aunt Margaret, but he's so like her with his matchmaking.* Grace waved to Andrew and Charlotte before they started their retreat up the beach toward the Cliff House.

Once settled back on the blanket, Grace helped herself to a few strawberries. Henry poured her a glass of water, which she accepted with a nod of thanks. Grace watched the waves caress the sand. They mirrored her emotions, which rushed forward and retreated like the water. Andrew was an attractive man, and if she hadn't known Charlotte, the jealousy Grace might have felt seeing him with another woman reminded her of what Frank must have felt when he saw her talking to Andrew that day in the Cliff House hall. *I understand now.* Grace munched on a strawberry, her eyes trained on several seagulls that wheeled and settled onto the water. *But I can't be with Frank. I will not live my life under the watch of a jealous man.*

Grace swallowed her bite and sipped her water. She gazed up at the Cliff House. Its grandeur loomed large like a beacon over the sea, much like her decision to part from Frank cast a shadow over her heart. *Just because I can't marry Frank doesn't mean I've failed during my time in California.*

When the seabirds lifted and whirled overhead, Grace's pulse quickened; she was circling and waiting. Now that she would be an unmarried woman attending school, she would need to arrive in Los Angeles a week before the term began to secure housing with an approved family. She gnawed on a fingernail; she wondered if those with whom she would live would be kind to her, like her relatives in San Francisco. She wondered if they would have a daughter close to her age, someone who might also enjoy sewing and playing the piano. She wondered, too, what they would expect from her if she was forced to help with domestic duties to cover her room and board.

Grace nibbled on a cracker, the gulls still tilting in wide circles overhead. At some point, she, much like the birds, would fly away. Grace only hoped that when she did, she would end up floating above the tumult instead of drowning in it.

THIRTY

Isabelle smiled at Josephine, who sat on a woolen blanket, a palm resting on her belly. Josephine's morning sickness had proven to be an unpredictable devil. It came and went when it pleased, but afternoons and evenings were when she usually felt best. She had handled the situation much as she had planned. She had changed what she ate for breakfast and retired to her room soon after finishing her meal. Josephine had also told Henry. He had arrived one evening at dinner, a bemused expression of awe and anticipation etched on his face. Josephine had also scheduled an appointment with Dr. Jenkins. Grace had reacted to the news with a curiously prolonged pause but had finally whispered her congratulations. The hardest part for Isabelle and Josephine had been convincing Margaret not to take out full-page advertisements in the *Chronicle* and *Call* newspapers. She had been so overjoyed at the prospect of being a grandmother that Isabelle had feared her mother might have another fainting spell.

When Isabelle and Grace rose to go for a walk, Josephine kissed Henry on the cheek, popped a strawberry into her mouth, and joined them.

Grace walked ahead on the sand, her gaze distant, while Josephine and Isabelle trailed behind.

Josephine leaned closer to Isabelle and whispered, "Grace likes Andrew Kepler even though she's trying to hide it."

Isabelle let out a derisive snort.

"She says all the right things and behaves like a proper lady, but the way she looks at him could melt steel," Josephine continued.

Isabelle gaped for a moment. *How would Josephine know such a thing? She only looks at Henry with adoration.* Isabelle shook her head at her sister's nonsense.

"Father said you'd landed a big fish when you brought Andrew down the beach to visit. But what if Grace landed him? Wouldn't *that* shock her parents?" Josephine snickered.

The notion of Grace landing Andrew Kepler struck Isabelle as possible and preposterous all at the same time. He had only seen Grace three times—at Violet's engagement party, in the Cliff House hall, and today—but hadn't Josephine only seen Henry a handful of times before she had burst into Isabelle's room and declared how much she loved him? Falling in love as fast as a pelican diving toward the water wasn't out of the question, though Isabelle highly doubted it would happen to her.

"Do you think he's the one sending her all of those secret letters?" Josephine continued.

Isabelle jerked her head around to face her sister. "What secret letters?"

Isabelle full well knew that Grace was receiving secret letters—she had caught Sarah scooting one under Grace's door barely a week ago—but Isabelle didn't dare share this with Josephine. Sarah was helping Isabelle too, and Isabelle couldn't risk Josephine blabbing to their mother and having Margaret scold, or worse yet, fire the maid.

With Grace several yards ahead and out of earshot, Josephine shared how Sarah hadn't been smart enough to keep the letters she collected from Grace's room from peeking out of her apron pockets. Josephine had racked her brain trying to figure out to whom Grace might be writing. When Grace had arrived, she had mentioned that she would be sending letters to a friend in Wyoming, but Josephine suspected that was a ruse. It would allow Grace to send and receive letters without suspicion. And if she was corresponding with her Wyoming friend, why was Sarah secretly mailing the letters?

Isabelle shook her head and watched a young child turn in circles, its arms floating at its sides like the wings of a bird. "I don't know."

Josephine tsked. "Even you have to admit, it'd be a little romantic if Andrew was writing to her."

Isabelle giggled. Despite not agreeing with Josephine about much of anything when it came to relationships, she did think Andrew Kepler would be a great catch. He had proven himself calm in times of crisis by helping Isabelle with Margaret's fainting spell at Violet's engagement party. He was also the sort of man who could go a long way toward restoring a young woman's faith in men, which was what Isabelle imagined Grace needed. "Yes, that would be romantic."

Isabelle and Josephine joined Grace at the water's edge, the surf lapping over their toes. The three women stood in silence, staring out at sea. Finally, Isabelle gazed up at the Cliff House and closed her eyes. With luck, she would have completed a year of school by next summer and be preparing to return to Los Angeles. Josephine would be a mother, her little one old enough to crawl on a blanket and wiggle its toes in the sand.

Josephine turned and ambled away from Isabelle and Grace, dabbing a sleeve to her cheek. Isabelle inhaled the salt air, her heart going out to her sister. Though Josephine still enjoyed her gossip, her pregnancy marked a point of no return, and a shadow of sorrow still clung to her. *This is her last summer of freedom, and in some ways, it's mine too.* Everything was about to change; in fact, it already had. Isabelle hoped that in time, Josephine could be as excited about her future as Isabelle was about hers.

THIRTY-ONE

Wicker picnic basket in hand, Henry climbed the front steps and followed his father-in-law and the women into the house. Lying on the warm blanket beneath the sun had done wonders to calm his ever-turning mind; he wished the family could have stayed longer at the beach. *When Josephine and I move into our new house, we'll visit the ocean more often. Especially now that there will be a baby.*

The thought of becoming a father sent prickles of nervous anticipation up Henry's spine. It excited him, but it also meant he would have much more responsibility. If he was going to look for a different job in San Francisco, he needed to do it now. When Josephine had told him she was most likely pregnant, he had swung from elation to resignation. He loved Josephine, probably a little too much. She would be an excellent mother, but with the news of this child, Henry watched his chances to move to Los Angeles—or anywhere else—fade like the late afternoon sun that now hung low on the horizon. With a grandchild on the way, Margaret would never allow Josephine and Henry to leave San Francisco. And Henry had to admit, it would be nice to leave their little one with family if he and Josephine wanted to go to the theater or the beach.

Grace, Isabelle, and Josephine excused themselves upstairs, and James headed to the study. Eleanor bustled into the foyer and relieved Henry of the picnic basket. Moments later, Sarah walked through the front door, rifling through a thick stack of letters. She froze at the sight of Margaret and Henry.

"You can leave those here." Margaret stood before the mirror and tapped her finger on the credenza, then removed her hat.

When Sarah hesitated, Henry furrowed his brow.

"I—would you like me to check for what might've come for Isabelle or for the ladies, madame? To save you an extra trip on the stairs?" Sarah asked.

That's a bold thing for a maid to ask. Henry wrapped his lips over his teeth. *She should've put the mail down and gone to the kitchen immediately. Why was she sorting through the letters and clutching them as if she had something to hide? Has she been delivering mail to the others all along? And why would she mention Isabelle? She doesn't have any secrets.*

Margaret tucked a stray wisp of hair back where it belonged and shook her head. "No, leave them here. I'll make sure they get what's theirs."

Margaret held out her hand, and Sarah paused for an unusually long moment. Finally, the maid handed Margaret the mail and hurried up the hall. At the kitchen door, Sarah lingered, her expression worried, then disappeared behind the door.

Henry started up the stairs. When he rounded the landing, he stopped and peeked down into the foyer. Margaret sifted through the mail, laying a few pieces aside on the credenza. She examined the front and back of one envelope, the mirror reflecting her clear displeasure. She glanced toward the kitchen door, and when she turned to look up the stairs, Henry instinctively pulled his head back. After a few seconds, he cautiously peered into the foyer again; Margaret folded the envelope and tucked it into her purse.

What's going on here? And where can I go to be alone to think? Henry climbed the remaining stairs and tiptoed down the hall.

He crept into the bathroom and locked the door. He didn't need to relieve himself, but the cramped room was the only safely unoccupied private space in the house. Josephine was in the room they shared, James was in the study, and Henry didn't want Margaret, Isabelle, or Grace joining him in the sitting room—or any other room—at the moment. He leaned on the basin, blew out his cheeks, and stared at his reflection in the mirror. *It's impossible to keep up with all the secrets the women in this house have.*

Henry took a precarious seat on the edge of the white clawfoot tub. *Grace's suitor situation is unsettling, and Josephine sometimes behaves strangely, but Isabelle?* He tried but failed to find a comfortable position on the narrow lip of the tub, his stare boring a hole through the rug in front of the sink. *She never has secrets. It's one of her most admirable qualities. Everyone else disapproves of her straightforwardness, but there's a type of genuine charm in it, and the world needs more of her charm.*

Someone tried the doorknob, and Henry shot up from his perch. "I'll only be a moment."

He pulled the toilet chain and mussed a nearby hand towel. *Just as well. All of this intrigue is exhausting, and I need a more comfortable place to sit.* When Henry opened the door, whoever had tried the knob had disappeared.

THIRTY-TWO

A few days after encountering Charlotte Gordon and Andrew Kepler on the beach, Grace stood before her dressing table and opened an envelope from her father. It contained a brief note and twenty-five dollars for the Red Cross, half of the amount she had requested. *At least he sent something.* Grace shook her head and sighed, smoothing the sleeves of her emerald-colored gown. *No one knows how much I asked for, so he won't come off as the cheapskate he is by only sending twenty-five.*

She sat down, wanting to take a few deep breaths to calm her frustration, only to be thwarted by her corset. She fingered the letter and narrowed her eyes. *I could keep part of this money for school, and no one would be the wiser.* Grace was dead set on ridding herself of Frank, but an unfamiliar sense of anxious irritation had set in, much to her dismay. She needed money so badly, but to steal funds meant to help others was wrong. And selfish. She grimaced; the entire notion reminded her too much of something Frank might do.

"I will *not* stoop to his level," she whispered, staring hard at her reflection. "I will not cheat the Red Cross out of money like Frank cheats men at cards."

Grace lifted her chin, rose, and tucked the letter and money into an armoire drawer.

"I'll enjoy my uncle's birthday party and make sure I give Father's donation to Isabelle when the time is right."

Downstairs, Grace paused between the dining and sitting rooms, the gaiety of Uncle James's birthday party swirling around her. The foyer chandeliers bathed the ladies' shimmering dresses in soft light, making them resemble Christmas ornaments reminiscent of those that often adorned the enormous pines at the Brown Palace during holiday gatherings. Everyone had been invited, or so it seemed. The house teemed with conversation, the tinkling of glasses, and the scents of soft, feminine perfume. Eleanor and Sarah had outdone themselves; the dining room buffet was bedecked with sprays of white roses and lavender hydrangeas. Trays of roast beef, mounds of shrimp, oysters, caviar, and crabmeat salad sat artfully arranged around platters of sliced chocolate cake. The scene reminded Grace of Violet's engagement party, minus the patio setting. Though she needed to subtly shift from side to side every so often—her infernal corset was digging into her ribs more than usual tonight for some reason—she strolled into the sitting room, confident that she was every bit as elegant as the other ladies in attendance.

Graham and Rosaline talked with Uncle James and Aunt Margaret in the far corner, and Henry chatted with Charlotte and Andrew near the room's entrance. Josephine stood with them, but given the greenish tint of her skin, she was positively ill. Her morning sickness had played a cruel trick on her, choosing the most unfortunate time to last the entire day.

A motion in the foyer caught Grace's eye, and her pulse quickened. Frank had arrived, an attractive woman with almond-shaped eyes and a high pompadour of blond hair clutching his arm. The woman's lavender dress gleamed like a pale amethyst. *Who is she, and where did he find her?* Grace's breath grew shallow, and she clamped her mouth shut, afraid she might have growled out loud. *He badgers me about talking to Andrew Kepler but has the nerve to bring another woman to my uncle's party? He truly is an awful man! But now I'm the one being jealous. Why do I feel this way if I know*

I can't marry him? Grace brushed her cheek with a palm, trying to quell her anger, and swept out of the sitting room.

"Mr. Buchanan." She approached Frank and his guest. "How are you?"

Grace shook Frank's hand and turned to the woman at his side.

"And who is your friend?" Grace forced herself not to glare at Frank's guest.

To Grace's surprise, the woman held her gaze without blinking.

"Grace, this is my sister, Mary," he said.

Grace stood in stunned silence for a moment, then bowed her head. Mary stepped closer and shook her hand.

"It's nice to finally meet you." Mary's kind voice melted Grace's anger. "I hope you don't mind my intrusion this evening."

Grace shook her head, still ashamed of having assumed the worst about Frank's companion. "I—no, not at all. It's lovely to meet you too. Please, come in."

Frank grinned at Grace, his hand resting on the small of Mary's back. Grace bit her lip, sorrow and nostalgia washing over her. She remembered why she had been so enamored with Frank: the protective way he always stood beside her, the affable smile, the eyes that hinted at danger and adventure.

"You look fetching as always." Frank winked at Grace.

Before she could stop herself, she giggled. "Thank you." She quickly sobered. "Graham and Uncle James are this way."

The trio wove through the sitting room until they reached Andrew, Charlotte, and Henry. Josephine had disappeared, undoubtedly upstairs to the bathroom. At an opportune moment, Grace tapped Henry on the arm, and he stepped aside, allowing her, Frank, and Mary to join the circle.

"Frank, a pleasure to see you. Good that you could make it tonight." Henry shook Frank's hand.

"Good to be invited," Frank said, then introduced Mary to the others.

With formalities out of the way, Frank surveyed the room, a gleam in his eye.

Don't gawk; you'll blow it. Grace willed him to focus on the conversation.

"We'll leave you to talk," Grace said. "Charlotte, would you like to come with me to get some punch?"

Andrew patted Charlotte's hand, and Grace noticed Frank's benign reaction. Frank had greeted Charlotte as if she and Andrew were a couple. Grace had no intention of correcting him.

In the crowded dining room, Grace and Charlotte filled four cups with punch. The ladies carried them into the foyer and sat them on the credenza. As the two women chatted, Grace glanced from time to time into the sitting room. Andrew and Frank remained engrossed in conversation. Though Frank appeared to be a high-rolling cattleman, Grace sensed he was a bit out of his depth. He hadn't grown up in "the big house," as he called it, in Kansas City. Instead, he had been sent to live with his industrious, penny-pinching uncle in Denver at a young age. Frank's business acumen, including the unsavory card-sharp and pool-playing skills, had undoubtedly come from his uncle. Frank wasn't accustomed to fine things, at least the level of fine things that Grace desired and that adorned the Hamilton households in San Francisco and Denver.

"I'm sorry I haven't had you over again for tea." Charlotte's apology jolted Grace's attention away from Frank. "We've been so busy, what with Andrew visiting."

Grace finished a sip of punch and waved her hand. "It's nothing. I'd love to visit again, but don't feel obligated. Should we take them their drinks now? Mr. Buchanan looks like he could use some punch." Grace waggled her eyebrows.

Grace and Charlotte both picked up two cups of punch and

crossed the foyer. *If others wouldn't think the drink was for me, I'd fetch Frank a glass of whiskey, but I'm not supposed to know what he favors.*

Grace and Charlotte maneuvered around a few guests and into the sitting room. Frank accepted his cup of punch without incident, but Charlotte accidentally stumbled forward, splashing almost all of Andrew's punch onto him.

"Oh, Andrew, I'm sorry." Charlotte patted his coat, her hand undoubtedly sticky as she looked around for a nonexistent napkin.

Grace immediately turned to Mary. "I got this for you. Would you hold my cup and excuse me? I need to show Mr. Kepler to the bathroom."

Frank narrowed his eyes and flared his nostrils when Mary took the punch cups from Grace. *Please don't make a scene, Frank. I'm simply helping him find the bathroom.* Grace's heart pounded.

She led Andrew out of the sitting room, and once through the foyer, they turned down a narrow hall to their right. Grace pointed toward the lavatory.

"Thank you for helping. Sometimes my cousin gets ahead of herself." Andrew brushed the left side of his coat and chuckled.

Grace tipped her chin and smiled demurely, then started back up the empty hall. When the bathroom door clicked behind her, she stopped and closed her eyes. *Having Frank and Andrew in the same house is awful! I have to pretend not to know one and not to like the other.* Grace smoothed her dress and made her way back to the sitting room. Her eyes searched for Frank, but instead found Mary chatting with Aunt Margaret. Grace soon spotted Frank sipping his punch and holding a glass, which she guessed was hers. Grace inhaled a shaky breath and approached him, pretending she couldn't read his feelings.

"Mr. Buchanan, thank you for keeping this for me." She took her cup of punch from him.

"You help him take the coat off?" Frank sneered.

Alarmed by Frank's tone, Grace's eyes widened, and she swallowed hard, hoping no one else had heard him. She quickly recovered, a smile resurfacing on her face. When she glanced across the room, Mary, having seen Grace and Frank's unpleasant exchange, returned her attention to Aunt Margaret. Grace gathered her courage and turned to Frank, her back to the others.

"Listen to me, Frank." Grace's smile belied the hard edge of her voice. "You're in a room full of people with very powerful connections, and once again, you're being hurtful. I'm part of this family, and as such, I'm a hostess to every man and woman in this house. It's my place—my responsibility—to help Mr. Kepler. When I'm *your* wife, and we're living in that large house you've promised me, I'll have the same responsibility. So, I'd appreciate it if you wouldn't accuse me of being inappropriate when all I'm trying to do is help you."

Grace sipped her punch, willing the hand that held the cup not to shake. *My God, that's the most audacious thing I've ever said to a man. My older brother would backhand his wife for such talk.* Grace stared out into the darkness through the nearest window and blanched. She didn't want to remember the faint bruises on her sister-in-law's cheek. The woman had sometimes come to Sunday dinner, her head bowed, purple and yellow blooming beneath one of her eyes. Given Grace's strong desire to fume at Frank's uncouth behavior, she understood how her sister-in-law might have ended up with her wounds. Grace couldn't fathom how the woman had stayed married to her brother.

Despite her shaken nerves, Grace refused to step away from Frank. He stared at the floor and ran his fingers through his hair. *He knows I'm right.* She remained silent and allowed him to collect himself. *He knows he can't make a scene even if he doesn't like what I've said.*

"I don't mean to be hurtful." His voice was apologetic. "But you shouldn't be going off with him. I know it's right and proper, but I still don't like it. I'm not proud, but seeing you leave with him got my blood up."

Grace's face softened, and she checked the room again. Aunt Margaret and Mary remained deep in conversation with Henry and Josephine.

"I know." Grace met Frank's eyes. "But you must always trust me. I can be your wife and a good hostess. That's going to be part of our new life together."

Frank shifted his weight to the other foot and hung his head like a scolded child. "I know. You're right, and I do trust you."

Do you? Grace crinkled her eyes. *Or will you say you do and never be able to, regardless of what I say or do?*

Grace leaned closer to Frank.

"I certainly know nothing about the beef industry, but I also thought it wise to stay in the good graces of Mr. Kepler because he's from Los Angeles. Wouldn't he be a wonderful business contact when we move there?" Grace stared up at Frank, her expression innocent and questioning.

Having taken the bait, he quirked a grin, much to her relief. "Yes. Yes, he would."

The high-pitched ring of a fork tapping against glass hushed the surrounding conversation. All eyes turned toward the sitting room entrance.

"It's time to wish James a happy birthday in the dining room. Let's all get ready to sing," Aunt Margaret announced.

Guests trailed out of the room, and laughter and the buzz of conversation resumed. Grace followed Frank and Mary toward the foyer, her heart still thudding in her chest. *I've smoothed things over for now, but I fear it won't last. I'll need to stay on his good side until I can end our relationship once and for all.*

THIRTY-THREE

Isabelle squeezed her way past a few guests in the crowded dining room and retrieved two forks and plates of cake. Josephine stood near the buffet next to Henry, a sickly smile on her face. While the mood was joyous—everyone had finished singing "For He's a Jolly Good Fellow" to her father—Josephine was not. Isabelle had clutched Josephine's hand and feared her sister might cry when Graham gave his moving toast. Afterward, Josephine had hurried from the room, most likely to empty the contents of her stomach into the upstairs toilet.

Isabelle returned to her sister and nudged her gently with her elbow. "I got you a small piece of cake," Isabelle said, her voice thick with concern. "I thought you might manage a little bit of it. Father would be disappointed if you didn't at least try."

"Thank you." Josephine took the fork and plate.

Henry excused himself and Josephine motioned for Isabelle to move a little farther away from the buffet table. "I have to get out of range of the oysters lest they send me running for the nearest bathroom."

Isabelle hurriedly stepped aside. She could barely smell the plate of glistening oysters that sat on the nearby table. Despite her excitement at becoming an aunt, Isabelle pitied Josephine. Isabelle couldn't imagine how exhausting it must be to fear the smell of certain foods. Isabelle smiled and bent her fingers in acknowledgment of a family friend. Grace stood talking near the dining room entrance with Frank Buchanan and the pretty woman who had accompanied him to the party. Andrew and Charlotte had ensconced themselves on the other side of the room.

"Looks like they're at it again." Josephine tipped her chin toward Andrew.

Isabelle sighed but caught Andrew stealing a glance at Grace. Isabelle downed a gulp of punch and focused on her cake.

"Did you see how she almost fell over herself to help him after Charlotte spilled punch all over his coat?" Josephine ate a small bite of cake.

Isabelle shrugged. "I thought she was being helpful."

Josephine's eyes rose skyward.

"What?" Isabelle's protest drew the brief attention of a few nearby guests.

"Keep your voice down." Josephine pulled Isabelle closer to the wall. "What I'm saying is, she isn't behaving like someone who just had *two* suitors *disappear.*"

Isabelle's eyes flew open. "What?" she breathed.

Josephine clutched Isabelle's arm. "Oh, that's right," Josephine hissed in excitement. "You were walking with her on the beach when Cora told the story."

While Josephine shared Cora's sensational tale of how both of Grace's suitors had disappeared, Isabelle gaped, slowly shaping her mouth into an O. When Josephine finished, the sisters shot furtive glances at Grace, who still stood chatting with Frank and his mystery woman.

"Why are you only telling me this now?" Isabelle said, astonished and perturbed that Josephine would keep something so immense from her.

Josephine ignored Isabelle's question. "I think she's a tease. I don't think she misses either of her beaus. She obviously likes Andrew, but she also seems interested in Mr. Buchanan." Josephine narrowed her eyes at Grace. "She's no innocent. I mean, she's innocent in *that* way, but she's mastered the art of stringing a few men along until she decides who she wants. And if I'm not mistaken, she wants Andrew."

Isabelle forked in another bite of cake and snuck a peek at Grace. "I hadn't noticed, but maybe you're right. Andrew *is* a nice man, though he does nothing for me. I don't know about Mr. Buchanan. Maybe she's trying to forget her beaus, or maybe she's happy to be away from home. I get the sense her parents are very strict. I don't think she means to, but she sometimes doesn't pay attention and comes off as only caring about herself."

Josephine patted her sister's arm and arched a brow. "We all can't be saints like you, Isa."

"I'm not trying to—" Isabelle objected.

"I'm not criticizing," Josephine interjected. "I appreciate how you care, like bringing me this cake and standing over here so I don't have to smell those abominable oysters. And you're right. Her attention floats away, and she can be standoffish or maybe a little unsure of herself. What I want to know is, what *really* happened to her suitor and to the man her family didn't approve of? If her parents think she's going to forget about either of those men just because they sent her away to visit family for a few months, they may be in for a rude surprise."

Isabelle cut a chunk of frosting off of her piece of cake and popped it into her mouth. The idea of suffering through a difficult situation with one suitor had been enough to pique her curiosity, but for Grace to have survived two suitors' disappearing? Isabelle eyed Grace with benign suspicion. *Is this how men behave when they stop courting a young woman? Did those men disappear into the night, much like the fog over the bay that disappears each morning? Surely Grace would have seen one of them at a social event.* Isabelle's fork scraped her plate with a screech and she pulled a face.

"What do you think happened to them?" Isabelle asked, her voice intent.

Josephine grinned. "You sound like Mother and Harriet in the women's parlor."

Isabelle scoffed in amusement at her sister's teasing.

"It doesn't matter." Josephine tilted her head in Andrew's direction.

He had broken off his conversation with Charlotte and was headed toward Grace, Frank, and Mary.

"This should be interesting." Josephine shifted to her left, angling her body to get a better view. "We must get to the bottom of the two suitors' stories, because a third man looks to be making his move."

THIRTY-FOUR

Dread tightened its grip on Grace, and her pulse quickened. Andrew was walking toward her. Mary stood quietly between Grace and Frank, his neck quickly turning the color of rare steak. *Frank will always be jealous, which means he'll never trust me.* The finality of that truth made Grace want to cry. There was no turning back; Frank would never change, no matter how hard she tried to please him.

"Hello, Frank," Andrew said. "I need to have a quick word with Miss Hamilton in private. Would you mind?"

Grace feigned a smile and inhaled a shaky breath. "I'll be right back, Mr. Buchanan." *I hope that sounded reassuring. I don't want to have to calm him down again tonight.*

Grace and Andrew exited the dining room into the foyer and turned down the side hall. Midway to the bathroom, Andrew stopped and turned to Grace.

"I wanted to thank you for spending time with Charlotte." His voice was thick with sincerity. "Her heart's fragile, and she's not always able to do many of the social things other girls her age do. She talked for days about how delightful it was to have you and Isabelle visit for tea."

Andrew's compliment calmed Grace's nerves. "She was a perfect hostess, and I was happy to visit. She's invited us back, although we haven't set a date."

"All the same," Andrew said. "I'm going back to Los Angeles

soon and wanted you to know how much I appreciated it. Charlotte doesn't like it when I make a fuss. The family tries to keep things as normal as they can for her, though sometimes that can be difficult." He walked up the hall a few paces and then turned back. "If you're ever in Los Angeles and need anything, please let me know."

Grace lifted a hand in acknowledgment and paused; she would remember his offer. "Thank you. I'll keep that in mind. I'll be back in a few minutes."

When Andrew disappeared around the corner, the demons of self-doubt crept forward like shadows from the dark corners of Grace's mind. She had yet to rid herself of Frank, didn't know Andrew that well, and didn't trust herself enough to stray from forging a path to school on her own.

Grace hurried into the bathroom and locked the door. She blew out a sigh and paced in front of the mirror. Finally, she sat down to relieve herself. She was attracted to handsome Andrew with his wealth and charm. She had fallen hard for those very things with Charles and Frank, but maybe that was the problem. Charm was one thing, but wealth was another. *Am I selfish for wanting a husband with money?* Grace bit her lip, her chest tightening. Marrying a man of her social station wasn't wrong; it was assumed she would do so. With Frank and Charles, however, she had found herself in similar predicaments. *I'm not shallow for wanting a husband of means; I'm simply not confident enough in myself to tell if the man I've chosen will respect me as much as he respects his money.*

Grace had also enjoyed her tea with Charlotte and Isabelle. It had become one of the highlights of her trip after she had recovered from the horror of nearly revealing that her parents wouldn't allow her to speak about going to school, let alone do it. But she *would* do it. Grace adjusted her dress, flushed the toilet, and smoothed her hair in front of the mirror.

"And I'll do it myself," she vowed, still unsure of how she would ever come up with the money.

Grace returned to the foyer, only to stop short when she spotted Frank and Mary. Blessedly, Frank's neck was no longer red, probably because Andrew now stood near the entrance to the dining room chatting with Henry.

"I was wondering there for a minute if you'd slipped and gone in," Frank laughed, walking toward her.

Grace's cheeks flared in embarrassment. *Did he ask Andrew where I was, or did he assume I was returning from the bathroom?*

"Do not make a scene," Mary pleaded quietly with Frank.

Grace mustered an appreciative smile at Mary, but a few guests had overheard Frank's comment and snickered.

"I—Mr. Buchanan, what an awful thing to say," Grace said, her eyes ablaze. *He's rude and uncouth and has no class! I cannot believe I ever thought of marrying him. He may tease his male friends this way, but he's made me look foolish, and I never want to see him again!* Grace, caught in the stares of Frank and a handful of other guests, struggled to remake herself into the good hostess she claimed to be. "Did you need something?" She silently prayed he would say no.

"I wanted to say goodbye, but I didn't think I'd have to hunt you down like a lost steer in a snowstorm to do it." He grinned again, patted Grace on the shoulder, and winked at a man standing nearby.

At that moment, Grace swore her corset had finally won the battle and was going to unceremoniously end her life in the middle of her aunt and uncle's foyer. *What is he doing?!* Her breath grew ragged, and she stepped back, her face hot, her eyes narrowed in fury. *He cannot speak to me in such a familiar way. It'll ruin everything and arouse suspicion. He must stop! How do I make him stop?*

Grace wanted to spit epithets at Frank. Instead, the perfect response struck her, and she shot him a steely grin. "I have no doubt, sir, that you would've spared no expense with your search and rescued me like you would've any of your prized cattle."

Mary giggled and clamped a hand over her mouth.

Frank's hearty laugh drew a chuckle from the bemused guests who had witnessed the entire spectacle. "Well said, Miss Grace, well said."

Grace smiled politely and escorted Frank and Mary to the door.

"Thank you for a most pleasant evening, Miss Hamilton," Mary said, clasping one of Grace's hands while George opened the door. "It was so nice to meet you, and I hope to see you again."

Grace thanked Mary, grateful for her kindness. "I hope so too. You both have a good evening." Grace waved to Frank and Mary, who descended the steps.

With Frank gone, Grace strode past the dining room, raising a hand in hello to Henry. She ascended the stairs to her room and, once inside, latched the door. She flopped onto her bed and screamed into her pillow. *What a disastrous night! One minute, I'm jealous because Frank brought a woman to the party who turns out to be his sister, and the next, I'm fending off his insults. At least Mary seemed nice.*

Grace sat up and tugged at the collar of her dress. She walked to the window and gazed at the inky sky. The stars were up there somewhere, twinkling down on her. As Grace tried to catch a glimpse of faint starlight through the clouds, her mind drifted to Charlotte and her damaged heart. *My heart's damaged too.* Grace smoothed her hair and prepared to rejoin the party. *I hope that, in time, I can trust myself enough to repair it.*

Henry stood next to Josephine in the entrance to the dining room, gripping his glass of port and shifting his weight from one foot to the other. The uncomfortable exchange he had witnessed between Frank and Grace had unsettled him. There was something about the man that still didn't sit right. The way Frank had spoken to Grace in the foyer before leaving had not only been rude, it had also been a little too familiar. *Maybe, like Andrew, he's interested in her.* Henry sipped his port.

When Frank had patted Grace's shoulder, Henry had tensed, thinking he might need to intervene. Given what had happened to his mother and that his brother had descended into the seedy world of organized crime, where strongarm tactics ruled, Henry hated physical violence, especially against women. But Grace had expertly handled the situation. Henry couldn't think of why Frank Buchanan would want to hurt her.

Unless he's jealous.

Henry straightened and downed the rest of his port. He had noticed Frank speaking with Grace earlier in the evening in the sitting room. Frank had looked none too happy when she had disappeared with Andrew after Charlotte had accidentally doused his coat with punch. Henry nodded at the man who was regaling him and Josephine with a harrowing tale of how he and his wife had fled to Seattle to live with relatives after the quake. At the mention of fleeing, Henry peered up the stairs. Grace had fled the party shortly after Frank and Mary had left.

When the couple excused themselves, Henry flashed the man a smile and returned to ruminating. *I still believe Frank Buchanan's dangerous, but I can't interfere unless he becomes violent or Grace asks for my help. This is another situation where watching and waiting will win the day.*

THIRTY-FIVE

A few days after James's birthday party, Isabelle and Grace sat in Charlotte's gloomy sitting room around an oval mahogany table littered with saucers and rumpled napkins. July had arrived along with an unusually thick cloud bank; the stormy skies outside mirrored Isabelle's emotions. The white cake squares and lavender tea had been delicious, but not delicious enough to drown out the bitter sorrow that had made itself far too comfortable within Isabelle.

"I don't know where it could be," Isabelle lamented.

Charlotte and Grace scooted to the edge of their chairs.

"I mailed my application *weeks* ago, and I can't imagine it'd take the hospital admissions committee this long to decide. Wouldn't they send me a rejection letter if I hadn't been accepted?" Isabelle shook her head and sipped her tea.

"I simply can't believe it," Charlotte fumed. "You're the best-qualified candidate in all of California—in the entire country!—and I have no idea why they wouldn't accept you. I think you should give it some more time."

Charlotte plucked a single sugar cube from the china bowl and splashed it into her tea. She flung a cube into Isabelle's teacup, and Isabelle laughed despite herself.

"Grace? A cube?" Charlotte teased, a brow lifted.

Grace declined. Charlotte ignored her and tossed not one but two cubes toward Grace's teacup. One landed on the saucer, the other in Grace's lap. She laughed, plucking the cube from the folds of her dress and dropping it into her teacup.

"All right, that's enough." Charlotte settled back into her chair, her spoon circling inside her teacup. "I'm sorry for the flying sugar, but I'm trying to amuse myself because I'm about to be stuck in this house like a caged bird again. Andrew's going back to Los Angeles soon, which means far fewer walks on the beach for me. There are weeks of warm weather left, but Mother and Father are so uptight they'll only let me visit the women's parlor every time the moon turns pink, or so it seems. You'd think I was climbing into the attics of the Cliff House instead of up a single flight of stairs."

Isabelle chuckled, and even Grace managed a weak smile.

Charlotte took a sip of tea and shot a coy grin at Grace. "And what have *you* decided about school?"

Grace licked her lips and stared at the floor.

"I'm still trying to figure out how it would work," she admitted. "I admire you, Isa, and I'm thinking about what you said—about me having talents to share—but it's still scary. I'll be unmarried and have to live with strangers. And then there's Mother and Father. I fear their disapproval, but who knows, they may not care what I do if they can make up a story that makes them look good. It's all so discouraging."

Isabelle forced herself not to scowl. *I'll be living with strangers in the Nurses' Home, but you don't see me griping about it.* Her expression softened when Grace's eyes grew glassy. The unsteady hand with which Grace held her teacup told Isabelle that her cousin was struggling much more than she was letting on. *So she is suffering from the loss of her suitors. How horrible it must be to lose someone you love. And if I'd thought I'd be living with a husband only to find myself having to pay for room and board, I'd be devastated too. I guess we're all feeling sorry for ourselves today.*

Charlotte finished a bite of cake and set her teacup and saucer on the table.

"You know, Andrew brought me a present from the beach the other day." Charlotte rose, retrieved an item from a nearby desk drawer, and returned to her chair. "It's only a feather, but it reminds me of the birds at the ocean, how free they are, how they can go wherever they want.

"I envy you two." Charlotte gently laid the feather on the table. "You have opportunities I'll never have, and though that could make me angry, it doesn't."

Grace stared at Charlotte so intently that Isabelle couldn't help but do the same.

"Those opportunities make me grateful that I can help people. I can give to the Red Cross or the Orphan Asylum, or maybe help you in some way, Grace? I'm not sure how, only to say that, though you may feel discouraged, know that you're freer than you believe."

Charlotte winked at Grace, who surprisingly didn't look away. Hope bloomed within Isabelle. *Maybe Grace will figure out a way to go to teaching school after all.*

Isabelle patted Charlotte's knee in thanks.

Grace helped herself to a bite of cake and spoke when she was finished. "You're right. I think we—I don't mean to speak for you, Isabelle, but I think you would agree—we're freer than we know. We can apply to school and attend if we're accepted, even if we're scared or have to figure things out, like singing for our supper or selling jewelry we thought we'd cherish forever. And thank you for offering to help me, Charlotte; you just did. I should be more grateful for my freedoms, however small, and I will be from now on."

Grace straightened in her chair, an expression of resolve etched on her face.

Isabelle swallowed one last bite of cake and tried to rally her flagging spirits. She wanted to remain hopeful that an acceptance letter would come. She doubted it, but without an outright rejection, she hoped there might still be a chance. Her chest swelled as she wiped her mouth with her napkin; she was secretly proud of Grace. *Maybe I've misjudged her all along.*

THIRTY-SIX

A week after her father's birthday celebration, Isabelle sat on the edge of a chair at Josephine's bedside next to their mother, ready to spring up at any moment. Grace sat with spellbound attention to Isabelle's right. Outside, the leaden sky mirrored the mood in the room; clouds had rolled in and blotted out the sun.

"Mrs. Rothwell?" Dr. Jenkins stood at Josephine's shoulder and spoke softly.

"Hmm," Josephine mumbled. She slid a hand to her head and lightly fingered the small lump on her temple.

"Mrs. Rothwell, it's Dr. Jenkins." The doctor swiped smelling salts beneath Josephine's nose and her eyes flew open.

"My—my hip hurts and my head . . . What happened?" She peered up at Dr. Jenkins.

"You fell, dear." Margaret patted Josephine's hand.

"Did I?" Josephine sniffed and rested her hand on her belly. "Is it still there?" Josephine's question hung in the room.

Isabelle held her breath, afraid of what the answer might be.

Dr. Jenkins adjusted his spectacles and patted her arm. "Time will tell, of course, but there's no bleeding, and I believe you're far enough along that your baby will be fine. Your sister spared you a worse tumble. She was smart to put you to bed and have your mother call me immediately. She certainly will make a fine nurse." Dr. Jenkins beamed at Isabelle. He stowed his stethoscope in his black doctor's case and snapped it shut.

Color rose in Isabelle's cheeks. *He really must stop or he'll ruin everything!* "I—thank you," Isabelle sputtered, clutching the bedspread. "Should we watch for anything? I mean, how will we know if we should call you again?"

Margaret rose and accompanied Dr. Jenkins to the door.

"Only call if she starts to bleed," Dr. Jenkins said. "Stay in bed for the rest of the day, and I'll be back to check on you later in the week."

Josephine smiled weakly at Dr. Jenkins, tears pooling in her eyes.

"Thank you for coming so quickly, Doctor." Margaret opened the door, and Eleanor met Dr. Jenkins in the hall. "I'm sure she'll be all right now."

Isabelle exhaled a sigh of relief; Josephine might have been sore and had a bump on her head, but her baby was safe. Tears ran down Josephine's cheeks, and she reached for her mother's hand when Margaret returned to her chair.

"Oh, Mother, I didn't mean for any of this to happen." Josephine choked out between sobs. "I was so dizzy and—"

"Well, no one means to fall out the front door onto the stoop," Margaret said. "You were lucky Isabelle was there. She rushed out and grabbed you before you could roll down the steps. If you'd made it any farther, you'd have tumbled into the yard."

Josephine sniffled and wiped her nose with the back of her hand. "That's not—that's not what I mean."

Josephine searched their mother's eyes, and Isabelle straightened in her chair. *What do we not understand? What does she want us to say?*

"Grace, can you go get a pitcher of water and a glass, please." Isabelle's tone was one a nurse might use when giving an order.

Grace rose quickly and left the room.

"I'm not ready." Josephine's eyes grew large. "I'm not ready to be a mother, and all of this is a mistake. Not that I don't love

Henry, I do. I love him so very much, and we want to have children someday. I know he's happy, but we were always so careful, and everything's ruined now, so very ruined. All of my time, our time, to have adventures is gone, and I'm going to be stuck with—"

"Please, dear, you're rambling." Margaret stroked a few strands of hair from Josephine's forehead. "No woman is ever ready to be a mother, even if she is excited. All of us will be here to help. And please don't say this was a mistake, especially in front of Henry. A child is a gift from God, and you insult Him and Henry by saying otherwise."

Josephine stared out the window and brushed away her tears. A few moments later, Grace returned with a glass and pitcher. Josephine sat up and winced, Margaret rearranging the pillows behind her daughter's head. Grace handed Josephine a glass of water, and she took a few sips.

"You rest for a little while longer," Margaret said. "Isabelle or I will come to check on you later."

Isabelle, Margaret, and Grace rose and walked to the door.

"Thank you, Isa," Josephine said gratefully.

Grace and Margaret exited into the hallway.

Isabelle winked at her sister. "I'll be back in an hour or so." Isabelle clicked the door closed behind her.

Isabelle stood at her window, a warm breeze wafting through the white curtains. She closed her eyes and laid a hand on her chest, her heart pounding. If she hadn't come out of the sitting room at the exact moment Josephine was half-walking, half-staggering out the front door, she would never have been able to save her sister from possibly falling head over heels down the concrete steps. Isabelle inhaled sharply and shivered. *Josephine could've lost the baby and might've even broken an arm.*

As the sun struggled to pierce the clouds, Isabelle sat down on her bed, her brow furrowed. *What did Josephine mean by "everything's ruined"? And what are the adventures she spoke of? She and Henry never go anywhere. She always wants to go to the Cliff House or to parties.*

Isabelle blew out her cheeks and lay back on her bed. *At least she thanked me.*

Isabelle had made peace with the notion that being a nurse would likely be a thankless job. She would hopefully never see her patients again after they left the hospital. Still, Josephine's thanks had made Isabelle feel appreciated and valued, emotions she rarely experienced given how different her ambitions were from those of the other young women in her circle.

"And speaking of ruining things, Dr. Jenkins almost ruined it for me," Isabelle whispered, and clamped a palm over her mouth to smother a giggle.

Isabelle had almost gasped after Dr. Jenkins had said, "She certainly will make a fine nurse." He had secretly provided her certificate of good health for her nursing school application. Thankfully, Margaret hadn't noticed his comment and let it pass. Time, too, was passing, ticking by with no word from the nursing school's admissions committee.

Isabelle returned to her window and closed her eyes, pangs of sorrow tugging at her. *I thought I'd be accepted, but maybe they rejected me. Maybe I'll be like Josephine. She started to say she'd be stuck with a baby. Maybe I'll be stuck here taking care of Mother and Father.* Isabelle sniffed and balled her hands into fists. *Either way, a letter will come. In the meantime, I can practice being a nurse by taking care of Josephine.*

THIRTY-SEVEN

When Henry arrived home that evening, Isabelle shared what had happened to Josephine. Henry bounded up the stairway two stairs at a time, burst into the room he and Josephine shared, and found his wife propped against pillows, sipping a cup of broth.

"How are you?" Henry hurried to the bed and sat down. He kissed Josephine's forehead, and she set the cup of broth on her side table.

"Much better," she said. "The doctor's going to come by again later this week."

Henry clasped her hands, a trickle of fear shimmying up his spine. *I can't imagine losing her.*

Josephine stared out the window, where evening light faded over the treetops, tears rolling down her cheeks. "I'm so sorry," she sobbed. "I didn't mean for this to happen. I know we both wanted a bit more time together before we had a child, and I feel like I've ruined—"

"No, no." Henry gathered her in his arms. "Nothing's ruined. How could you even think such a thing?" *Does she not want this child?* He pushed the thought away as sheer lunacy.

She dabbed her tears, her eyes full of sorrow.

"Josephine, you're going to be a wonderful mother." Henry swallowed the lump in his throat, recalling how much his own mother had loved him and his brother despite the abuse and hardships she had faced. "We'll be in our new house soon, and we can even get a new puppy."

The mention of a new dog made Josephine chuckle, her face momentarily brightening. Henry clutched her hand once more.

"You'll get to prepare a nursery, and we'll need to make up one of the guest rooms right away for our new tenant." Henry winked.

Josephine furrowed her brow.

"Because your mother's going to want to move in once the baby arrives," he whispered.

Josephine chuckled again, despite her tears. Henry kissed her tenderly on the lips. *She thinks I'm joking, but there's more truth to that statement than either of us wants to admit.*

"I'm going to let you rest, but I'll be up after dinner," he said. "Should I have Eleanor send up anything else?"

Josephine picked at a loose thread on the bedspread. "No, I've already had something."

Though Henry was famished, and the tantalizing scent of hot rolls and garlic-roasted pork was wafting up from downstairs, he sensed he should linger. "Is there something else?"

Josephine shook her head. Her smile warmed his heart, and his stomach fluttered. The same smile had attracted him to her only a few years ago.

"No, nothing," she said.

Henry rose and walked to the door. As he opened it, Josephine spoke. "Please thank Isa again for taking such good care of me today. The doctor said I was far enough along that the baby should be okay. But if I'd fallen down the front steps, that would've been . . ."

Henry stared into the hall, his eyes darting left, then right, alarm bells clanging in his mind. *Far enough along? How many months has she been pregnant?*

He composed himself and faced his wife. "I'll tell her."

Henry left the room and clicked the door closed behind him.

Needing a place to think and be alone before dinner, Henry found himself sitting in the study. In an enormous breach of etiquette, he propped his feet on the edge of the desk, pungent cigar smoke rising like a cloud of deception that had just been lifted. He had done the math, and unlike his wife, math never lied. He didn't know when or where it had happened, but the most devastating and pressing question was: who was the father of Josephine's child?

How could she deceive me like this? Henry exhaled a trail of smoke, tears filling his eyes. *How could she deliberately destroy me like the raging fire that reduced our city to ash? Was I a fool to think she loved me all of this time?*

Henry stubbed out his cigar, rose, and paced in front of the cold fireplace. He would have to handle this carefully, but damn it, how it burned him that the apple hadn't fallen far from the tree. Henry knew of James's dalliance, but *Josephine*? James was a man, and Josephine most certainly was not. Henry stopped and stewed, absentmindedly drumming his fingers on the mahogany mantel. What galled him, and what he feared most, was that he had done this to himself. He had been distracted by what distracted most men, and he had married it. Only now, he was having to pay the most painful price imaginable for his distraction. Strangely, something in the back of his mind also told him he might have married the wrong sister.

As the accountant for Hamilton Holdings and a supposed father-to-be, he had to be employed, but would that mean remaining a cuckold? Bile rose in his throat at the despicable notion. He had thought that knowing as little as possible about James's financial and real estate dealings had been the biggest challenge he had faced since he came west, but this revelation certainly topped that. For now, he had a pregnant wife who was carrying someone else's child, and so he returned to what was sure—the math—to figure out the father.

Henry resumed his pacing. He had once believed that he could trust all the women in his life. He had trusted his mother and aunt in Pennsylvania. And he had never known Margaret or Isabelle to keep secrets. Then again, Henry spent so much time at the office with James, he wasn't at home or with the ladies when they paid their social calls. Henry raked his fingers through his hair, scolding himself for his naivety. His love for Josephine had blinded him. He had believed that she never had the opportunity to be alone with a man, but he had been horribly wrong. *What else have I been wrong about?*

Heat crept up Henry's neck, a plan forming in his mind. It began as a faint light, like a train coming through a dark tunnel, but quickly picked up speed. He had almost convinced himself there were other ways out of his predicament when a knock sounded at the door.

"Sir, dinner's ready," Eleanor called from the hall.

THIRTY-EIGHT

Concerned that her brother-in-law hadn't seemed himself during the evening meal, Isabelle popped her head into the study after dinner. Henry motioned her inside and offered her *The Jungle*, which she laid on a nearby table. She made herself comfortable on the tufted leather sofa while Henry paced in front of the fireplace. Outside, a few stars pinpricked the sky with faint light.

"Is something wrong?" Isabelle scooted to the edge of the cushion. "You looked upset and didn't talk much during dinner. I wanted to see if you were all right."

Henry frowned hard and blew out his cheeks. "I—thank you for coming to check."

He sat down in James's high-backed leather chair nearest the sofa and stared at the ceiling.

Something's terribly wrong. This is not Henry. Did something happen between him and Josephine? Though Isabelle wanted to pepper Henry with questions, she remained silent.

"I—did the doctor say—" He snapped his fingers and pointed at Isabelle. "Josephine thanks you for taking care of her today. I forgot to mention that at the table."

"It was nothing. I enjoy helping," Isabelle said.

She sensed Henry was on the cusp of saying something important, something she needed to know, but he wasn't quite ready to do it.

Henry leaned forward and clasped his hands together. "Can I tell you something?"

Isabelle nodded; his secretive tone unnerved and excited her.

"No, I shouldn't. This is between Josephine and me." He leaned back in his chair.

"I won't say anything," Isabelle assured him. "You know that if there's anything I can do to—"

"I'm not the father of Josephine's baby," he whispered, his voice strangled by a sob.

Isabelle opened her mouth and then quickly closed it, horror descending over her like a black cloud.

"*What?* Henry, no, that can't be." She laid a hand on his knee. He covered it with one of his. "Why would you say that?"

Henry wiped away a few tears that snaked down his cheek and inhaled a shaky breath. "The doctor told her she was *far enough along* in her pregnancy that she didn't lose the baby when she fell. Not to be impertinent, Isa, but the timing doesn't add up to this being my child."

"Oh." Isabelle's eyes flew open, and she pressed her fingers to her lips, the enormity of Josephine's betrayal hitting her full force. *Dear sweet Henry is the most amazing man. How could Josephine do this to him?* She sniffed and bit the inside of her cheek to quell her tears. *And, more important, who's the father of her baby?* "I'm so, so sorry," she whispered. "She doesn't deserve you. You're such a wonderful husband. I have half a mind to march upstairs and give her a good talking-to."

Henry shook his head. "That won't help."

"No," Isabelle agreed, "but it'd make me feel better."

Henry huffed out a chuckle, rose, and wandered to the fireplace. "What is it with the women in this house and all of their secrets?"

Adrenaline knifed through Isabelle. She clutched one hand in the other and avoided making eye contact with Henry, focusing instead on the bookcases across the room. *That's a bold question. Does he mean Josephine's secrets, or does he know about mine too?*

Henry returned to his chair, and Isabelle worked up the nerve to meet his gaze.

He motioned her closer. "I think something's going on with Grace. I don't know what, but I think it involves Frank Buchanan or Andrew Kepler."

Isabelle chewed on her lip, recalling Sarah tucking a letter under Grace's door. Was it from Andrew or Frank or her Wyoming friend? Images of Violet's engagement party, James's birthday party, and trips to the Cliff House also clicked through Isabelle's memory. But Grace was always gracious. The only time Isabelle paid attention to her cousin was when she was or was not helping in a medical crisis, such as Margaret's fainting spells or the accident with the girl at Walters Dress Shop. *Exhausting as it is, I must do a better job of noticing people.* Isabelle pressed her lips into a hard line, internally scolding herself. *If I'd been paying attention, maybe I'd know who the father of Josephine's baby is!*

"I don't—I don't know," Isabelle admitted. "Grace is always so proper, but I sometimes wonder if it's because she's unsure of herself or simply playing the part her parents want her to play. She's never mentioned Mr. Buchanan. I think she likes Andrew well enough, but she has other ambitions."

Henry opened his mouth to speak, but Isabelle stopped him with a shake of her head. "Please don't ask about her plans. She seems determined, and I told her I'd keep them in confidence. And then there's the whole suitor situation." Isabelle raised her eyebrows.

Henry clearly caught her meaning. "Can I ask you something?" Henry sounded like himself again, having conquered his emotions, at least for the time being.

"Of course, anything."

"Do you have a secret?"

Isabelle stared at her hands, her heart thudding in her chest. *Good gracious, he knows, but how? Sarah wouldn't say anything, and Grace doesn't talk to Henry unless the family is together. She also wouldn't gain anything by blabbing.*

Isabelle licked her lips and slowly nodded.

"You can tell me. After what we've shared this evening, I promise I won't tell a soul," he said.

Of course he won't. Isabelle smiled sheepishly, like a child caught stealing the last cookie from a tray without permission. *He's probably the only person in this house I can completely trust.*

"I applied to the California Hospital School for Nurses in Los Angeles," Isabelle whispered with barely contained glee.

Henry tilted his head; it was his turn to curve his mouth into an O of surprise.

"But that was weeks ago," Isabelle lamented. "I thought they'd send back a reply much sooner, even if I wasn't accepted, but nothing's come."

Henry lurched forward in his chair and clapped his hands once, as if struck by a bolt of lightning.

"What?" Isabelle prompted, her voice urgent. "Do you know something? Did Mother or Father say something, or did Sarah not give—"

Henry waved his hand. "No, no. Nothing like that." *I want to tell her, but what if I'm wrong about my suspicions? Damn! Yet another time I must be silent!*

Henry relaxed into his chair, a sly grin tugging at his lips.

"You're much more devious than I'd imagined, Isa," he teased. "How *did* you do it?"

Isabelle giggled and fidgeted her hands together in her lap.

As she quietly explained how she had ever so cleverly collected all of her application materials, Henry listened with more anticipation and interest than he ever had in any of his business meetings with James. He also squirmed when the flash of insight he had had earlier resurfaced: *Maybe I married the wrong sister.* What Isabelle had done was a little more than endearing. What he also found endearing and more disturbingly attractive was that he and Isabelle wanted to make a difference in the world for many of the same reasons.

Henry had experienced life in a household that needed medical care but couldn't get it. His mother had nearly died at the hands of his father. Isabelle wanted to change that by being on the front lines helping others. She wasn't sitting around having her life dictated to her. She was trying to make that life happen, even if it involved some secrecy and a bit of harmless bribery with housemaids that wouldn't land anyone in jail. Unlike Josephine, who hadn't been brave or honest enough to tell Henry the truth about the parentage of her child, Isabelle lived her truth. She had tirelessly tended to the wounded who lived alongside the family in Lafayette Park after the earthquake. She had tried to educate herself on how to be a nurse. And she had thrown herself into raising money for the Red Cross.

Henry steeled himself and rose. "I think you'll be accepted."

Isabelle sighed. "I hope so, but I don't know why it's taking so long to hear from them."

Henry nodded at her reassuringly. He couldn't help Josephine, but he could help his sister-in-law. *I'm confident that the letter from the California Hospital School for Nurses is already in the house. Now all I have to do is figure out a way to make sure Isa gets it.*

THIRTY-NINE

race closed her bedroom window, the dark void of the night sky mirroring the foreboding that coursed through her. She had found a letter tucked under her pillow before dinner but had put off opening it for fear of what it might say. She and Frank hadn't parted on the best of terms after Uncle James's birthday party. Grace crept to her dressing table and took a seat on her chair, her stomach churning. Slowly, she opened the envelope, removed the single sheet of paper, and unfolded it with closed eyes. Hoping against hope, she began to read.

> *Dear Grace,*
>
> *Before I started this letter, I downed a bit of whiskey. The color was up on my neck and I cud feel my temper burnin. I have thought long and hard about what to write about what happened at yer unkels party. I know you're right in thinking that Andrew Keplur is a good person to know for my bisness, but even if we are married, it will not do for you to flirt with him. It will not do for you to flirt or talk to any uther men because it will only be me and you one of these days. You need to leave all bisness dealings to the men from now on.*
>
> *When you left with him after Charlut spilt the punch on his coat, I wanted to drag you back into the room becuz it was not yer place to go. Yer place is with me*

and only me. I know you said you were the hostess, but it was Charluts place to help as he was with her.

Yer running off with uther men hurts my heart Grace becuz it makes me question yer love and devotion. Remember how you said I did hurtful things to you? I feel that now too. I still want to marry you and I know that once we are joined by God, we can put all this talk and bother about uther men behind us.

The real estate deal with Graham is coming down the track right quick and when I'm sined onto that I'll come for you. You wanted notice so this is it. Have yer bag ready. We're about to be off on our new adventure to Los Angeles soon!

Graham has a pretty spot of ground I'm going to buy to bild my restraunt. He also knows sum people in Los Angeles that can help us get a house. Our new place will be just as nice as yer aunt and unkels and I'm going to buy you one of those big hats and umbrellas so we can walk by the oshen every day. I can't wait for it to only be us in Los Angeles. Won't that be grand?

I need you to respect me by not seeing Andrew anymore. I'll say agen what I said at the party. I'll hunt you down like a steer in a snowstorm, only this time it won't be to say goodbye, it'll be to show you how much I love you.

I need a few more weeks to take sum more munny off these boys at cards and then we'll be able to make a proper go of it.

Frank

Grace's throat went dry, and she laid the letter aside with a shaking hand. She stared hard at her reflection in the dressing table mirror. Not only was Frank dishonest, he was threatening. His letter had made clear that he wanted to possess and control her, the very things she was trying to flee by leaving Denver with him. She shook her head and huffed out a sigh. Frank had fooled her with promises of travel and approving of her becoming a teacher, but his sweet whispers had been nothing but lies. Grace flinched, her sister-in-law's bruised cheek flashing through her mind. By asking Grace not to see Andrew Kepler anymore, Frank was no better than her older brother, who abused his wife.

Grace pressed a palm to her cheek, hoping to calm her fears, her pulse pounding. *It's impossible for him to think that I won't see other men in Los Angeles given the social circles we'll build there. Does he expect me to be rude to others at parties and not even greet women's husbands? I must end our relationship so I can start a whole new life and go to school.*

Grace stowed the letter with the others in the armoire and removed her boots. She didn't need anyone downstairs knowing she was pacing around like a nervous prisoner awaiting a firing squad. As she marched between the bed, the armoire, and the dressing table, ideas about how she could attend school without needing Frank's—or any other man's—help flitted through her mind. She growled when she thought of Jacob; her younger brother hadn't replied to her letter with a donation. She had also vowed not to lower herself and keep the twenty-five dollars her father had sent for the Red Cross.

"*I* have to figure this out. *I* have to make it work," Grace muttered to herself. "Which will be next to impossible with no money."

Still pacing, Grace tried to reassure herself by reviewing what she remembered from the California State Normal School's *Annual Catalog* about the two-year kindergarten training course. There were three school terms each year, beginning in late August and ending in late June. Tuition was free, but books would cost five dollars per term, and instruments, stationery, and materials would run up to twelve dollars for the two years.

"Forty-two dollars for books and materials isn't terrible; it's the board that's outrageous," Grace whispered.

At a maximum of twenty-five dollars per month, the board for one year would cost three hundred dollars, a small fortune. Grace could reduce the monthly fee by helping the family with whom she boarded with housework. But if she did that, the school strongly suggested that she extend her studies by one or two terms to not risk overwork. Grace scowled; she didn't have the time or money to extend her studies. She needed to finish the training course in two years and begin teaching immediately.

After a few minutes of circling, she accidentally stubbed her toe on the bedpost. "Ow, ow, ow." She hopped onto her bed, clutching her foot.

When the pain in her toe receded, Grace lay back on her bed and steeled herself. She would sell the earrings she had inherited from her grandmother. She would help the family with whom she lived with domestic duties. And she would take Isabelle's advice. Grace would teach piano and voice lessons to anyone willing to pay.

"I'll make it work," she promised herself. "I'll graduate in two years and be the best darn kindergarten teacher that city has ever had."

Despite her inability to shake her unease, Grace thrilled at the idea of going to school. If she could bring her plan together, it would be the ultimate triumph: making her own money would allow her to escape from Frank and her parents once and for all.

FORTY

Several days after Grace's unsettling encounter with Frank, she arrived in the Hamiltons' empty dining room for dinner. She sat down in her chair and admired the manicured side yard. The weather mirrored her mood; the clouds refused to clear and blanketed the city in gloom. The rest of the family filtered in, Aunt Margaret bringing up the rear of the brigade. Before she sat down, she placed an envelope addressed in neat script next to Grace's plate. Grace knew what it held; she and Isabelle had worked hard to plan the event. Still, it was all Grace could do not to tear into it in curiosity. When Uncle James settled himself at the head of the table and began the evening prayer, Grace bowed her head and said one of her own. *Please let Jacob send me a bit of money soon.*

With prayers finished, the others passed bowls of wild rice, shrimp, and delicious-smelling curry sauce around the table. Despite Grace's formidable appetite, she quietly opened the envelope and gasped.

"It's so beautiful." Grace swept her fingers over the elegantly swirled black script and official red lettering of the Red Cross gala invitation. Reluctantly, she passed it to Isabelle.

Isabelle tried to chew and smile simultaneously and brought her hand to her mouth when a few grains of rice escaped onto the front of her dress.

She can be so unladylike, but I admire her dedication. Grace wanted to laugh. *I only hope I can be that determined when I start school.*

"It's quite pretty," Isabelle agreed. "I'm so excited to visit with Charlotte again and talk to Andrew one more time before he goes back to Los Angeles."

Josephine and Aunt Margaret grew quiet, their intense gazes boring into Isabelle. Grace pressed her lips together to stifle a giggle.

Aunt Margaret clasped her hands together. "Yes, Isa, that'd be splendid. I thought I'd seen you speaking to him again at your father's party. Do be sure to wear your blue dress to the gala. It sets off your eyes."

Isabelle cocked her head and spoke to her mother with all the interest she would have shown a tire salesman. "Yes, Mother, I'll do that. I'm sure blue is his favorite color, and he'll be instantly smitten. Really, I'm so exhausted by all of your meddling."

Aunt Margaret scowled, and an errant chuckle escaped Josephine. It was all Grace could do not to burst into laughter. *Aunt Margaret is so full of hopeful delusion. Isabelle doesn't like Andrew in that way, but he's such a gentleman that he'd talk to her about Los Angeles for an hour if he thought it might make her happy.* Grace tucked the invitation back into its envelope and laid it next to her plate.

The family fell into easy conversation. Henry and Uncle James held forth about a potential business deal while Isabelle and Josephine traded barbs about the upcoming Red Cross gala. Grace mentally reviewed the dresses she had brought from Denver. If Isabelle wore blue, Grace would need to wear a different color. She pulled a face, hoping none of the others would notice. Her burgundy dress was far too dark for the occasion; the color reminded her too much of blood. She had already worn her emerald-colored gown, so lavender it would be.

Grace cut her shrimp and dipped a bite into the curry sauce. The Red Cross gala would possibly be the last event she would attend in San Francisco before she left for Los Angeles. It would possibly be her last chance to wear a satin gown, her gold earrings adorned with seed pearls, and her hair combs embedded with abalone. It would possibly be her last chance to mingle with society before she entered the unknown world of living in a house with strangers who had been kind enough to take her in, sight unseen. Because she would be boarding for the duration of her studies, she needed to report to the school a week before the beginning of the term to line up lodging with an approved family. Despite the anxious uncertainty over where she would live, she jutted out her chin in silent pride. She envisioned herself in a classroom full of other eager girls engrossed in English literature and composition, physiology, and kindergarten theory.

"Don't you think, Grace?"

Caught daydreaming once again, Grace startled and blinked at Josephine. "I—I'm sorry. What were you saying?"

Isabelle huffed out a disgruntled sigh and shook her head at Josephine. Though her cousin hadn't heard Josephine's comment, Isabelle had. And despite not wanting to admit it, Isabelle dreaded events where she had to play "all the little games," as she often called them.

"I said that Charlotte might be a good person to ask for help so that Isabelle can ask people for donations without running them down like a woman fleeing a fire." Josephine waggled her eyebrows and forked in a bite of rice.

Isabelle snorted in protest. "I don't do that."

Josephine shot Isabelle a "yes you do" look. Isabelle stuck her tongue out at her sister. When Grace unexpectedly laughed, Isabelle's temper boiled over.

"Why are you all being so mean?" Her bitter tone stopped James and Henry midsentence. Isabelle glared at her sister and cousin, her cheeks burning. "I'm only trying to help, and you're all making fun." Isabelle stabbed a piece of shrimp with her fork. *I hate whining, and I know I'm upset because I haven't heard about school. Why can't I be myself without everyone wanting me to change?*

James and Henry resumed their conversation. Grace laid a hand on Isabelle's arm, but Isabelle pulled away.

"I'm sorry if you mistook what I did as making light of you," Grace said. "It wasn't meant to. I was simply laughing at how you and Josephine tease each other. I don't have sisters, and being here with you two has been such fun."

Isabelle lowered her head, ashamed that her frustration had gotten the better of her. *She only has brothers and, from what she's said, the world's most buttoned-up parents. We probably are a breath of fresh air.*

"I don't want to upset you further, but Maude told me about what happened when you asked the ladies at the Cliff House women's parlor for—"

Isabelle gasped. "Oh, please tell me she didn't share that." Isabelle covered her mouth with her napkin, her cheeks flushing again. *This is terrible, so very terrible! I want to crawl under the table and hide like I used to when I was little and Josephine teased me until I cried.*

"You've been so helpful to me during my time here." Grace's voice cracked.

Isabelle finally met her cousin's eyes, her heart heavy with empathy. *She's talking about me keeping her secret about wanting to be a teacher. I know the pain of wanting someone to be excited about your dream.*

"The least I can do is give you some pointers, but only if you'd like. I want to help, to thank you for all you've done," Grace said.

Isabelle smiled weakly at Grace, having forgiven her cousin for her earlier laughter.

Margaret finished a bite and raised her fork. "That's kind of you, Grace, thank you. Really, Isa, you mustn't think we're trying to goad you on like a lumbering beast in the street, but you can be quite—what's the word—overly *enthusiastic*. It isn't the best way to speak to others, dear."

Isabelle rolled her eyes.

"Isa," Josephine sighed, "I know you don't enjoy playing all the little games, as you call them, but ask Charlotte for advice, and Grace too. With Violet planning her wedding and Grace going home soon, you'll need someone to help with the cause."

Josephine raised her eyebrows and shot Isabelle a "consider this, dear sister" look.

Isabelle stared at her plate and drummed her fingers on the napkin in her lap. Josephine had a point. Isabelle hated all the little games—the sideways crablike advances, the flowery half-speak, the excessive deference—but those things usually helped secure donations. *Maybe it's because my passion overwhelms people. Maybe I'd have more luck if I were a bit more daft.*

"Josephine's right." Henry raised a bite of shrimp to his mouth, narrowly missing landing a dollop of curry sauce on his tie.

Henry agrees with Josephine and Grace? Isabelle sobered and sat forward in her chair, hanging on his words.

He wiped his mouth and continued. "Approach is everything. Your father and I were talking about that today with one of our deals. From what we hear from a few of Andrew's business associates in Los Angeles, he's a man of integrity. Having him as an ally can only help your cause. A well-placed word with him or Charlotte could go a long way."

Isabelle wiped the burning curry sauce from her lips and took a bite of salad. Though her sister and cousin had suggested the same, Henry's advice about how to speak to others somehow carried more weight. Isabelle crunched her bite of lettuce and nodded at Henry in thanks. He sat next to Josephine as if nothing in their relationship had changed. *How does he play that game?* Isabelle's heart went out to him. *He has to be in so much pain; how does he bear it?*

Isabelle sniffed and straightened in her chair. She still hated the idea of having to contort herself into someone else with Andrew and others in their circle who would most decidedly be at the Red Cross gala. Isabelle sipped her water and recalled telling herself that she—and the city—needed the ladies in the women's parlor. Their approval and donations were important if San Francisco was to continue its recovery. Learning how to appeal to others for the cause was something Kitty Felton did, and Isabelle admired her more than anyone. Isabelle scooted a piece of shrimp around on her plate and wondered if there was a middle ground. *Could I temper my enthusiasm and still impart the values of the Red Cross? Could I say something to Charlotte or Andrew and not have them think I'm pandering? Would playing the game as Henry suggested be so bad since it's for a good cause?*

"I'll keep that in mind," Isabelle said, then turned to her cousin. "I'm sorry for snapping at you, Grace. I'd appreciate your help."

Margaret patted James's hand. She pinned him with an intense stare, as if expecting him to speak. When he pulled away, his expression one of annoyed consternation, a sly grin stretched across Isabelle's face. She recognized the game her mother was playing.

"Yes, well—I—you do have a certain charm, my girl," James sputtered. "Sure it'll go a long way with everyone at the gala."

Isabelle beamed at her father and returned to her dinner. Eleanor had been generous with the curry powder, and Isabelle struggled to keep her throat from catching fire. *Maybe they're right.* Isabelle dipped another bite of shrimp into the spicy sauce. *There's no harm in asking Charlotte for a few pointers and mentioning my work to Andrew. Charlotte's been one of my closest confidantes, and she could help me once Grace is gone and Violet is married.*

FORTY-ONE

L ate on a Wednesday afternoon, Henry, Graham, and James relaxed at their usual table at the back of the Fairmont Hotel dining room. The place was all but deserted; the only sounds were of waiters moving about the room, resetting tables with crisp white tablecloths and fine china.

James and Graham were still discussing what Henry deemed to be their doomed real estate venture. When Graham said he had been in contact with a particular businessman who Henry knew had barely avoided jail, a curtain descended in Henry's mind. He needed to plan his escape from the Hamilton family, regardless of what it would mean for Josephine. A lump rose in his throat. *I loved her. I love her still, but I can't be with a woman who could so easily cast aside the sanctity of our marriage.* He would need to send out feelers to a few contacts in Los Angeles, but getting hired without a good word from James might be a challenge. And if James discovered what Henry was doing, he would surely be incensed. The family would never approve of Henry and Josephine leaving San Francisco. Thankfully, that wasn't what Henry had in mind.

Henry scribbled a few notes in his notebook and eyed his father-in-law. Henry would need to break the news of his plan delicately. If he waited until the right moment, he could pull James aside and lay out what he intended to do. *It'll be hard for Josephine, though.* Pangs of guilt gnawed at Henry. *Society can be so cruel, especially to women.*

Henry flipped to a blank page in the back of his notebook and made seven bullet points. He wrote the names of five businesses, the name of a lawyer he trusted, and the name of a car dealership next to the bullet points before flipping back to the page that held the day's meeting notes.

"Write down that we won't be cutting Frank Buchanan in on this deal." Graham waved a finger at Henry's notebook.

Henry paused, pen poised over the page. Dutifully, he noted, "No F. Buchanan for r.e." With his senses now on high alert, Henry focused solely on the current conversation.

"Had a hell of a time tracking down folks in Denver and Cheyenne who could vouch for him," Graham said. "Goes by Benjamin in Colorado and Wyoming, apparently."

James arched an eyebrow and puffed on his cigar. "That's interesting."

Graham nodded, his face grim. "Seems Mr. Buchanan is known around the Rockies as a bit of a strongarm."

One end of Henry's mouth quirked up, validation sweeping over him. He had been right about Frank's hands. Mr. Buchanan wasn't the smooth businessman he pretended to be. He had acquired his crooked finger and abnormally large knuckles through violent means.

James inhaled another drag of his cigar and shook his head. "Can't have that kind of attention around right now, especially with land dealings."

A knowing look passed between the three men.

"Too bad," James continued. "Liked his swagger and that steer tiepin. He on the level with the beef operation?"

Graham nodded vigorously. "That he is. Angelo Del Monte over at Fior d'Italia got a shipment in a few weeks ago. Said customers have been raving about the filets."

Graham's devious smirk caused a sense of foreboding to descend over Henry.

"Frank also seems to be in a rush to find a place where he can open a restaurant before he moves on to the Los Angeles market. Told him I have a nice spot of ground I can sell him. Not that I own it, but then again, maybe I do." Graham's wide grin made James laugh.

Henry swallowed hard and managed a smile. *Yes, I must get away from all of this. Maybe I should take my own advice and put in a good word for myself with Andrew. Nothing could be as bad in Los Angeles as it is here.*

FORTY-TWO

Less than a week later, Isabelle dabbed her cheeks as she sat at her mother's bedside. Outside, the late-morning sun blared down, its intensity mirroring the stark reality in which Isabelle now found herself. The shock of Margaret's heart attack—the loud thump when she had fallen upstairs, the anxious horses stamping when the attendants had loaded Margaret into the ambulance, the diagnosis that the attack had nearly ended her—still weighed on the family, most of all on Isabelle. Though Margaret had returned home only yesterday, Isabelle's energy was already flagging. Her passion and cursed knowledge of nursing had crashed down upon her immediately when James had assured Dr. Jenkins and the doctor at the hospital that his daughter could handle anything Margaret might need. In Isabelle's eyes, this assurance absolved her father of further responsibility toward his wife. With Josephine struggling with morning sickness and Grace vacillating between being helpful and being paralyzed by the sight of her pale and unmoving aunt, Isabelle had been left with the brunt of Margaret's care.

While Margaret dozed, Isabelle rested her head on her crossed arms on the edge of the bed. A few tears escaped down her cheeks as she sobbed, her dream dying. She wondered if her nursing application had gotten lost in the mail. *It doesn't matter now. There's no way I can leave. Grace will be gone soon, and Henry and Josephine will be back in their new house in a matter of months. With a baby to take care of, Josephine won't be able to help with Mother. It'll all fall to me. Life is so unfair.*

Grace sat in the sitting room quietly stitching her needlepoint, her ears tuned to the movement within the house. She tried to ignore the faint echo of a cupboard bumping shut or a pan clanging every now and again from the kitchen. Instead, she was most interested in the goings-on upstairs, which had fallen eerily silent.

The near finality of Aunt Margaret's heart attack had terrified Grace. She had watched the ambulance race away from the house, the horses' manes flying as they rounded the street corner, the driver having to slow them to apply the brake, losing precious seconds as they descended the hill. The family's stricken reaction had reminded Grace of the sometimes desperate emotional outbursts she had overheard from where she perched frozen on her bed upstairs at home. A few of her father's patients' family members hadn't been able to contain themselves while the patient howled in pain or gasped as they inhaled their last breath hidden behind his office door. Someone those people loved—someone worth saving—had been in the throes of death, and there was nothing they could do to save them. Grace shivered; a sensation of powerlessness swept over her, and the hair on her arms stood on end.

She paused, her needle poised above her canvas. The idea of someone worth saving disturbed her now. Aunt Margaret wasn't a sinister character in one of Grace's horror novels; she was a beloved and integral part of the Hamilton family. *She deserves to live, unlike some people.* Grace sniffed and pulled her needle through her canvas. Grace hadn't understood the difference between those who did and didn't deserve to survive until Aunt Margaret's crisis. The notion that bad people might be better off dead had felt wrong, sinful, and unkind. Hadn't the minister at Grace's church assured his congregation that all souls were redeemable? Hadn't Grace silently prayed for those who had perished despite her father's best care? And yet, hadn't her father mumbled more than once that maybe it would have been better for everyone if one or two of his patients died? At the time, Grace had found his cold dismissal of death off-putting. The longer she reflected, however, the more she begrudgingly wondered if he was right.

Grace had initially thought he had meant it was better for some of his patients to die because they would be free of pain, but maybe it was because, as people, they didn't deserve to live. Maybe it would be better or safer for a spouse or child if that person passed on. Maybe it would be better for society if that person was no longer around. *Maybe I was wrong to believe everyone was redeemable.* She tied off her yarn and pulled another strand of burgundy wool from the hank. *Maybe that also applies to Frank.*

Grace shook her head, trying to rid herself of such a damning thought. So far, she had managed not to spend more than a few moments in Aunt Margaret's presence. The sight of her aunt made Grace queasy: her wan skin, her weak voice, her chest rising and falling beneath her covers, possibly to cease forever at any moment. Though Grace loved Aunt Margaret and wished for nothing more than her speedy recovery, Grace wasn't Isabelle. The more she could avoid her aunt, the better.

FORTY-THREE

I sabelle woke with a start. She wanted to be with Margaret every minute, but couldn't. What she needed was more rest and help. She rose from her chair, her fists clenched into tiny balls, frustration and anger rising in her chest. She tiptoed across the room and into the hall, closing the door behind her silently.

Downstairs, Isabelle strode into the sitting room. *She sits there as if nothing has happened,* Isabelle fumed in silence at her cousin, *and I'm not putting up with her sad little act any longer!* A startled Grace set down her needlepoint canvas.

"I'm taking a proper nap," Isabelle announced. "I'll tell Eleanor you'll take some broth up to Mother when she wakes up. Sit with her until I've finished resting."

"But I—" Grace started.

"I've had it with you acting like a scared little rabbit," Isabelle hissed. "Pull yourself together, or I'll tell Mother you're getting secret letters from someone I suspect isn't your friend in Wyoming."

Grace gaped and her eyes widened. "Please don't say anything about—"

"Then help me," Isabelle admonished her cousin. "Mother's not going to die if I'm not with her every moment. I'm so tired I can barely stand up."

Grace hopped up and pitched her needlepoint canvas onto the chair. Isabelle stalked out of the room in triumph, Grace scurrying behind her. Isabelle left Grace in the kitchen with Eleanor and met Josephine, who was descending the stairs.

"Why aren't you with Mother?" Josephine's voice registered alarm.

"You and Grace are in charge," Isabelle said. "If you're well enough to be up, you're well enough to sit with Mother. I expect to find you with her when I'm done resting."

Josephine spluttered a reply, but Isabelle ignored her and continued her hurried climb up the stairs. Once inside her bedroom, she bumped the door shut and locked it. Without removing her boots, she collapsed onto her bed, and her eyes fell shut. *Spoken like a nurse running her own ward.* Isabelle's smile faded, and she fell fast asleep.

A few hours later, a somewhat revived Isabelle stood in the hall outside her mother's bedroom, her ear pressed to the door. The muffled voices inside the room assured her that Josephine and Grace had followed her orders. *So they can help if they're forced to.* Isabelle sighed. She opened the door a crack, and all heads turned in her direction. Margaret sat propped against pillows, Josephine spooning broth into her mouth. To Isabelle's astonishment and delight, additional chairs had been brought into the room and were arranged in a row at Margaret's bedside. Isabelle sat down in the chair next to Grace.

"How are you feeling?" Isabelle asked her mother. Josephine tried to hand the bowl of broth to Isabelle, who shook her head. "You're doing fine."

Josephine flared her nostrils and returned her attention to their mother.

"Better." Margaret concentrated on a mouthful of soup.

Isabelle turned to Grace. "Thank you for helping. I'm sorry I was cross with you earlier. Truly, I—" Isabelle scrubbed her cheeks with her palms. *I'm still so tired, but she has helped, and I need her to give me some pointers to make the Red Cross gala a success.* "I can't do this all by myself."

Grace stared at the floor. "I know. I'm sorry. I'll try to do better."

Isabelle furrowed her brow. *Will you?* Though Isabelle doubted Grace would ever willingly offer her help, she was too exhausted to challenge her cousin. Instead, she accepted Grace's apology and hoped Grace would be as good as her word.

Margaret tutted out a huff of protest. "You're not doing it by yourself, Isa. Eleanor and Sarah can see to me along with you."

Isabelle inwardly sighed. *She doesn't understand. She'll never understand.*

"I'll stay if it's all right," Grace reassured her aunt.

Margaret blinked wearily. "Do stay, child. It's so nice having all you girls here together."

When Margaret shifted her weight and winced, Isabelle felt a different type of pain. It was clear her mother would not side with her when it came to understanding that she was the only one who would know what to do if Margaret had another heart attack. Sorrow descended like a blanket, smothering Isabelle. *The most important thing is that she gets better, even if I am stuck taking care of her mostly by myself.*

Josephine set the bowl of broth down on the side table, readjusted the pillows behind Margaret's head, and paused. Josephine licked her lips and made a chewing sound. Isabelle grasped the bottom of her chair, poised to spring up and fetch the empty washbasin. *Please don't throw up*, Isabelle silently begged Josephine. *The smell alone will kill us all.* Blessedly, the moment passed, and Josephine helped her mother scoot farther under the covers.

"We'll let you rest now," Isabelle said, and rose. "Do you need anything else?"

Margaret shook her head.

Josephine kissed her mother's forehead. "You need to rest so you can be full of energy by the time this baby arrives."

"That's the perfect reason to get better." Grace rose and followed Josephine to the door.

Isabelle's gaze locked on to her sister's belly, sadness lingering within her. *I'll still love her child, but there's far less joy in this niece or nephew because it isn't Henry's.* Isabelle painted on a kind smile for her mother's benefit.

"Isa, can you stay?" Margaret waved goodbye to Grace and Josephine.

Isabelle returned to the chair nearest her mother's bed, and Margaret grasped her daughter's hand. The mixture of gratitude and devotion in her mother's eyes caught Isabelle off guard.

"I wanted to thank you," she said. "You've been such a blessing during all of this. I don't know what I'd do without you."

Isabelle's chin quivered, tears welling in her eyes. "Thank you." Her voice cracked. "We were all so afraid, especially Father. He wouldn't—none of us would know what to do without you."

Margaret touched Isabelle's cheek. "No, I imagine he wouldn't. But there'll be no more talk of that now. I'm going to be fine." Margaret motioned to the pillows behind her. "Can you take these away?"

Isabelle rose, removed the pillows from behind her mother's head, and pulled the covers over Margaret's arms.

"I'll be back later to check on you." Isabelle brushed a few strands of hair from her mother's forehead, then padded to the door.

When she turned back, Margaret's eyes had closed.

Father wouldn't know what to do without you, and even though we don't always see eye to eye, I wouldn't either. Isabelle swiped a tear from her cheek, stepped into the hall, and closed the door silently behind her.

FORTY-FOUR

That evening after dinner, Henry stepped into Isabelle's room and closed the door. His sister-in-law sat at her dressing table, her head in her hands. She had mentioned during the meal that she had taken a nap, but her sagging shoulders told him she was still exhausted.

At the sound of her door closing, she stood, her eyes weary yet concerned. "Do you need something?"

Henry shook his head and motioned for her to return to her chair. It wasn't the best decorum for him to be in her room with the door closed, but he didn't care. He had had his fill of what was going on with the women in the household and had decided it was time to say his piece.

"I know this is hard for you." He sat on the edge of the bed behind her chair.

Dark circles ringed Isabelle's eyes, her face somber. Nothing had been said at dinner, but Henry had sensed that Isabelle, Grace, and Josephine had quarreled earlier in the day, most likely over Margaret's care.

"Know that I—that all of us—are very thankful for what you're doing," he continued.

Isabelle covered her mouth with her hand, her eyes glassy. Henry feared she might cry. *I want to gather her up and hold her like the frightened yet brave child she is. But she's not a child. She's the capable, responsible adult this family needs, and for that, I love her even more.*

Henry rose and motioned for Isabelle to lie down on her bed. She did, tears staining her cheeks. He settled onto her dressing table chair, his heart aching.

"I'm never going to be able to go to school," she sobbed. "Mother's sick. You and Josephine will be leaving soon. Father needs me here."

Henry scooted his chair closer to the bed and patted her hand, intent on reassuring her. He would not let her dream die, not while he believed it was still possible that she had been accepted into nursing school. And certainly not when he believed James would let her go.

"Don't give up," he said. "Margaret's going to get better, and plenty of women could use the work as an aide. I think this is one of those times when patience will win the day."

Isabelle wiped her cheeks with her sleeve but remained silent.

Henry stood and walked to the door. "Stay the course, Isa. My mother always used to say it was the darkest right before the dawn, and I believe that's true in this case."

Isabelle sniffled and smiled weakly at him.

She understands, and she'll soldier on. I just don't know for how much longer. Henry lingered at the door.

"I hope so," she said, "and thank you. I want to believe the letter will come."

Henry winked. "I feel confident it will."

Once in the hall, Henry walked toward the door to the bedroom he shared with Josephine, his stomach clenched in worry. *I better be right about who has this letter. If I'm not, Isabelle will be completely devastated.*

Henry entered the room he and Josephine shared and clicked the door closed behind him. His wife sat on the edge of their bed, unlacing her boots.

"Were you talking to Isa?" She pointed toward the wall as if she had overheard voices, then plunked a boot onto the floor.

"Yes." He sat down next to her and removed his shoes and tie. "Why?"

Henry rose and walked to the armoire, where he began unbuttoning his shirt. "She seemed like she needed a little encouragement."

Josephine audibly sighed. In the reflection of the armoire mirror, she shook her head and pursed her lips. Henry's neck flushed, anger rising within him.

"Again, why?" she asked.

Henry covered the distance between the armoire and the bed in an instant, his eyes narrow, his nostrils flared. Josephine recoiled in fear, tucking her feet beneath her and leaning against the headboard.

"Because she's been caring for you, *our child*, and your mother nearly nonstop, and that deserves a little appreciation and respect," he snapped, his hands planted on his hips.

Josephine remained frozen, her eyes still pleading, when Henry backed away.

"I—I thanked her." Josephine's voice verged on desperation. "When I—when I fell. I thanked her for taking care of me, and I told you to thank her again for me. I'm grateful for what she did after my accident." She unlaced her remaining boot with trembling hands.

Henry returned to the armoire, removed his dress shirt and suit pants, and hung them inside. Something had changed within him since he had learned of Josephine's pregnancy. Once he had discovered the truth, that change had been most unwelcome. He and Josephine had suffered disagreements during their marriage, but the way she had provoked him tonight was a first. Henry hung his head and blew out a long breath, his anger fading. He was not proud of his behavior.

He resented Josephine's pregnancy not only because the child she carried wasn't his, but also because it was yet another secret he had to keep. Deep down, the idea of being a father thrilled and terrified him. Because Henry's father had been the epitome of who not to be as a parent or spouse, Henry had long ago vowed to be different. One day, he would have a child with a woman who honored and respected him. When that day came, could he become the father he wanted to be?

Josephine rose and crept to her dressing table chair.

"I'm sorry." Her oval dressing table mirror reflected Henry in his pajamas, sitting in bed, his back propped against a pillow. "Now that I'm feeling better, I should try to help more with Mother."

Josephine pulled her hairbrush gently through her hair, tilting her head to one side. Henry smiled. She *had* recovered quickly from her tumble, but he suspected she hated being alone with Margaret. Her mother's weakened condition served as a blatant reminder of how fragile life was. It was one thing to ignore the piles of rubble that still lay strewn throughout the city. It was another to have one's parent lying at death's door only steps away.

"I'm relieved you're feeling better and can be up and around. Work has kept me so busy. I'm sorry if I've been neglectful." He met her gaze in the mirror.

Josephine laid down her brush and ran her fingers through several long strands of hair. She joined him under the covers but startled when he wrapped his arm around her. He grimaced and sniffed. *I'm not my father, and I must never be menacing to her again.*

"You're not neglectful," Josephine said, finally settling her head against his shoulder. "What happened with Mother was so dreadful and scary, and Isa knows more about helping than I do. Still, it's not an excuse. I *will* try to do better."

As the pale moon glowed through the window, a watchful unblinking orb high in the onyx sky, Henry lay beside Josephine, his back to hers, his eyes open. Several minutes had passed since he had turned off the light, and Josephine's slow, steady breathing told him she was asleep. He had never spoken to her the way he had tonight, and had almost apologized afterward. The entire spectacle had disgusted him. It reminded him of how his father sometimes spoke to his mother. There would be a comment delivered in a warning tone, and as a child, Henry would instinctively retreat either under the kitchen table or to his room before his father became violent.

But Henry wasn't a violent man. It certainly hadn't been his intention to sound violent this evening. And yet, as he lay in the dark, the moonlight dimming behind a cloud, he pressed his lips together into a hard line. He had finally said exactly what he had wanted to say, exactly how he had wanted to say it. *I've had Josephine up on a pedestal all of this time, and this is what happens when I take her off of it.*

Henry closed his eyes but found himself absentmindedly chewing on his lip. He wasn't proud of how he had spoken to his wife, but her panicked response about thanking Isabelle told him he had hit the nail on the head. There was no reason for Isabelle to be caring for Margaret alone. Though Grace was family, she was a guest and not expected to help, although it would be appreciated. Josephine had recovered quickly from her fall and could most certainly be doing more for her mother.

This doesn't bode well for her child.

Henry adjusted his pillow, a knot already forming in his neck. Josephine claimed she cared about children because she supported the orphanage, but that was patronage, not passion. How Josephine felt about the orphans and how Isabelle felt about the Red Cross were like night and day. What would happen when Josephine's child arrived? Henry's mind drifted back to his mother, who had tried her best to love and raise her sons. Not that leaving them in the care of others had been a choice. Henry's parents were poor; they could barely put food on the table most of the time, let alone hire a nanny. Henry shifted under the covers, unable to get comfortable. He would have liked a wife who at least wanted to play with their child, not simply hand it off to hired help.

Josephine stirred in her sleep, and Henry sighed silently. *What I'd really like is a wife who's carrying* my *child.* He clenched his jaw.

Henry shifted his weight, turning the predicaments in his life over in his mind. Josephine was pregnant by another man. His mother-in-law had recently suffered a near-death health crisis— and if truth be told, probably wasn't out of the woods yet—and his father-in-law was heading back down the path of corruption that might land him, and possibly Henry, in jail.

And yet . . . *My damned sense of loyalty.* Henry rolled over, desperately wanting to distance himself from the evening's events. *I can't believe I have to sort out alliances with yet another family.* When Henry finally drifted off to sleep, an image of his brother standing on the docks on the last day they had seen each other floated before him. His brother had waved, but Henry had simply turned and walked away.

FORTY-FIVE

The night of the Red Cross gala, Isabelle stood with Grace in Charlotte Gordon's foyer, an irrepressible smile spread across her face. While quiet laughter, warm conversation, and the tinkling of crystal filtered throughout the space, Isabelle gazed up at the two enormous chandeliers. Their dim light illuminated the shimmering tapestries on the walls and set off an exquisite silver vase that held a large spray of burgundy roses on the sideboard. Isabelle's stomach fluttered. Tonight was important because she would get to test out all the tips she had received from Charlotte and Grace about how to approach people for donations. Isabelle tried to steady her nerves. She vowed to enjoy herself regardless of how the evening went.

Isabelle glanced around the foyer, and her eyes fell on Charlotte. *It's a rare woman who can pull off that color, but she looks like a freshly plucked flower.* Radiant in a pale shade of yellow, Charlotte began to make her way through the clusters of people toward Isabelle and Grace.

"Hello!" Charlotte gushed. "It's so good to see you both again. Isabelle, you look especially beautiful this evening."

Isabelle's chest swelled with pride. She had worn the blue dress her mother had suggested and adorned her high honey-blond pompadour with three hair combs inset with abalone that Grace had offered her at the last minute. The touch added a veneer of reserved sophistication to which Isabelle wasn't accustomed.

"Thank you." Isabelle's calm and contained response caused Grace to raise her eyebrows. "Everyone's gathered in the library or the sitting room before dinner," Charlotte said. "Let me take you back to see Andrew."

Isabelle, Charlotte, and Grace threaded their way up the hall, greeted by various acquaintances, many of whom frequented the Cliff House women's parlor. Though her heart pounded with excitement, Isabelle returned their hellos without gushing.

Once in the sitting room, Charlotte left them to collect Andrew. Isabelle smoothed the front of her dress and tried to mimic Grace, who relaxed into short conversations with a few other ladies who passed by. Isabelle spotted Maude and Harriet across the room and lifted a hand in acknowledgment. Harriet gave Isabelle a quick once-over, her expression one of barely concealed surprise. Isabelle smothered a giggle. Harriet was clearly impressed by Isabelle's unusually feminine ensemble.

"Ladies." Andrew joined them and shook Isabelle's and Grace's hands in turn. "Good evening. So good to see you."

"You as well," Isabelle greeted Andrew. She wanted to talk to him more about Los Angeles, but since she hadn't been accepted into nursing school, there was no point. Isabelle bit her lip, sorrow creeping forward from the edges of her mind. Her smile remained, though she dug her fingernails into her palm. She would not have her evening ruined by worrying about her application. She had worked too hard to help plan the gala and deserved to celebrate.

"How's Margaret?" Andrew's question jolted Isabelle back to the present.

"She's still weak, but the doctor thinks she'll recover with time."

"That's good to hear." Charlotte's voice was full of relief.

"Yes," Andrew agreed. "Very good, indeed. And speaking of good, I've been remiss. Would you like something to drink?"

Isabelle shook her head. "Not right now, thank you. If you'll excuse me, I see some ladies I need to speak to." Isabelle dipped her chin and stepped away, leaving her cousin alone with Andrew and Charlotte.

Isabelle joined Maude, Harriet, and a few other women on the other side of the room. Harriet was tempting her enthralled audience with a juicy piece of gossip, dangling it like a T-bone steak in front of a dog. This time, the meal consisted of adultery mixed with legal intrigue and served with a healthy side of spousal suspicion. Maude stood silent and attentive, much like Grace usually did in social situations. *I should be furious with her.* Isabelle still couldn't believe Maude had tattled to Grace about Isabelle's disastrous attempt at asking for funds from the ladies at the Cliff House. *But I'm sure she didn't mean any harm. Given her limited prospects and that her mother is an incorrigible gossip, I really shouldn't be surprised.*

"I heard she spurned him, though," the woman next to Isabelle whispered. "The mistress, I mean. Something to do with her husband."

Isabelle made a half-hearted attempt to feign interest; pretending to care about gossip was a part of the game she could barely stomach. At the first break in the conversation, she moved on to mingle with some of her and Violet's friends. As they chatted about how much the city had recovered, the topic of the Red Cross inevitably surfaced, which gave Isabelle the opportunity to use what she had learned from Grace and Charlotte.

Step one: name-drop.

"As some of you know, Mrs. Kitty Felton spoke to us about the city's new initiative for supporting those still in need." Isabelle surprised herself with her steady yet dispassionate delivery.

Step two: play on emotion.

"And unfortunately, it's usually the children who suffer most when a natural disaster strikes," she continued.

A few women crinkled their eyes, their brows creased with pity. And then the unthinkable happened. The woman to Isabelle's left asked how Isabelle was involved with the Red Cross. Isabelle paused for a moment, her toe tapping on the floor hidden by her long skirt, and recalled one of Grace's tips. Isabelle sidestepped asking for funds and instead offered specifics. She calmly explained that she, Violet, and Grace helped collect clothing, blankets, and linens along with planning events such as the gala. The woman opened her purse and handed Isabelle a quarter.

"You take that, dear, for the children." The woman patted Isabelle's hand.

Two other women followed suit, and before Isabelle knew it, she had over two dollars in coins that she hadn't even tried to solicit. Money in hand, it was time to end the game.

Step three: defer and depart.

"I hadn't expected this." Isabelle's sincere gratitude almost allowed her emotions to get the best of her. "Your generosity will go such a long way."

She graciously excused herself and hurried up the narrow hall off of the foyer to the bathroom. Once safely inside, she danced in a circle, then leaned against the door and sighed. *How exhausting this is, but it's something I'm going to have to do now that I'm doomed to be a spinster who must live at home forever and take care of her aging parents.*

Isabelle walked to the sink. Despite her momentary elation over the donations she had received, the face in the mirror reflected a weary and resigned woman: resigned to waiting for a letter that would never come, resigned to not becoming a nurse, resigned to living in a broken city trying valiantly to rebuild. *I don't want to wallow in self-pity because I know life isn't always fair, but why can't something good happen? Is that too much to ask?*

A knock sounded on the door, and Isabelle jumped. "I'm—I'll be just a moment."

She smoothed her hair and stared at herself again in the mirror. *At least I can be successful at the game, even if I don't like to play it.*

Several minutes later, Isabelle waited for dinner to be announced alongside Grace in the foyer, both women holding glasses of punch. Isabelle had assured Charlotte that she didn't need to donate to the Red Cross this evening but recognized and appreciated her enthusiasm. Isabelle caught a motion out of the corner of her eye; Charlotte descended the grand staircase, her hand wrapped around what Isabelle considered a more-than-generous number of bills.

Charlotte pulled Isabelle and Grace aside and handed Isabelle the money. "I must tell you, I'm also quite passionate about their cause. What they've done for everyone during this horrible year has been nothing short of a miracle, and I don't understand why more people can't see that."

For a moment, Isabelle struggled to contain her excitement. She feared she might break out of the staid and stifled character she was playing and hug Charlotte right there in front of the other guests. *She gets it! She's donating because she wants to, and that's the most meaningful part. And Josephine—silly Josephine—was right. Charlotte's the perfect person to help me now that Grace is leaving and Violet is going to be busy with her wedding.*

"I know, and thank you again for helping me tonight." Isabelle struggled to keep her voice calm, her eyes widening. "They're such unsung heroes, and I'm thrilled I'm not alone in my views on that." *I'd love to ask if she'd like to help me plan events for the upcoming winter holidays, but tonight isn't the time.* Isabelle sipped her punch. *This stupid game of social niceties requires me to wait until a more appropriate moment.*

Isabelle glanced up in time to see Andrew walking toward them. Charlotte pulled him aside so they could speak privately. Moments later, the pair rejoined Isabelle and Grace.

"Isabelle, Charlotte's been telling me about your work with the Red Cross, and I want you to have this." Andrew pulled out his money clip and removed several ten-dollar bills.

Dear heaven, that's a lot of money! Isabelle forced her eyes not to bulge when he handed her his donation.

She stowed the bills in her purse in one slow, smooth motion. "You're so very generous. Mrs. Felton and the rest of the volunteers thank you."

Charlotte grasped Andrew's arm and squeezed it while Isabelle bit her tongue; Grace's expression of sheer astonishment at Isabelle's performance was priceless.

The butler gingerly approached and caught Andrew's attention.

"Yes, dinner's ready. I must let the others know," Andrew said.

Isabelle, Grace, and Charlotte trailed up the hall behind the other guests. At the dining room entrance, Charlotte excused herself. Isabelle took a sip of punch and turned to Grace.

"I don't know about you, but this has been the most successful evening." She giggled.

Grace laughed and clutched Isabelle's arm, the two young women huddling together like gleeful children. "It really has."

At home after the gala, Isabelle sat at her dressing table in her long white nightgown and gently removed the hairpins and combs that held her hair in place. Her purse lay on her bed, and she gazed at its reflection in the mirror. The evening had been successful in more ways than one. She had secured an enormous forty-dollar donation from Andrew and thirty dollars from Charlotte, and had also accepted smaller donations from several ladies, all without directly asking for the money. *Did those women donate to be seen?* Isabelle carefully laid Grace's combs aside. *Or because they want to help?*

Isabelle ran her fingers through her hair, her eyelids growing heavy. Margaret was getting better, and though Eleanor and Sarah tried to help as much as they could, the dark circles around Isabelle's eyes told the truth; she still shouldered much of her mother's care alone.

Isabelle crawled into bed and turned off her light. She sank into the soft warmth beneath her covers, a faint smile tugging at the corners of her mouth. Charlotte had been the bright spot of the evening with her unexpected donation and enthusiasm. And Grace's advice had ultimately helped Isabelle win the day. By controlling her excitement and remaining calm—traits that Grace possessed and that Isabelle could only dream of consistently emulating—Isabelle had secured funds for the Red Cross along with a healthy dose of sorely needed self-confidence.

"At least someone understands me," Isabelle mumbled, drifting off to sleep, "and thanks to Grace's helpful suggestions, maybe I can learn to at least tolerate the game."

FORTY-SIX

Nearly two weeks after her mother's heart attack, Isabelle sat at the dining room table, her head about to slump forward into her bowl of vegetable soup. Though Margaret was now allowed out of bed, the doctor hadn't wanted her to navigate the stairs more than necessary. Despite her protests, James had insisted that Margaret stay in her room most of the time. Isabelle wondered if it was out of caution or because he couldn't stand seeing his wife in her diminished state. In either case, it meant more work for Isabelle, Eleanor, and Sarah.

A motion in the hall distracted Isabelle, and she turned to find Sarah beckoning her. Despite Isabelle's exhaustion, her spirits soared. Had her acceptance letter arrived? She rose without excusing herself and turned back when she left the dining room. No one had said a word. *They're such ingrates.* She tsked in disgust.

"She says she's not feeling well this evening," Sarah said as she and Isabelle ascended the stairs. "I gave her some soup and aspirin, but—"

Isabelle waved a hand, she and Sarah continuing down the hall. "You did the right thing by telling me. It's Father. He's treating Mother like a china doll, and she needs to move. No one's going to feel well if they have to sit in bed all day."

Isabelle tapped on her mother's bedroom door and opened it.

Margaret's wan face greeted her daughter. "Oh, Sarah, you shouldn't have fussed."

"I'm sorry, madame, but I—"

"Mother, we need to get you out of bed." Isabelle strode to the edge of the imposing four-poster.

"I'd have been up earlier, but your father—"

"Father has a case of the vapors." Isabelle whipped the covers off of her mother's legs.

Isabelle closed her eyes and pressed her hands together in front of her mouth.

"I'm sorry." She took her mother's hand. "I'm tired, and it's making me cross. Dr. Jenkins is right. You shouldn't go up and down the stairs too often, but you must move. I'll talk with Father and tell him you simply can't stay cooped up in here any longer." Isabelle turned to Sarah. "Can you walk up and down the hall with her a few times? I'll be back to check on her after dinner."

Sarah helped Margaret out of bed and into her robe.

"I'd like to come downstairs." Margaret steadied herself against her dressing table chair.

It was all Isabelle could do not to scream in exasperation. Her soup was getting cold, and she was certain that by the time she returned to the dinner table, Josephine would have inhaled all the grapes and mashed potatoes. Her pregnancy left her so sick in the morning that she gobbled her dinner like a starving horse.

"Why don't you walk the hall first?" Isabelle suggested. "I'll help you with the stairs when I come back."

Isabelle shot Sarah a weary yet grateful smile and left the room.

Downstairs in the dining room, Isabelle returned to her vegetable soup and commandeered the bowl of fruit in time to swipe the next-to-last handful of grapes. She savored the black spheres of sweetness, none of her family daring to meet her eyes. *Maybe they feel guilty. But if they do, why don't they help more?*

Isabelle had just polished off her grapes when a muffled thump sounded upstairs. Isabelle and Henry both jumped up, and Grace scooted her chair back but remained seated. James's face went ashen, and he gripped the tablecloth so suddenly that Isabelle feared the candlesticks in the centerpiece would topple over and ignite the cloth. Josephine clutched her husband's hand; his stricken expression and the fear in his eyes pained Isabelle.

"Thank you, Henry!" Isabelle hurried out of the room and bounded up the stairs. "At least someone else in this family cares about my mother!"

Isabelle rushed down the hall and burst into her parents' bedroom to the sight of an overturned chair. Margaret sat on the far side of the bed, holding Sarah's hand.

"I lost my balance for a moment, but I'm all right," Margaret assured Isabelle.

"We walked the hall twice." Sarah fretted the hem of her white pinafore between her fingers. "She grabbed hold of the chair while I was helping her back to bed. When she turned, the chair fell over."

Isabelle laid a palm on her chest, her heart fluttering like a caged bird.

"It's nothing," Margaret insisted.

"Mother, let's go downstairs." Isabelle helped Margaret up from the bed. "You can sit at the table and talk to us. It's entirely too quiet down there, and I think it'd do everyone good to see you." *It'd do everyone good to sit and stew in their fear, and I am not apologizing for yelling at them.* Isabelle bit her tongue.

Isabelle and Sarah helped Margaret down the stairs. When the trio appeared at the dining room entrance, Henry was the only one who immediately rose to help Margaret into her chair. She thanked him with an expression of admiration that Isabelle hadn't seen before. It was an expression Isabelle mirrored as she took her seat across from him and Josephine. Moments later, James grumbled and blustered at Margaret for being out of bed. Isabelle almost shrieked.

"Father, please," she scolded. "Mother *cannot* be confined to bed all day anymore; it isn't healthy."

"But Dr. Jenk—"

"Dr. Jenkins would be the first person to say that she needs to be up and about in a safe way for her circulation. He said she should take it easy on the stairs, and she has. She must move to get better, and walking up and down the hall and coming down to see us are perfectly normal parts of her recovery." Isabelle spooned in another measured bite of lukewarm soup.

James scowled. Isabelle avoided his hard stare by helping herself to a roll.

"Well, what was the banging? Did you fall?" His tone softened, and he turned to Margaret.

She shook her head and shrugged. "I tipped over a chair. Really, I feel fine. Now then, I'd like some grapes."

Henry passed the bowl to Josephine to send on to her mother. Grace commented on how Margaret's color had improved. It had, but only a little. With Margaret by his side, James finally calmed himself long enough to fall into a conversation with Henry about a parcel of land near the shipyards.

When Eleanor came next to the dining room, Margaret asked for soup and more grapes. Isabelle giggled when Eleanor admitted the grapes were gone, and Margaret teased Josephine about stealing all the fruit. Even Grace laughed, and Henry put his arm around his wife. With dinner conversation returning to a semblance of normalcy, Isabelle grinned at her mother. *She's the glue that holds our family together, and it's as if nothing ever happened. That'll last until she needs something, and then it'll all fall to me again.*

With peach slices substituting for grapes, Margaret chatted contentedly with Josephine and Grace. Isabelle finished her soup, her mind wandering. She watched her parents relax back into their familiar banter and tried to picture herself living with them for the rest of her life. The prospect nearly brought tears to her eyes. She loved San Francisco, and that love had literally been shattered and pieced back together over the past year. But the idea of living at home as a spinster sent her spirits so low that her vision blurred, and she brushed a sleeve against her cheek to quickly wipe away a stray tear. *I simply can't do it, but how do I escape? I can't see a way out.*

She cleared her throat, only to discover Henry staring at her in concern. She smiled weakly and focused on a peach slice. *He's so perceptive. I hope he doesn't ask what's wrong.* She chastised herself for allowing her emotions to get the better of her.

Isabelle tried to distract herself by counting the miniature roses printed on her china plate, but her exhaustion finally overtook her. "I'm going up. It's been a long day."

James's head jerked up.

"But she'll need you to—" Josephine began.

"I'll help Margaret back to her room when she's ready." Henry's authoritative tone comforted Isabelle.

"I'll help, too," Grace added.

"Thank you," Margaret said, casting grateful glances at her son-in-law and niece.

Father should be the one helping. She's his wife. Heat crept up Isabelle's neck.

On her way out of the dining room, Isabelle paused and mouthed "thank you" to Henry and Grace. James cut his eyes away and lowered his head.

At least Henry is enough of a gentleman to answer the bell when a man's needed. Isabelle dragged herself up the stairs. *And given all that's happened, he may be the only gentleman in this house.*

FORTY-SEVEN

A few weeks later, Grace and Isabelle waited outside the doors to the main dining room of the Cliff House at a quarter past seven. Josephine stood nearby, her fingers tucked around Henry's arm. The setting sun had started to paint streaks of orange and yellow across the sky, which perfectly highlighted Josephine's new russet A-line gown. Grace suspected Josephine had insisted on that style of dress to cover the hint of her growing belly.

Henry opened the door, and Grace, Josephine, and Isabelle stepped inside. It was the beginning of August, and though Grace had visited the Cliff House several times in the three months she had been in California, she continued to be impressed. The dining room had been transformed into a place to eat and dance, the tables arranged around the outer perimeter of the space. The sparkling white china, the twinkling crystal, the rich mahogany wainscoting, and the crisply ironed ivory tablecloths represented the finest San Francisco had to offer. It was an environment in which Grace belonged.

Grace spotted her aunt and uncle talking with a few people she recognized from her uncle's birthday party. Grace's breath caught in her throat. Aunt Margaret spoke animatedly to the woman across from her. Grace had hoped that Josephine would be allowed to announce that she was having a child when she was ready. Aunt Margaret, however, had been so excited to learn of Josephine's pregnancy that Grace wasn't sure her aunt could keep the joyous news under wraps much longer.

Grace, Isabelle, Henry, and Josephine greeted Aunt Margaret and Uncle James. Grace excused herself and crossed the room. She spoke briefly with Andrew and Charlotte, who stood near the windows overlooking the sparkling ocean. Grace's heart pattered faster than usual when Andrew focused his undivided attention on her. Sensing she was being observed, Grace turned and acknowledged Josephine and Isabelle, then rejoined them.

"How are they this evening?" Josephine asked Grace.

"Doing quite well." Grace stole a glance over her shoulder, then looked to her left and right.

Josephine tilted her head. "Do you . . . are you looking for someone?"

Grace shook her head and quickly composed herself. "I—no, sorry." Grace's stomach tensed. *That was close. I mustn't raise suspicion.*

Josephine looked down her nose at her sister. Isabelle stared at the floor, her face somber. Grace crinkled her eyes. *It must be discouraging not to have heard from the nursing school. I'm so lucky to have already received my acceptance letter.*

"Can you at least pretend to be enjoying yourself?" Josephine whispered to Isabelle. "This is the first time we've been out of the house in weeks. Why aren't you more excited?"

Isabelle's stony expression belied what was bothering her. "Unlike some people, I have nothing to be excited about."

Josephine frowned. "What does *that* mean?"

Isabelle shook her head and feigned interest in the painting of an imposing ship on the wall.

Andrew and Charlotte drew near, Andrew holding two glasses of champagne. Isabelle and Grace accepted them with words of thanks.

"We decided it was safer for him to carry them," Charlotte

joked in reference to her punch-spilling episode at Uncle James's birthday party.

Charlotte's humor broke the gloomy spell Isabelle was laboring under, and she chuckled. The string quartet in the far corner began a Beethoven arrangement, and a few moments later, Josephine clutched Grace's arm.

"What?" Grace's eyes widened.

Josephine shook her head and slowly turned around. Her parents, along with Graham and Rosaline, stood at her elbow.

"Here they are." Margaret's smug smile alarmed Grace. *No, no, no! She's going to tell!* Grace nearly held her breath.

"Good evening." Graham addressed the group, his eyes lingering on Josephine. "Good to see everyone out and about again. Wasn't sure we'd get the pleasure of having you with us, Margaret." He took Aunt Margaret's hand in both of his, and she blushed.

"Yes, I—I'm much better," she sputtered.

Grace's pulse quickened. Graham McCormick's amorous attention had unnerved Aunt Margaret. The man could so easily make one feel like she was the only woman in the room.

"No drinking or dancing, but there's so much to celebrate," Aunt Margaret said.

Grace clutched her champagne flute tighter and said a silent, futile prayer. Rosaline searched Aunt Margaret's face in the bemused way a child might stare at someone who had teased them with a secret. Graham arched his eyebrows.

"I'm going to be a grandmother!" Aunt Margaret squealed.

Rosaline gasped and clasped her hands together. Josephine struggled to keep her chin from quivering. Thunderstruck shock and surprise spread across Graham's face. Grace painted on a pleasant smile. *Josephine wanted to tell him in private. He knows it's his, and he'll want nothing more to do with her. Josephine's such a foolish woman. What did she think would happen? Did she think he would leave Rosaline for her? That would be entirely too scandalous.*

At the thought of scandal, Grace's stomach dropped, and she bowed her head. What she was about to do to Frank was scandalous too. Not only was it scandalous, but it was also wrong in ways that sent people to jail and their souls straight to hell. It was wrong in ways that made Grace doubt she could go through with it. She shivered and swallowed hard. *But I can't see another way out. I did nothing wrong with Charles, and I can't let Frank ruin my reputation.* She also couldn't imagine spending the rest of her life with him. Grace stared out the window at the vast ocean and fidgeted, Aunt Cora's condemnation echoing in her mind. *I'm not selfish. I'm simply seizing an opportunity like Isabelle and Josephine did. And I will not have my evening ruined by another woman's folly.*

Josephine tore her gaze from Graham when Rosaline grabbed one of her hands and squeezed it.

"Such wonderful news!" Rosaline exclaimed. "How thrilled you must be." Rosaline beamed at Henry and patted his arm.

Graham had finally comported his face into calm composure. "Yes—that is, congratulations to you both." He nodded at Josephine and shook Henry's hand.

"We're delighted." Josephine's voice quavered.

To his credit, Henry wrapped his arm around his wife's waist. But whereas he usually drew Josephine close—a tender yet protective gesture Grace had noticed and once longed for with Frank—Henry stood unmoving at his wife's side. Grace remained rooted in place by a rising tide of suspicion and dread. *Does Henry know the baby isn't his? Has Josephine confessed, or has he figured it out some other way?*

"It's wonderful, isn't it?" Rosaline pressed closer to Grace, jolting her from her thoughts.

"I—yes," Grace replied with a nervous, breathy laugh. "We're all very happy."

Grace chatted quietly with Andrew and Charlotte, the music and conversation in the room growing somehow louder. The din pressed against Grace, and she winced. She guessed the shame that weighed on Josephine to be at least a thousand times worse. The news would be all over the room in minutes. And between Rosaline and Aunt Margaret, everyone from the shipyards to the Presidio would know of Josephine's pregnancy in less than a week.

Beside Grace, Josephine sniffed and held her head high, her eyes glassy. Graham and Rosaline excused themselves and moved on to speak to another group of friends. Josephine whispered in Henry's ear, and he excused himself. As he walked away, Josephine shot one last lingering glance at Graham. He looked through her as if she weren't there.

The string quartet began a new song, and when Andrew asked Grace to dance, she demurred, but he insisted. *It might be one of the last times I'm at the Cliff House, and there's no harm in dancing once dance with him.*

"Would you hold this for me?" Grace handed Charlotte her glass of champagne and joined Andrew and several other couples in the center of the room.

FORTY-EIGHT

enry sat at a table with Isabelle and sipped his gin and tonic. He had no interest in doing the rounds with James, Margaret, or his wife now that Margaret had spilled the beans about Josephine's pregnancy. Instead, he relished sitting quietly with sister-in-law. Her grim expression mirrored his emotions. If he could have, he would have driven home and locked himself in the study to stew.

A few minutes later, Frank Buchanan walked through the dining room doors, the same striking woman who had accompanied him to James's birthday party on his arm. Frank stopped short, the couple behind him almost bumping into him and his guest. Impeccable in a charcoal-gray suit, his necktie adorned with the gleaming tiepin with a steer in the center, Frank leveled a narrow-eyed stare at something or someone across the room. Frank clenched his jaw, and Henry straightened. *Does he see Graham? Has he told Frank he's out of the real estate deal yet?* Henry searched the room for Graham McCormick and found him standing along the far wall talking with a group of men. Graham, however, was not the object of Frank's intense gaze. Henry continued to scan the room in the direction of Frank's stare. In an instant, Henry saw her. Grace and Andrew twirled by, a couple amongst many, Frank's unblinking eyes following her like a hawk stalking its prey. *This is like when he hunted her down to say goodbye at James's birthday party.* Uneasy pressure built in Henry's chest. *But why is he so jealous if there's no connection between them?*

Frank remained inside the door, his companion shifting nervously in her shimmering garnet-colored gown. Henry set down his glass and ticked off what he knew about Frank and Grace. They had both appeared in San Francisco at roughly the same time, which could be coincidental. Grace had shaken Frank's hand as if she hadn't known him when they had met, and she had been nothing but polite and appropriate all the times Henry had seen her and Frank together.

But Josephine had whispered something about letters.

Grace had supposedly received several from a friend in Wyoming. Henry had caught Sarah going through the mail that fateful day that Margaret had tucked an envelope into her purse. Graham had mentioned that Frank was from Cheyenne and that there had been a mix-up with Frank's name when Graham had called a few businessmen to learn more about him.

Could Sarah be secretly delivering letters from Frank Buchanan to Grace? It made no sense . . . unless . . .

The thought hit Henry so hard that he drummed his fingers on the table loudly enough to elicit a confused stare from Isabelle. *Is Frank Buchanan the second missing suitor that Grace's parents disapprove of?* It was a preposterous notion, but it would explain why Frank still stood near the dining room doors, a vein in his neck bulging. If so, it was the most outrageous and exhausting case of female chicanery Henry had ever been privy to, and that was saying a lot given what had transpired with his wife, his mother-in-law, and his sister-in-law over the summer.

Henry had wondered at James's party if he might need to protect Grace from Frank. It appeared that he would, but how? The man was half a head taller, obviously stronger, and more experienced with grappling than Henry. A physical confrontation simply wasn't an option. The main dining room of the Cliff House wasn't a dark alley next to the docks. Henry needed to defuse the situation and had more to consider than his bodily health. As Grace floated across the floor in Andrew's arms, a radiant smile spread across her face, a solution dawned on Henry.

He turned to Isabelle, who sat quietly, picking a speck of lint off of the tablecloth. "Would you like to dance?"

His invitation brought on an unexpected smile, and she joined him when he rose.

FORTY-NINE

race danced with Andrew, envisioning her future. She would become a teacher and eventually find love again. More important, she would learn to trust herself when it came to men. Andrew had been nothing but a gentleman, and she hoped against hope that she would meet someone equally kind and sincere in Los Angeles at the end of her two years of schooling. Andrew smiled down at her, and when he twirled her away, Henry and Isabelle whirled by. Grace beamed at her cousin. Maybe dancing would help Isabelle not feel so discouraged about not hearing from the nursing school.

Isabelle, the picture of a polite yet detached young woman who dutifully visited the women's parlor, swept across the floor with Henry. When Henry whispered something to Isabelle and she laughed, Grace grinned. *She needs someone like him. I'm no expert, but Henry cares for her. They would be such a good match, much better than him and Josephine.*

Grace twirled again, her hand in Andrew's. When her eyes passed over the dining room doorway, her breath caught in her throat. Frank Buchanan stood glaring at her, Mary at his side.

Andrew spun Grace back toward him, his brow furrowed. "What? Is everything all right?"

Grace forced a smile. "Yes, I—I think I may need to sit down when the song ends. I'm feeling a little dizzy."

While Grace and Andrew danced, Frank strode to the buffet,

Mary hurrying behind him. They helped themselves to plates of crab cakes and romaine salad and took their seats at a table in the corner. When the music finished, Grace and Andrew retired to a nearby table. Andrew left to retrieve Grace's glass of champagne from Charlotte, and Frank made his move. He closed the distance between him and Grace like a predator, stopping only to speak with Graham along the way. Grace gripped the edge of her chair so tightly that her knuckles hurt. *Please don't cause a scene, Frank. It'll end us both*, she prayed.

Without asking, Frank pulled up a chair and sat down beside her.

"I thought I told you to stay away from him," he hissed, his neck growing redder by the second.

"I—he asked me to dance, and it would've been impolite to—"

"It's impolite for *you*—my future wife—to dance with anyone but *me*," he continued, his low voice filled with contempt. "I told you, it'll only be us in the future, no other men."

"Frank, please don't," Grace whispered. "I'm sorry I upset—"

"Don't worry. I won't cause a stir here, but if you're not in the hall in five minutes, I'll make sure Andrew knows exactly what kind of woman you really are."

Grace gasped, then quickly closed her mouth. She struggled to recover from his insinuation, her blood boiling. "I've *never* done anything wrong, and you know—"

"Mr. Buchanan." Andrew arrived at the table.

Frank smoothed his suit coat and rose. "Hello, Mr. Kepler." Frank's tone had changed so suddenly that Grace wondered if he wasn't the living embodiment of Dr. Jekyll and Mr. Hyde. How was it possible that she was listening to the same man who had just threatened to destroy her reputation by spreading insidious lies?

"Would you like to join us?" Andrew sat two glasses of champagne on the table and motioned to the chair from which Frank had risen.

"No, I need to speak to some other gentlemen." Frank tipped his head toward Graham, Uncle James, and a few other businessmen. "I may come ask for a dance from Miss Grace a bit later, though."

Frank's smile was the same one that had initially won Grace's heart. Now it only made bile rise in her throat. *How could I have ever thought I loved him? He's an awful, vile man.* Vowing not to let fear get the best of her, Grace pried her fingers from her chair, rose, and rested a palm on the table to steady herself. "That'd be lovely, Mr. Buchanan." She narrowed her eyes at Frank, and his face sobered. "I'm sure I'll see you again this evening, and we can talk further."

Grace threw a little wave in Mary's direction. From across the room, Mary returned the gesture, trouble etched on her brow.

"Yes, well, I'll take care of some business and come see about that dance." Frank grinned.

Grace and Andrew took their seats and sipped their champagne. Though she tried not to fidget, Grace couldn't help herself. She was truly between what her father would call "the hammer and the anvil." She wanted to talk to Mary, but it would have been rude to leave Andrew after he had brought her champagne. At the same time, she had to keep a close eye on Frank. After the most uncomfortable few minutes, Frank exited the dining room.

Grace leaned closer to Andrew. "Please excuse me. I'll be right back." Her pleasant tone belied her fear.

Grace passed through the frosted glass double doors and spotted Frank partway down the hall near one of the short corridors that led to several private sitting rooms. With the party in full swing, the hall was deserted, and the ominous, dimly lit space stretched out before her. *He doesn't want to be seen, and no one will be here to save me if something happens. Just like with Charles . . .*

Grace shivered and started down the hall, her pulse racing. The closer she grew to Frank, the more she wanted to retreat. The color that stained his cheeks told her his temper hadn't cooled since he had left the dining room. When she was close enough, he grabbed her arm and yanked her into the dark corridor.

"Ow, Frank, stop, I—" Grace grimaced and managed to pull away.

"You will not dishonor me by dancing with that man—or any other man—again," he spat. "My last wife tried my patience on that, and I put a stop to it once and for all. You cannot go around throwing yourself at other men and acting like a common whore!"

Grace glared at him, her nostrils flaring. "I am *not* a whore, and you know it, Frank. I've done nothing wrong, and you insult me by—"

Suddenly, he grabbed her arms and pinned her against the wall. Her head thumped against the paneling, and she winced, the pressure of his body forcing the breath from her lungs.

"You're such a tease, Grace," he sneered, his breath smelling of whiskey. "Charles always said you were a tease, and if your brother and I hadn't been there, he would've made you regret it."

Grace tried in vain to push Frank away, her eyes clamped shut, her heart thundering in her chest. Visions of Charles at her parents' house the fateful night of the food poisoning roared through her memory: one hand wrapped around her neck as he held her against the wall, the other hand hiking up her dress and ripping down her bloomers. She had struggled with him like she was now struggling with Frank. Charles had gotten his pants unbuttoned and forced his thigh between her legs the instant before she kneed him in the groin at the exact moment Frank and Jacob had burst into the room.

I'm an honorable woman, and you will not live long enough to tell Andrew Kepler otherwise. She gritted her teeth, still pushing against Frank's chest.

A burst of men's laughter and music echoed up the corridor, and Frank released one of her arms. He held her against the wall with the other, and she dared not move. He stepped sideways and peeked into the main hall. Finally, he released her, and she massaged her arms where he had gripped them, blood still roaring in her ears. Footsteps approached, and Frank stepped to Grace's left. She shied away, still hidden behind him, her cheeks burning. She couldn't imagine the humiliation of prying eyes discovering them together in the dark corridor.

Once the men had passed, Frank checked the main hall and returned to Grace. She stood plastered against the wall, breathless, still rubbing her sore arms.

"You be ready." His stare made her tremble. "I about have enough money scraped together to go in on a deal with Graham, and when I do, I'm coming for you."

Still shaking, Grace eased away from the wall. She had to execute her plan soon; she couldn't endure any more cruelty. Most of all, she feared Frank might finish what Charles had started.

"I—I will," she whispered. "I won't go near him again after tonight, I promise."

"Good." Frank grasped her hands a little too tightly, and she grimaced. "I love you, and all this is going to be forgotten when we're together proper. So, no more carousing with Mr. Kepler, right?"

Grace nodded and shrank away when he leaned down to kiss her cheek.

"We'll be the talk of the town," he whispered in her ear. "You wait and see." Frank released her hands and walked into the main hall. "Soon." He winked and disappeared.

Grace closed her eyes and stifled a sob. Her legs were so weak she feared she might crumple into a heap in the corridor, only to be found by an errant waiter. *Why do men always hurt me?* A few tears leaked from her eyes. *Is Frank right? Am I a tease? I don't mean to be; I just want someone to love me and be proud of me. Is that too much to ask?*

It wasn't, but the shame of poor judgment and of making two terrible choices in suitors made Grace wonder if she would ever trust herself—or another man—again.

She tiptoed to the end of the corridor and peeked into the main hall. Unable to keep her hands from shaking, she hurried back into the shadows. She couldn't return to the party looking as if she had been assaulted, which she had been, for the second time in her life.

Grace allowed her silent tears to fall and wiped them away with the back of her hand. With no one in sight, she took a tentative step out of the corridor and began walking back to the dining room. The music and laughter grew louder from behind the glass doors; Grace could make out the shapes of Andrew and Charlotte chatting with friends at their table.

Grace paused outside the dining room doors, trying to calm her churning stomach and temper the unfamiliar inferno of rage building inside her. *That man will never hurt me or any other woman again.* Though Grace had no idea how long her terrifying interlude with Frank had lasted, she stepped through the dining room doors, her face etched with a polite smile, unshakable resolve blooming in her heart. She wasn't sure how she would explain her absence to Andrew or her family, but she would think of something. Grace approached Henry and Isabelle at a nearby table, admiring her cousin. *I've helped you with your little game, Isa. Now I need you to help me with mine.*

FIFTY

Two days after the celebration at the Cliff House, Isabelle sat at her dressing table, late-morning sun streaming through her window. Josephine and Grace had asked her to go shopping with them—Graham had announced his oldest daughter's engagement at the party, and Josephine was using the upcoming event to buy yet another dress—but Isabelle had declined. Though Dr. Jenkins had given Margaret permission to resume most of her activities, Isabelle still felt beholden to her mother. Margaret had encouraged Isabelle to go with Josephine and Grace, but Isabelle had no interest in dress shopping and had remained in her room instead.

Isabelle rose and opened her bedroom window to allow in a late-summer breeze, a few tears rolling down her cheeks.

All was lost.

She wasn't accepted at home unless there was a crisis, and now the one place where she felt she would fit in most had rejected her; a letter from the nursing school had never arrived. She wiped away her tears with her sleeve and sniffled. *If this is my fate and I'm not meant to be in Los Angeles, then why do I feel so awful?*

A knock sounded at her door, and she jumped. She grabbed her handkerchief off of her dressing table, dabbed her eyes, and crossed the room.

She expected her mother, but when she opened the door, Henry greeted her, a book in the crook of his arm. "I thought— Why are you crying?"

She pressed a forefinger to her lips, motioned him inside, and closed the door. He sat down on her bed while she returned to her window. She envied the freedom of the sparrows who flitted from branch to branch in a backyard tree.

"The letter from the nursing school never came." She blotted her cheeks again.

Henry exhaled in a way that made her wonder if he was upset. She turned to him, but his staid expression belied whatever emotions he might have been hiding. *I wish he'd say something. It's not like him to not comfort me. Then again, maybe he's trying to find the right words.*

"I brought you this." He offered her *The Garden of Allah*. "I found it in the study downstairs and thought you'd like it. I read it a couple of years ago."

Isabelle thanked him more out of duty than interest and set the book on her dressing table. *There's no garden with God in it for me now.* She returned to her window, unable to hold back more tears.

"What am I going to do?" she choked out.

Henry rose and enveloped her in a gentle embrace. "I know the last month or so has been hard for you."

Isabelle laid her cheek on his lapel. "It's not just that."

Henry rubbed her back, and at that moment, Isabelle allowed herself to cry. All the exhaustion, frustration, and discouragement she had experienced over the past weeks with her mother, coupled with the crushing rejection of the undelivered letter, burst forth in waves. To his credit, Henry remained silent and allowed her to weep until she had no more tears. When she had finished, she gazed up at him, her eyes still blurry.

"Sorry." She wiped her cheeks with her handkerchief. "I've been such a terrible mope all of this time, and I don't mean to blubber.

I know I should be grateful. We have so much, and others don't. Mother could've . . ." Isabelle shuddered and rushed on. "I could look into going to school here, but I'm sure the term has already started. And with the hospital only recently readmitting students, I doubt they have any spots left. I feel so stuck and can't see a way out."

Henry hugged her again and gently grasped her shoulders. "No one else may tell you this, but you saved her, Isa." His eyes shone with an intensity that made her pulse thrum. "Without your quick actions, we would've lost her, and I—"

His eyes became glassy, and Isabelle cradled his forearms in her palms. "I know. I can't imagine life without her either."

Henry cleared his throat. "Your father, Josephine, and I were terrified. In many ways, we still are. It's why we've leaned on you, too hard, honestly."

He released her, and they lingered in the warm light, facing one other. As the silence grew, so did Isabelle's unease. She had never shared a moment like this with anyone, let alone a man, and wasn't sure if she should say something. Henry reached for her hand but closed his at the last moment. He withdrew it as if he had caught himself in a breach of etiquette and walked around the bed toward the door.

"I think . . ." He turned and furrowed his brow. "I think you should be patient and have faith. I know it's hard, but it's like with Margaret. We hoped she'd get better, and she has. I know that isn't the same, but . . ."

Isabelle shook her head. "No, it's not the same."

Henry showed himself out. Isabelle remained at her window, his words echoing in her mind. *Oh, how I wish I could have faith.* But faith wouldn't solve the problem that loomed over her, much like the Cliff House loomed over the Pacific. Even if she was accepted into nursing school, could she bring herself to leave, given her mother's fragile state? Isabelle had lamented that concern to Henry once before, and he had assured her there were plenty of women they could hire to help with Margaret.

But those women weren't Isabelle.

Deep down, the only person whose approval mattered to Isabelle was her mother, and Margaret was the person most against Isabelle's attending nursing school. *No. I'm rightly and truly stuck.* Isabelle closed her eyes and raised her face to the warm sun. "The sooner I can accept my fate, the better off I'll be," she whispered, trying to swallow the rising lump in her throat.

FIFTY-ONE

After leaving his sister-in-law's room, Henry descended the stairs, his emotions swinging from determination to resentment to impending dread. His conversation with Isabelle had made it clear that he couldn't wait any longer. Despite his trepidation, he needed to talk to James. Henry walked to the study, but when he laid his hand on the doorknob, he paused to gather his courage. *It'll be all right. I've been through worse, and I'll make the best of whatever happens.*

Henry stepped into the study to the scent of cigar smoke. James sat in his usual leather chair near the cold fireplace, buried in his newspaper.

James lowered his paper and removed his stogy from his mouth. "Fine day today, don't you think, my boy?" James nodded at Henry and returned his attention to his paper.

"I'm afraid not." Henry sat down on the end of the sofa nearest James's chair.

James furrowed his brow and rested his cigar in the ashtray on the side table. "What has you troubled?"

Henry wiped his mouth. *There are so many things I hardly know where to begin.*

Henry clasped his hands together and crossed his legs. It was a casual gesture that disguised his jangled nerves and the revelations he was about to spring on James. Henry had watched other men do it over the years, confident men who had no trouble telling the truth from a place of power and certainty. And while Henry had decided what he would do regardless of the consequences, he couldn't help but squirm. His father-in-law's reaction stood to make or break him personally and professionally.

"I believe Isabelle has been accepted into nursing school in Los Angeles, but Margaret has her acceptance letter," Henry said.

James arched his brows and drew back in his chair.

"I can't prove it," Henry continued, "but I saw Margaret tuck a letter into her purse several weeks ago. I hesitate to accuse her, of course, but not knowing is making Isabelle miserable, especially with what's happened to Margaret in the last few—"

James held up a hand. "Isa applied to this school without telling us?"

Henry hated revealing Isabelle's secret, but telling the truth had now become imperative. "I think she was afraid to."

James pursed his lips and folded his newspaper. Henry remained frozen on the sofa. The same perturbed expression that sometimes clouded James's face during particularly difficult business meetings when he was challenged by something he didn't like but knew might be true had suddenly materialized.

Henry had tired of trying to gauge when it might be best to speak, so instead of waiting, he continued. "Honestly, I was shocked when she told me."

He neglected to bring up the afternoon at the office when James had said he would support Isabelle if she were admitted to nursing school. He hoped James would remember. If not, Henry would remind him.

James shook his head. "She's determined, I suppose, but Los Angeles . . ."

"Yes." Henry rose and wandered over to one of the large windows that overlooked the backyard. "My fear is that if Isabelle's been accepted but doesn't know, she might miss her chance to attend, and her spot could be given to another girl." *With what I have to say next, I don't feel like I should order him to ask Margaret about the letter, but I'd like to.*

James sniffed and slapped his folded newspaper on the side table. He puffed twice on his cigar and mashed it out with a firm thump in the ashtray. Henry chewed on his lip. *Is he angry with Isabelle or Margaret, or both?*

James rose and walked toward the study door. Henry spoke before James could open it. "There's more."

James eyed Henry suspiciously, then crossed the room to the fireplace and removed a fresh cigar from the gilt-edged box on the mantel. Henry returned to the sofa and waited for James to cut the end off of the cigar and light it. When James finally made himself comfortable in his chair, Henry took a deep breath and winced. *I never imagined I'd be saying these words.*

"I'm divorcing Josephine," Henry said, his voice cracking.

"By God, why?" James thundered, his face reddening with fury as he gripped his chair arms.

Henry stared hard at the study door, his mouth pulled down for fear others in the house had overheard James's outburst. James mashed his new cigar into the ashtray and wiped his face with his hand.

"Because the child she's carrying isn't mine." Henry leaned back and ran a hand over his hair.

He had thought saying it—that finally admitting it aloud—would cause his heart to splinter into so many pieces again. Instead, he was left with only relief and lingering sadness.

James hoisted himself out of his chair and headed toward the door. "I'm not listening to any more of—"

"I've done the math, James. It isn't mine," Henry said. "I haven't confronted her yet because I have a proposal that affects the family. I'd like you to hear it before I put it into play."

James whirled around, his eyes narrowed.

He heard me say I'll put my plan into action without asking him, and he's trying to call my bluff. Hope bloomed within Henry. James stalked back to his chair and sat down heavily. He relit his partially mangled cigar and shifted in his seat before dipping his chin for Henry to continue.

"As part of the divorce, I'll renounce ownership of our new house. You can use the proceeds from the sale to hire help for Margaret and for Josephine when the baby arrives. I've not only been your son-in-law but also a loyal and *discreet* employee over the years, and I'll expect a letter of recommendation before I leave the business. I'll let this serve as my notice of resignation, which should give you plenty of time to find a new accountant."

James puffed on his cigar, and Henry held his breath in anticipation, his heart thundering in his chest. *It's more than a fair offer, and he knows it.*

James rose and stumped over to the window. The longer he stood without speaking, the more Henry's spirits rose, much like the curls of cigar smoke that wafted into the air. James hadn't blustered and protested, which meant he was at least considering Henry's offer.

James exhaled a throaty sigh of resignation and turned to Henry. "I regret it's come to this."

Henry lowered his eyes. *What does he mean?*

James returned to his chair and stubbed out his cigar. "It's hard for a father to hear these things, but we both know I haven't exactly been perfect either."

Henry bit his tongue to keep from smirking. James's comment was a strange and fascinating way of saying "like father, like daughter."

"And you have indeed been loyal and discreet," James said. "I've not thanked you for that, but I *have* appreciated it."

A look of mutual respect passed between the men. Henry wanted to speak, but he needed his letter of recommendation, and James hadn't agreed to provide one for him yet.

"Who do you think it is?" James asked. "The father, I mean."

Henry wiped his mouth, bile rising in his throat. "I don't know."

His eyes grew glassy, and he examined his hands, the same ones that had caressed Josephine on their wedding night. That she could still evoke such a reaction despite her betrayal left him more anguished than he cared to admit. Henry swallowed hard and glanced up when James blew out his cheeks.

"It'll cause quite the sensation," James admitted, "but your plan's a generous one. The house will fetch quite a sum. Don't know what I'll do without you at the office, though. What are your plans?"

Henry hesitated. He didn't want James to think he was in cahoots with Isabelle, but he owed James the truth. "I've called a few of our contacts in Los Angeles." He watched James closely for a reaction. "A couple have shown interest."

A wry smile spread across James's face. "Well played, my boy, well played. It's a city on the move, and as I know, they could use a man like you."

Henry appreciated the compliment but sobered, trying to wrestle away an ominous sense of foreboding. *They can use a man like me because I won't tell anyone they're cheating on their wives or taking money under the table. How I hope I can escape those kinds of deception and underhanded dealings when I leave this place.*

James leaned forward and offered his hand to Henry, who shook it.

"You'll have your letter of recommendation." James rose and headed across the study for the third time.

When James reached the door, Henry spoke. "And Isa? Will you at least ask Margaret about the letter?"

James paused. "I will." He left the study, closing the door behind him.

Henry resumed his position at the window and gazed up at the clouds. He closed his eyes and exhaled a long breath, basking in the sun's warmth. He had done it. He had proposed his plan, and James had agreed to give him the letter he needed to make a new start in Los Angeles. Henry pressed a palm to his throat and swallowed, trying to calm his breathing. *That went better than expected.* Henry whispered a silent word of thanks to the robin's-egg-blue sky, then surveyed the room. He admired the rich wood paneling and soft leather furniture. A family photo of the Hamiltons taken before Henry and Josephine were married sat on a table at the far end of the sofa. Henry walked over and picked it up. He stared at Isabelle, his mind turning. If she was accepted into nursing school, James would pay for whatever she needed, but she wouldn't know anyone in a new city. *I'll visit her. When I find a job, I'll make sure she doesn't feel alone.*

The thought of spending time with Isabelle made Henry smile despite himself. That smile faded when his eyes fell on Josephine, her beauty radiating out at him from the photo. He sat the picture down and returned to the window. *She'll accept my decision.* The richly hued flowers along the fence line, alluring in their delicate beauty, made Henry wince. They reminded him of his soon-to-be ex-wife. *She'll accept it because she has to. The question is, will she tell me the truth? No. The real question is, will I ask who the father of her child is, and do I want to know?*

FIFTY-TWO

Early that afternoon, Grace stood with Josephine at the counter of Walters Dress Shop, having finalized their latest orders. Grace had chosen mallard-blue cotton, while Josephine had settled on gold satin.

"I'll need that cut in an A-line again, like the other one I recently purchased." Josephine laid a delicate hand on her midsection. "And I don't mean to press, but could it be ready in a week? We have an engagement party to attend at the Cliff House, and I'd—"

Mr. Walters waved a hand and stepped closer to Josephine and Grace. "It won't be a problem at all. I usually send rush orders out, but I'll have Emelia make yours." He tipped his head toward the shopgirl, her arm fully healed. She sliced the satin from the bolt, her scissors parting the fabric like a hot knife through butter. "She's my finest seamstress, and thanks to a stern scolding and your sister's help with her arm, her work is the talk of the town. I'll have her start on it right away."

He pressed a palm to his chest and addressed Grace. "I apologize, Miss Hamilton. I hope you won't be offended to have your dress made by one of our other seamstresses."

Grace shook her head. "My dress doesn't need to be done for the party. I'm taking it home to Denver."

Having finished cutting the fabric for Josephine's dress, Emilia set down her scissors.

Josephine blushed and motioned the shopgirl closer. "Maybe

with a little more room in the bust and waist," she whispered, her eyes dancing.

"Yes, ma'am." Emelia grinned. "I'll add a half inch to the bust and an inch to the waist to make sure it drapes properly with the gathers."

I suppose she's going to start getting bigger much more quickly now. Grace stifled a giggle. *I almost envy her being able to eat and breathe in a looser-fitting corset that isn't trying to squeeze the life out of her.*

"Mr. Walters," Grace said. "Would you know of a nice gentleman's store where I could buy a flask? I'd love to get one as a gift for my father."

Mr. Walters tapped his chin. "I believe the best place to do that is at City of Paris. They've set up a temporary store in the Hobart mansion at Van Ness and Washington. If Mrs. Rothwell doesn't know where it is, I can tell you."

"I know where it is," Josephine assured him. "We can stop there on the way home."

Mr. Walters wrapped the mallard cotton in plain brown paper and tied it with a length of string. Grace waited patiently and drew back with a start when Mr. Walters rang up Josephine's purchase. The cash register was so loud it could probably have been heard on the beach below the Cliff House.

"And, Mrs. Rothwell . . ." Emelia's address of Josephine startled Mr. Walters. He knit his brow, his lips pressed together into a hard line. "Please thank your sister again for helping with my arm. The doctors said her putting that magazine around it and tying it to my side was a good bit of quick thinking, and I'm plenty grateful."

Josephine feigned a polite smile at Emelia, which made Grace want to swat her cousin for being rude and uncaring. *Without Isabelle's help, the girl would've been left with a crippled arm and would undoubtedly be doing much more unsavory work than sewing.* Grace shook her head, trying to force away the repugnant thought.

Grace sighed inwardly when Mr. Walters rang up her purchase.

The total was over half of what remained of the allowance that Aunt Cora had left with her. Grace clenched her fist around her purse, silently praying she would have enough money left to buy a flask. *When I'm a teacher, I'll make and spend my money as I please.* Grace handed Mr. Walters the bills and change.

"Thank you for everything, sir," she said. "I'll be sure to recommend your shop to any of my friends who are traveling this way."

As George drove Grace and Josephine home from the City of Paris department store, Grace clutched the brown paper package in her lap. She had had barely enough money to purchase a silver-plated flask; the only coin that remained in her change purse was a nickel. She didn't wonder how her father would feel about how she had spent the last of her allowance. He wouldn't care. At this point, he would never know. *I will never again be beholden to a man for money.* Grace narrowed her eyes, her triumph crumbling away slowly. She tilted her head and reconsidered. If she ever trusted another man enough to marry him, she might be, but maybe that wasn't the problem. *If I play my cards right, I won't feel beholden. That's the difference.*

George rounded a corner a little too quickly, and Grace grabbed the door frame of the Winton. The sudden need to brace herself reminded her of her time in San Francisco; it had been quite the wild ride. One minute she had been sure Frank was meant for her, and then her world had spun on its axis. She had discovered not only that Frank was an underhanded businessman, but that he was also a jealous and vengeful brute who had no qualms about hurting her. *But he won't ever hurt me again.* Grace swallowed hard and straightened in her seat.

George pulled alongside the curb in front of the Hamiltons'

home and parked. Grace gripped her package tighter and thanked him when he helped her out of the car. She climbed the front steps, a smirk curling on her lips. *Thanks, Father. You have no idea how happy your money has made me.*

Upstairs in her room, Grace stowed the flask in the armoire. She spied an envelope peeking out from underneath her pillow, and apprehension shot through her. *I can't bear the thought of another letter from Frank.* She hurried to her bed, the handwriting on the envelope filling her with relief and elation. She opened the envelope and discovered a twenty and a five-dollar bill. Tears pricked her eyes as she read the brief note from her brother, Jacob. Though she had hoped he might send more, twenty-five dollars would buy her a train ticket and cover all of her school supplies for the next two years. *What would I do without him?* Grace twirled in a circle, the bills held high overhead. She gazed out the window toward the ocean in the distance. *Thank you, Jacob. You, Andrew, and Henry have gone a long way in helping me have faith in men and myself again.*

FIFTY-THREE

On a Friday evening, the Hamiltons arrived at the Cliff House to attend the McCormicks' engagement party. Grace entered the main dining room with her family. She appreciated Josephine's shimmering dress. The satin gleamed in the warm light of the chandeliers, the shade of gold matching the band that ran around the rim of the china plates on the tables. The color also coordinated beautifully with the pale yellow roses that burst forth from two vases, one on each end of the dessert table.

Grace spotted Graham and Rosaline standing with their daughter and her new fiancé on the far side of the room. Couples were filtering by, paying their respects. At some point Grace, Josephine, and Isabelle would need to do the same. Grace cleared her throat. *I'm sure Josephine would rather not, but she can't be rude.*

"Can we find someplace to sit?" Josephine asked Henry.

He guided her, Isabelle, and Grace to a table near the buffet.

Suddenly, Josephine laid a hand over her mouth, her eyes wide. "I—can we move? I'm a little too close to the oysters."

Henry scanned the room but shook his head; all the other tables were occupied. He immediately motioned to a chair on the other side of the table, but Josephine declined. "I'll go with Mother to speak to Rosaline and her daughter."

Isabelle sat down facing the doors, and Grace took the chair opposite her. Grace sipped from her water glass and tried not to imagine how hard it had to be for Josephine to be in Graham's presence. Josephine had made a disastrous choice and was now suffering the consequences. Grace nearly cringed; Josephine had reached the receiving line and smiled primly at Graham. Grace doubted Josephine had wanted to become a mother yet, but she would be a good one. She had learned her lesson the hard way and could pass that wisdom on if she had a daughter.

Henry and Uncle James excused themselves to talk to several businessmen. Grace spotted Andrew and Charlotte several tables over, chatting with friends. Grace scooted her chair closer to the table. It wasn't that she especially wanted to talk to Isabelle. She sensed her cousin was struggling to endure yet another social event where she had to pretend to be happy for another woman when nothing was going right for her. But Isabelle had a view of the doorway; Grace needed that tonight. She couldn't be caught unaware when Frank arrived. That had cost her dearly the last time she had visited the Cliff House, and she had vowed not to let it happen again.

Grace picked up her water glass and purse and scooted around to the chair to Isabelle's right. The seat afforded her a view of the doors and of Andrew and Charlotte. *I need to talk to Charlotte about her offer to help me, but I'm afraid of going anywhere near Andrew. I can't afford another misstep with Frank.*

From her new vantage point, Grace perused the room and clutched her purse in her lap with gloved hands. Her fingers gripped the bag a little tighter than usual, the outline of the flask distinct inside it. Sarah would probably wonder why the whiskey decanter in the study was lower than usual. The whiskey, along with the flask, were gifts Frank would appreciate. *He said to be ready, and I am, but he certainly isn't.* Grace inhaled a shaky breath, making sure a pleasant smile remained on her face for Isabelle's sake.

"Are you excited to be going home soon?" Isabelle's question jolted Grace back to the present.

Grace tapped her foot on the floor, scrambling for a believable answer. "I—um, yes. Well, maybe not as much as I should be. I'll miss everyone, and I'll miss this place. It'll be cold and snowy in Denver before long, and I'm sure I'll miss the ocean and the warm weather."

Isabelle chuckled, and Grace eyed the dining room doors. Frank still hadn't arrived.

"You said something." Grace turned to Isabelle. "The first day we came here, about the Cliff House being a place where you could dream."

Isabelle's face brightened momentarily, then dimmed. "Yes, I used to do that here, but not so much anymore."

Grace laid her gloved hand on Isabelle's. Grace wished she could have done more to help Isabelle, to thank her for the courage she had instilled in Grace. How unfair it seemed for Grace to be chasing her dream while Isabelle wouldn't be able to pursue hers.

"You were right." Grace paused to soak in the decadent ambiance of the dining room. "This is a place where someone can dream." *And now part of my dream is coming true. I'm going to school, I'm going to become a teacher, and I'm ridding myself of the only man who can ruin my life.* "This place, along with our time on the beach and our teas at Charlotte's, is what I'll remember most."

Isabelle nodded, but Grace sensed her cousin was only being polite.

Grace leaned closer to Isabelle. "You're going to be a nurse one day, Isa," Grace said, her voice edged with intent. "You're the bravest woman I know, and you *will* be rewarded for it. Maybe not in Los Angeles, and maybe not right away, but you'll be the best nurse any hospital could have. I'm so thankful we've had this time together to get to know each other."

Isabelle's eyes grew glassy.

Grace patted her arm. "You've inspired me to do things I never thought I could."

Isabelle wiped away a tear and whispered a thank-you to her cousin.

"Now then," Grace said, straightening in her chair. "I'm going to go talk to Maude. Would you like to join me?"

Isabelle declined. "I'm going to take a minute and then go talk to Rosaline's daughter."

Grace and Isabelle parted ways, Grace scanning the room, almost afraid of spotting Frank in the crowd. He still hadn't arrived, but he would. This time, she was ready.

Having spent the last twenty minutes speaking to Maude, Grace glanced up as Frank Buchanan strolled into the dining room. She had nearly missed him thanks to being distracted by Harriet's latest piece of gossip. Grace had shifted around to the side of the group, but when she noticed she was facing the dark ocean, she had startled. She had pulled Maude aside to talk and, in the process, repositioned herself to face the doors.

Despite everything that had transpired between Grace and Frank, the sight of him still tugged at her heart. He had outdone himself tonight in a black suit and burgundy tie. *He is handsome, but handsome men sometimes do terrible things to women.* She swallowed hard and excused herself from her conversation with Maude. She crossed the room, a smile blooming on her face. By the time she stopped in front of him, she was beaming.

"Mr. Buchanan, how nice to see you tonight." She extended a gloved hand. *Oh, those wolfish eyes and that sly grin. How they used to thrill me with the promise of adventure and more.* He took her hand and kissed it, her pulse quickening. "Would you have a moment?" she asked in her most innocent voice. "I have something for you."

A smile quirked at the edge of Frank's mouth.

"Wonderful. Let's step into the hall."

Frank motioned for Grace to go ahead, and the pair left the dining room. Grace walked down the hall, her head held high despite the terror that coursed through her. She wondered if she might faint. *My future hangs in the balance, as does my reputation and possibly my life.* She turned down one of the dimly lit corridors that led back to a few private sitting rooms, Frank close behind her. Though she could sense his interest in being near her was based on curiosity and attraction, she still couldn't forget how he had pinned her against the wall. It was all she could do not to shrink from him.

"Frank, I wanted to—" Grace stopped and faced him, pausing to collect herself. What she would say next galled her. "I wanted to apologize for how I behaved with Andrew the last time we were here. It was wrong of me to do something that made you not trust me, and I've—"

"I need to apologize too." Frank wiped his mouth with the back of his hand and stared at the floor. "I—my temper—I said some things I shouldn't have. It's just, I love you, Grace, and I—"

She laid a gloved hand on his arm and gazed into his eyes, heat rising on her neck. *I can't believe I apologized for something that wasn't wrong, and I can't believe I have to comfort him for a lily-livered apology that doesn't include him admitting he should've never threatened me.*

"I know you love me." Her steady voice barely masked the fear mixed with anger rising within her. "And I know your temper sometimes gets the best of you. I want to let bygones be bygones, so I bought you this."

She opened her purse and withdrew the flask; the silver plate gleamed in the dimly lit corridor.

"Now, this is very special," she said, "and you must promise me that you won't drink from it until you get home."

Frank eyed the flask like a greedy child would a bowl of candy.

"I filled it with the good whiskey from Uncle James's study." Grace giggled with devilish glee and handed Frank the flask.

He accepted it and chuckled. When he unscrewed the cap, Grace held her breath. *He can't take even one sip!*

"What did I tell you?" she teased, her heart hammering in her chest.

When she reached for the flask, Frank pulled it away.

"I wanna smell it." He ran the flask beneath his nose. "That *is* the good stuff. You're a clever one. I'll have to watch you close, or you're liable to pull more wool over my eyes when we're married."

Grace smiled slyly at him. "I'll do no such thing."

"Yes, you would." Frank grinned.

He recapped the flask and stepped forward, causing Grace's breath to catch in her throat. For a terrifying second, she wondered if he might be so bold as to kiss her on the lips. Instead, he gently touched her shoulder and leaned forward, his cheek brushing hers.

"What do you think about a week from Tuesday?" Frank whispered in her ear. "That be too soon?"

He studied her face, and Grace forced herself to hold his gaze.

"That'd be fine." She laid her hand on his arm again.

But it won't be soon enough.

Frank's toothy grin assured her that she had played the moment to perfection.

"Remember, this is only for you." Grace motioned to the flask as Frank tucked it into an inside coat pocket. "I think you're really going to enjoy it."

"I know I will." He waggled his eyebrows.

Grace convinced Frank they shouldn't be seen returning to the dining room together. She lingered in the corridor, the sounds of his retreating footsteps swallowed by the carpet. *I've done it, and there's no going back.* Blood roared in her ears. *I can only hope Frank behaves himself and doesn't drink from the flask until he gets home.*

With the coast clear, Grace hurried up the hall and into the lavatory. She checked the pins in her hair in the mirror and inhaled a few ragged breaths. *Please don't send me to hell for this, Lord. It was a dastardly thing, but it was my only way out of this terrible situation.* She cleared her throat and tried to steady her shaken nerves. *It's done, and it's going to be all right. Now all I have to do is write to Charlotte and have her help me with the next part of my plan.*

FIFTY-FOUR

The Monday evening after the McCormicks' engagement party, Henry stood before the armoire mirror in Josephine's childhood bedroom and removed his tie. He had spent the better part of the afternoon at work trying to decide how to best tell Josephine he was divorcing her. To James's credit, he had intimated nothing to the family and had told Henry he would have a letter of recommendation ready for him by the end of the week. When James had left for lunch, Henry had called and reserved a room at the Fairmont Hotel.

Henry hung his tie on a hook inside the armoire and turned when Josephine walked through the door. The way she could light up a room was one of the things he still loved about her. It would also make it harder to do what he knew he must.

"How was your day?" Henry attempted to make idle conversation.

"It was good." She sat down at her dressing table. "Now that the morning sickness is settling down, I'm feeling a little better."

Henry winced. *Feeling better will be short-lived after what I'm about to say.*

He closed the bedroom door and took a seat on the bed behind Josephine's chair.

She faced him, her brow furrowed. "What's wrong?"

"Josephine." Henry's heart beat wildly in his chest. "I know the baby isn't mine."

Her eyes widened, and the color drained from her face. Her

fingers gripped her chair back until her knuckles turned white. "What—what do you mean?" she sputtered. "Of course it's—"

Henry held up his hand. "I know it isn't because I have an outstanding memory, and I can count. And as much as it pains me, I've decided not to ask whose it is. I will ask that you at least honor me by admitting the truth."

Tears sprang to Josephine's eyes, and she lowered her head. Henry fretted his hands; it was all he could do not to take her in his arms and comfort her. But this wasn't like comforting Isabelle, whose honorable intentions hadn't come to fruition. This was his wife, who had devastated him in the worst possible way.

"It's not." A sob nearly choked Josephine, and she joined him on the bed. "I'm so terribly sorry. I do love you; I really do. Can you please forgive me? I was such a fool, a fool who made a terrible mistake."

Henry's hands trembled. *Fool or not, my heart's shattered, and I can't forgive her.* "I'll be serving you with divorce papers. I'll also be leaving San—"

Josephine gasped and covered her mouth with both hands, more tears spilling down her cheeks. Henry grasped her shoulders for fear she might scream. Had she believed he would stay despite knowing the child wasn't his? Henry shook his head. Josephine had been a fool who had made a terrible mistake, but Henry refused to compound the situation by staying and being a cuckold. Like Josephine, his heart was broken, albeit for vastly different reasons.

"I'll be leaving San Francisco, and our new home will be sold. I'm leaving you all the proceeds," he said.

Sobs continued to rack Josephine's body.

"You can live here with your parents or find other suitable arrangements."

Her eyes widened again, which confirmed Henry's suspicions. There were no other suitable arrangements. Having discovered Josephine's pregnancy, her lover had spurned her. She would be left to live with her parents until she could find another man willing to marry a woman with a child. But why had she done it? A lump rose in Henry's throat, and sorrow welled in his chest. Josephine continued to weep quietly. *Why did she have to be so cruel when all I ever did was love her?* Though Henry hated what Josephine had done, he still loved her and probably always would. But the illusion of the type of love he thought he had with her had been irreparably destroyed.

Henry rose, Josephine's eyes pleading with him, tears still streaming down her face.

"Dinner will be ready soon. I'm going to let you collect yourself before then," he said.

He walked to the door and reached for the knob.

"How long do I have?" Josephine asked.

He turned, his heart aching. She wiped her cheek with the back of her hand. *She means how long does she have until she has to admit what she did to her mother.* Henry inhaled sharply. *My heavens, this may end Margaret, but I simply cannot stay.*

"I'll be moving out in early September." Though Henry wanted to hurry from the room, he found himself rooted in place.

"Does"—Josephine wiped her nose with her finger—"does anyone else know?"

Henry paused. *If she's angry at me for telling James first, so be it.*

"Only your father, and only recently," Henry said. "He's agreed to my proposal about the house and knows when I'm leaving."

Josephine nodded and wiped away more tears.

"I'll see you at dinner." Henry left the room and clicked the door closed behind him.

FIFTY-FIVE

Two evenings after telling his wife he was divorcing her, Henry sat at the dining room table in his usual spot next to Josephine. He winked at Margaret when she asked him to pass the steaming bowl of new potatoes in cream sauce. *How comforting to have her back eating with us, and how painful it'll be when I go. She's been like another mother to me, and I'm still not sure if she'll forgive me for leaving Josephine.*

He passed the potatoes and then concentrated on his roast chicken and broccoli.

"We won't talk shop at the table long." James waved his fork in the air before plunging it into a piece of chicken. "Did you file the paperwork with the lawyers for that project down at the shipyards, my boy?"

Henry bit his lip to keep from smiling. It had infuriated him that James sometimes referred to him as "my boy" once he had married Josephine. Over the past two-plus years, however, Henry had begun to view the term as complimentary and mildly affectionate. Over time, James had come to remind Henry of his uncle in Pennsylvania. Both men had made him feel like a welcome and valued member of the family. *I'll miss James, even though I won't miss the corruption.*

"I did," Henry said.

"Good, good . . . ," James mumbled, stuffing a large piece of chicken into his mouth. He chewed for a moment, then waved his fork again. "Forgot to tell you." James hadn't quite finished his bite, and a morsel of chicken escaped his mouth and landed on his plate.

Margaret drew back in her chair and tutted in displeasure.

"Graham called," James continued. "Said Frank Buchanan didn't show up at a meeting earlier today. Strange really. He was always so eager to be in on the action."

Grace coughed several times, choking on her bite of food. "I'm sorry, excuse me," she squeaked. She patted her chest twice and reached for her water glass. Several sips later, her coughing ceased.

Henry blinked, alarm bells sounding in his head. Before he could ponder the matter further, Margaret spoke. "Maybe he was sick. The girls and I took tea at the Cliff House today, and the parlor was aflutter."

Henry leaned so far forward in his attempt to hear his mother-in-law that he almost baptized his tie in cream sauce.

"Harriet said something was amiss with the oysters at Graham and Rosaline's daughter's party. Several people became quite ill, including Maude," Margaret said.

Henry swallowed hard. He could have been one of those people. He had downed four oysters and found them delicious.

"That's terrible," James said.

"It *was*," Margaret continued. "Harriet said the head chef was fit to be tied, and the entire kitchen staff was called to account by the management."

Margaret returned to her chicken and potatoes, her face etched with smug satisfaction at having been able to contribute a tasty morsel of gossip to the conversation.

"They should've been," James blustered, nearly knocking over his water glass. "Can't have people getting sick, especially there. One of the only decent places left to eat in this town since the disaster."

Henry chewed his bite of chicken, struggling to determine what was more important: that Frank Buchanan hadn't shown up at a meeting or that people had gotten sick. He decided that Frank's absence was the greater mystery. Frank had never missed a meeting or the opportunity to rub elbows with Graham and James's business associates. Graham had also grumbled a couple of times that he had lost more than his fair share of money to Frank at cards. Henry struggled to swallow his mouthful of chicken, a sense of unease overtaking him. *I hate to think the worst, but something's happened to Frank. I doubt he was at home sick from eating oysters.*

Grace cleared her throat and Henry darted his eyes in her direction, his breathing growing shallow. Hadn't Cora mentioned a food-poisoning incident at a party held at Grace's house? And hadn't Grace's then-suitor disappeared after that party? Henry's pulse ticked faster. Had Grace tried to poison Frank Buchanan? Was Frank lying dead in a motel somewhere? More important, why and how would she do that?

Henry had certainly noticed odd moments of tension between Grace and Mr. Buchanan during their few times together. But nothing had come of it. Grace had appeared more interested in Andrew Kepler than anyone else, and Grace and Frank had rarely been in each other's company. Henry arched his eyebrows and took a bite of broccoli. *I may never know.*

Henry pushed sordid thoughts of Frank Buchanan aside and watched the others enjoy their dinner. His spirits sank when he contemplated his future. Regardless of the chaos at the office and in San Francisco, the Hamiltons had always eaten as a family each night around a lovely table full of food. It was so much more than Henry had experienced as a child. Meals had been plentiful at his aunt and uncle's home, but the conversation hadn't. The Hamiltons provided both. Henry picked at what remained of his chicken. He would be eating simple fare when he moved to Los Angeles and desperately wanted to delay the inevitable loneliness that would accompany his return to bachelorhood. *I won't miss the drama of working for James, but I'll miss this family. And despite her crushing disregard for our marriage, I'll miss Josephine too.*

FIFTY-SIX

Grace had wondered if she might suddenly expire from choking on an exceptionally dry bite of roast chicken when Uncle James had mentioned that Frank hadn't shown up for their business meeting. What had shocked Grace most was the coincidental food poisoning at the McCormicks' engagement party. Josephine had expressed apologies about Charles's disappearance shortly after Grace had arrived in San Francisco, so the family knew that there had been a similar incident in Denver. But Charles hadn't been sick at the party, and Grace still didn't understand why he had disappeared or what had become of him. She cut her eyes toward her aunt, uncle, and eldest cousin. *I hope they don't think I poisoned the oysters.* She shifted in her chair, struggling to calm her frayed nerves. *It's terrible that others got sick. It was such a lovely party, other than what happened to Frank afterward.*

With the second, and blessedly last, of her volatile and pugnacious beaus gone, Grace was torn between immense relief and soul-crushing shame. The cure to both ailments, of course, was more apple brown Betty. When Sarah returned to the dining room, Grace asked if there was any more whipped cream. Josephine might as well have licked the bowl when she had scraped nearly every last bit of it onto her dessert. To Grace's delight, Sarah appeared minutes later with a fresh batch of the delicious topping. Grace helped herself to a large dollop. As she savored the buttery crumbs and sweet apples, she tried to steady herself, her emotions unwinding. Despite risking eternal damnation, her plan had worked. She would never need to worry about Frank Buchanan again.

There was enough strychnine in that flask to kill a couple head of cattle.

Grace forked in another bite of dessert, willing her hand not to shake. Rye whiskey was the perfect drink to mask the taste of bitter strychnine. She had suffered through a nerve-racking comedy of errors when she had ground up the fifteen one-sixtieth-grain tablets of strychnine using only the heel of her boot and Frank's letters as a base. One tablet had escaped from beneath her boot heel, ricocheted off the foot of the dressing table, and disappeared under the armoire. She had retrieved it along with a tuft of dust, only to have another tablet fly under the bedside table. In the midst of grinding up the tablets, she had stopped and covered her face with her hands, tears rolling down her cheeks. She was going to kill the man who had saved her from Charles, the same man she had once loved. What she was doing was so egregiously wrong that she had nearly vomited and abandoned her plan.

Despite her father's enduring disinterest in Grace, the man possessed certain medicines that could cure and kill. Thankfully, he had also practiced medicine at home since she was a child. Grace had made a careful study of the purpose of each substance he regularly kept on his shelves. At the prescribed dosage of one-sixtieth of a grain, strychnine gave Grace's heart the boost it needed in Denver's thin air. It also helped stimulate her appetite. There was no mystery as to why she was losing weight. She couldn't eat a thing once she discovered Charles was nothing more than a brute in sheep's clothing and a tawdry cad with no regard for her reputation or feelings. That was how a bottle of one of the most potent substances known to man had come with Grace to San Francisco. That bottle, still stowed in the bottom of her train case, had provided her with the perfect solution to an otherwise unsolvable problem.

Grace tried to savor her last bite of apple brown Betty. Her mouth was not quite empty; a crumb tumbled onto her plate, and Isabelle giggled. Grace wiped her mouth with her napkin and took a sip of water. She swallowed hard, a bit of dessert lodged in her throat. Though Grace enjoyed the gruesome mystery novels her younger brother read, she had never thought herself capable of killing anything, let alone another human being. But Frank had all but insisted. In his letters and actions, he had prescribed the type of future they would have together. Grace would be trapped like a prisoner in a gilded cage, her world limited to what Frank deemed appropriate. And to Grace's horror, he had also insinuated at the Cliff House that he might have killed his previous wife. The prospect of an isolated existence and the threat to her life were beyond what Grace could tolerate. *I would've ended up like my sister-in-law or worse.* Tendrils of revulsion and disgust shimmied up Grace's spine, and she winced, recalling the occasional bruises she had sometimes spied beneath her sister-in-law's eye.

Grace scraped the remaining dessert crumbs into a pile and scooped them onto her fork. She wanted to trust that she had done the right thing. The knowledge that she had killed a man would be a burden she would bear until the day she died. But it would be a different burden than being Frank's wife, and she could live with that burden knowing she had saved herself and possibly others from his cruelty. Frank would never hurt her or any other woman again. As dreadful as the deed was, ending Frank Buchanan might have been the most unselfish thing Grace had ever done.

Having finished her bite of crumbs, Grace set her fork on her plate, her nerves refusing to settle. Chances were good that Frank had downed a little of the whiskey on his ride home. He would have felt the effects immediately and had probably died at Mary's house. Grace exhaled a silent breath. She had avoided all the nasty business surrounding Frank's demise: the struggle after he had taken the first few sips from the flask, the reaction of his overwhelmed body as it went into paralysis, the sight of his pale and lifeless corpse, like those she had seen through the keyhole of her father's office. She licked her lips, her mouth dry. If the knowledge of her misdeed and the risk of an irredeemable soul were the prices to pay for her crime, she would find a way to endure them with dignity and silence. They had purchased her freedom, and, she hoped, a life of peace.

Grace wiped her mouth with her napkin and took a sip of water. Her time in San Francisco was drawing to a close, much more quickly than anyone else in the dining room knew. Her wary eyes swept from one family member to the next, nostalgia welling within her. *I'll miss them. They've shown me how wonderful a family can be, or at least a family that cares about me and doesn't treat me like something to be fobbed off like a broodmare.*

After dinner, Grace returned to her bedroom and discovered an envelope peeking out from under the edge of her pillow. For once, her pulse didn't race in fear. *It can't be from Frank, thank heavens. And it also can't be from Charlotte; I just mailed something to her today.*

Grace picked up the letter and sat down at her dressing table. The elegant script on the envelope could only belong to a woman. Grace tore open the envelope, and when she unfolded the letter, two one-hundred-dollar bills and a twenty-dollar bill fluttered to the floor.

She gasped and scrambled to retrieve the money. "What's *this*?" She laid the bills on her dressing table and began to read.

> *Dear Grace,*
>
> *It is with the greatest sorrow that I write to you today. Your fiancé and my beloved brother, Benjamin, died early Sunday morning. The police are still investigating, as it seems he was poisoned. By the time he crawled through our front door, he could no longer speak. He*

passed quickly, though I'm crushed to say, in great pain. I may never forgive myself for not accompanying him to the Cliff House the night before his death. I didn't feel it proper to attend the engagement party, as I didn't know the McCormicks well.

Though I loved my brother, you and I both know that he, at times, was not the kindest of men. It aggrieved me to watch how disrespectful he was to you at your uncle's birthday party. I also feared he might have had words with you at the Cliff House when you left the dining room with him for a short time. He assured me that nothing in your conversation was untoward, but I'm not proud to admit that I have my doubts.

Ben was a man of many vices, but his love for you was not one of them. I was honored to keep his engagement to you a secret, and in that vein, I wanted to send along some of the money he recently won playing cards. I hope you don't find the money tainted, given how it came to him. In my heart, I believe that Ben would have wanted you, as his betrothed, to have this money.

Know that you are in my thoughts and prayers during this difficult time, and I wish you nothing but safe travels as you return home to Denver.

With sincerest sympathy,

Mary

Grace set the letter aside and scowled. She grabbed the three bills from the dressing table, stowed them in her train case, and returned to her chair. Grace was relieved beyond words that Mary hadn't accompanied Frank to the McCormicks' engagement party. She was also astonished and thankful that Mary had chosen to send her Frank's gambling winnings. What stung and angered Grace, though, was that Frank had clearly not mentioned to Mary that Grace would be attending the California State Normal School for teachers. *Had he planned on making me give up my place at school?* She stared hard at herself in the mirror. *Probably.*

Grace rose, pulled her white shawl from the foot of her bed around her shoulders, and gazed out the window at the twinkling stars. She tapped a fingernail on the glass.

I must be careful.

She shivered and goose bumps rose on her arms. She was so close to freedom, so close to starting her new life. Her escape would scandalize her family, in both San Francisco and Denver. The letter she would send to her parents from Los Angeles would shock them, but they wouldn't object to her schooling in the end. They would smooth away any gossip, speculation, or raised eyebrows by concocting a story to their liking. Her mother would worry quietly while her father would shrug and return to his medical practice.

"It'll all be worth it," Grace whispered. "Once I'm a teacher, I'll be more than someone they can ignore like a servant or sell off like a prized heifer. I have a chance to fulfill my dreams, and I have Jacob, Isabelle, Mary, and the rest of this family to thank for it."

FIFTY-SEVEN

On August 23, the Friday after the McCormicks' engagement party and the mysterious disappearance of Frank Buchanan, Grace sat at her dressing table after breakfast and drummed her fingers on her thigh. Her eyes burned with exhaustion thanks to spending the last several days wondering if she would be able to escape San Francisco unscathed. She reread Mary's letter, courage building in her chest.

The two hundred and twenty dollars from Mary, the twenty-five dollars from Jacob, and the money Grace could make from selling her grandmother's earrings would more than cover room and board for her first year of school. By the time that year ended, she would have met enough people that she should be making some money by teaching piano and voice lessons. *It's the best I can do, and I will graduate.* She rose, hurried to the armoire, and tucked the letter into her carpetbag.

Charlotte had invited Grace to accompany her and her family on a supposed overnight trip to Yosemite National Park. That Grace wasn't actually going to the park made packing that much easier. *I can buy a new cotton dress or two when I get to Los Angeles, but I'd like to take a few of my satin ones in case I'm invited to any parties.* She tucked her bloomers and stockings into her train case and stared at the new mallard-blue cotton dress that had been delivered from Walters Dress Shop the prior day. *It'll be a wrinkled mess, but I must have something nice to change into to meet the faculty secretary about approved lodging. And I certainly don't want Father's money going to waste.* Grace snickered, rolling the dress up and mashing it into the train case.

"Grace?" A knock sounded on the door, and Grace's stomach leaped into her throat. Had the police arrived to speak to Uncle James and Henry about Frank's disappearance? What if they wanted to speak to her?

"Come in." Grace forced her voice to remain steady.

Isabelle opened the door carrying a long black coat, which she laid on Grace's bed. "I hear it can get chilly in the forest this time of year, especially in the evening."

Relief washed over Grace, and she held up the garment. *She's so kind, always thinking of others. I must make sure she knows how she can retrieve it.* "Thank you. I'm sure it'll be useful."

To Grace's dismay, Isabelle made herself comfortable on the bed. "Are you excited to see the sequoias? I've heard they're spectacular, but we've never been."

"I am," Grace lied, returning to the armoire. "We have pines in Colorado, but nothing like the giant trees in Yosemite."

I wonder if she's jealous and confused about why Charlotte didn't invite her. Grace forced a prim smile, willing her cousin to leave. *I'm sure she also finds it odd that Charlotte's parents are hauling their weak-hearted daughter into the wilds of California for an outdoor trip, but it was the best story Charlotte and I could concoct on such short notice.*

Grace glanced at her train case; it sat on her bed nearly stuffed to the brim. She pulled open two more armoire drawers as if searching for something, the silence in the room growing so loud Grace almost couldn't stand it. *I'm happy to have spent the summer with her, and there's so much I need to tell her, but not right now, and certainly not in person. I know I'm being rude, but she simply must get out!*

A few moments later, the silence must have finally become too much for Isabelle, because she rose and walked to the door. "I'll let you get back to packing."

"Thank you again for the coat," Grace said. "It'll come in handy."

Isabelle closed the door behind her, and Grace blew out her cheeks.

Fifteen minutes later, Grace had repacked her train case so it had a much better sense of order. It was still overstuffed, but she couldn't very well arrive in Los Angeles with only the dress on her back. She paused in her dressing table chair, her heart a tangle of emotions. She needed to find the words to thank the Hamiltons for welcoming her into their home and treating her like a beloved member of the family. Leaving San Francisco, however, was the only way she would be able to put the terrible business with Frank Buchanan to rest once and for all.

Most men had flasks like the one she had gifted Frank. There had also been so many people at the engagement party that Grace couldn't imagine anyone would suspect her of killing him. And if Frank's letters were any indication, he had made plenty of enemies amongst the men with whom he played cards. Grace had spent the last few days trying to convince herself that one of those men would be the prime suspect in Frank's death.

Grace stared at the blank page before her, her pen poised. *I'll pay Sarah to deliver the letter promptly at four thirty, and I will not mention Frank.*

After a few moments of debate, Grace began:

> *Dear Isabelle,*
> *Thank you for the most incredible summer. I will always be in your debt, you being so kind as to show*

me the beauty of San Francisco. It's a lively city, and I'm certain that men like your father, Graham, and Henry will make business boom here again.

What I have to say next may come as a shock, but I felt it only proper to tell you first. I, like you, secretly applied to school. I've been accepted into the California State Normal School, beginning my first term in September. I'm going to be a kindergarten teacher, Isa. Can you believe it? I had expected to be married when I arrived at school, and sadly, as you know, that is no longer the case. Despite my doubts and fears, the encouragement and support from you and Charlotte convinced me that I can complete my studies as a woman on my own. Because of you, I'm bravely forging ahead, more determined than ever to attend school and teach in Los Angeles.

Though I'll miss you all terribly, I depart on this afternoon's train. I'm hopeful that my time in school will be the beginning of a new and happier chapter in my life. Charlotte has your coat, and you may call on her to retrieve it whenever you like. Please don't be angry at us for our deception. Also, please don't scold Sarah for not giving you this letter sooner. I paid her to deliver it once I knew I would be away.

Know that I wish you all the happiness in the world, Isabelle. I will never forget our times together at the spectacular white palace perched by the sea. The Cliff House is truly the best place to dream. I'm confident you will become a nurse, and I look forward to hearing about your studies, whether they be in Los Angeles or San Francisco. The fine people of either city will be better off having someone so caring and devoted as you watching over them in their time of need.

> *Please ask your parents not to call Mother and*
> *Father. I will write to them and share my joyous news*
> *when I settle in. Give the rest of the family my best and*
> *thank them for being so kind to me during my visit.*
> *Best wishes and many thanks from your cousin,*
> *Grace*

Grace blew on the letter, folded it carefully, and slid it into an envelope. She tucked it into her pocket alongside a dime. Grace straightened in her chair, her breath tremulous. Her choice to strike out alone was one in a long line of choices she had made in California. It was one in a long line of choices that had finally convinced her that she had to begin to try to trust herself again. Though the prospect of going to a new city as an unmarried woman frightened her a little, most of all, it thrilled her. *It's not the first decision that has both frightened and thrilled me, and it won't be the last.* She smiled to herself.

A knock sounded on the door and Grace startled.

"Miss Grace?" Sarah called from the hall. "Miss Gordon is here."

Grace rose and hurried to the door. When she opened it, she was greeted by the maid and the butler.

"Yes, George." Grace motioned behind her. "The train case and coat are all I'm taking. Please stay a moment, Sarah."

George picked up the two items and disappeared down the hall, leaving Sarah alone with Grace.

Grace pulled the letter from her pocket and handed it to Sarah along with a dime. "For Isabelle, but not until four thirty. That is all."

"Yes, miss." Sarah tucked the coin and letter into her pocket and padded away.

Grace surveyed the room one last time, her eyes lingering on the two satin dresses she had left in the armoire. *Isabelle can have them. She'll be the best-dressed nurse in all of San Francisco.*

Grace stepped into the hall, closed the door, and walked toward her future.

FIFTY-EIGHT

ater that afternoon, Isabelle trudged up the stairs, her hand resting on her stomach. She, Josephine, and Margaret had recently returned from a gathering at Harriet and Maude's, where Isabelle had indulged in too many slices of chocolate cake. She was so full she felt like she was carrying a sack of potatoes. Not that she had ever carried a sack of potatoes before, but she imagined this was the herculean effort it took to move one up a flight of stairs.

In her bedroom, she sat down at her dressing table and checked her hair in the mirror. Moments later, Sarah's reflection appeared behind her. The maid stood outside the door, an envelope in her hand. Isabelle's heart leaped; was it her acceptance letter from the nursing school? She hopped up and hurried across the room.

"She said not to give it to you until now," Sarah said, her eyes solemn.

Isabelle's spirits sank when Sarah handed her the envelope. It wasn't the letter she wanted, but that wasn't Sarah's fault.

"Thank you." Isabelle closed the door and returned to her bed.

Isabelle frowned and opened the envelope. *Why would Grace leave a letter if she'll only be gone for the weekend?*

Isabelle began reading and gasped. "She applied to school in secret and got in!" she whispered in an excited hiss. "And she's right; running off to Los Angeles alone is a shock."

After Isabelle had finished reading, she had every intention of taking Grace's letter downstairs and sharing it with her mother and sister. Instead, she remained on her bed. Grace's letter was yet another reminder of what Isabelle didn't have. Her dreams of becoming a nurse were all but gone. *Grace is one more woman getting what she wants while I'm not. Why is life so unfair sometimes?*

Though jealousy threatened to dampen Isabelle's excitement, what she felt most for her cousin was pride. Isabelle had underestimated Grace. Not only had her cousin been brave enough to apply to school, but she had also been daring enough to go without help or the approval of a husband or either of her parents. *But how will she ever pay for it?* A wan smile spread across Isabelle's face. Grace could play the piano, sing, and also draw. *Maybe she took my advice and plans to offer lessons.*

Isabelle crawled off of her bed and crossed the room. When she reached the door, she stopped. *I'm happy for her. I'm happy that despite losing her beaus and not getting married, she decided to follow her heart and go to school.*

Though nagging doubts about her own future still clouded Isabelle's mind, she opened her door and stepped into the hall. *I'll figure out how to make my dream come true, one way or another.*

FIFTY-NINE

Henry and James returned home from work that evening only to be waylaid in the foyer by the women of the household. Isabelle kept saying how shocking and exciting something was, while Margaret's dismayed comments added only worry and intrigue to the mysterious subject. Meanwhile, Josephine chattered nonstop and tugged first at Henry's arm and then at her father's. Henry wondered if it was because she had something to add to the conversation or was simply annoyed by their lack of attention.

"What's this, what are you—stop talking over one another," James blustered. He removed his suit coat and handed it to Sarah.

Margaret held up her hands, and the family fell silent. "Everyone into the sitting room."

The Hamiltons strode out of the foyer, Margaret clutching James's arm. "You simply won't believe what she's done," she whispered.

We won't believe what who's done? Henry trailed behind the others, his concern growing.

In the sitting room, Margaret pressed James into an armchair, and Isabelle parked herself on the edge of the chair opposite her father. Josephine pulled Henry awkwardly onto the settee. He landed with a thump and grunted in protest, extricating his arm from his wife's clutches.

"Grace has gone to Los Angeles to go to teaching school!"

Isabelle clasped her hands together, her face the picture of sheer delight.

Margaret huffed out an indignant snort. "Isabelle, I should've been—"

"It was in her letter to me, Mother. I should be the one to tell."

Henry almost laughed. Isabelle abhorred gossip but obviously had no trouble sharing it when it suited her. And Grace! She had apparently given up her "unsuitable" suitor from Denver and stunned everyone by running off to pursue an education.

James raised his eyebrows and tilted his head. "Well, that's quite the shock. Can't say my brother will be pleased. I think he was hoping she might find a fellow here, someone like that Andrew."

Henry bit his tongue to keep from grinning. James had been right that day on the beach. Andrew was a big fish, but instead of Isabelle or Grace landing him, Grace had tossed him back and sailed away alone. *But it still doesn't explain who sent Grace those letters, and I refuse to believe they were from a friend in Cheyenne.* Henry frowned.

Josephine sighed in exasperation. "Father, it's *scandalous*! She's going to a new city alone where she doesn't know anyone except Andrew. What if something happens to her? And what if you're right? What if she actually has run off with Andrew? He never properly called on her. Don't you see what this will do to her reputation? People may think the story about her going to school is a ruse and that she left town quickly for all the wrong reasons." Josephine arched a brow at her father.

Isabelle waved a hand and scoffed at her sister.

Henry caught Josephine glancing at him. *She can't look at me because she's ashamed. She hasn't told her mother about her illegitimate child and our divorce. If she were genuinely concerned about a scandal, she wouldn't have behaved the way she did.*

James narrowed his eyes at Josephine. "Yes, but she made

her choice, didn't she, and now she'll have to live with whatever consequences come with it."

Josephine audibly inhaled and looked away. Henry admired James in silence. *That was close to the bone. It's true for every woman in this room and might be the most honest thing he's ever said.*

"Father, that's unkind," Isabelle protested. "We need to tell the truth. People will believe that she went to Los Angeles to go to school if we say she did. Women go to school all the time now. There's no reason for others not to believe Grace is going to be a teacher."

Josephine rolled her eyes, and Isabelle pulled a face at her sister.

"Girls." Margaret leveled a hard stare at her daughters. "We need to decide what to say," Margaret continued, her voice thick with urgency. "We can't have people thinking the worst." Margaret waved a finger at Josephine.

"I—what?" Josephine sputtered, her eyes widening.

"What you said, dear, about the wrong reasons."

Josephine rubbed her ruffled collar. Henry clenched his jaw in withering silence. *She thought her mother knew about the baby, and her heart was about to burst out of her chest.*

As the women and James figured out the story they would share about Grace's hasty departure, Henry's mind wandered back to the events that had recently transpired at the Cliff House. Grace had been polite but not flirtatious when she had danced with Andrew Kepler. Frank Buchanan had arrived and become angry with Grace. People had fallen ill thanks to tainted oysters. Frank had attended the McCormicks' engagement party and hadn't been seen since. Had Grace poisoned the oysters in an attempt to kill Frank? Or had she killed him another way? Henry swallowed hard, his stomach clenching. It was awful to think that she had killed him at all, but Henry doubted Frank had been called back to Cheyenne on business.

Henry returned his attention to the conversation, where Josephine and Isabelle were debating the finer points of reputation.

"But don't you see? That's how we can explain it," Isabelle insisted. "Grace wasn't impulsive, and she was always proper. That's what makes all of this more exciting. That she—"

"We could wait." Josephine's eyes gleamed in a way Henry had never seen before. "We could tell everyone that she had to return to Denver because Aunt Cora or her beau became ill and died unexpectedly. Charlotte's the only other person who knows what Grace has done, and she won't say anything to anyone if we ask her not to. In the meantime, you could call Uncle, Father, in Denver and find out where Grace is living. I'm sure it's with a family and not in some shady boardinghouse. We could say that after the funeral, she came back to California to go to school. That'd still be shocking and surprising, but it'd keep people from questioning her virtue or wondering if she had any connection to Andrew."

Henry haltingly turned to face his wife, a sinking feeling of horror overtaking him. *My God, no wonder she was able to carry on an affair without my knowing. Her mind works like those of many of the corrupt businessmen that are now rotting in jail.*

"Hmmm," James muttered, patting his vest pocket as if searching for something. "I—I need—"

"We're almost finished, dear, and then you can have a smoke," Margaret assured him.

Henry snickered. When James faced serious problems at work, the first thing he would reach for was a cigar. It reminded Henry of himself as a small child. He always sought his most cherished stuffed bear for comfort in times of distress.

James licked his lips and finally rose. "Well, you all decide what we'll say and let me know if I need to call my brother. I don't think the girl meant to cause anyone grief, but she could've handled the situation better. It'll be for her parents to sort out now. And someone speak to that Charlotte. Maybe she can shed more light on if anything was going on between Grace and Andrew."

James left the sitting room, and none of the women objected when Henry followed. As Henry trailed James up the hall toward the study, he was torn. He was surprised by what Grace had done and proud of her, prouder than he thought he would be given that he didn't know her very well. While he agreed with Isabelle that what Grace had done was exciting, he also understood Margaret and Josephine's concern. People would talk, and eyebrows would undoubtedly be raised. Some of those who had met Grace might believe she had secretly run off with Andrew Kepler. Grace's character might be questioned, but somehow Henry doubted it.

Josephine's concern about reputation is hard to swallow. Henry flared his nostrils. He followed his father-in-law into the study and bumped the door closed. *At least I won't be here when she decides what to tell her friends about her child.*

SIXTY

On Saturday, September 7, Isabelle and her family strolled along the beach, the Cliff House towering over the Pacific in the distance. Heat had settled over the city, the late-afternoon sun glowing behind a bank of clouds, the sky the color of thick cream.

Isabelle tiptoed to the edge of the surf and stared out at the water, her spirits ebbing like the ocean at low tide. The Cliff House had closed a few weeks earlier for improvements, and she wasn't sure when it would reopen. Though she didn't miss the mindless chatter of the women's parlor, she longed to stand on the balcony and pretend that she could fly away like the sandpipers that circled overhead.

"Look!" a man down the beach shouted.

Isabelle whirled toward where he was pointing and gasped. Smoke poured from the fourth-floor balcony of the Cliff House. Moments later, flames shattered the third-floor windows. In the distance, seals lounging on Seal Rocks roared in fright and flung themselves into the water. Isabelle's heart seized in her chest and she sprinted toward the fire.

"Isa, no!" Henry shouted from behind her.

Isabelle staggered to a halt and sank to her knees. Tears rolled down her cheeks, and she panted in exhaustion. She reached a hand toward the Cliff House; orange and yellow flames stretched toward the sky, enormous plumes of black smoke roiling behind them.

"No! Please, no!" Isabelle screamed, and buried her face in her hands, sinking farther into the sand.

The Cliff House, which had survived the inferno that had claimed most of San Francisco a little more than a year ago, was now being consumed by fire. Isabelle's last vestige of certainty and hope in a city that had endured so much loss would be gone in less than two hours. *It was where I could dream, and now, like my dream, it's gone, too.* Isabelle bent forward, tears streaming down her face. A keening wail rose deep within her. When she could no longer contain it, it burst forth so suddenly that she feared her lungs might explode.

A hand grasped her shoulder, and she flinched.

"Isa, come away." Henry knelt beside her and clutched her hand.

A few onlookers hurried past on their way to watch the fire.

Isabelle cried out and buried her face in Henry's chest. He helped her to her feet, and she wrapped an arm around his waist. She gulped for air through her sobs. How could this have happened? And where were the fire trucks?

"We're going home now. It's all going to be all right," Henry said.

Isabelle shook her head. *Nothing will ever be right again.*

"Come, dear. I'll help you to the car." Margaret wrapped her arm around Isabelle.

Isabelle shook as she shuffled through the sand next to her mother. At the edge of the beach, James helped Isabelle and Margaret into the backseat of the Winton. Isabelle sagged against the tufted leather, unable to bring herself to face the chaos at the far end of the beach. James hoisted himself into the driver's seat and fired the engine. He pulled the car onto the road, and Isabelle peeked one last time at the Cliff House. The beautiful white edifice that sat atop the rocks was now engulfed in roaring red tongues of flame.

Henry followed his in-laws home in the Buick, Josephine beside him, a trembling hand fluttering at her throat. Sorrow welled in Henry's heart and he bit the inside of his lip to keep tears from spilling onto his cheeks. With no word from the nursing school and one of her favorite places burning to the ground, Isabelle had to be devastated. Henry sniffed and tried to swallow away the lump in his throat. He, too, would miss the Cliff House. It was one of the few nice places one could go to enjoy a good meal and escape the pressures of daily life.

Cars rolled by and the Buick passed two couples out for a walk, the ladies' green and gold parasols now dull beneath the muted afternoon sun. Henry had missed his outings to the Cliff House. With his and Josephine's divorce not yet announced, he usually confined himself to the study at home and only ventured outside to get some air during his lunch hour on weekdays. A good long stroll on the beach, capped by a noon meal at the Cliff House, would certainly have lifted his spirits.

The car rounded a corner and Josephine spoke. "I wonder how the fire started."

Henry shook his head. In truth, he didn't want to know. What was important was that the Cliff House was gone, and with it, Isabelle's happiness.

"I'll miss it." Josephine's voice cracked.

Henry's brow furrowed for a moment. Isabelle had never been shy about sharing her love for the "gingerbread palace," but the emotion in Josephine's voice surprised him.

"We all will, Isa especially," Henry said.

"Yes," Josephine said, her voice distant. "She was right, you know. It really was a place of dreams."

Henry gripped the steering wheel tighter. He had had dreams once too, but the one he had shared with Josephine had shattered.

She had assured Henry she hadn't yet told her mother about their impending divorce or the reason for it. Henry licked his lips and inhaled a shaky breath. He was still deeply concerned about how Margaret would receive the news given her fragile heart. But the family had survived worse with Daniel's death. Somehow, they would survive again.

Henry turned left, and the car climbed up the hill, the streets devoid of people. Maybe it was better the Cliff House was gone. Word would spread quickly enough about his and Josephine's divorce. His neck warmed, and he clenched his jaw. He hoped Josephine would do him the honor of telling the truth about the parentage of her child; luckily he wouldn't be in San Francisco to find out. Much as the Cliff House would be rebuilt, a sentinel standing guard over the sea, Henry would heal his wounded heart, rise from the ashes of his broken marriage, and start anew in Los Angeles.

SIXTY-ONE

The Winton rolled to a stop along the curb, and Isabelle staggered out. She rushed up the front steps, burst into the house, and thundered up the stairs. Once in her room, she banged the door closed and lay sobbing on her bed. She shuddered and squeezed her eyes closed, willing away the horrible memories.

Everything was lost.

Grace had escaped to Los Angeles and, worryingly, hadn't been heard from since. Josephine and Henry would move into their new home in a few months. *But I won't be going anywhere.* She felt herself sinking into an unfathomable pit of desolation. Her dreams and the place she loved most had been reduced to piles of ash. Through her tears, Isabelle struggled to remind herself of how lucky she was. Her family had survived the earthquake, as had their home. Her mother was recovering well from her heart attack. Isabelle guessed that she could even bring up going to nursing school in San Francisco again, but feared that would only lead to more arguments with Margaret. Isabelle told herself she should be grateful, but grief numbed her senses, leaving her listless. She would remember this day as one of the worst of her life.

A knock sounded on her door, and Isabelle sat up and wiped the tears from her cheeks. *Please go away, Mother. I don't want to talk about it.* "Yes?"

Margaret opened the door and joined Isabelle on her bed.

"I'm truly sorry, dear," Margaret said, trying to soothe her. "I know you liked it there, and we had such fun times with the others in the parlor."

Isabelle bit her tongue to keep from screaming. She didn't miss the women's parlor with its gossip and talk of weather. She missed her majestic refuge with its ocean views.

She missed the idea of the place.

The Cliff House represented strength and solidity, a beacon able to withstand earthquakes, corrosive salt air, and the beating sun as it set each evening. Secretly, Isabelle believed she represented something much like the Cliff House: a nurse in a white uniform unharmed by danger, able to provide comfort to those who came to her in need of solace and healing. Isabelle sniffled and wiped her nose with the back of her hand. *If only it were as simple as missing Maude, Harriet, and the other ladies in the parlor.*

Margaret laid her hand on Isabelle's. "With it being closed, we can only hope that no one was hurt. In the meantime, we'll simply have to find another place to gather with our friends. Maybe that's something you and Charlotte and Violet could help plan. Would that make you feel better?"

Isabelle nodded, despite wanting to shake her head. *Mother will never understand.* It was as if 80 percent of the city hadn't been reduced to rubble in the past year, or as if the Cliff House hadn't consisted of so much more than wood and glass. Maybe Margaret couldn't understand Isabelle's devastation because the Hamiltons' house had been damaged during the quake but had survived. Or maybe it was because Margaret had gotten what she wanted. She had married, had children, and enjoyed her place in society. Her home—her place of dreams—was where they lived. But the Cliff House had been Isabelle's place of dreams, with its expansive balcony, long halls, sweeping views of the ocean, and regal turrets. It was gone now, much like Isabelle's hope for a better future.

Isabelle sniffled again. The Cliff House would never be rebuilt in the image of the one that had burned. Sometimes, when a city was reduced to dust or a dream or a building burned to ash, it might be rebuilt, but its soul would only live on as a shadow of its former self. It would never again recapture the spirit of the old city, the old dream, the old building. *And the sooner I start accepting that, the better off I'll be.*

Resigned, Isabelle stared at her hands. "Charlotte and I can plan a tea party soon."

"Thank you. That'll be nice for everyone." Margaret rose from the bed. "Now then, I'll ask Sarah to bring you up some tea. You rest for a while and we'll see you downstairs for dinner in a bit."

Isabelle smiled weakly at her mother, who left the room. Isabelle rose and wandered to her window, her gaze unfocused, tears still leaking from her eyes. *I'll figure something out. I'll accept my fate and bide my time and somehow make a new plan.* If Grace was brave enough to set off on her own, Isabelle would do the same. It was just a matter of how and when she could do it.

SIXTY-TWO

Isabelle sat in the sitting room on a Friday afternoon, her nose in a book. She had tried to concentrate but had reread the same two paragraphs without absorbing them. September was almost over, the green already bleeding from the leaves. Low clouds dotted the horizon. Isabelle had resigned herself to her fate of living at home while she tried to pick up the pieces of her life.

The sound of fire engines rose and fell in the distance, and Isabelle pressed her eyes closed. Two weeks had passed since the Cliff House had burned to the ground. Her throat clotted with emotion as she remembered reading the newspaper the following day. She had growled in frustration; the article had provided no additional details other than that the fire had started on the lower level of the building.

Isabelle sniffed and tried to find a more comfortable position on the settee. She had almost succeeded in losing herself in her book when Sarah appeared at the entrance to the sitting room.

"There's a letter for you, miss," the maid said.

Isabelle set her book aside and motioned for Sarah to enter the room. The maid handed Isabelle the letter and left.

Though Isabelle had given up on receiving anything from the California Hospital School for Nurses, a jolt of adrenaline coursed through her when she tore open the envelope. She opened the letter and let out a cry of surprise; it was from Grace.

Dear Isabelle,

I've settled in with a nice family in Los Angeles. There are two children in the house, a boy, aged five, and a girl, aged ten. The little girl tries but isn't very good at playing the piano. I'm pretending she is a student and am helping her learn her chords. The little boy is a lively fellow who is often into mischief. Still, he minds his parents and can be quite charming when he wants to be. I'm always relieved when he goes to bed each evening and the house is quiet.

School is proving to be as challenging and interesting as I had hoped it would be. Most of the other girls are as thrilled to be here as I am. Almost all of my classmates are from California, but a few are from Kansas or Iowa. At least I'm not the only one so far away from home. I'm going to join the Glee Club next term and can't wait to meet more first-year students like myself as the term progresses. I'm working off some of my board by helping with housework. It's taught me a lot, and so far, I've been able to do it and keep up with my studies without being too tired.

As you can imagine, Mother and Father were quite shocked and disappointed when I wrote and told them I was no longer in San Francisco. Mother scolded me so harshly on the phone that I almost cried. But now that I'm here, I have no intention of going back to Denver any time soon. Father's refusal to speak to me left me more wounded than I would care to admit.

Though it has taken some time, I've made peace with the choices I've made in California. Some of them were quite difficult but will serve me well both now and in the future. It has sometimes been very hard to accept *that I won't have a husband for the time being, but I'm enjoying my days more than I could have imagined.*

I hope you were able to use the dresses I left in the armoire. Maybe you wore one to the Cliff House for a special evening?

Please give Henry, Josephine, and your parents my best and tell them I think of them often. Also, please write when you get a moment and let me know how you are and what you're doing.

With many warm thoughts from your cousin,
Grace

Isabelle set the letter aside and stared out at Lafayette Park through the large window. She envied Grace and her life full of schoolwork and meeting new girls from faraway places. She envied her being in a bustling city full of sun and warmth. Isabelle shook her head. Grace had been so lucky.

Isabelle recalled the last few lines of Grace's letter with sadness. The dresses Grace had left behind hadn't fit, and Isabelle doubted Grace had read about the horrible demise of the Cliff House. Grace would mourn its loss, but not like Isabelle did. Isabelle would also need to find a way to give Grace's well wishes to Henry. It had been over a week since he had moved out, and Isabelle hadn't realized how much she would miss him. Margaret had become so hysterical when Josephine had told her, James, and Isabelle that Henry was divorcing her that Isabelle had feared the shock and scandal—and this was a true scandal, much more so than what Grace had done—surrounding Josephine might end her mother. After many tears shed by both Margaret and Josephine, Margaret had at least pretended to accept the sin her eldest daughter had committed. As if losing a second son, Margaret had embraced Henry for an agonizingly long minute on the day he had left.

Despite already knowing the truth, Isabelle had wept when Josephine had bared her soul to their parents that fateful evening. Josephine had insisted that she not be asked to reveal the name of the child's father. When Margaret had protested, James had intervened and spared Josephine. Afterward, Isabelle had eyed her father with suspicion. She had also expected him to bellow and insist on knowing the man's identity. That he didn't told Isabelle that Henry had already told him of Josephine's indiscretion, and that James had worked through his customary bluster and bellow. James had chosen not to press his already devastated daughter for an answer.

Isabelle picked up her book and ran her fingers over the cover. It was one Henry had gifted her. She chewed on her lip, envisioning his empty dining room chair. *I never knew how much I'd miss him. He kept Father steady, and without him, Father grumps around like an old bear who's just awakened from hibernation.*

Fabric rustled against the marble floor, and Margaret appeared in the sitting room entrance. "Let's go upstairs and talk, dear."

Isabelle left her book on the settee and ascended the stairs behind her mother. *What have I done now?* Isabelle searched her memory for whatever inadvertent social faux pas she might have committed over the last several days. She followed her mother into Margaret and James's bedroom. Margaret motioned for Isabelle to sit in one of the brown leather wing chairs near the dressing table opposite the door. Margaret seated herself in a matching chair that faced Isabelle.

"As you're well aware, we find ourselves in a bit of a *situation*." Margaret fretted her hands in her lap.

Isabelle arched her brows. *That's one way of putting it.*

"I've also found myself in a predicament and have decided to do the right thing," Margaret continued.

What on earth is she talking about? Isabelle licked her lips and frowned.

"I, I—" Margaret lowered her head.

She looks like a guilty child. Isabelle sat still as a stone, bewildered by whatever had come over her mother.

Margaret finally met Isabelle's eyes. "It's taken me some time to come to terms with what your sister's done and the effect it'll have on the family."

Isabelle nodded, still unsure where her mother was going with their conversation.

"I'm afraid, Isa, afraid for what it'll mean, but I know now that it's wrong to deprive you of the life you want." Margaret rose and walked to the enormous wooden dresser that sat against the wall to the right of the door.

Isabelle's eyes darted from side to side. *The life I want? What does she know that I don't?*

Margaret retrieved an item from the dresser and crossed the room. She handed an envelope to Isabelle, who gasped. It was from the California Hospital School for Nurses.

"You had it all this time and kept it from me?" Isabelle cried. "Mother, how could you!"

Isabelle leaped out of her chair and tore open the envelope so fast that she nearly ripped the letter in half. As she read, she paced between her chair and the bed, her eyes growing as wide as the grin on her face.

"I've been accepted!" She jumped in the air, her boots slamming against the floor with a loud bang.

The smile fell from her face moments later. "But I have to be there by the end of the month. Someone dropped out, and I can have her place, but only if I report by September twenty-seventh." *Applicants can start any time during the term if someone drops out.* Isabelle recalled the rules for admission. *And I'm the lucky bird who gets one of those spots.*

"I didn't know it worked like that," Margaret whispered, a solemn expression of horror spreading across her face.

Isabelle reread the letter, her mind racing. Henry had been right; she should have had faith and been patient.

"I'm so sorry." Margaret's voice cracked, her eyes filling with tears. "You were so helpful after my heart episode, and now with Josephine staying and a baby on the way and Henry gone, I—I didn't want to let you go." Margaret grabbed a handkerchief from her dressing table and dabbed her eyes. "It was so selfish of me, I know."

Isabelle froze, letter in hand. What her mother had done was unforgivable . . . almost. It had been incredibly selfish of her to think of Isabelle as only a helper and not a woman with her own dreams and aspirations. And Margaret hadn't opened the letter. If she had waited much longer to give it to Isabelle, the deadline for Isabelle to report to school would have passed. Isabelle would have been doubly crushed: she would have been accepted but would have missed her chance to attend because of Margaret's inability to face her fears and overcome her stubborn unwillingness to let go of long-held notions about who women should be.

I want to scream at her, Isabelle thought, stewing. *She betrayed me in an unimaginable way, but she did the right thing. And this family doesn't need more anguish right now.*

Margaret dabbed her cheeks, unable to meet her daughter's eyes. Isabelle pulled her wing chair closer to her mother's and sat down.

"I—I am angry," Isabelle said, choosing her words carefully. "This is the one thing I've wanted to do for so long, and you kept it from me. But I'm so happy, too, I don't—"

Isabelle's head was such a jumble of thoughts that she didn't know where to begin.

"I know you're afraid." Isabelle clasped one of her mother's hands in both of hers. "I know you think something else might happen with your heart, or to Josephine or the baby, or that I won't be safe in a strange city. But being a nurse is what I'm meant to do. The program is only for three years, and—"

Margaret sobbed again and wiped her eyes.

That must seem like a lifetime to her, but it feels like the beginning of a new life for me. Isabelle squeezed her mother's hand.

"Just because I'm going to Los Angeles doesn't mean I'm going to stay there," Isabelle said. "I'll visit when I can, and maybe when I'm finished with my training, I'll move back. Three years isn't forever."

Margaret's sobs quieted, her eyes full of regret. "I know, but my family's falling apart, and you're the one I can always count on."

Isabelle pressed her lips together to smother a smile. *Father throws up his hands and blusters while Josephine charms her way out of doing anything useful. With Henry gone, I am the only one she can count on other than the butler, the cook, and the maid.*

"We're not *really* falling apart," Isabelle said. "Father and Josephine are still here, although you're right. They're not much help."

Isabelle giggled, and Margaret choked out a laugh.

"I guess you'll have to set them straight when I'm gone." Isabelle winked.

Margaret sighed, her face etched with doubt.

Isabelle stuffed her acceptance letter into the torn envelope and walked to the door. She turned to her mother, her eyes glassy. "Thank you. Thank you for letting me go after my dream."

SIXTY-THREE

Isabelle rushed down the hall, brushing away tears. Once in her bedroom, she reread the letter and laid it on her dressing table. She hurried to the stairs, and as she descended, she almost tripped. She caught herself on the railing and stopped, her heart pounding. *That was close, but I must tell someone. Grace isn't here, but I'll write to her tonight. Josephine has her own problems and certainly won't care. And the Cliff House is in ashes, not that anyone in the women's parlor would've done anything other than judge me as a daft woman whose chances of finding a husband have dwindled to nothing. Which leaves Father and Henry.*

Isabelle tilted her head to one side and crinkled her eyes. It was strange how she wanted to share her news with Henry first. She continued down the stairs. *I'll make sure he knows, even if George has to drive me to the Fairmont Hotel so I can tell him.*

Isabelle walked down the hall toward her father's study. *Does Father know about the letter?* She slowed to a crawl and finally stopped. *What if he won't let me go to school?*

With the enormity of that invisible danger, her tears returned. She stepped into the bathroom and blotted her face with a towel. *I vowed to Charlotte and Grace that I'd go whether or not Father wanted me to, but I hope this once he can be as excited about my dream as I am.* She narrowed her eyes in resolve and stared at her reflection in the mirror. "He *will* let me go," she whispered aloud.

Finally, she emerged from the bathroom, knocked on the study door, and stepped inside. James sat in his usual high-backed leather chair across from the fireplace, hidden behind a newspaper. A glass of brandy rested on a side table, cigar smoke rising from a nearby ashtray.

He set his paper down and puffed on his cigar. "Isa, you look positively miserable. What's the trouble?"

Isabelle laid a palm on her cheek. She gingerly walked to the sofa and sat down. "Do I? I don't mean to."

James stared at her with his usual "get on with it" expression, and Isabelle cleared her throat.

"Father." Her voice quavered, and she cleared her throat again. "I've been accepted into the school for nurses' training at the California Hospital in Los Angeles. Someone has dropped out, and I've been given the honor of her spot. I need to be there by the afternoon of the twenty-seventh. To do that, I need your help with train fare, books, and supplies."

There, I've done it. Isabelle's pulse raced. *I hate having to ask him for money. Being able to make my own way in the world is one of the reasons I'm going to school.*

James blew out a trail of smoke and rested his cigar in the ashtray. He knitted his brow and steepled his fingers together in front of him. "So you applied to this, this training school without asking." It was more of a comment than a question.

"I did," Isabelle admitted, sinking back into the cushion.

James sniffed. Surprisingly, his face was peaceful, a far cry from the blooming blush of red that was usually followed by an outburst. *Did he know Mother had the letter?* Isabelle frowned and looked away. *I don't dare ask because I can't bear the thought of another parent conspiring against me.*

"Seems all the women in my house have kept things from me," James lamented, "but I admire you most."

Isabelle's head jerked up.

"Sometimes, we have to take risks to get what we want." His wistful gaze gave Isabelle hope. "God knows I've done it over the years in business."

James rose and retrieved another cigar from the box on the mantel even though his current cigar lay, still lit, in the ashtray. "I commend you, my girl, and would be proud to help you become a nurse."

Isabelle leaped up and rushed to her father. She wrapped her arms around his more-than-ample midsection, causing him to almost drop his new cigar. "Thank you so much, Father!" She gulped a sob. "I'll make you proud, I promise. I'll be the best—"

James gently drew back and held her at arm's length. "You've always made me proud, Isa. I've just done a poor job of telling you."

Relief washed over Isabelle and tears rolled down her cheeks. She hugged her father again. *Finally, someone who appreciates me for who I am and who I want to be. I feel like I could fly to Los Angeles, and I'll be the best nurse that school has ever seen.*

James laid the unwrapped cigar on the mantel. "See now. There must be a gathering to celebrate, small of course, but this is an accomplishment, and people need to know. Invite your friends, and that Charlotte too." He raised his eyebrows, and Isabelle laughed. "Buy yourself a new dress if you like, and—"

Isabelle shook her head and grinned.

"Right, then. Tell Eleanor what you'd like, and we'll make sure to have all the trimmings." He wrapped an arm around Isabelle's shoulder and squeezed.

"I can't believe I'm going to be in Los Angeles by October," Isabelle breathed.

James resettled himself into his chair and then puffed on his still-lit cigar.

Isabelle returned to the sofa, her tears fading, her joy melting into trepidation. "There's one other thing."

James waved his cigar in the air as if to say "out with it."

"I want to invite Henry. Having him here may be awkward, but he's my friend. Can you call him? Josephine won't dare be angry if you do it."

James licked his lips and frowned, then took another pull on his cigar. "I'll make sure he's here."

Isabelle eased back into the sofa. Perhaps it was because she had mentioned Henry, or because her father had admitted he was proud of her, but James now sat silent, his expression pensive. Isabelle inhaled a shaky breath, hesitant to break the spell.

"Would you be able to give me the money for train fare and books now?" she ventured.

Torn from his thoughts, James fished around in his breast pocket. "Yes, these enterprises do take a bit of capital." He pulled two ten-dollar bills from his wallet and handed them to her. "Will that be enough?"

Isabelle almost choked; twenty dollars would more than cover her train fare, books, and all the supplies she would need for her first year. "Yes, that's—that's quite generous, Father. Thank you."

"It's all a good investment, my dear, and I must say again how proud of you I am."

Isabelle's chest nearly burst with the promise of opportunity. "Thank you. I'm so nervous I almost can't sit still, but I'm also so very grateful that Mother finally relented and gave me my acceptance letter. And not a moment too soon." Isabelle arched her brows.

James cleared his throat and rose. He wandered to one of the windows that overlooked the backyard. "Yes," he said, his voice distant. "Not a moment too soon."

Isabelle studied her father, unsure if she should join him or remain on the sofa. *He says he's proud of me, but is he upset like Mother because I'm leaving?*

James returned and lowered himself into his chair with effort. "There have been secrets." He took a sip of brandy and sighed. "I'm not good at this, Isa." He fluttered a hand. "When Henry told me he was . . . that he and Josephine were divorcing, he also told me about the letter. Mind you, he didn't know what it was, only that your mother had stuffed something into her purse and that he had suspicions."

Isabelle's mouth curved into an O. *Of course it was Henry.* Isabelle's heart swelled. *That's why he kept telling me to be patient and have faith.*

"I should've asked her about it sooner, but I didn't want to believe that you'd go behind our backs and do such a thing," James said.

Isabelle stared at the floor, gripping the ten-dollar bills. "I'm sorry that I—"

"No, *I'm* sorry." James patted her knee. "I was afraid to let my little girl go, but I know now that was wrong. You'll make a fine student and a fine nurse, and we'll muddle on without you here, me alone again in this house of women."

Isabelle giggled. James had survived being the only man in the house after Daniel had died, which was before Henry had joined the family. "You never know, Father. Maybe Josephine will have a boy."

James chortled and downed the rest of his drink. "That'd be grand, just grand!" He thumped his glass down on the table, and a wide grin spread across his face. "Not that your mother and I haven't had enough trouble keeping you and your sister in hand, but a *boy*? Why, I'd be delighted!"

Isabelle's laughter died when James's grin faded. *He's thinking about Daniel.*

"I don't think it matters what Josephine has." Isabelle squeezed her father's hand, both of them rising from their seats. "What matters is that we're all going to be all right, regardless of what the future holds."

James carried his empty glass to the credenza beside the fireplace and poured himself another drink. "Well said, my girl, well said." He raised his glass to her.

SIXTY-FOUR

Henry strolled through the Fairmont Hotel lobby only to be waved down by the gentleman behind the front desk. *Has something happened to Margaret?* Henry's stomach flipped, and he snatched the folded message from the attendant with a word of thanks. Though Henry would soon be off of his father-in-law's payroll, he had splurged and booked himself a room at the finest hotel in San Francisco. With its city views, plush double bed complete with neck roll, and warm chandelier lighting, the Fairmont was a far cry from the spartan boardinghouse room in which he would be stuck in Los Angeles. *It'll take me half a lifetime to get back to how I lived when I was with Josephine, but it'll be worth it to be away from all of James's antics.* Henry's heart threatened to shatter again, and he shivered; he didn't want to think about Josephine's antics.

Alone in his room, Henry read the note and bounced up and down on the balls of his feet. *I knew Margaret had the letter! And Isabelle got accepted. I must get her something.* He laid the note on a side table and walked to the window. From where he stood, he couldn't see the Hamiltons' house, but he still gazed in its direction.

Living at the Fairmont had been a shock to Henry's system. Despite the luxurious room and decadent meals, Henry was alone again to enjoy both, much like when he had first arrived in California from Pennsylvania. Dinners at the Fairmont were sumptuous, but the food didn't taste nearly as good as it could have because it wasn't accompanied by the lively conversation he had become accustomed to with the Hamiltons. Even though Josephine had wounded him in the worst way, there were moments when he missed her. Henry ran his fingers through his hair. *I don't miss her; I miss being a part of that family.* It was a family he had never imagined he would have to give up.

Henry walked to the chest of drawers, picked up his wallet, and eyed the cash inside. He had sold his car the week before and held out a little money to pay for incidentals until he left town. He had tucked the rest of the bills under a shirt in the chest; it would be used for train fare, a new suit and tie, and a new automobile once he arrived in Los Angeles.

Much to Henry's surprise and relief, he had secured a job at an attorney's office that did business with Hamilton Holdings. James had been as good as his word, and the man who had hired Henry had mentioned that he was "thrilled to be bringing on someone who comes so highly recommended." While the comment flattered Henry, it also left him wary. He hoped this man wouldn't put him in compromising positions like the ones he had endured while working for James.

The real estate deal involving James, Graham, and several of their friends had moved forward apace, and Henry was relieved to be leaving Hamilton Holdings at just the right time. He had a sneaking suspicion that Graham had acquired the land using tactics that weren't entirely on the level but were kept quiet enough to prevent the local authorities from snooping around too much.

Henry stuffed his wallet into his coat pocket and returned to the window. Shopping for Josephine had always been simple. She liked parasols and hats, hair combs and flowers. Isabelle was different. She didn't care about the usual things other women cared about, which meant her present would take more thought. *I should get her a book, but that isn't enough. A coat would be nice, but is it too much?* Isabelle would soon be his ex-sister-in-law, and Henry didn't want to arrive at her going-away party with an ostentatious gift.

Eyebrows would be raised enough when others discovered he was no longer part of the family. To his knowledge, no one knew he had moved out, let alone filed the papers to divorce Josephine.

A truck belching smoke passed by on the street below. The driver beeped the horn, and a few men hustled out of the way. Henry snapped his fingers. *I know what I'll get Isabelle.* It would be the perfect gift for a student and one she could use after she finished her studies. *And I know exactly what I'll put in it to make it special.* He walked to his bedside table and grabbed his room key. *I only hope she doesn't cry when I give it to her.*

SIXTY-FIVE

Dressed in her finest burgundy gown, Isabelle stood next to her father in the sitting room late on a Saturday afternoon and beamed. Though clouds clotted the sky and threatened to spit rain, Isabelle couldn't stop smiling. Everyone important to her had accepted the invitation to her going-away party, and the room was filled with her closest friends and family. Eleanor had outdone herself; apple tartlets and individual lemon puddings, along with slices of Isabelle's favorite chocolate cake, sat elegantly arranged on a table in front of the unlit fireplace for guests to enjoy.

It's finally my turn. Isabelle's chest swelled with pride.

Margaret talked quietly with Henry while Josephine mingled with Violet, Maude, and Harriet. A few of Isabelle's school friends were also in attendance, along with Miss Pritchard, the Sunday school teacher who had written one of Isabelle's letters of character. James had assured Isabelle she could invite whomever she wanted to her party, and she had almost burst out laughing when Miss Pritchard had arrived. Given that James and Margaret didn't know Isabelle had even applied to nursing school, the revelation that an oddly tall and slim God-fearing woman with a beaklike nose had helped Isabelle without their knowledge had left Margaret momentarily stunned. James's face had turned the color of a ripe tomato when he sputtered out a polite greeting.

James tapped his highball glass with his fork. It gave off more of a clunking sound than a melodious tinkling, and the conversation faded.

"Here now, yes." He cleared his throat. "Isabelle would like to say a few words."

Isabelle turned to her father in mortification. She had known she would need to give a speech, but her father's lack of notice had put her in the most unfortunate position. She had just taken a bite of chocolate cake, half of which was now mashed into a ball in her mouth. Isabelle ran her tongue over her teeth, hoping to remove whatever leftover frosting might be there, and swallowed the bite.

"Thank you, Father." She took a sip of punch and peered out at the smiling faces around her. "I want to thank everyone for coming to help me celebrate. I also want to especially thank Violet and Miss Pritchard, who wrote letters on my behalf."

Isabelle dipped her chin toward the two women. She bit her tongue to smother a giggle when Harriet eyed Violet with shocked surprise. *Harriet thinks scandals are only for unfaithful cads and corrupt businessmen. She hadn't counted on a woman like me who takes matters into her own hands.*

At the thought of unfaithful cads, Isabelle stole a glance at Josephine. The family hadn't announced that she and Henry were divorcing yet, and the couple stood together, yet miles apart, near the sitting room entrance. Josephine smiled politely at Isabelle, her expression unable to entirely mask her pain. Isabelle's heart went out to her sister. *I can't imagine how devastated and afraid she must be, but she has Mother to lean on.*

"I'd also like to thank my parents for allowing me to follow my dream." Isabelle wrapped her arm around James, amused when his face flushed. He hastily took a sip of whiskey. Margaret's thin smile and glassy eyes told Isabelle she was still struggling to be happy for her daughter.

"I'll be leaving the morning of the twenty-seventh for Los

Angeles, but I'll come home whenever I can." Isabelle squeezed James, and he bashfully put his arm around her. "Please enjoy the cake and other refreshments, and thank you all again for being here."

Violet sidled up to Isabelle, who hugged her best friend. Isabelle's emotions almost overwhelmed her, her throat closing when she whispered thank-yous in Violet's ear. Isabelle briefly greeted two other guests as she threaded her way across the room toward Josephine. Isabelle had been so stung by Josephine's betrayal of Henry that she had almost gone out of her way not to speak to her sister after Henry had moved out. But time was growing short, and Isabelle had no intention of leaving town without at least extending an olive branch to Josephine. Isabelle clasped her mother's hand and squeezed it as she passed by and continued to where Josephine now stood, beautiful as ever but bereft and alone. Henry had moved on to speak with Miss Pritchard.

"Thank you," Isabelle said, pulling Josephine aside. "This must be hard for you, but know that I'm grateful. I know that looking after Mother and Father wasn't—isn't what you had in mind, but I—"

Isabelle paused when Josephine looked away, her chin quivering.

"Please don't give up hope," Isabelle whispered. "Times are different now, you'll see. Be patient and have faith."

Isabelle laid a hand on Josephine's shoulder, struck by the irony of her words. *That was what Henry once told me, and now I have to use it to comfort his soon-to-be ex-wife.*

"Thank you." Josephine sipped her punch. "I am happy for you, Isa, and I hope you're right."

Isabelle squeezed Josephine's shoulder. "I am."

Isabelle turned her attention to Henry, who talked with James near one of the floral upholstered armchairs. Her father motioned to her, and Isabelle made her way across the room, stopping to say a few polite words to Violet, Harriet, and Miss Pritchard on the way. Finally, Margaret took James's arm and led him away, leaving Isabelle alone with Henry.

"I have to go, but I have something for you," he said, not meeting her eyes.

"Thank you for coming," Isabelle replied. *Being back in this house and pretending to be pleasant around Josephine must be terrible.*

Isabelle followed Henry into the foyer. A large rectangular taupe paper box tied with a pale blue ribbon sat on the credenza.

"I don't know if this is something you can use, but I wanted you to have it," he said.

Isabelle removed the bow and opened the box. She gasped at the burgundy and navy brocade carpetbag with a thick mahogany handle. "It's beautiful. Thank you." She carefully lifted the bag from the box. When she held the carpetbag at her side, something rustled within. She laid the bag on the credenza, dug around inside it, and removed a small package tied with another pale blue ribbon.

"I thought you might want these to remind you of home," Henry said.

Isabelle untied the package and pressed her hand over her mouth, tears springing to her eyes. A collection of postcards, one with an image of the Cliff House on the top of the stack, greeted her. "Oh, Henry. Thank you." She slowly flipped through the postcards, nostalgia tugging at her.

Not only had Henry collected several postcards of the Cliff House, but he had also included ones of prominent buildings that tragically no longer existed thanks to the quake. Isabelle wiped away a few stray tears and stared at him in gratitude. *He's the most thoughtful man I know. He must've spent half a day going around the city to find these.*

"I'm going to go." Henry fidgeted and cast one final glance over his shoulder into the sitting room. "I'm sure you'll do very well in school, and I hope you'll be happy there."

Henry walked toward the front door, Isabelle close behind him.

"Thank you again." Isabelle stopped when George opened the door for Henry, who stepped onto the front stoop. "I appreciate you being here."

Henry waved to Isabelle but didn't linger. He descended the steps quickly and didn't look back, striding down the walkway toward the street. *This cannot be the last time I see him.* Isabelle closed her eyes, a pit growing in her stomach. *I must ask Father where Henry will be working in Los Angeles so I can look him up sometime.*

SIXTY-SIX

A few days before Isabelle was to leave for Los Angeles, she and Josephine stood in Isabelle's room, her bed covered with stacks of items she would take to nursing school. The sisters had returned from a whirlwind afternoon of shopping, and the sun hung low in the west, warming the room and cutting shapes on the wall. Though those admitted to the nurses' training program owed no tuition, they were required to complete a two-month probationary term. If they were deemed to have an aptitude for the work and general fitness at the end of that term, they were admitted to the school to begin their actual training.

Isabelle had memorized the California Hospital School for Nurses Annual Announcement, including the clothing supplies she would need to take to school. She could barely keep from dancing a jig admiring the black cape, white linen collars, crisply ironed aprons, and three "wash dresses of quiet color." Isabelle had chosen pale blue dresses. Young women who passed their probationary term and were admitted to the training program wore the school uniform of plain blue gingham. Isabelle wanted to get accustomed to seeing herself in that color.

"Thank you for going with me today." Isabelle continued to mentally check off the items on the bed. "I know it probably wasn't as much fun as going to see Mr. Walters and buying another satin dress, but I—"

"It was fine." Josephine eased herself onto Isabelle's dressing table chair, her hand resting on her belly.

Isabelle pushed the stack of aprons aside and perched on her bed across from her sister. It was moments like these that left her torn.

"Is everything all right?" Isabelle clutched the bedspread. *What if something happens to Josephine or Mother and I'm not here to help? I would never forgive myself.*

"This baby is making me tired, that's all." Josephine leaned back in the chair. "Otherwise, I feel fine."

Isabelle breathed a small sigh of relief and scooted farther back onto her bed. She had wanted to ask Josephine a hundred questions when she and Henry had announced their divorce but had held her tongue. She had been so angry that she could have smacked Josephine hard, right across the cheek. How Josephine could have hurt Henry so grievously still puzzled Isabelle. Josephine had everything she wanted, and Isabelle had never understood how she could have carelessly thrown it all away.

"Can I ask you something about the baby?" Isabelle ventured.

Josephine started to rise, but Isabelle stopped her. "No, it's not about the father; I won't—I'll never ask about that."

Josephine remained in her seat, her eyes guarded.

"Why did you . . ." Isabelle didn't want to come across as accusatory, but there was simply no other way to ask the question. "Why were you unfaithful to Henry?"

Josephine sighed heavily and gazed out the window. The silence in the room grew to where Isabelle only heard a crow caw as it flew by, and the faint bump of a door downstairs as Eleanor or Sarah moved around in the kitchen.

"I suppose I wanted an adventure too," Josephine finally said, her voice echoing defeat. "He was—it was dashing and daring and *lustful.*" Josephine pressed her palms to her temples for a moment. "I was so naïve. I think I believed in some small way that I could get away with it. At first, I didn't care if he stayed with his wife, but over time, I wanted him to leave her. Of course, that doesn't make it right because I loved Henry. I still do. It started as one thing, and then I built it into something else, and . . ."

Josephine lifted her teary eyes to Isabelle. "Henry was nothing but caring and kind to me, Isa, and I threw away the most honorable man I know because I was selfish, so very selfish. I wanted *more*, more than he could give me, but I never meant to hurt him. I wanted fiery passion *and* I wanted Henry, too. He saved me from being trampled after I stepped off of the cable car, and I'll forever be grateful for that, but I wanted something beyond the love we shared."

Isabelle bit her tongue to keep from shrieking at her sister.

"It thrilled me to have a secret," Josephine admitted, her chin trembling. "It was dangerous and exciting, and for a while, I had both. I had Henry and I had—" Josephine abruptly pressed her lips together, tears leaking down her cheeks.

Did she almost reveal her lover's name? Isabelle slid off of her bed and crouched beside Josephine's chair. Josephine cried, her hands covering her face.

"I never thought Henry would leave," Josephine managed through sobs. "I thought I could convince him the baby was his. I tried to make sure that we, well, you know, and I thought even if he questioned it, he'd stay because he loved me, but he didn't."

I have half a mind to shake her silly! Isabelle remained crouched on the floor, her legs aching. *I want to smack her yet again for betraying Henry like that, but she knows now what she did was wrong.*

Isabelle finally reached behind her, grabbed an apron off of her bed, and offered it to her sister. Josephine took it and dabbed her tears.

"I'm not proud of this, but I was also jealous of you and Grace," Josephine said.

Isabelle returned to her bed, a frown creasing her brow. "Why would you be jealous of me and Grace?"

"Because the two of you were getting what you wanted. You'd finally learned to get Red Cross donations from people without acting like an eager child, and Grace showed up and charmed everyone and then shocked us all by running off to school."

Isabelle spread her hands and exhaled a breathy protest. "Are you daft? I wasn't getting anything I wanted. I constantly fought with Mother about nursing school. Mrs. Felton shunned me in favor of Grace at first, and there were times I felt lucky that Grace even asked me to help her organize the gala. It was hard for me to change who I was so that people would donate to the Red Cross. And the only place I loved—where I could dream despite the absolutely *dreadful* conversation in the women's parlor—burned down!" Isabelle clasped Josephine's hands and stared deeply into her sister's eyes. "I was accepted into nursing school because I took matters into my own hands. Do you know how ashamed I felt when I went behind Mother and Father's back with Dr. Jenkins and Miss Pritchard from *church*? And Mother nearly cost me my spot because she stole my acceptance letter and almost didn't give it to me!"

Josephine gasped and withdrew her hands.

"Believing I hadn't been accepted into school made me feel like *everything* was lost. I watched you and Henry announce your pregnancy and felt like you were getting what you wanted. I watched Grace befriend everyone so easily and found out she'd been accepted into school. And she went despite the messes with her suitors and both of her parents not approving. I thought everyone was getting what they wanted except for me."

Josephine blotted her cheeks with the corner of the apron again. "I didn't know about your acceptance letter."

"I felt like a servant after Mother had her heart attack. If she hadn't given me my acceptance letter when she did, I'd be stuck here." Isabelle took one of Josephine's hands in hers and squeezed it. "I didn't get what I wanted at all this summer until Mother mercifully gave me that letter. Until then, I was drowning in the belief that I would have to live here forever and take care of her and Father. Do you know what that feels like?"

Josephine patted Isabelle's hand, a wry smile on her lips. "Yes," she chuckled, her sobs fading. "I do, and it's downright terrifying."

Isabelle and Josephine both laughed.

"If we've learned anything this summer, it's that things aren't always what they seem to be and that having pity parties for ourselves doesn't make us feel any better," Isabelle said.

Josephine nodded. "I think that's all so very true."

Isabelle sighed. She had gotten what she had wanted, but her heart still ached for Josephine.

"You know, Maude said something to me at your party," Josephine continued. "She said you were an inspiration to her because you were going to school *and* to a new city."

Isabelle blushed with pride. She had encouraged Grace to go to school without the support of her family. Might sweet, plain-faced Maude do the same and avoid becoming a spinster who lived at home with her parents?

"She said what you're doing is progressive, even though Harriet told her it'd ruin her chances of having a husband." Josephine crinkled her eyes. "Maude wasn't so sure."

Isabelle bit her lip. She wasn't sure either. Maybe, like Emma Sutro Merritt and Katherine Felton, she too would one day meet and marry a man who would love her for who she was and what she wanted to accomplish outside the home.

"What you're doing *is* progressive, Isa." Josephine wiped her nose on the apron and brushed away a few more tears. "I've never understood your odd notions about wanting to work or to be around wounded and sick people. The thought of blood and vomit and broken bones and open wounds is repulsive, but maybe a different type of progress might save me. Do you think a man might love me and my child one day?" Josephine stared at the floor and sniffled.

A lump rose in Isabelle's throat. Josephine was afraid: afraid of facing the shame that would undoubtedly dog her, afraid of raising a child as an unwed mother, afraid of never being loved again. And while working as a nurse or a teacher was a far cry from bearing an illegitimate child, deep down Isabelle knew Josephine would remarry in time. *She wants to believe. She wants to believe that she'll meet someone who will accept her for who she is and that she won't have to live with Mother and Father forever.*

"Yes." Isabelle struggled to speak, her emotions clotting her throat, an unshakable certainty rising within. "Someone will love you and your child one day. You won't always be alone, Josephine. You'll meet another man. You'll love him and honor him, and the two of you will be very happy together."

What Isabelle couldn't say was that Josephine had paid the heaviest of prices for her betrayal and greed. She had learned how not to treat one of the best men they both had ever known. Josephine would never hurt another man that way again. She would never take for granted the type of love she had shared with Henry.

Josephine met her sister's gaze and held it, her eyes cautious.

"Let Mother and Father enjoy this baby while they can," Isabelle said. "Let them spoil it and look after it while you get back on your feet."

Josephine straightened in the chair and stretched her neck. She tilted her head as if considering Isabelle's advice. Isabelle took the apron from Josephine and tossed it behind her.

"Sorry." Josephine pointed to the apron.

Isabelle grinned and climbed off of her bed. "Trust me, there'll be much worse things on it in the future."

Josephine pulled a face. She rose and hugged Isabelle. Josephine walked to the door, then turned back to her sister. "You're going to be a wonderful nurse," she said, her eyes shining. "And if anyone deserves to get what they want, it's you."

Isabelle hurried across the room and hugged Josephine once more. "Thank you. So do you."

SIXTY-SEVEN

The following morning, Isabelle gripped the edge of the backseat while George navigated the streets to the train station. Enormous white clouds floated through the bright blue sky, sunlight sending sparks off of the bay in the distance. With James sitting in front next to George, Margaret had insisted on mashing herself between her daughters and now held Isabelle and Josephine's hands. *This is the last time we'll be like this as a family. So much is going to change.*

Isabelle smiled to herself. Grace had gotten at least part of what she had wanted. She didn't have a husband, but she was going to school. Of the three women, Grace had probably suffered the least. She had been immediately accepted by the ladies in Isabelle and Josephine's social circles, taken inspiration from Isabelle and Charlotte, and mustered up the courage to follow her dream. *Oh, to have it that easy.* Isabelle shook her head. *No matter, I'm finally getting what I want and couldn't be more excited.*

Isabelle smoothed her navy dress and wiggled her toes inside her best black boots. During her probationary term and training, she, along with other hopeful apprentices and young women from all over the country who had already been admitted to the program, would live at the Nurses' Home near the hospital. Her chest swelled in anticipation. She couldn't wait to meet the other girls. None of them would want to talk about the weather; they would all be as eager as she was to get into the hospital and start helping patients.

Once at the train station, the family waited on the platform while Isabelle purchased her ticket. Steam rose from chimney stacks, whistles blew, and other passengers hugged relatives before boarding their trains. George handed Isabelle's suitcase to a porter. She clutched her carpetbag close by her side, the set of postcards Henry had gifted her safely in the bottom. Isabelle cast a hopeful glance around the platform, tears pricking in her eyes. *I wish he was here to see me off with the rest of the family.* With Henry nowhere in sight, Isabelle hugged her mother.

"You must write." Margaret patted her cheeks with her handkerchief. "And don't talk to strangers on the train. I wish one of us could—"

Isabelle laid a reassuring hand on Margaret's arm. "I'll be fine, Mother. Young women travel alone all the time now."

Isabelle hugged Josephine and marveled at her sister's growing child; a hard ridge protruded from Josephine's belly. *It must be a boy.* Isabelle sent up a silent prayer. *Mother and Josephine would love a girl, but Father needs a grandson so very much.*

A stiff breeze swept across the platform, and Josephine planted a palm on her hat. "Good luck. I hope you'll be happy there."

"I will be," Isabelle assured her. "Please take good care of yourself."

Josephine's brave smile told Isabelle that Josephine was struggling more with her sister's leaving than she wanted to admit.

Isabelle then embraced her father. He engulfed her in such a crushing hug she feared he might squeeze all the air from her lungs. Afterward, he held her gently by the shoulders and looked her straight in the eye. "By thunder, you'll be the best one of them. Do come back and see us when you can."

The train whistle blew, and Isabelle stepped away from her family, wiping a few tears from her cheeks. "I'll write!" Isabelle called, hurrying down the platform. "I love you, and I'll come back to visit as soon as I can."

Isabelle boarded the train and chose a bench midway up the car. As the train rolled away from the station, she waved and dabbed at a few more stray tears, her pulse thrumming. *I'm doing it. I'm really doing it!* Isabelle settled into her seat and quickly removed *The Jungle* from her carpetbag. She had chosen an empty bench near a young couple and hoped to read in peace until it was time to go to the dining car for lunch. Isabelle read the first two paragraphs of the first chapter but was so enthralled by the sway of the train and the sight of the bay as it gave way to rolling hills that she set her book down and stared out the window. Two firm taps on her shoulder startled her. *I do not want to be bothered by some strange man who thinks he can chatter in my ear all the way to Los Angeles simply because I'm a woman traveling alone.*

She straightened and pursed her lips, poised to rebuff whoever was bothering her. When she turned, her stern veneer dissolved into a delighted grin.

"Henry!" Isabelle nearly jumped up and hugged him.

"May I join you?" he asked.

Isabelle scooted over, allowing him to sit down.

"How did you—how are you *here?*" she implored.

"You mentioned when you'd be leaving at your party." He removed his hat and settled in next to her.

Isabelle darted her eyes from side to side, a slow grin spreading across her face. "I guess I did, didn't I."

A conductor distracted the pair long enough to collect their tickets.

"I should thank you." Isabelle turned to Henry in seriousness. "Father told me about how you thought Mother had my acceptance letter."

Henry blushed like a bashful child. "It wasn't my place to accuse her or to insist that James ask her about it, but I couldn't bear the thought of you missing your chance because Margaret wanted to keep you at home."

Isabelle's heart thudded when Henry's eyes met hers.

"It wouldn't have been right," he continued. "The world needs more people like you, Isa, good people who aren't afraid to stand up for others and help them. I think you're going to be a fine nurse."

Isabelle clutched *The Jungle*, her stomach fluttering. Henry had given the book to her. *I can never let him go. He's the one person who appreciates me for who I am, and he wants me to succeed. He always has.*

"So, where are you staying in Los Angeles?" she asked, the train continuing to wend its way south.

As they talked, Isabelle knew that Henry Rothwell would always be in her life. Not only had he made sure that she had received her acceptance letter, but he had also shown that he was interested, possibly in more than whether she was admitted into school. Isabelle leaned back against the bench and relaxed into their conversation, unable to stop grinning. *Despite the trials and tribulations, I finally got what I wanted. Though the Cliff House is gone, I'll find another place to dream and dare and create new memories alongside those I love.*

AUTHOR'S NOTE

The majestic white Victorian Cliff House stood on a rock outcropping overlooking the Pacific from January 14, 1896, to September 7, 1907. The palatial building had four floors, two attics, a central tower, and four turrets. Built on the original Cliff House site, the "gingerbread palace" was visited by multiple presidents and survived the great earthquake of 1906 with almost no damage.

Before it burned, the Cliff House had gone through bankruptcy and changed hands. The new leaseholders closed the building in June 1907 with plans to renovate it at the cost of $60,000 and reopen it on August 1. Sadly, renovations ran behind, and a fire broke out before they could be completed. Because of the total devastation of the building, the origin of the fire was never discovered. Suspicions were that either a steamfitter working in the basement had left a firepot burning or a cigarette butt had been discarded too close to flammable material. Despite heroic efforts by firemen, two blasts sealed the Cliff House's fate. Powder being used to widen the road down to the beach was stored in the basement and exploded, as did turpentine and painting materials a short time later.

Though the Cliff House was technically closed during the time period of the book, the verbal descriptions of the interior, including Grace's impression of the shabby carpets, were taken from actual visitor recollections. The claim that the owner, Mr. Adolph Sutro, had cleaned up the reputation of the Victorian Cliff House is also true. Though the Cliff House was open to the public, Mr. Sutro tried and mostly succeeded in attracting a more upscale crowd. Like Graham and Josephine, they were more discreet in their dalliances than the former gun-firing, garter-snapping rabble-rousers who frequented the previous Cliff House.

Today, the Cliff House remains one of San Francisco's most treasured historical structures. After it closed in December 2020, during the height of the COVID-19 pandemic, there were rumored plans to convert it into an office building. In a hopeful turn of events, those plans were scrapped, and a new concessionaire plans to reopen the building in 2024.

One of the most maddening challenges in writing this book was that only a single known interior photograph of the Cliff House taken after 1900 exists. That black-and-white photo—of a dining room decked out in what was probably red, white, and blue bunting, likely in anticipation of a presidential visit—was the only visual reference I had to create the ambiance of what was once a spectacular place to eat and socialize. That photo and detailed building blueprints helped me reimagine the real-life women's parlor that Isabelle, her mother, her sister, and her cousin Grace frequented.

Though the hospital housing the UC medical school on Parnassus Avenue had been hastily rebuilt after the quake and its first nursing student entered the UC San Francisco training school for nurses in June 1907, Isabelle might not have been patient enough to wait for the hospital to be rebuilt or to begin offering nurses' training again. That impatience, coupled with her desire to make a clean break from her family, led me to choose a school in another city for her education.

The California Hospital School for Nurses, originally located at 1414 South Hope Street in Los Angeles, was one of the premier institutions for nurses' training in the early 1900s. I pulled all application requirements, supply lists, and terms of admission directly from their charming and informative six-page 1906–1907 annual announcement. Their mandate that "candidates should have their teeth examined and put in good condition before entering the school" still makes me giggle. Apparently, the hospital deemed it essential that patients recover aided only by nurses with straight teeth, which likely made for pleasant and dazzling smiles.

The Los Angeles State Normal School for teachers was the southern campus of the California State Normal School, which was, ironically, located in San Francisco. Because Grace was unmarried and had no family with whom to live, the requirement that she arrive at school a week before classes were to begin to receive a list of school-approved families with whom to board would have applied to her. That requirement, along with the details of her two-year kindergarten training course, was taken straight from the school's (unexpectedly intimidating and detailed) sixty-five-page 1906–1907 *Annual Catalog and Circular of Information*.

Writing a book set after a major natural disaster also posed significant challenges. Landmarks had been destroyed, and many stores had been either reduced to ash or reestablished in temporary locations. That I. Magnin (the model for Walters Dress Shop), City of Paris, and so many other businesses could reopen, often in tents or surviving homes such as the Hobart mansion, is a testament to the will and spirit of the people of San Francisco during that tragic and difficult time.

The corruption that so appalled Henry Rothwell continued after the quake and the sentencing of crime boss Abe Ruef while the city raced to rebuild in time to host the 1915 Panama-Pacific International Exposition. When city hall was destroyed, real estate records and birth certificates perished with it. This provided unsavory opportunities for those crafty and nervy enough to return to bribery and corner-cutting as the city struggled to regain its footing.

Katharine "Kitty" Felton was one of only two women on the Committee of Fifty (also known as the Committee of Safety, Citizens' Committee of Fifty, or Relief and Restoration Committee of Law and Order) and chaired the Relief of Sick and Wounded subcommittee. She dedicated her adult life to humanitarian causes, mostly helping neglected and orphaned children. At age twenty-eight, she became the first director of Associated Charities of San Francisco. After the disaster, the army, the Red Cross, and Associated Charities directed the entire Earthquake Relief Program, and Associated Charities briefly merged with the Red Cross. It was during this time that Isabelle and Grace would have planned and attended the fictional Red Cross gala. Associated Charities reestablished itself as a separate entity in 1908, with Mrs. Felton continuing as director.

The lack of antibiotics in the early 1900s would have made Charlotte Gordon's scarlet fever horrible to endure and her permanently damaged heart a very limiting reality. And though it's nearly impossible to believe, strychnine in minuscule doses was prescribed to help stimulate a person's heart and increase appetite. Those tiny pills certainly helped Grace in more ways than one.

Handsome and polite Andrew Kepler could have been one of a privileged group of young men plucked from a city on the rise. In the 1890s, Los Angeles had a population of fifty thousand, and during that time, some of the most productive oil fields in history were discovered there. By the 1930s, LA produced nearly one-quarter of the world's oil output, and the population had swelled to 1.2 million people.

The elegant and inspiring Cliff House of the early 1900s truly could have been a place for dreamers. The ambiance, the ocean views, and the allure of something beyond the ordinary would have been a balm to the souls of young women like Isabelle and Grace, who sometimes found themselves stuck in a women's parlor talking about the weather when they would rather have been healing the sick or educating young children. My hope is that readers, much like Isabelle and Grace, will find their own place to dream as they continue forward with bravery, initiative, and perseverance.

ACKNOWLEDGMENTS

Ideas for books often come to me unbidden, usually through old photographs. I was flipping through *Lost America: From the Mississippi to the Pacific* by Constance Greiff one afternoon only to stop and gasp in awe at a photo of a palatial building, its windows shining like beacons, the night sky illuminated by a bolt of lightning. I poked the page with my finger and exclaimed (to no one… in my living room), "that place needs a story!"

It takes a team to send a novel out into the world, and I am indebted to those who have helped me go from idea to publication. Sun Cooper, who has read everything I've ever written and always encourages me to take my writing further, provided critical critique and developmental editing expertise that tightened and shaped this book into something I'm very proud of. Aja Pollock, my eagle-eyed copyeditor, polished this manuscript with care and kindness. Roseanna White not only created a lovely interior book layout but also a gorgeous cover.

I used so many sources to research this novel, but two deserve special attention. *The San Francisco Cliff House* by Mary Germain Hountalas and Sharon Silva provided a concise and meticulously researched history of the various Cliff Houses over the decades. In addition to numerous pictures, the book offered menus, recipes, and anecdotes from visitors which helped me get a feel for what it must have been like to relax and dine at such a spectacular place. Secondly, the Cliff House Project website (www.cliffhouseproject.

com), maintained by Gary Stark, provided timelines, photos, building blueprints, and newspaper articles. Dedicated specifically to the Adolph Sutro Victorian Cliff House, the Cliff House Project website is truly a treasure trove for history lovers. I could not have written this book without these two invaluable resources.

To those in my writer's brainstorming group, as always, I am thankful for your humor and ideas. Kim MacLean, Kim Taylor, and Holly Hammond can always be counted upon to fill plot holes, assure me that my ideas aren't terrible, and celebrate with me when my books are finally published.

You, my dear readers, make all of this work (especially the seemingly endless rounds of editing!) worthwhile. I also salute the countless librarians and booksellers who help connect readers to new stories every day. Without you, our world would be a much sadder and duller place.

Finally, thanks go to my parents for instilling a love of books in me at a young age and encouraging my creativity. Thanks, Mom, for asking to read this book so many times, and for being patient while I the massaged the first draft into something coherent enough to share. Dad, thanks for everything. I know you're watching over me and I miss you every day. As books go, I think you would've liked this one.

ABOUT THE AUTHOR

Brooke L. Davis was born and raised in Indiana. Needing an outlet for her never-ending creativity, she began writing seriously in 2013. Stories would often (and still do) come to her unbidden, usually through old photographs. After over twenty years working in finance and cash management, she left corporate America in 2015 and is fortunate enough to be a full-time writer. She has lived in the American West for over a quarter-century and (dreams of) splitting her time between Colorado and Montana.

Visit Brooke on the web at:
www.brookedaviswrites.com
Instagram: @brooke.davis.writes

www.ingramcontent.com/pod-product-compliance
Lightning Source LLC
Chambersburg PA
CBHW070838260626
47170CB00007B/2425